The Weaver's Daughter

Donna Baker

Myriad Books Ltd
35 Bishopsthorpe Road
London SE26 4PA

ISBN 1 904154 19 0

Printed and bound in Great Britain

To

CAROLINE SHELDON

with many thanks for her

encouragement and guidance

Author's Note

For the original idea for the story of this book, I would like to thank my friend Joyce Sutcliffe, and Professor Maurice Beresford. For assistance and advice in research, I thank Mr Jim Bennett of Adams Carpets, Kidderminster, and must also acknowledge the following sources: *The Story of British Carpets* by Bertram Jacobs; *Carpet Weavers and Carpet Masters* by L D Smith; *Kidderminster Since 1800* by Ken Tomkinson and George Hall; *London's Underworld* by Henry Mayhew, edited by Peter Quennell. I am grateful to the excellent museum at Wilton, for displaying the old looms and machinery. Any mistakes in the text are entirely my own work.

Prologue

On the day that Rebecca Himley was born, Admiral Lord Nelson won the Battle of Trafalgar and was killed in the doing of it.

There were those in Kidderminster who were following the reports of the wars in their daily newspapers, and those who gleaned news from neighbours and workmates; but they were not of the Himley household. William was too occupied at his loom, for he had been forced to 'play' for the whole of the previous week and needed to complete his piece by Thursday fall day. And Fanny could think of nothing but the pain tearing through her body. Battles far away were nothing to the screaming muscles of her womb, and even the carpet on which their livelihood depended would take second place until the pain was over and the new baby here at last. A new son or daughter – to live or die.

Bessie was with her, only five years old but already a handy little thing – her face white as she watched her mother's struggles, yet still able to do the midwife's bidding and lend a hand, ready with the rags Mrs Davies had demanded, and quick to hold a cracked cup of water to her mother's lips when she gasped for it. Bessie – the last child Fanny had borne to live more than a few days. And even though she seemed healthy enough now, who was to say she would ever grow up to bear her own children? Only the very fortunate survived accident, disease or plain starvation in these hard times.

'Nearly there now, Mrs Himley.' The midwife's voice was encouraging. 'Here, give me that rag, Bessie girl. That's right . . . One last good push now, and it's born. You'll have your baby in your arms any minute.' She knew as well as Fanny that the baby's chances of living were no better than those of any of the other babies born in the past four years. And that if it did survive the birth, it would probably not see its first birthday. Yet the will to bring a new life into the world was as strong in her now as it had ever been, stronger than it was in Fanny herself, who just wanted the whole business to be over and done with.

With one last tremendous effort, Fanny gathered her strength to meet the rising wave of pain. Her body embraced it, welcomed it, used it with a thrust that had her half off the pallet of straw on which she lay. She felt the hard head open her as if she were a door, the shoulders widen the opening until she knew she must split in two; even two tiny elbows pressed into her flesh as though the baby itself shared her urgency to have done with it. Briefly, she knew she could stand no more, that the baby must be born now or both of them die. And then, with one final surge of flesh and blood and water, it was over. There was an exclamation from the midwife, a cry from Bessie; and, after a moment's breathless silence, a roar of fury from the one whose voice had never been heard before, who had until this moment had no voice nor any breath to use one.

Son or daughter? Fanny lay back, exhausted. There were women who found birthing easier the more they experienced it, who dropped their babes as casually as if they were setting down a bucket of water. She had never been one of them.

'It's a girl,' Mrs Davies said. 'A fine one, Mrs

Himley. Big and strong. Here. Have a look.'

Weakly, Fanny lifted her head. A girl. Another one to suffer as she had suffered, as Bessie would suffer, as all women must. And big and strong – likely to live.

She would be better drowned, like a kitten.

'Hold her,' the midwife urged, and mechanically Fanny held out her arms.

The baby was placed against her breast. Almost without meaning to, Fanny folded her arms around the slippery body, feeling its warmth, its trembling, the beating of the tiny heart against her own. The shape of it was moulded against her abdomen as it had, until moments ago, been inside the same wall of skin and flesh and muscle. Her daughter. Living – and, after all, as likely as not to go on living.

Slowly, she turned her head and looked down at the tiny, naked body, still covered in its greyish slime.

Rebecca looked back at her mother. Her eyes were dark even then, brown as the horse-chestnuts young Tom played with in the autumn, and their glance was straight and direct. Above them were dark brows, thick as the hair which covered the small, pulsating head like black velvet. And the mouth, the soft, baby mouth which was only minutes old, was already set in determination.

Fanny caught her breath. She had borne many children, and so far only two had lived. Of the others, some had been born already dead, some had sighed for a few minutes, a few hours, before drifting out of reach. Two had seen their first birthdays, one even learning to walk, and another, born already damaged, had hung on in misery until he was eighteen months old.

3

None of them had looked like this.

None of them had looked at her with eyes that were already wise, telling her so clearly, in the first moments of life, that they meant to survive.

Chapter One

The clatter of her father's loom had been in Rebecca's ears from the moment of her birth. She grew up to take for granted the cumbersome iron frame that stood at one end of the cottage with the bobbins of coloured wool ranged beside it. The sight of her father working feverishly from early morning until late at night was one she had always known. The spectacle of first Tom, then Bessie, working beside him as his drawer was familiar as that of her mother winding the bobbins in the warehouse where she went each day, taking Rebecca with her until she was old enough to stay at home to learn in her turn to be a draw-girl.

'Seems there ought to be more than this for you,' Fanny said as they hurried along the banks of the Stour where freshly dyed yarn was being washed. 'I don't know what . . . Service, that's hard work but at least it's out of the way of the looms. I grew up in service. But your father'd not hear of it. He's like all the weavers; independence means more to him than a full belly, though he'd soon squall if it were ale he lacked.'

Rebecca hardly heard her. She was gazing at the men as they perched on their small platforms over the river, holding brightly coloured skeins of wool in the water on long poles. Loose dye swirled out of the bundles, turning the water to a gaudy, shifting pattern of red, green, yellow and blue. Too soon, the colours merged into each other and the river became a turbid flux of murky soup. But for those first few moments it was a brilliant display; a hint of the patterns that would be woven later by weavers like her father.

The yarn came from out in the country, her mother said, from sheep that grazed in the fields. Some of it came from much further away, from Yorkshire, but Fanny was vague as to exactly where Yorkshire was. The yarn came to Kidderminster, that was all that mattered, brought by carts from spinners or their agents to the dye-houses near the carpet manufacturers' warehouses. But there was always too much dye to be absorbed by the wool, and it was this excess that Rebecca saw being washed out in the Stour.

'Water's good for dyeing hereabouts,' Fanny observed, pausing too to watch as the skeins were swished about in the running water. 'They say it's because of the ironworks up the way . . . Come on, Rebecca, do. I'll be late, and you know what that means – no money and we don't eat tonight.'

She grasped Rebecca tightly by the hand and dragged her on along the riverbank to the workshop. Most of her fellow-workers were already there, taking off the sacking that served them as coats and sitting down at their winding-frames, their busy fingers beginning to wind the coloured wool around the spindly wooden frames and on to the bobbins.

Rebecca sat on the floor in a corner, playing with a few scraps of wool. She watched her mother and the other women, listened to conversation she did not understand and let her mind stray outside again, to the river that ran so clean into the town and so dirty as it left it. Where did it come from, that river, and where did it go? Her world was small and narrow, yet there were disturbing hints of something bigger outside the boundaries of her own knowledge. Places with names like Yorkshire and Scotland, Birmingham and Wilton. There was another place, too – London, where the King lived.

Rebecca wasn't too clear about the King. He was a very important man, she knew that, and she pictured him as being rather like Mr Bradwell, her mother's employer, only somewhat fatter, and riding everywhere in a carriage made of gold.

But there was something strange about the King. Her mother and the other women were talking about it now.

'Gone mad, they say. And the Prince is going to be Regent in his place. Look after things for him.' The speaker shook her head. 'It just shows, even folks like royalty are just like the rest of us really. Doesn't matter how rich they are.'

'Well, I wouldn't mind some of their gold all the same for that,' Fanny said. 'Mad or not . . . At least he'll be comfortable. Warm and fed. Looked after.' She sighed and Rebecca saw without understanding the tired lines on her grey face. '*He* won't have to sit winding bobbins all day and wonder how to feed a family, or if there'll be any money left over on fall day, when his man's been at the tavern till all hours.'

The other women yelped with laughter at the picture she had conjured up, and Bill Saunders, the overseer, came into the shed, his face stern. 'What's all this noise, then? You should be getting on with your work, not gossiping. I want all these skeins wound by dinner-time, there's a new batch just come in from the dye-house and Mr Bradwell's in a hurry for it.' He marched around the shed, glancing with disapproval at the work being done. 'You idle lot! You're winding too loose – look at this. I suppose you think I won't know?' His face red with anger, he wrenched Fanny's bobbin from its spindle and tossed it the length of the shed. As it rolled away, it unwound a trail of blue yarn, undoing all the work that Fanny had done that morning. She watched hopelessly, knowing that it would be docked from her wage, meaning effectively no pay for that day, and Rebecca saw her eyes mist with tears she was already too exhausted to shed.

A feeling of helpless rage rose in the child's heart. She jumped up from her corner, knocking over one of the winding frames as she did so. Bill Saunders was already halfway down the shed but at the sudden commotion he turned and Rebecca flew at him, her fists clenched as if she were about to pummel him. He caught at her wrists and held her away from him so that her flying feet could not reach his shins.

'What's this then? Who is this little spitfire?'

Fanny got up hastily and came forward, her face anxious and frightened.

'It's my Becky, sir. She don't mean no harm – she's got a bit of a temper but we're taming her. Her father'll take the strap to her, sir, the minute we get home – she won't cause no more trouble—'

'She'd better not—' the overseer began, but his voice was drowned by Rebecca's cries as she struggled against his callous strength, trying to wrench her wrists away from his hands, wriggling frantically in her efforts to get at him.

'Let me go! Let me *go*! You ent got no right – me mam's done her best, she's worked hard all morning and now you've gone and spoilt it. She *weren't* winding loose, she never does, it's just you, you're cruel and hard and—'

'Becky, *stop* it!' Fanny's voice was agonised. She pulled at her daughter's shoulders, trying to drag her away, trying at the same time both to quieten her and calm her. 'Be quiet, for mercy's sake. You'll lose me my job. *Becky*!'

'But it *ent* fair! It's always him as is right – never us. You has to work and work and nobody cares – it ent *fair*!' Rebecca renewed her struggles and actually managed to catch Saunders a sharp kick on the shin. He swore and jerked her closer, giving her a slap on the ear with one hand before he began to rub his leg. Fanny took the opportunity to pull Rebecca away and dealt her a smack on her other ear. Rebecca put her hands up to her head and began to cry, staring at her mother in astonishment and dismay. Why had *Mam* hit her? Hadn't she been trying to help? It *wasn't* fair – none of it was fair. Why shouldn't she say so?

Fanny turned to the overseer.

'Mr Saunders, I'm that sorry. She don't understand – she's only a little girl. Please, don't throw me out – we can't do without the money and I'll work twice as fast, I swear I will. Her dad'll leather her when we get home. She won't do it again, I'll see she won't—' Her voice went on, begging and pleading, while Rebecca listened, her mind cringing at the quavering subservience in Fanny's voice. Her mam was worth six of that man any day. All he did was walk about shouting while women like her mother slaved at their winding frames, their fingers raw and bleeding from handling the yarn. Why should Fanny have to beg and plead like that? Why shouldn't Rebecca say what was no more than the truth?

But she did not speak again. Her head was ringing from the blows she had been given and she didn't want any more. One of the other women came forward and slipped her arms around Rebecca's shoulders, leading her back to her corner. She sat Rebecca down and went back to her own work, keeping her eyes on the yarn she was winding. The other women did the same. Nobody wanted Bill Saunder's fury to be turned on them.

'Please,' Fanny whispered, 'don't turn us away, Mr Saunders.'

Bill Saunders stared at her. His face was red with anger, his small eyes bulging. But Fanny was one of his best workers and he knew that if he were to lose her it would mean getting another woman and training her. And the work was needed. The weavers would be wanting those bobbins.

'All right,' he said grudgingly, and Fanny heaved a sigh of relief. 'All right, we'll overlook it this time. But you keep an eye on that girl of yours. See she behaves herself in future. I'm not having no bit of a wench flying at me the way she did – kicking and scratching and all. Does it again, she'll be out, and you with her. So mind.'

'Yes, sir, I will, I swear. Thank you sir.' Fanny hurried back to her frame and began to wind a new bobbin, her fingers trembling. The overseer watched her for a moment, his face hard; then he gave Rebecca one last glance and turned away.

Rebecca sat very still. She looked at the scraps of wool she had been making into a doll, trying to come to terms with what had just happened.

It *wasn't* fair. But nobody seemed to think that it should be. And a lot of other things weren't fair either, and nobody seemed to think they ought to be put right.

But why was Bill Saunders so much better than her mother? What made him the one who could shout and throw things and never get into any trouble for it? What was the difference between him and her mother,

her father, the rest of the weavers and dyers and bobbin-winders?

On her eighth birthday, Rebecca became her father's draw-girl.

She scarcely needed instruction, knowing the process as well as she knew how to draw water from the well in the yard that served the little row of cottages.

'Are you listening?' William Himley growled, and she snapped to attention, watching as he demonstrated what she must do. 'There's thirteen hundred of these "simple" cords, going through these brass eyes to the box of bowls where the pulleys are – d'you see that? Five colours – that's two hundred and sixty ends of each. The lashes are tied here, see, and what you have to do is catch hold of that first lash and pull all the cords towards you. That separates them from the others, so you've got all the yarns of one colour.' He gave her a sharp look. 'Have you got that, girl?'

'Yes, Father. And then I pull them down so that the ends are up above the new bit of carpet.'

'Hm. I see you've been watching your sister. Now, this is the sword, this bit of wood. You put that in through the width of the weave and hold the yarn up so you can get the terry wire in.' He slid a long, thin blade, much more like a sword than the five-inch-wide wooden board, into the raised pile and withdrew the sword. Then he worked the big wooden treadles with his feet so that half the linen was raised above the surface. Taking the wooden shuttle on which the yarn was wound, he passed it behind the raised chain, lowered it, gave the weave a couple of blows with his steel comb to force it closer together, raised the other half and threw in the next 'shoot'. 'That's woven in that

11

lash. And now we start again. You think you can manage it?'

'Yes, Father.'

Rebecca spoke with docile obedience, knowing that her father's short temper would tolerate nothing else, but even so he gave her a second sharp glance, as if suspecting her of insolence, before grunting: 'Right, let's try it then. And remember, you're going to have to work all the hours I do, it'll be no use complaining you're tired or hungry. This is proper, grown-up work; you're not a baby now.'

'No, Father.' Rebecca scarcely understood what he meant; she had never felt like a baby. Always, she had been expected to do whatever jobs she could manage – helping to sort the coloured yarns at the winding-shed, keeping the smaller children quiet as she grew older, scrubbing potatoes for the family supper.

As for being tired and hungry – these were a natural part of everyday experience. Since 1808, when Rebecca was only three, life for carpetmakers had been growing steadily harder, and there was no sign of any improvement. Half the weavers in Kidderminster were out of work; one of the largest manufacturers, Mr Broom, had laid off half his workforce of seven hundred; and it was no better in the other big carpet factories. Men roamed the streets, living on a poor relief that was stretched to its limits, and the soup kitchens were besieged by starving weavers and their families.

'Serves 'em right for giving up their independence,' William grunted. 'Weavers shouldn't be working for masters – we've always been our own masters. Look at me, got my own loom and as long as the yarn's there I can weave it and no one to tell me different.'

12

'That's all right so long as there's someone to buy your piece,' Fanny snapped. 'What do you do if you go back on fall day and Mr Taylor says he don't want it? Going to set up as agent on your own, are you?'

William glowered at her. 'That'll never happen. They've supplied us with the yarn, they're honour bound to buy it back.'

'So long as you take it back in time,' Fanny said bitterly. It had happened more than once that William had been late with his piece – and if it were not returned at precisely the correct time on fall day (either Thursday or Saturday) then it would be refused. And that meant another week on only Fanny's wage, a week of potatoes and little else, with no yarn to weave; a week of gnawing hunger and 'play' as the weavers bitterly called such enforced idleness, with William's temper growing worse as he slumped out of the house each morning to loiter in the streets with other idle weavers, and spend the few farthings he had managed to keep to himself in the tavern.

'Always money for drink,' Fanny said caustically. 'You never go short of that, never mind if the boy needs boots or Bessie a pinafore. Never mind that we didn't eat at all yesterday and if it weren't for old Mag giving Rebecca a crust now and then she'd be in her grave with the rest of the babbies. Ah, and lucky to be there too, if you want to know.'

'I don't. And you can stop your groaning, woman. We don't live so bad – there's plenty worse off than us. Only three children, and with young Tom bringing in three shilling a week from Butts, and Bessie due to start as draw-girl there now Becky's old enough to work for me, we don't do so bad.'

'No, not until there's more lay-offs and we're all at home to play together. And nothing coming in at all.

It'll be the parish for us then, Will Himley, independence or no. Independence!' she snorted. 'A fine thing for them as can afford it.'

Her husband gave her a black look and stamped out of the house. Rebecca, watching from the heap of sacks where she sat in a corner, heard his footsteps go away up the cobbled street. Fanny sighed and turned to the sagging basket which held the potatoes she had saved for tonight's supper.

'Why aren't people buying carpets now?' Rebecca asked. 'Have they got enough?' She had tried often to picture the kind of house where people lived who actually bought the carpets her father wove. Where they laid them on the floor – on the *floor*! – and walked on them, apparently oblivious of the mud that must come off their boots and obscure the beautiful colours. There was nothing on the floors Rebecca knew, other than an occasional length of Kidderminster 'stuff' – rough, of no particular colour or pattern but serving to soften the worst of the chill hardness of the floor.

'People never have enough – people with money,' Fanny answered vaguely. 'No, it's not that – it's summat to do with these wars we're having with the Frenchies. Don't ask me why a lot of queer foreigners should have anything to do with us here in Kidder, but that's what they say.' She dropped a potato in the pan of water she had placed ready by the fire. 'Not that it matters to us – whatever happens, we'll always get worst of it.'

'You used to work in a house with carpets, didn't you, Mam?' Rebecca asked, knowing the answer but wanting a story and wanting, for a moment at least, to take the grey weariness out of her mother's face.

As she had hoped, the tired lines softened and the eyes brightened a little.

'Ah, up at Mr Pagnel's – I were in service there, could've done well for myself too. I hoped to rise to be parlourmaid and would have if I hadn't wed your father.' She sighed. 'Oh, it's a fine place, the Pagnels' house – big rooms, bigger than this whole row of cottages put together, and carpets spread over all the floors – such colours, you wouldn't believe. The housekeeper told me some of them came from places like Turkey and Persia. Not that we had carpets in the servants' quarters, mind. And we worked hard – oh yes, we worked all right. Up at five in the morning, I was, to clear out the grates and blacklead and polish them before the family was about. And never off my feet till I went to bed at ten, if I was lucky. But you got good meals there, and clean clothes to wear, and a proper bed to sleep in, even if 'twere freezing in winter and roasting in summer up under that roof. Ah.' She looked back with the rose-misted spectacles of nostalgia to days that had been harder than she remembered. 'We had some good times there. That were when Mr Jeremiah were a lad, of course.'

'Why doesn't Bessie go into service, instead of being a draw-girl?' Rebecca asked. 'Our Tom comes home too tired to stand when he's working twelve and twelve, and he's three year older than she. Wouldn't she be better up at Mr Pagnel's?'

Another potato dropped into the water. Fanny's mouth tightened. She disliked the twelve and twelve system as much as anyone and resented the broken nights when Tom came in dropping with fatigue at one in the morning, having worked since one the previous afternoon. The system which required weavers to share a loom, keeping it working between them for the full twenty-four hours of each day, was universally unpopular and ate away at the independence of

15

which weavers were so jealous. But there – nobody was truly independent, and if you wanted the work, and the wage, you had to do as you were bid. And with both work and money short at present, even twelve and twelve would have been welcome. As it was, few weavers went to work without the fear that today might be the day they were sent home again with nothing in their pockets.

'Bessie go into service? Your father'll not hear of it. He's like the rest of them – sees himself a cut above the folk who have to take orders from others. Though what he thinks he's doing when he goes to collect his yarn and bobbins of a Tuesday morning . . .' She dropped the third, and last, potato into the water, and felt in the pocket of her skirt. 'Here, child, here's a farthing – go and see if old Thomas will let you have a bone for some gravy to go with these potatoes.' She watched Rebecca scamper away up the muddy street. 'And what'll become of you, my girl?' she muttered to herself. 'A draw-girl like your sister until some young cock gets you in the family way? And then slave and grind away, with a babby a year and never a sight of anything better . . .' She turned away and lifted the pan on to the fire. 'Service . . . it might be hard, but it's bound to be better than this – if only Will could see it.'

But William Himley could not see it. And this week, Bessie had gone with Tom to begin working as a draw-girl in the factory and Rebecca had taken her place at her father's side, inserting first the wooden sword and then the thin blade of the terry wire to raise the pile for him. Over and over again, for hour after hour – first the sword, then the wire, now the sword, now the wire . . . until she felt she would scream with the sheer tedium of it, and from the growing ache in her legs and back.

16

But there was nothing to be done about it, no use in complaining. At the slightest hint of flagging, the slightest droop of her eyelids, her father would cuff her back into attention. And the gnawing in her belly, the aches and the pains and the boredom would all have to be relegated to the back of her mind as she concentrated once more on her work. Sword, wire – sword – wire – sword – wire – until once again she thought she must scream or go entirely mad.

And again, did neither; simply acquired another layer of toughness, another fibre of determination never to give in.

Bessie was delighted to be leaving her father's loom and going to work in the bigger shed owned by Mr Butts down near the river. There were other girls there, girls and boys too of her own age, working on the looms that Albert Butts kept clattering day and night. Twelve and twelve wasn't new to Bessie; she had worked long enough hours when William, after keeping St Monday too well at the beginning of the week, had been forced to stay at his loom until late into the night in order to finish his piece by fall day. She had even helped him with the shears sometimes, wielding the big, heavy tool almost as dexterously as he did himself to snip off long ends and make the pile of the carpet smooth and even.

But it had been a lonely life with only her father for company, and William Himley was a silent, taciturn man. His weaving was good because that was the way he earned a living, and because he saw himself as an independent man, licking no master's boots. He was a weaver because his father had been a weaver, and his grandfather too, in the days when Kidderminster had been known for its worsteds, its silks and bombazines, its poplins and prunellas. He had never thought of taking any other trade and it did not occur to him that any of his children would do so. And so each one, on reaching the age of eight, became his drawer and went on to work in the trade, bringing in the extra few shillings that enabled Fanny to buy bread and meat and sometimes a pair of second-hand boots or a shirt or shawl for one of them.

Bessie knew quite well that she wouldn't be allowed to keep more than a penny or two of the money she earned. But on that first morning, stepping jauntily through the narrow streets to the carpet shed, she cared nothing for that. It was the company she was looking forward to – the chatter of other girls, the glances of the boys. At thirteen, Bessie was as big as a girl three or four years older, her slightly protuberant blue eyes bold, her red lips pouting. For months now she had been restless, eager to be out of the house at every opportunity, impatient with Rebecca and half-shy, half-flirtatious with her brother Tom.

Near the factory, she saw another girl, a year or two older than herself, and hurried to catch up with her.

'Nell! Thought you were going to call for us.'

The girl turned and her eyes brightened. 'Well, Bess, so you'm come. I wondered if your dad'd let thee. You've been working for he long enough.'

'Too long,' Bessie said, tossing her tangled yellow hair. 'Time our Becky did her turn. I been shut up with him till I thought I'd go mad with it. Now – tell us. Who's your fancy-boy this week?'

Nell giggled. 'And who's to say I've got a fancy-boy? We're not all like you, Bess Himley, down by the canal bridge of a night.'

'And how would you know I'd been there if you hadn't been yourself?' Bessie dug her elbow in her friend's side and they both yelped with laughter. 'Hey-up, look at this. I've not seen him before.'

They both stopped and stared as a young man crossed the road ahead of them, making for the door of Butts' shed. Taller than most of the weavers who were thronging the river-bank now, he was thickly built with broad shoulders and a neck like a bull's. His head was covered with black curls that looked as if they had been greased and polished, and when he turned to glance back along the rutted road the girls saw that there was a handsome arrogance in his face. As they came closer, slowing down for a better look, his black eyes moved over them carelessly and they nudged each other and giggled again.

'I wouldn't mind drawing *his* sword,' Nell muttered, and Bessie let out a squawk of mirth. The dark eyes moved back to her, and she caught her breath as his glance drifted across her face and lingered on the swelling figure beneath her shabby dress. She felt an odd twinge inside and reacted without thinking about it, lifting her chin a little and meeting his gaze boldly. For an instant, his look sharpened and she felt the heat in her cheeks; then he turned away and disappeared into the shed.

'Well!' Nell whispered as they followed him. 'I'd say you made a mark there. Hey-up – there's another one.' Her eyes widened as a second young man passed them. Although a few years younger, he was almost as tall as the first, but more slender; fair, with a pale complexion and eyes as dark as the indigo dye used in the dyeshops along the riverbank.

With the two girls still half blocking the doorway, he was forced to slow his pace. Again, Bessie bridled, moving her shoulders and lifting her chin. But the dark blue glance passed over her without interest.

Politely, the young man stepped aside to let them through. With a feeling of chagrin, Bessie followed her friend into the shed.

'Well, there's a couple of good-lookers for you,' Nell giggled. 'What did you think of the fair one, eh? Still waters run deep there, I'd say . . . Wonder who they are. Don't look like weavers to me.'

'They're not,' said one of the other women as they crowded into the shed. 'The dark one's Mr Vivian – Jeremiah Pagnel's boy. You won't find *him* at a loom. And the other's his cousin Francis – son to the schoolmaster up at the Grammar School. They must have come to see Mr Butts about summat.'

Bessie looked around the shed. She had been here before, when her father had brought her to Albert Butts a week ago to arrange for her to start work, but she had taken little notice of the looms. She had been more interested in the people operating them and her eyes had roved over the weavers, wondering which of the men she would draw for. But now she was more interested in the arrogant Vivian Pagnel, and her blood stirred as she caught a glimpse of him at the far end of the shed, talking with Mr Butts while his cousin stood by listening.

However, she was not to be allowed to stare for long. As the weavers and their assistants settled into their places, the overseer came bustling down the shed and caught at Bessie's arm with one hand. A short, squat frog of a man, he stared up into her face and she turned her face away from his pungent breath.

'Come on, girl, come on—' even his voice was like the croak of a frog '—you don't have no time to stand there gawking. We're not on holiday here, you know. Might've had it easy, working at home, now you're going to learn what real work is.' He dragged her past

20

several looms to one which had only one man sitting before it. 'Here you are, Jabez, here's your new draw-girl. She ought to know how to do it, she's been drawing for her father since she were eight, so I won't expect you to work any slower for the sake of having to teach her naught.' He gave Bessie a little push. 'All right, get started, you've lost time already and it's me that'll get stick if production goes down.' He stepped back and his eyes flickered over them. 'Didn't you hear me, then? Get *started*.'

He scuttered away down the shed and Bessie turned to look at the man she would work with. Jabez Gast – she had heard of him from Tom. Her heart sank a little. Jabez was known to have a sarcastic tongue and a mean temper. Her picture of a day filled with chatter and laughter with the other girls began to fade.

Jabez's small, hard eyes watched her. He was a tall, spare man, lanky as a spider, with thin, pale hair lying like old hay across his small, lumpy head. He jerked his head at the sword and the terry wire, lying ready for Bessie to use.

'You know how to use them?'

She nodded.

'All right,' he said, and checked the bobbins and lashes to see that all was ready. 'Don't let's waste any more time.'

Bessie opened her mouth to make a retort, and then caught his eye and thought better of it. She had been warned by both Tom and her mother that her over-ready tongue would serve her ill here. 'Save your cheek for outside the doors,' Fanny had said, and with Jabez's cold eye on her as she took the lashes in her hand, Bessie knew that it had been good advice.

All the same, she meant to enjoy whatever she

21

could of this new life. And she was aware when Vivian Pagnel walked back along the shed and passed the loom; aware too of a perceptible slowing in his pace and a brief touch of his arm against her back. She was thankful that Jabez was absorbed in his weaving at that moment, so did not see her sudden flush.

Vivian Pagnel was out of her class, of course. She'd probably never see him again, so close. But he was just a taste of what there was out there and Bessie, already a woman and well informed on what that meant, intended to make the most of the attributes Nature had given her.

She had no intention of following in her mother's footsteps – marrying a weaver, falling for a baby every year, spending three-quarters of her life dragging a swollen body around only for a mess of pain and blood at the end of each miserable pregnancy. No – for Bessie, there was to be something more. A life that was more comfortable, with a proper house, a fire whenever it was cold and enough food to fill her belly.

How this was to be achieved, she was not yet sure. But she knew that the long, yellow hair which curled down to her shoulders, the bold blue eyes so unlike her mother's anxious glance, and the bouncing figure which had begun to draw the men's glances when she was only twelve, were all weapons to be used to gain her object. And now that she was out of her father's cottage, she could begin to practise the use of them.

There being no other material available at the moment, she began with Jabez Gast. When he next looked up, she smiled slowly at him and let her tongue appear briefly on her lower lip. Then, as if confused, she glanced away; and knew that his gaze rested on

22

her for a second longer before he too returned his attention to his work.

While Rebecca stood beside her father's loom and Bessie began work with Jabez Gast, their brother Tom was in another part of the shed, weaving his own piece of carpet.

Tom wasn't yet a full weaver. He had been apprenticed to Samuel Hooman, one of the journeyman weavers employed by Albert Butts, at the age of thirteen, after working as draw-boy for two years. The premium demanded by Hooman had cost William and Fanny dear, but for once William had not begrudged the money. For Tom to make any kind of a living, he had to be a trained weaver. William looked forward to the day when he and Tom would work together, a loom each, with the two girls as drawers until such time as Tom would marry and produce his own children to take on the work.

As an apprentice, Tom had to live with Hooman's family. The rules were strict, as for all apprentices – his allegiance now must belong to his master, he must not get married (or 'commit fornication', a term which had puzzled him until he was enlightened by the other apprentices) nor play cards nor dice, nor 'haunt Taverns or Playhouses'.

How an apprentice could be expected to haunt such places when he was paid nothing but the occasional ha'penny or farthing, tossed to him as a dog might be tossed a bone, Tom didn't know. There were, of course, opportunities to make money. Yarn could be stolen, tools left carelessly lying about filched and sold.

It was a risky business, but some boys were ready to take the chance, nevertheless. Tom, when invited to join them, shook his head.

'Come on, Tom – old Sam'll never know, he's half blind anyway.'

'He knows what yarn he's got all the same. It'd be more than my place is worth—'

'And what's that?' Will Hatherley sneered. 'Slaves, that's all we are. Paid nothing, worked like dogs from dawn till dusk, half starved and beaten if we dares to say aught. Why shouldn't we make what we can when we gets the chance? I can get a good price for a few bits of yarn. Don't you want a sup of ale down the tavern, like the rest of us?'

'Aye, and what happens if we get caught? Magistrates' court and hard labour, and that's if you're lucky. You could find yourself on ship and bound for Australia. It's not worth it.'

'Ah, you're too good to be true,' Will said in disgust. 'I suppose you're looking to be a half-weaver. Hev old Sam said aught?'

'Not in so many words,' Tom said reluctantly. 'Anyway, it's not that. I just don't see stealing from him—'

'Gawby! What's he ever done for thee? Fed thee, aye, when he had to, to keep thee alive to work all the hours God sends. That in't stealing – 'tis your right. Everyone does it.'

But Tom simply shook his head again and left them. He had set his face against even the pettiest of pilfering from his master. Not that Samuel was a particularly kind master – he imposed a strict discipline on his apprentices and, as Will had truly said, he extracted every ounce of work from them. But he was fair, and Tom knew that he was hoping to be offered a second loom, on which he could employ Tom as a half-weaver. He had already hinted that there might be a shilling or two a week as pay, and Tom was working hard to improve his weaving at the prospect of this advancement.

He was too busy, then, to keep an eye open for his sister on her first day at work, or to notice the glances of the other boys when they caught sight of her. Nor did he take much notice of Vivian Pagnel as he talked to Albert Butts and moved slowly through the shed, his dark eyes taking everything in.

Tom's world was small and narrow, confined to his loom, his master and his family at home. He did not understand that a much wider world could affect him; that stones thrown into a pool from different points could start ripples that would reach, touch and change his life. Vivian and Francis Pagnel, Jabez Gast – they moved around him in a circle, unnoticed, unregarded. Yet each had a part to play in the lives of Tom, Bessie and Rebecca. Each would reach out a finger and set those lives on a different course.

There was no sign on that October morning in 1813 that anything had changed. But in truth, everything had.

Chapter Two

On the day that Rebecca had her eighth birthday and
started to work as her father's draw-girl, another
birthday was celebrated in Kidderminster. Vivian
Pagnel was twenty-one and the Pagnels gathered
together in the house on Mount Pleasant to toast his
health.

Isabella, slender as a rod, sat up in her chair with a
back as stiff as if there were a sword sewn into her
dress. She glanced with pride at her son. Totally
unlike her, with her silvery fair hair and air of brittle
fragility; so much like his father, with those black
curls and laughing, arrogant eyes.

For a moment, she allowed her mind to dwell on the
days long ago, when she and Vivian's father had been
first married. But thoughts like that were unsettling.
That first, youthful marriage had been so different
from the life she now shared with Jeremiah. Vivian's
true father, her first husband, had been so unpre-
dictable, so full of energy, of sudden ideas . . .
whereas Jeremiah was so safe, so reliable. A good
husband, she knew, and she valued him even while she
sighed, occasionally, for the heady excitements of
youth.

But those had been firmly put away now. She
turned her mind quickly away and looked again at her
family.

Who would have thought that she, so delicate as a
child, would bear five robust children? A pity that
four of them had to be daughters – but Vivian was

27

son enough. Even for Jeremiah, surely. She glanced at her husband, sitting in his favourite armchair and talking with his nephew Francis, and frowned a little. Francis was a nice enough boy, she had nothing against him, but there were times – and this was one of them – when it seemed that those two were too close. This was Vivian's day. It was to him – his *son* – that Jeremiah should be paying attention.

'You're looking very solemn, Mamma,' a voice said softly in her ear, and she looked up quickly, her face alight with pleasure.

'Vivian. How handsome you look. And so grown up.' She sighed a little. 'It seems only yesterday that you were a little boy, in frocks. What happens to the years? You – and your sisters, all grown up. I feel quite old.'

'You look no older than a sister to me,' he responded with the smile that had caught the attention of Bess Himley that morning. 'Why, look at Jane and Edith – nobody can believe they're your daughters. Married women of twenty-five and twenty-three – it's absurd.'

'And you're absurd, Vivian,' she said, laughing. 'Flirting with your own mother. Are there no young ladies for you to practise your charms on?'

'None as beautiful as you, Mamma.' He turned as his cousin Francis came over to them, awkward with the lankiness of adolescence. 'And here comes young Frank to tell you all about our visit to Butts' carpet sheds this morning. Now there were plenty of pretty young ladies there, weren't there, Frank?'

'Were there? I suppose so.' Francis bent to take his aunt's hand. 'They were all working so hard, I didn't care to stare at them. And they looked so young – only children, younger than Isabel, some of them.

28

Uncle Jeremiah says they work full hours, as long as the weavers, even the twelve and twelve system.' His dark blue eyes were troubled and he frowned a little.

'Well, and why not? You mustn't let yourself be swayed by sentimentality.' With a flourish, Vivian took out the snuffbox that had been one of his birthday presents, then remembered his manners and put it away again. 'The working class is different from us, Francis. Stronger. They're accustomed to hard work. It's their life.'

'Is it? They looked as human as you or I. I can't believe they wouldn't appreciate a little more leisure.'

'More leisure!' Vivian gave a crow of laughter. 'Why, they have as much leisure as anyone could wish for. Haven't you heard of St Monday – kept as religiously as any Sunday. And some of them even keep St Tuesday too, when they've a mind. They work when they like, that's the truth of it, and when they've earned enough money to fill their bellies at home and their pots in the alehouse, they take their leisure again. Isn't that right, Mamma?'

'Quite right,' she said, smiling fondly.

'Of course it is. Why, what do they call it when they can't work, for whatever reason? Play. *Play*. That shows you how much they care for hard work.'

'That may be true of the independent weavers. But those in places like Butts—'

'Albert Butts has a rent to pay on his sheds and on his looms too,' Vivian said carelessly. 'It's in his interest to keep those looms working. Especially now that I'm putting the rent up.'

'Putting the rent—' Francis stared at him. 'Did you tell him that this morning?'

'Of course not. I simply let him think that I was

29

coming in to look over the place, since Father had assigned it to me on my birthday. Which was nothing other than the truth, after all.' Vivian smiled. 'But he seems to have a very efficient operation running there. He must be making quite a fat profit. I don't see why I shouldn't benefit a little from that.'

'But you heard what Uncle Jeremiah said – the recession has made everything difficult. If Butts is doing well—'

'I should share in his good fortune,' Vivian said smoothly. 'After all, the business is mine now, effectively. The premises and all the equipment belong to me. If Butts doesn't like my terms, I've no doubt there are plenty of other manufacturers who will be pleased to take it on.' He smiled at Francis. 'Anyway, why should it bother you, cousin? You're hardly of an age to understand such matters.'

'I'm almost fifteen,' Francis said. 'And I shall be coming into the business as soon as I leave school. Uncle Jeremiah—'

'Jeremiah has been very kind to you, we all know that,' Isabella interposed swiftly. 'And I'm sure he will be pleased to take you on in some capacity, if you should still be of the same mind when you come to leave school. But won't your father want you to follow in *his* footsteps – become a schoolmaster?'

'In any case, you're not likely to have the same kind of responsibilities as I shall have,' Vivian said coolly. 'I shall be inheriting the business – the factory, the rented sheds, everything. And I intend to build it up into something much, much bigger than it is at present.' He glanced at the big man who stood at the other end of the room, head bent as he listened to something his stepdaughters were saying to him. 'Father has done very well, but he doesn't realise that

30

the time for expansion is drawing near.'

'But the recession—'

'There is always someone,' Vivian said, flicking a speck of dust from his jacket, 'who will make money from a recession. I intend that Pagnel's should be that someone. It's simply a matter of watching what happens, and being ready when the moment comes.'

Isabella looked at him with fond admiration. 'And I'm sure your father is right to begin to give you more responsibility, Vivian.' She turned her smile on the younger boy. 'And no doubt there'll be a place for you, too, my dear, when the time comes. But I still think your father would prefer you to follow his own calling. After all, you've inherited his talent, haven't you.'

Francis bowed his head non-committally and as his aunt and cousin began to talk again of Vivian's prospects, he let his mind wander. They weren't really interested in him, he knew that. He wasn't exactly a 'poor relation' but the gulf between his home and Jeremiah's household was wide, particularly as far as Isabella and her son were concerned.

Sensing himself forgotten, Francis drifted over to the big window that looked down over the town of Kidderminster. It was dark now and only a few lights could be seen: mostly those of factories which were still working, illuminated by candles or oil lamps. The narrow streets were lost in the heavy murk that so often descended over the town, especially in the autumn and winter.

Somewhere in the darkness was the carpet shed where he had been that morning. He remembered the clatter of the looms, the drawn, tired faces of the weavers and their assistants. Some of them were, as he had remarked, no more than children. Younger than

31

himself, younger than his cousins Sarah and Isabel, as young as eight or nine years old. Francis stared down as if trying to pierce the darkness, to see into the carpet sheds and factories, into the cramped houses that clustered about them.

And not far away was the street where he lived with his own parents. Church Row, rising from the Bull Ring to the open space in front of the red sandstone of St Mary's Church, was generally accepted to be one of the best addresses in Kidderminster, with its grand new houses built on both sides. It was not in one of these, however, that the Pagnels lived; as under-master of the King Charles I Grammar School, Geoffrey Pagnel occupied one of the old timbered buildings, their upper storeys leaning drunkenly out over the street, that had been built two hundred years ago when Kidderminster had been already flourishing as a manufacturing and market town.

Geoffrey was in the room now, talking to Jeremiah, and Francis watched them covertly, wondering as he so often did how it was that two brothers could be so different. There were years between them, of course. Geoffrey, the elder, was tall and thin, with mild blue eyes and a vague air that was often miscon-strued by the boys in his class. He was not really a born teacher; he would have preferred to be a scholar, studying and writing. But old Joseph Pagnel had not yet achieved success with his new carpet weaving busi-ness when Geoffrey had left school, and since he was clearly quite impractical and unsuited to business life, the position of under-master at the Grammar School had been seen as an opportunity not to be missed. Only later, when Jeremiah's better-developed busi-ness sense had brought prosperity to the family, did Geoffrey's life seem at all lacking.

'Not that he sees anything amiss,' Jeremiah had observed to his wife once when they had not been married long. 'He'd rather be shut up in that cramped little house of his with his books than making money, if it means noise and dirt and smells. And that wife of his encourages him.'

'Enid thinks of nothing but Francis,' Isabella said, forgetting that her own son was the apple of her eye. 'I suppose it's natural, if you have only one child.' She spoke with the complacency of one who has been successful in raising several children. 'Even though Francis isn't really her child – one tends to forget that. I wonder where he did come from.' She looked at her husband.

Jeremiah moved in his chair, then got up to walk to the window. 'Geoffrey and Enid will never say, I'm certain of that. And it hardly matters – Francis passes easily for their son. Why, he even resembles Geoffrey, with that fair hair and slender build. And shows every sign of being just as bookish, though I believe he's beginning to display quite a talent as an artist.'

Isabella gave him an arch look. 'Do you suppose Francis *is* Geoffrey's son? I wonder if Enid—'

'No!' Jeremiah spoke brusquely. 'I don't suppose any such thing. The matter's simple enough and you know the story as well as I do. Francis was the child of some poor young woman of Geoffrey's acquaintance who died in giving birth to him. Geoffrey and Enid were glad to take him as their own son, but he is *not* Geoffrey's by-blow and I don't want to hear such a suggestion on your lips again.'

'Well, of course not, Jeremiah. But when nobody knows the mother's name or the circumstances—'

'They're nobody else's business. *Nobody's*. Geoffrey and Enid agreed that the unfortunate woman's name should be kept a secret. It's much the best way.'

'Well, of course, my love,' she murmured, looking down at her hands. 'You know I'd never dream . . . especially in our own situation . . .'

She could not see Jeremiah's face, but knew from his sudden stillness that she had struck a nerve. He had never quite recovered from his apparent inability to father sons, even though he had agreed when they were married to adopt her own son Vivian as his heir, and had never given any sign of regretting it. But every man wanted his own son; it was natural. And she had done her best, nobody could say otherwise. It was her misfortune – and his – that they had been able to produce only another two daughters to add to the three children, Vivian and his sisters Edith and Jane, that she had brought with her from her previous marriage.

Francis knew nothing of this conversation, nor of the implications it had held for himself and his cousin. He knew, of course, that Vivian was not Jeremiah's true son but the son of Isabella and her first husband, Alfred Faulkner, who had died leaving her with three children and a very useful fortune. And he knew too that he was not the true son of Geoffrey and Enid Pagnel. But that had never disturbed him; they were all the parents he had ever known or wanted.

He looked now at the man he knew as his father, stooping already into old age though he could not be more than fifty, and at the hearty, robust uncle who had brought Pagnel Carpets to the forefront of the Kidderminster industry.

As Francis looked across the room, Geoffrey lifted his head and their eyes met. As if aware of a shift in his brother's attention, Jeremiah glanced up too. The two men and the boy, separated by a room filled with people and by the gulf of years, stared at each other.

Francis was aware of a tiny prickle at the back of his neck. For a brief space of time, he felt he was on the edge of grasping some elusive truth, something that was important to him. And then it was gone, leaving him with no more than a sense of unease, as if a ghost had passed across his vision.

He turned away quickly and was thankful to find his youngest cousin, eleven-year-old Isabel, at his side. Together, they began to discuss the latest addition to his butterfly collection.

Over the next two years, Bessie's hopes of seeing more of the handsome Vivian Pagnel faded slowly. He seldom came to the carpet shop, other than for the occasional visit when he sauntered past the looms with Butts in servile attendance, glancing with his bold, dark eyes at the girls who worked with swords and wires to draw up the pile as it was woven. Whenever he passed her, Bessie would do her best to meet his gaze, but since that first morning he seemed to have forgotten her and would pass her with no sign of recognition. For a moment, she would stare after him, deflated and angry, but a sharp word from Jabez would bring her back swiftly to her task and she knew that for the rest of the day the weaver's tongue would be even harsher than usual.

Her first excitement at going to work in the carpet shop had quickly evaporated. Each morning, as she hurried through the streets, she had to accustom herself all over again to the rancid smells of wet wool and boiling dyes. Once inside, the smell was even stronger, worsened by the tub of size which stood in one corner. On that morning two years ago, when she had first seen it, Bessie had drawn back, revolted by the stench of leather and gelatine.

'Ugh! What's it for?'

'It stiffens the chain,' Nellie explained. 'Makes it easier to work. You gets used to it.'

Bessie wrinkled her nose and wondered, and her doubts were increased when she saw a second large tub which stood at the doorway. The odour which came from this was unmistakable and she soon saw why, when one of the men left his loom, went to the tub and, unfastening his trousers, proceeded to relieve himself into it. Bessie stared and the man, catching her eye, grimaced rudely. 'Seen enough?' he asked, and some of the others laughed. Her face burning, Bessie turned back to the loom and found Jabez watching her sardonically.

'You'll hev to get used to that too,' he remarked. 'Master needs the piss to make dye, so we has to give him that as well as the sweat off our backs. Seems the Himleys are brought up too delicate to work with us common folks, your dad being an *independent* weaver.'

Bessie flushed but said nothing. She had found very quickly that it didn't pay to answer back. So far, Jabez had not struck her, but his tongue was abrasive and she feared the look in his small, hard eyes. And she had seen several of the other weavers beating and even kicking their draw-boys and girls; she didn't imagine that Jabez would be any more gentle if the mood took him.

'I reckon our Rebecca's got the best of it after all,' she told Nellie as they sat eating their breakfast. After over two years in the carpet shop, a good deal of her original bounce had left her. 'Doesn't have to come out in the cold, no stink in her nose, only one loom

. . . Didn't know when I was well off.'

'Well, her turn'll come,' Nellie said, chewing on a crust. 'There's naught else for the likes of us around here. What is she now, ten, eleven? Won't be long now before she's at the looms with the rest of us and your ma drawing for your dad.'

'I dunno so much.' Bessie was thoughtful. 'Our ma seems to think there's summat special about our Becky – like she's too good for the carpet shop. She's talking about putting Becky in service.'

Nellie sniffed. 'Service! Your dad'll never stand for that. He's like the rest of the independents – thinks weaving's summat better than serving other people. He wants to come down here and see little girls being belted round the shop, and worse. And that's nothing to what goes on when we're working twelve and twelve.'

Bessie nodded and wrinkled her nose. ' 'Twouldn't be so bad if they kept to twelve and twelve,' she said. 'But old Jabez, he sent me home at ten the other night and wanted me back here at two in the morning. Just because he'd spent the Tuesday drinking and had to finish his piece by Thursday. I was too bone weary to eat my supper and only had three hours in my bed.'

The overseer's froglike face appeared before them and the two girls looked up. 'We've got five more minutes yet,' Nellie said defensively.

'Not if I say you haven't,' he sneered. 'Get back to those looms – we've a big order on, and that new pattern ent turning out right. Too much blue in it. We've got to throw away all that's been done so far and start again – you're in for a late night tonight, doxies, so I hope you haven't laid on anything special for this evening.'

'Just settin' down peaceful for half an hour'd be

summat special,' Nellie muttered as they hurried back. 'Did you hear that? All to do again – and no extra time allowed, you can be certain. By the time this lot's finished, you'll think yourself lucky to get three hours in bed, Bess.'

Bess did not reply. She could see Jabez already at the loom, his cold, pale face set in even harsher lines than usual. He gave her a brief look as she took up her position, and began work without a word. Her heart sank as she grasped the sword and watched the shuttle. When he put his mind to it, Jabez could work faster and longer than any weaver in the shop – and he made no allowance for any fatigue on the part of his draw-girl, who was forced to stand for hours at his side, her hands moving mechanically to insert the broad wooden sword and the narrow blade of the terry wire, her back aching and her calf-muscles screaming for relief.

Working to a new pattern was always difficult. The quills and bobbins had to be wound and ranged in a different order, and the automatic knowledge of the pattern, gained through hours of repetitive motion, had to be relearned. Several times, Jabez cursed as he reached out for the wrong colour and as the hours wore on and they both grew increasingly weary, so his temper worsened.

Matters were not improved when there was a stir at the doorway and Bessie glanced round to see Albert Butts coming in with someone else close behind him.

'Now what do *he* want?' Jabez muttered. ' 'Tis all we need – the master looking over our shoulder just when we're racing time to get the piece finished. *And* young cock-of-the-walk Pagnel, too.'

Bessie felt her heart give a little jump. Vivian Pagnel? She stole another quick glance and saw that he was indeed there, walking beside Albert Butts and stopping at each loom to examine the newly woven carpet.

'Not bad,' she heard him say as he drew near. 'Not bad at all. I like this new design, yes, I like it very much. It'll do well in my new drawing-room.' He came to Jabez's loom and stopped beside Bessie. 'How are you finding this new pattern?'

Jabez gave him the briefest of glances. 'Well enough, when we're allowed to work on it.' He barely paused in his work, his hands moving swiftly, feet on the treadles, almost as if he were playing a church organ. Vivian Pagnel smiled a little, and turned his dark eyes on Bessie.

'And you? You enjoy working here?' His glance was like a caress and she shivered and touched her lips with her tongue, not knowing what to reply. Enjoy working in a carpet shop? Enjoy working at all, in any job she had ever heard of? She was suddenly aware that her hands had stopped moving and that Jabez was glowering at her, and went hastily back to her work. Vivian laughed and passed on and she heard him murmur something to Albert Butts, who answered him with the obsequious tone in his voice that would change to harsh tyranny the moment his young master had left the shop.

Bessie worked on in a dream, hardly conscious of the weaver's cursing. For a brief space of time, she was back to the first day when she had come into the carpet shop, when Vivian Pagnel and his young cousin Francis had been there and she had first met the glance of those dark, arrogant eyes. Her heart was beating hard, just as it had then; and now she had something else to savour. The words that she had heard Vivian Pagnel murmur to Albert Butts, barely

39

audible under the clatter of the looms yet burning in her ears as if they had been shouted.

'That's a fine piece of goods, Butts,' Vivian Pagnel had said. 'And I don't mean the carpet, either. What's her name?'

She hadn't heard Butts' reply. But she hugged the question to her as she thrust the sword into place with one hand, the wire with the other.

He'd noticed her. Vivian Pagnel had *noticed* her – Bessie Himley. He'd wanted to know her name.

There was a sudden heavy pain in her hand as Jabez struck her hard with a rockatee rod, and she jerked back to attention, her eyes filling with agonised tears. She stared at him, shocked and sickened.

'Get your mind on your work,' he snarled, and the look in his eyes was so coldly furious that she trembled. 'I know what you're thinking, Bess Himley – and you can forget it. The likes of young Pagnel ent for you. And mind this—' he lifted the rod again and Bessie flinched '—if we don't finish this piece tonight, there'll be more of Master Rod to keep thee in order, and he'll not be so gentle next time, either.'

He gave her a final glare and picked up his shuttle again. And Bessie, trembling with pain and fright, set her bruised and shaking hand to her own tools. Vivian Pagnel was forgotten.

But she did not forget him for long. The look in his eyes, almost as if he were touching her, the ringing quality of his voice, the swagger in his walk, returned to her mind again and again. She clung to them, conjuring up their memory to help her through the long, wearying hours. And as she dragged her exhausted body through the streets on her way home, or stumbled half-asleep to the factory after no more than a few hours' sleep, the possibility that she might catch a glimpse of him kept her drooping eyes open and her tired heart thudding.

She was aware too of the changes that were taking place in her body. The flow of blood that the other girls had talked about with a mixture of knowingness and resignation had begun soon after her fourteenth birthday, but even earlier than that her breasts had begun to blossom and she had seen the eyes of the boys and men in the carpet shop follow the sway of her rounded hips as she walked past the looms. Excited by an attention she had never known before, she reacted to it, exaggerating the movements of her body, flaunting its new ripeness. And she had been rewarded by that sharpening of interest in Vivian Pagnel's dark, assessing eyes.

Surely he would seek her out? Surely he would come to the carpet shop again? He had asked her name – he *must* be interested.

Her thoughts and dreams were filled with him and with a growing fantasy in which he bore her away to some dark place where he took her in his arms and kissed her . . . Her fantasy never went much further than that, but she knew that there would be more to come and her body ached and quivered and grew warm and moist with the sensations conjured up by her dream.

But Vivian did not come. And Bessie stood at the loom, her legs throbbing with fatigue, her hands moving swiftly and mechanically, and yearned. And never noticed the different look in Jabez Gast's small, hard eyes, or the way his thin lips slackened as he glanced at her burgeoning body and yellow hair.

The new pattern was mastered at last, and the shop

in full production. Even Albert Butts seemed satisfied, but this brought little pleasure to the weavers and their assistants, who found themselves working harder than ever to produce yards and yards of carpet. They worked twelve and twelve for week after week, living in a daze of clattering looms, flying shuttles, spindles, quills and bobbins. Jabez worked harder than most. With no wife or family and, unlike most of the weavers, seldom inclined to spend his money in the tavern, he had little outside the carpet shop to occupy him and his only interest appeared to lie in making more and more money.

'He's naught but an old miser,' Bessie declared one day to Nell. 'If he could get away without paying me my wage, he'd do it. It's always cold in the shop when it's his turn to buy the firing, and he won't get the candle out until we can hardly see the loom. He must have pounds stacked in that cellar of his.'

'Still, he don't beat thee much, do he?' Nell said feelingly, rubbing an arm bruised by her own master's latest outburst of temper. 'Old Ben never has his hand off his rod. He seems to think I'll work all the faster for a bit of beating. Still, I'd rather that than what happened to Daisy Smith t'other night.'

'Why, what—' Bessie began, but at that moment the bell was rung to send them all back to their places and, fearing another beating, Nell scurried back to the loom where Ben Willis was already waiting, his face thunderous. Bess followed, not really needing to ask what had happened to Daisy, a thirteen-year-old who had started work in the shop only a few weeks earlier. Everyone knew what her master was like and what would probably happen to her. Walt Harris never kept a draw-girl for more than a few weeks, and Bess knew that her own brother Tom had objected strongly when it had once been suggested that Bess herself should be drawer for the big weaver. Even now, Tom still kept an eye out for her. It annoyed her at times – wasn't she fifteen years old, and well able to look after herself? – but she knew that the other girls admired Tom, and she couldn't help feeling proud that he was her brother.

Arriving at her loom, she set her hand immediately to the sword, hardly noticing the expression on Jabez's face. They began to work, steadily increasing the length of the carpet that inched its way up the heddles, and Bess wondered what time she would be allowed to leave tonight. Twelve and twelve had little meaning for Jabez these days; he would work on past midnight if the mood took him, or if fall day were close at hand, and take no account of Bessie's condition.

The pieces had to be finished by next morning; anything not completed and handed over by ten wouldn't be paid for that week. The other weavers, less assiduous than Jabez, had worked only normal hours and had their pieces completed by eleven. But Jabez, determined to complete not one, but two lengths, had kept Bess working late every night that week and his second length was still only partially ready.

'We'll never finish it by midnight,' Bess moaned, shifting from one foot to the other. 'Can't I go now, Mr Gast? I'm that weary.'

He flung her a black look. 'Go home? We'll go when this piece is done, and not before. I said I'd do two this week, and that's what I'll stick by – aye, and you too, so keep those hands moving, I can't afford no mistakes.'

Bessie sighed, feeling herself near tears of pure exhaustion. Her head ached and her eyes were blurred; the wires of the frame shifted and merged before her, the noise battered at her ears. Her hands moved almost of their own volition, inserting first the sword and then the wire in wearisome repetition.

One by one, the other weavers finished their work and sent their drawers home. Their looms stopped and a quiet descended on the shed. And still Jabez, his face grim with determination, worked on. He seemed tireless, as if he were made of some different cast from his fellows. He did not even glance at Bess.

She felt someone touch her elbow, and Tom's voice said in her ear: 'You all right, Bess?'

'She'm all right,' Jabez growled before Bessie could answer, and he thrust in the shuttle with extra force. 'She'll be even better if she's let alone to do the work I pays her for.'

'I only asked because she's my sister, Mr Gast,' Tom said quietly. 'I know she gets tired, working these late nights.'

'Then the sooner thee lets her be, sooner she'll be home.' The weaver's hands and feet never ceased in their rhythmic movements and after a moment, Tom shrugged and moved away.

'I'll be off, then,' he said, but Bessie only nodded; she was too tired now to speak, dared not take her eyes from the frame and knew that if she paused for only a second, she would falter and spoil the work – with what consequences, she dared not imagine.

She and Jabez were now alone in the darkened shop. Their only light was the candle Jabez had placed beside the loom. The other looms stood silent; the completed pieces were rolled neatly, ready to be handed over. The floor was littered with flights and ends, which would be collected up by some of the weavers or their drawers and sold. The smells from the cauldrons of urine and size were unnoticeable now, though they had struck at her nostrils with all the familiar pungency only a few hours earlier, and would do so again when she came in tomorrow.

Jabez threw in the shuttle for the last time. Bessie slid in the terry wire and lifted the pile. The weave was battered down with the iron comb and Jabez fastened off the end and sat for a moment, staring at the finished piece of carpet.

Its colours glowed. Red, blue and green, mixed together in a swirl of pattern. On this carpet, over which they had laboured so long and intensively, other people would walk. Boots and shoes would tramp in mud and dirt, dogs would roll on it, children play. Food would be dropped on it, wine spilt, and tired housemaids would brush and sweep it. And none of them would give a thought to Bess and Jabez, momentarily united in fatigue, almost too exhausted to leave it and go home.

But they couldn't leave it yet. There was the shearing to do, and like most weavers Jabez considered this the hardest task of all. But it must be done, and done now; there might not be time in the morning.

Moving slowly and stiffly, assisted by Bess, the weaver lifted the heavy piece of carpet away from the loom and spread it out. It lay on the floor – the only time either of them would ever see it as it was intended to be seen. Jabez took up the heavy shears and began to work over it, clipping the pile to an even depth, ensuring that there were no long ends to spoil it. It was heavy work, needing both strength and dexterity, and he grunted with the effort.

'There,' he said at last – the first unnecessary

words he had spoken all evening. 'That's done. That's finished.' He stood back and looked down at his work with the pursing of his lips which was as near to pride as he would ever allow himself.

'It's lovely, Mr Gast,' Bessie said. She had never seen a carpet like this before – so glowing with rich colour, spread out on the floor of the big weaving shop. She had never been here when it was so quiet, empty of other people, with nobody but the man she spent all her working time with and yet knew so little about.

She bent and fingered the thick woollen pile. It felt soft and springing under her touch. Bemused, she leaned over it, letting her hand trace the pattern. Its texture enticed her nearer; she thought of the rough sacking that made her bed at home and longed to lie down here, on this carpet that would be so much more luxurious a resting place than any she had known. Weariness washed over her like a tide and she felt tears sting her eyes.

'Be thee going to sleep down there?' Jabez asked suddenly.

Bessie jumped and began to scramble to her feet. For a few seconds, she had forgotten Jabez, forgotten everything but the carpet and the aching muscles which cried out for rest. But as she moved, her legs gave way beneath her and she fell back in a sprawling heap on the soft coloured pile that she and Jabez had worked so hard to create.

For a moment she lay breathless, unable to move. She looked up at Jabez, at the thin, wiry body, the small round head and the hard eyes and mouth. She saw his expression change as he stared down at her; saw a lasciviousness she had never suspected creep into the slate-coloured eyes, saw the mouth work a

46

little and the movement of the Adam's apple in the scrawny neck.

Her heart seemed to stop for a moment, and then begin to thud. She began once more to scramble up. And Jabez reached out a long, spidery arm and pushed her down again.

'Mr Gast—'

'Don't say you're not ready for it,' he muttered, and Bessie flinched as he dropped down beside her on the carpet, his hands on her shoulders, thrusting her over on to her back. 'I've watched thee – eyeing up the lads, aye, and hot for that young Pagnel – if it was him here now you'd be begging and panting for it . . . But it's not him.' His face was close to hers now, his thin, strong body pinning her down. 'It's me – and why not? Haven't I had to teach you all you know about weaving, aye, and put up with your mistakes, your broken cords and lashes, the days when you were too idle to work as fast as I wanted, the days when you were late? Don't I deserve something for my trouble?'

'No!' Bessie gasped and fought him, trying to push his body away from her. She felt his hand on her knee, pushing up under her skirt, and she squirmed and twisted beneath him, but her fear only seemed to inflame him the more. His eyes were glittering wildly, his face distorted, lips drawn back over his teeth in a snarl of lust. He laid one hand against her forehead, jerking her head back as he laid lips and teeth against her neck; with his other hand, he forced her thighs apart. She felt his legs between hers, keeping her spread wide; and then the blunt warmth of something hard and alien, ramming its way inside her, splitting her skin, tearing and thrusting with ruthless urgency.

It was over in moments. With a final grunt, Jabez wrenched himself away from her. Bessie, sobbing with pain and fright, twisted away from him, drawing her knees up and covering her face with her hands. She lay for a few seconds, trembling; then she heard a movement by the door and took her hands away from her wet face.

And looked straight into the eyes of her brother Tom.

For no more than a heartbeat, the three of them remained perfectly still, a frozen tableau. Bess, half lying, half crouching on the brilliant carpet. Jabez, arrested in the act of rising to his feet, his hands at the waist of his breeches as he dragged them up his thighs. Tom, framed in the doorway, his eyes black with fury in a face as white as chalk.

'You . . . *bastard*—' he growled, and launched himself forward.

Jabez twisted and turned but there was no escape and he was forced to defend himself as Tom, a maelstrom of whirling fists and feet, hurled himself upon the weaver. Bessie shrank back, her hand to her mouth, as the two men fought, crashing against the looms, tripping over the rolls of carpet, staggering and swaying as they clutched each other in violent embrace.

'Tom,' she whispered, kneeling upon the carpet, watching in horror as her brother forced the older man backwards over a bench and drove his fist into the gibbering mouth. 'Tom – no . . . You'll kill him . . .'

But Tom wasn't listening, and she remembered an earlier occasion, when they were children, and her normally quiet brother had erupted with a similar rage. It had been over a pair of cats then, caught by some boys and hung over a washing-line with their tails tied together, to claw each other to death. It was a familiar game in the streets of Kidderminster and nobody took much notice, but Tom had exploded with rage and waded into the crowd of boys, all bigger than himself. He'd arrived home eventually with a bleeding nose and black eye, but had given as good as he got; at least two of the boys had given him a wide berth from then on, bigger though they were.

But this wasn't a fight between children and Tom wasn't defending a kitten now. And Bessie, seeing the fury in his eyes, was afraid.

Jabez was up now, taking advantage of a slight pause in Tom's onslaught. He was breathing heavily, one eye already swelling and blood trickling into the other from a cut on his forehead. Half-blinded, he felt around him for a weapon, and Bessie saw his hand close over the end of a terry wire.

'Tom!' she shrieked, on her feet as she lunged towards them. 'Tom, look out—' She reached forward and tore the wire from Jabez's hand. The long, narrow blade quivered in her grasp. He reached out, trying to wrench it back, and she pulled it sharply away. At the same moment, Tom laid his hands on the weaver's shoulders and jerked him up from his half-prone position. The end of the wire caught against his hand and he twisted his fingers around it. Jabez twitched suddenly and arched in an effort to escape, and Bessie felt the blade of the wire touch and scrape against skin, against flesh and bone. There was a sickening drag on its quivering tension and a fountain of blood arched outwards from Jabez's throat. He gave a cry, a gurgling scream of pain, his body jerked once, twice, and sagged in Tom's arms. Appalled and terrified, Bessie felt the dead weight against her body and knew what they had done.

Tom dropped the wire on the floor. He looked

down at the draining white of Jabez's face, at the lolling head, at the bright red blood that gushed from the grinning wound. He looked as white and sick himself, and Bessie, hearing her own blood roar in her ears, sank dizzily to the ground.

The blood pumped from Jabez's thin, spidery frame until there was no heartbeat left to force it from his veins. It gathered in a thick pool on the carpet over which he had laboured so long and hard, and the rich, glowing pattern merged into a dark, steaming mass.

Tom lowered the body to the floor. Slowly, he reached out for Bessie's hand and drew her away. They backed out of the shop, past the looms, past the rolls of carpet, past the tubs that held their stinking cargoes, past the bobbins that stood as silent witnesses to the horror that had just taken place. They slid out of the door that Tom had entered only minutes before, into the darkness of the night.

Then they turned and ran.

Chapter Three

There was more than a touch of winter in the air when the watchman came to the Himleys' cottage and asked for Bessie. And when he departed, the chill that came with him through the door stayed to eat into the bones of Rebecca and her mother and to bring a white fury to the face of William Himley.

'Our Bess?' Fanny quavered, staring at the wooden-faced watchman when he first knocked on the door and, without invitation, stepped inside. 'No, she ent been home all night. I thought old Jabez was keeping her at the loom. I know he had a piece to finish – today being fall day—'

'They did finish it,' the watchman said grimly. 'Not that it'll ever be used now, spoilt as it is.'

'Spoilt?'

'Aye. Blood's none so easy to get out of dyed wool – not when it's dried.' His cold, hard eyes watched as if looking for a reaction, and Fanny staggered suddenly and put out a hand. Rebecca, still barely half awake, caught her mother and helped her to sit down on the broken-backed chair, and William left his loom and came forward.

'What's all this? What are you saying? Hev aught happened to our Bess?' His jaw thrust out aggressively, but the watchman stood firm.

'If it hasn't, it will once the magistrate has her. And rightly so, too. Saw it myself, I did – old Jabez lying there in his own blood and never a—'

'*Jabez*?' Fanny gasped. 'Hurt? But what—'

'Not just hurt,' the watchman said with grim relish. 'Dead. Dead as mutton. And your girl never come home, you say? 'Tis easy to see what happened, then.'

'It's not – it's not at all! Our Bess would never have – have done that.' Rebecca saw that her mother's face was the dirty white of new, undyed wool. She drew nearer, chilled by a fear that she couldn't yet name, and felt her mother's arm grip her waist tightly. 'Will – tell him.'

William stepped forward threateningly, but the watchman stood firm. He was a big man and accustomed to rough-housing; few days or nights passed without some scrap, and he fought to win. He met Will's eye without flinching, merely changing his stance slightly, and the weaver hesitated.

'Let's hear what you hev to say then,' he growled. 'And you'd better be sure what it is.'

'Oh, I'm sure enough. Your girl Bess was the last one left working in the carpet shop last night, her and Jabez. This morning when the overseer went in, the door was wide open and Jabez's piece spread out on the floor – with Jabez hisself spread out atop of it. Covered in blood, like I said.' The watchman paused. 'Had his throat cut, he had. Near took his head off an' all. They'll never use that carpet for Master Vivian's new drawing-room for when he's wed, that's certain.'

Rebecca gasped as her mother's arm tightened convulsively about her. She stared at the watchman, sickened by the picture conjured up in her mind. Bessie – *Bessie* – had done that? She thought of her sister, bouncing her way to work, giggling with Nellie, eyeing the boys . . . Bessie, dragging home white-faced and exhausted after a long day's work;

grumbling as she got up next morning after too little sleep to go back. Bessie, careless and good-natured, who only wanted a little fun and seldom got it.

'I don't believe it,' Fanny whispered. 'She wouldn't . . . she *couldn't* . . . Not our Bess . . .'

'So why ent she come home, then? Why int she here?' There was a note of triumph in the watchman's voice. 'Run away, that's what she've done. Well, I found out what I come for – she ent bin home all night. That *is* the truth, innit? You ent holding out on me?'

Fanny shook her head. 'No,' she said dully. 'It's the truth. We haven't seen Bessie all night. She's never been near us.'

The watchman moved away.

'Well, I'm off now. The magistrate'll send out a summons for her and she'll be watched for. I dare say she's not got far – they'll hev her in before you can say Jack Robinson.' His glance fell on Rebecca, standing at her mother's knee, her dark eyes huge in her ash-white face. 'There'll be a job going for a handy draw-girl down at Butts',' he said with heavy irony. 'But I don't see them taking on another Himley girl – not now. Wouldn't take the risk, would they?'

'Get out,' William said, raising his fist again and lunging forward. 'Get out – afore I throws you out.'

The watchman looked at him, a sneer forming on his lips; but at the expression on William Himley's face he backed quickly away. One hand came up, palm outwards in a warding-off motion. He felt behind him for the door, jerked it open and almost fell out into the yard. Beyond him, Rebecca could see a ring of curious faces. His arrival had not gone unnoticed. Probably they even knew why he was here.

Already, she thought, her sister was marked as a murderer.

William slammed the door after the watchman and turned to face his wife and daughter. They watched him in silence; Rebecca could feel her mother trembling.

'So that's why she never come home,' he said at last, heavily. 'Done Jabez in and lit out of Kidder. They'll catch her, you know, and bring her back. And then she'll be a Jack Ketch's pippin, all right.'

'Oh, no!' Fanny covered her face with her hands. 'They'll never hang her, Will! Not our Bess! Why, she's nothing but a wench – she'll not even have known what she were doing. And why did she do it anyway? What did Jabez do to *her*, that she had to strike out like that?'

'Aye, it's easy to guess that,' he agreed. 'We all knows what goes on in the carpet shops of a night. But she didn't hev to *kill* him, Fan.'

Fanny shook her head. 'I still can't believe it. Not our Bess. It must've been an accident, Will.'

'And is anyone going to believe that?' he demanded. 'No – all we can hope for is that she'll get clear away. But there's not much chance of that. She'll be picked up afore sundown – see if she int.'

Fanny's head drooped and tears began to fall on to the hands Rebecca had laid on her knees. She looked at them and wiped them away, then seemed to realise for the first time that Rebecca was there, still close beside her. She raised her head and looked up at Will.

'What that man said – about our Becky going to work as a drawer,' she said. 'I'll not have it, Will. I'll not have another girl of mine working in that place. I don't care what you say – our Rebecca's going into service. And if you need a drawer, I'll draw for you – but I'm getting her out of this hellish trade, just as soon as we can find her a decent place.'

William stared at her, looking for a moment as if his own shuttle had leapt from the loom and defied him. But before he could answer, there was another knock on the door.

Fanny gasped and clutched Rebecca to her. William turned to face the door. They watched it as if it were the entrance to hell.

'It's her . . .' Fanny breathed. 'They've got her already . . . oh my God . . .' She let go suddenly of Rebecca. Her hands were fists at her mouth. And as William moved slowly to the door, the terror transmitted itself to Rebecca's shivering body. She gripped her mother's arm, afraid of whatever fresh horror might be coming to them but determined to face it.

She heard her father open the door, heard the murmur of voices, the whispering from the growing crowd outside. And then the door closed again, and Rebecca was aware of her father crossing the room and felt the weight of his hand on her mother's shoulder.

'That were Sam Hooman,' he said heavily. 'He says our Tom's disappeared, too. Seems they were both in it together somehow. And they've both gone.'

Bessie and Tom, leaving the carpet shop in a blind, panic-stricken run, had no idea where to go, or what to do next.

Hand in hand, with Bessie tripping over her skirts and sobbing as she ran, they scuttled along the riverbank. It was dark and cold, with a thin film of ice on the stones; they stumbled, skidded and once almost slipped into the river. Bessie clutched her brother's hand tightly. They had not run together like this since they were children, but now he was all she had in the world and she dared not let go.

'Oh, what are we going to do, Tom?' she panted when they stopped for breath and he drew her into the shadow of a warehouse. 'They'll find Jabez and hang us both. Everyone knows I was there with him.'

'You must go home at once. Pretend nothing's happened – they'll think it was someone else, some intruder. There's nothing to say it was either of us.'

'There is,' she whispered miserably. 'His blood – it's all over me. And you. And I've nothing else to wear, only my Sunday dress and it's in pawn . . . Tom, *what are we going to do?*'

She saw the glimmer of his eyes as he stared at her in the darkness. 'I dunno,' he said wretchedly. 'I dunno what to do, Bess . . . We'll have to get out. We'll have to leave Kidder now. You're right – they'll be after us in a few hours and then it'll be all up. Oh, God, Bess, I never meant to kill him, I swear I didn't – though when I saw what he was doing to you, I felt like murder.'

'I know. I know you never meant it – it was an accident.' She glanced fearfully about. 'But *they* won't believe that. Tom, where can we go? There's nowhere they won't find us.'

'We'll have to get right away. Somewhere big. London. They'll never find us there.'

'London? But we can't go to London! We don't know the way. And it's hundreds of miles.'

'Not that far. There's a coach.'

'A *coach*? But that costs money.' Bess felt in the pocket of her skirt. 'Look – sixpence, that's all I've got. And I'm supposed to buy some dinner with that, for our Dad and Becky.'

'We'll have to walk, then.' Tom stepped away from the shadow of the wall and Bessie stared at him. He looked young, determined – and afraid. Misery welled up inside her. Somehow, this was all her fault. If she hadn't been there with Jabez – what was it he'd said? That she'd been asking for it? She shook her head uncomprehendingly. What had she done but what all the girls did – eyed the men, giggled and flirted in the few moments that were spared to them during their long, tedious, back-breaking day? Was that really so wrong?

It must be, since it had resulted in this. Jabez dead and her own brother likely to be accused of his murder.

And me, too, she thought with a sudden rush of terror. Girls could hang as well – girls younger than she had been hanged, and for less than murder.

'Come on, Bess,' Tom said. 'It'll be getting light soon – people'll be about. We've got to get away afore anyone sees us.'

He pulled at her wrist and started off up the road and Bess stumbled after him. Tears burned her eyes. Were they not even to go home, just for a moment – to tell their mother what had happened, to say goodbye?

'No,' Tom said sternly, 'we can't. Don't you see, that'll be the first place they goes to. And if Ma knows where we've gone, they'll make her tell. And it'll take too much time any road. We've got to get *away*, Bess – fast.'

He was almost dragging her along the rough track now, taking no heed of her entreaties to go more slowly. 'You've got to keep up, Bess. We've been lucky no one's seen us so far – we could get caught at any moment. Why, they might have found old

57

Jabez already – the watchman might be looking for us this very minute.'

'But, Tom, I don't think I can—'

'You've *got* to,' he repeated, and jerked her roughly after him.

The streets were dark and silent. A candle glimmered in the occasional window, where some weaver, tailor or milliner worked late into the small hours. A cat or two whisked across their path after rats; once, a dog growled threateningly from a doorway. They met a few men stumbling home from a drinking den, and almost fell over an old beggar, crouched in a corner. None of these were new to Bessie, who encountered them every night on her way home, but each brought a fresh scream to her throat and she pressed her hand to her mouth to keep silent.

'We'll have to go back past the carpet shop,' Tom said after a few minutes. 'It's the quickest way. We didn't think when we ran out of there . . . Keep in the shadows, Bess, and let's hope nobody's been by yet.'

Trembling and cold, Bessie crept after him. They came within sight of the long building which Albert Butts rented from Vivian Pagnel. There was no sign of life . . . The thought brought a sickness to her throat. No glimmer of light; the stub of Jabez's candle had burnt out, as surely as had his life. She felt Tom's fingers tighten around her own and knew that he was shaking, too.

Suddenly, he stopped. Bessie bumped against him in the darkness and again almost screamed. She clung to him, shivering. 'What is it, Tom?'

'There's someone about,' he breathed. 'By the doorway – see? Something moving . . . a sort of dim light . . .'

'Oh, my God! It's Jabez's ghost! He've come back

to haunt us, Tom.' Her voice rose in hysteria. 'Tom, what're we going to do, he'll find us wherever we go, he'll haunt us for the rest of our lives, he—'

'*Shut up*!' Tom's whisper was fierce and low and he clapped a dirty hand over her mouth. 'You'll have everyone in Kidder awake. Just keep still and keep quiet – I don't think he's seen us.'

They pressed together in the shadow of the dye-house. Bessie's body was trembling so much that she could hear her own teeth rattling. She buried her face against Tom's shoulder to deaden the sound, and a whimper rose in her throat. In another moment she would scream . . . she wouldn't be able to help it. She must scream . . . she *must* . . .

'Who's that?' The voice was sharp and loud. 'Who's there?' Bessie drew in a breath and Tom pressed her head so hard against him that she could take no further air at all. 'I know you're there – by the dye-house,' the voice went on, drawing closer. 'Come out at once, or I swear I'll shoot you.'

The sobs burst from Bessie's throat and she struggled in her brother's arms. He swore softly and gripped her hard, but her panic was beyond control and she fought blindly to be free. Jerking back her head, she caught a glimpse of his face in the dim glow of a lantern and knew that they had been seen and must be recognised. Moaning with terror, she fell to her knees and clasped her hands, raising them in involuntary prayer.

'Please – please don't shoot! We didn't mean to do it – it were an accident. He attacked me, Jabez did, and Tom hit him for it, but that were all. We never meant to kill him – we never did. Please, please, sir, don't shoot us – let us go, please.'

Tears shook her voice and streamed down her

face. Still on her knees, she scrambled across the rough ground and, hardly knowing what she was doing, pawed at the legs of the man who stood just beyond the shadow. She felt him shift a little, moving back as if too fastidious to tolerate her touch; then he bent and grasped her hair with one hand, pulling her head painfully towards him.

'So! As I thought – it's the pretty wench who draws for Jabez. Bess, isn't that your name? And who's your partner in crime – your lover, is it, taking exception to Jabez's whim?'

Bessie stared, a sob caught midway in her throat as she realised that it was Vivian Pagnel who held her. She opened her mouth but could not speak; the sob shuddered on its way and fresh tears spilled from her eyes. Vivian jerked her hair impatiently and then released her, so that she fell sideways, and Tom started forward from the shadows.

'I'm Bessie's brother Tom, Mr Pagnel, and I'll thank you not to hurt her. I've already killed one man tonight for her, and they'll not hang me twice if I send you after him.'

Vivian stared and then laughed. 'Well! It's a proper firebrand, isn't it. I've seen you in the carpet shop, too, haven't I? Apprenticed to Hooman – yes? So . . . you've killed one man, have you, and proud of it, too, by the sound of your voice. And what do you mean to do now? It's hardly sensible to stand here and wait for the watchman to take you.'

'We were trying to get away,' Bess whispered from the ground. 'We were going to go to London . . .' She sniffed and wiped her face on her sleeve. 'Please, Mr Vivian, please let us go. If we don't get away soon—'

'You'll be caught and hanged.' Vivian spoke with a kind of dispassionate relish. 'There's no doubt about that. Well, so what shall we do about it, hm? I suppose my duty is to take you to the watchman straightaway. Or to the magistrate.' Bessie caught the sudden gleam of teeth in his shadowed face. 'Who just happens to be my father! Well, what an interesting evening this is turning out to be.'

Bessie stared up at him and felt her heart weigh heavily in her breast. Hopelessness dragged at her veins. She sank her face into her hands.

'So that's it, then,' Tom said, and she heard the same miserable despair in his voice. 'Well, let's get it over with then. Turn me over to the watchman – or to your father, whichever it's to be. But let Bessie go, sir. She never touched Jabez. It was an accident – but it was me.'

'No, that's not true!' Bessie burst out. 'It was both of us – but it was Jabez just as much. He got in the way of the wire, or something, I don't know *what* happened, but we never meant to kill him. And if he hadn't jumped on me when I was down on the carpet, Tom would never—'

'Oh, leave it, leave it.' Vivian's moment of amusement seemed to have passed. He sounded bored, impatient. But there was a flicker of mischief back in his voice as he went on. 'All the same, he was a cantankerous old swine, and no doubt someone would have done for him someday. And I don't see why a pretty girl like you should hang . . .' His eyes moved over Bessie's crouching figure. 'Get up, girl. Let's have a look at you.' He reached down and helped Bessie to her feet. 'Hmm. Light's not very good, but you've an ample enough figure and as I remember it your face is pretty, for a weaver's wench. Yes . . .

61

you may do, you may do very well. So . . . you want to go to London, do you?'

'We don't *want* to, sir,' Bessie said quaveringly. 'But Tom says it's the only place where they won't find us. Only if we don't go soon, it'll be too late. And we haven't got the money for the fare, and it's a long way to walk – near two hundred miles – so I don't know *what* we're to do . . .' She began to cry again and Vivian moved impatiently.

'Stop your snivelling, girl, and listen to me. So you want to go to London. Well – how would you like me to arrange it?'

Bessie stopped sobbing and stared at him. Beside her, Tom moved a little closer. She felt him, tense with disbelief, at her elbow.

'*You* arrange it, Mr Vivian? I don't understand—'

'You don't have to. Just be satisfied that I'm prepared to help you – yes, both of you.' His eyes glittered. 'Now, look, we've lingered here for too long already. You've got to get away – and so must I. Nobody must know I've been here. Listen – do you know where the old woolshed is? Where the skeins are stored before dyeing?'

'Yes, sir, we knows,' Tom said cautiously. 'But—'

'*Listen*, I said. Go there now. At once. The door's not locked. Nobody will be going into it tomorrow – you can hide all day. I'll come to you as soon as darkness falls and set you on your way to London. Now, does that satisfy you? Oh, stop your *snivelling*, girl, and go before I change my mind!'

'But—' Tom began, and Vivian set his hand in the middle of Tom's back and pushed.

'Go, I said – *go*. I'll come tomorrow night – and don't either of you dare to set foot outside before then, hear me? Or I'll swear I saw you kill Jabez and

62

gave pursuit and then lost you. D'you understand?'

'Yes – oh yes!' Bessie grabbed Tom's hand and dragged him away. Still reluctant, he hung back and she could sense that he was about to speak again. She gave a sudden fierce jerk that had him almost off his feet.

'Come *on*, Tom. Can't you see, this is our chance – our only chance. There's naught else we can do now.' She turned to Vivian. 'We'll be there, sir, in the woolshed.'

'And remember what I said.' She could see his face, dimly, and realised with a shock that the darkness was already fading from the sky. Morning was coming and with it soon would come the first of the workers. 'Don't move a step outside until I come.'

'No, sir. We won't. Tom—' She pulled his hand again and this time he followed her. They moved slowly, cautiously, out of the shelter of the warehouse, then began to run. And as they ran, panic caught at them both and they scuttled as desperately as if the hounds of hell were after them, along the riverbank and into the door of the woolshed.

'Why isn't it locked?' Tom muttered as they slipped inside. 'There's summat funny about this, Bess. What was Mr Vivian doing along here at this time of night, anyroad? I don't like it.'

'Tom, don't be such a fool. What do you *think* he was doing here?' Even at this moment, Bessie could feel jealous of the unknown girl who had received Vivian's favours that night. A girl no better than she herself – or why would he have brought her to a woolshed? It could have been me, she thought, and then remembered Jabez's body forcing itself into her and shuddered.

'Well, I'm still not happy. How do we know he

means what he says? He might be off at this very moment to fetch the watchman along. He could have been laughing up his sleeve the whole time – and sent us here to wait like mice in a trap for him to come along and catch just when it suits him.'

'And what else do you think we can do?' Bessie snapped. 'It's nearly light out there now – d'you want us to go out and meet all the others, coming in to work? Or maybe you think we ought to go back to work ourselves – pretend we didn't even *know* about Jabez.'

Tom stared at her. 'Maybe that *is* what we ought to do,' he said slowly. 'After all, Bess, who's to know it's not true? Nobody saw us. Nobody knows but what you left Jabez in the shop, all hale and hearty, and someone else came in and did for him after you'd gone.' He gripped Bess's hand. 'Let's do it, Bess. Let's just go in with everyone else and make out we're as surprised as they are. Look – they're coming now, you can see them. We've just got time – if we don't go now, it'll be too late.'

But Bessie shook her head and refused to move. 'It's too late already, Tom. Mr Vivian saw us. He *knows*. We told him. And we've got *blood* on us. If we don't do what he says now—' She shivered, remembering the careless impatience in Vivian's voice. 'Look, it's just a bit o' fun to him, helping us get away – I'm sure that's all it is. If he's going to shop us, he'll do it anyroad, whatever we do. But I don't think he's going to – not if we do as he says.'

Tom sat down on a bale of wool. 'I dunno, Bess. I still don't like it. How do we know we can trust him? He might—'

'He might do anything. He might forget all about us and never come back. We *don't* know, Tom. But it's almost broad light now – there's nothing else we can do but stay here until tonight. Tom, we *can't* go to work. Neither of us went home last night. Ma'll be wondering what happened to me – and if Sam Hooman sees you now, there'll be hell to pay. And once everyone knows we didn't go home—'

'They'll know we did for Jabez. All right, Bess, you've got the right of it, I'll admit that. We got to stay here till tonight. But if he don't come—'

'Then we make our own way.' Bessie looked around the shed, dimly lit now by the increasing daylight that crept in through the few grimy windows. 'Well, I suppose there's worse places. At least we can be comfortable.' She picked her way through a maze of piled bales into a far corner, out of sight of the door. 'Come over here, Tom, and let's try'n get some sleep. I'm dog-tired.'

'Sleep?' he said, though he followed her and helped her to arrange a few loose skeins into a comfortable nest. 'I'm never going to sleep again. Every time I blink, I see Jabez lying there in his own blood.' He shuddered. 'I never meant to do it, Bess. Truly, I never.'

'It's all right,' she comforted him. 'I know you never. You were just trying to help me, that's all, and it were an accident. You couldn't help it. It was Jabez's fault.'

He nodded gratefully and lay down beside her. Bessie stretched her arm out and he rested his head on it. Within seconds, in spite of what he had said, he was asleep.

But Bessie lay awake for a long time. Tired as she was, her mind would not rest. It ranged backwards and forwards over the last few hours. From the instant when she had looked up to see the frightening lasciviousness on Jabez's thin, cruel face, to those horrifying seconds when the wire had scraped across his throat, cutting it as easily as a cheese; from their first terror-stricken flight across the yard, to the throat-catching dread when Vivian had first called out to them. Her blind panic as they ran, the fear when she knew them to have been seen; her disbelief when Vivian offered his help, so carelessly holding their lives in his hands.

And through it all, the sight and sound of the wire across Jabez's throat, the horrific gurgling of his death, and the warm, sickening smell of his blood on the newly woven carpet.

As dawn broke, she slept at last, heavily and throughout the short winter's day, her sleep tormented by a series of nightmares from which there seemed to be no escape. She was running through dark roads and passages with no way out, her legs swollen, her feet turned to lead; she was back in the carpet shop with Jabez leering over her before the grin on his face turned to a wide red wound, dripping hot blood; she was standing in front of a jeering crowd of people and a rope was being fitted around her neck.

And Vivian Pagnel was there, too. Not jeering; not calling insults. Merely watching, with that cool smile on his arrogant lips and a lift to his black brows. As if the sight gave him amusement. *Pleasure.*

'Bess! Bess, what is it? Wake up – you're dreaming, Bess.'

Bessie felt Tom's hand, rough on her shoulder as he shook her awake. She stared at him, dazed. Tom? What was he doing here? It was so long since he had

66

lived at home, she was not accustomed to seeing him as she woke. And where were her mother and Becky? And the sound of her father's loom, already rattling in the corner . . . ?

The horror of her dream flooded back into her mind, and then the worse horror of reality. She started up, her eyes wild, and Tom pushed her back on to the wool.

'Ssh . . . we mustn't make any noise. Someone'll hear us. There's folk about . . .' He paused, listening. 'Bess – it's nearly dark. You bin asleep nearly all day. I've been lying here listening – there's been noise all day, people searching, shouting. It can't be long before they look in here . . . Mr Vivian said he'd be back – but I reckon we'd be better off to get away by ourselves. As soon as it's clear. I don't trust him.'

'Why not? He haven't given us away yet.'

'I know. All the same . . . He had a queer look on his face, Bess. As if – as if he had some sort o' plan for us. Why should he help us, after all? His dad's a magistrate – it could mean a lot of trouble for him, if it got out. He must have a reason.'

'Well, maybe so, but we got to get away and I don't see no other way. They must have found Jabez this morning – they'll have the hue and cry out on all the roads. He's our only chance now, Tom. We just got to trust him. It's that, or–' The gallows in her dream struck at her imagination and she shuddered. 'Oh, Tom, why did it have to happen?'

'Things do happen to people like us,' he said grimly. 'It's only folk like the Pagnels that can choose . . . *What's that?*'

Bessie felt a chill freeze her skin. She sat perfectly still, only her eyes moving as she looked first at Tom, then at the piles of wool which surrounded them. They were well hidden here . . . but now she could hear what Tom had heard. The scrape of a door across a rough stone floor. A stealthy footstep.

Someone was in the shed. Someone was searching the bales. Coming nearer.

Looking for them . . . But was it Vivian Pagnel? Or the watchman?

Tom's hand was still on her shoulder. She felt it tighten, heard his quick, shallow breathing. She knew he was tensed, ready to leap, to fight, and wondered sickeningly if this were to end in yet another death . . . If only she had done as he wanted; if only they'd escaped while they had the chance. She closed her eyes.

The footsteps were near now. Slow and soft. Bessie's heart thundered in her breast. Beside her, Tom was taut as a spring.

A hand, dimly seen in the gathering dusk, parted the skeins of wool that lay piled around them. A tall figure appeared in the opening. Bessie felt Tom gather himself, ready to leap, and she gripped his arm hard. She found she had been holding her breath; her words came with a rush.

'Tom – no! It's Mr Vivian . . .' She peered into the darkness. 'It is you, isn't it, Mr Vivian? You've come.'

'Ssh – not so much noise. Yes, I've come.' He slid into the space they had made for themselves and looked down at them. 'Did you doubt me?'

Bessie did not answer. Now that the long day was over at last, she felt sick and weak, and her eyes burned with tears.

Tom spoke, boldly, as if he had nothing to lose now. 'Look, we reckon we ought to be getting away.

It's no good staying here. Someone's going to find us. And we've not eaten or drunk all day.'

Vivian laughed softly. 'So the birds would like to fly, would they? Well, and why not? Everything's arranged. And I've brought you food and drink.' He produced a bag and tossed it carelessly to Bessie. 'Eat quickly – there's no time to lose. And I'll tell you what you're to do.' He watched as they fell on the bread, cheese and beer he had brought. 'Bring it with you if you can't finish it now – it'll need to last.'

'Where are we going?' Bessie asked with her mouth full. 'Where are you taking us?'

'Why, London, of course.' His teeth gleamed as Bessie gasped. 'Wasn't that where you said you wanted to go? Now – no more questions. Put the rest of the food back in the bag – we've got to hurry.' He moved stealthily through the bales of wool towards the door. Bessie and Tom crammed their mouths full of food and followed him, stopping as he paused to look out into the yard.

'There's no one about,' he muttered. 'It should be safe enough. Keep close now and don't make any noise. We're making for the Birmingham road.'

He slipped out of the shed and moved noiselessly along the shadow of the wall. Hardly daring to breathe, Bessie crept after him, with Tom close behind her.

There were people about, but darkness came early at this time of year, and the factories were still working. In another two hours the streets would be filled with those going home from work; exhausted children dragging themselves along already half asleep, weary women anxious about feeding their families, men thinking of the tavern and the drink that would

69

ease their aching muscles for at least a while.

No one took any notice of the three who slid through the twilight. Jabez's death was a matter for gossip, for speculation, but nobody was concerned with looking out for the culprits. That was the watchman's job now. The townspeople had their own more pressing affairs to attend to.

All the same, Bessie expected at any moment to hear a shout of recognition, a cry of 'Murderers!' Her skin tingled with fear, her legs shook and waves of panic threatened to overwhelm her. Why was Mr Vivian going so slowly – didn't he know she wanted to run, to put as much distance as possible between herself and the river with its dyehouses and woolsheds and carpet shops? Didn't he know she was terrified, that a picture of the gallows haunted her mind, that she could almost feel the rough, hairy rope scraping at her neck . . . ?

But there was still one corner of rational thought left in her mind, one tiny reminder that if they ran it would draw attention to them, that their safest course lay in moving slowly, unnoticed, through the growing darkness. It was enough to keep her behind Vivian, trembling but obedient to his orders, so that when he stopped she stopped; when he moved on, she followed.

They reached the Birmingham road. There were few people about here and Vivian led them quickly to a darkened corner. Bess heard the scrape of a horse's hoof and a soft whicker. Her eyes now accustomed to the darkness, she could make out the shape of a cart. Suddenly nervous, she drew back.

'It's all right,' Vivian said impatiently. 'It's only Carter Higgs. He's going to take you to Birmingham. Then you can get the coach to London, and when you arrive go to this address—' he produced a packet and handed it to Tom '—and give the woman there this letter. She'll give you accommodation and feed you until I arrive, but you'd better start looking for work at once – I don't intend to keep you like pampered lap-dogs. Now, do you understand what to do?' His voice was sharp, peremptory. 'Higgs will show you where the coach leaves from and there's money here for the fare. You'll have to ask the way when you get to London . . . You can read, can't you? You know what the address says?'

'Yes, sir, I can read a bit,' Tom said, taking the packet. 'And thank you, sir, for all you're doing. But, I don't understand—'

'Don't understand what? Come on, man, we haven't got all night. I want to get you clear as soon as possible. I've other things to do with my time besides help felons to escape the law.'

'I don't understand why you're doing this,' Tom muttered. 'Why should you help us? It's costing you money – it could make trouble. Why should you bother?'

'Oh, it's no *bother*,' Vivian said softly. 'No bother at all . . . Let's say I'm just doing it for the novelty of it and because I think you might be useful to me in London.'

'Useful?' Bessie heard the sudden wariness in Tom's voice. 'How d'you mean, useful?'

Vivian showed his white teeth in a laugh. 'Why, in all sorts of ways. You'll be grateful to me for keeping you out of trouble – you'll be glad to wait on me when I come to London, I'm sure.' The undercurrent in his voice brought a shiver to Bessie's spine. Just what did he expect of Tom in London?

And of her . . . ? She caught her breath as the dark eyes turned her way. 'As for your sister, she'll have her own uses . . . Now, up into the cart. And don't worry about Higgs – he won't give you away. He owes me a favour, too, don't you, Higgs?' He watched as Tom climbed up into the cart, and then turned to Bessie. 'Haven't had much time to speak to you, have I?' he said, still in that soft voice. 'Never mind, we'll put that right when I come to London. Meanwhile—' So suddenly that Bessie gasped, he drew her hard against him and placed his mouth on hers in a harsh kiss. His teeth grated against hers and she felt his tongue thrust against her lips. Startled, she flinched and felt his hands grip harder, more cruelly as his mouth hardened and his tongue delved deeper. And then he let her go and thrust her towards the cart.

'I'll see you in London,' he muttered and Bessie, too shaken to answer, merely nodded and scrambled up beside Tom. Her heart thumping, she turned and looked down into the shadow.

Vivian's eyes and teeth glittered. He lifted one hand and gave the horse's rump a sharp slap. The cart lurched forward and swayed slowly along the road.

Bessie twisted in her seat but Vivian had merged with the darkness and become invisible. Unbelievingly, she touched her bruised lips with her fingers.

Vivian Pagnel had kissed her. She wasn't sure that she'd enjoyed it . . . but maybe that was what kissing was like anyway. And if he'd done all this for her – given her and Tom money, arranged for them to be taken to Birmingham, made sure there would be somewhere for them to live in London – well, it

72

must mean something, mustn't it? She'd known he'd noticed her in the carpet shop. She'd heard him asking her name.

The horse trotted off into the night and Bess, who had never been in a cart before, sat clutching her brother and dreaming. Tom seemed to have noticed nothing. He hadn't seen the kiss, didn't know what was going on in her mind. He was still worrying about Jabez, about what might happen even yet if they were caught.

Bessie's worries had evaporated. She felt lifted up, secure. Mr Vivian wouldn't let anything happen to them. Mr Vivian had arranged it all. As long as they did what Mr Vivian said, they would be safe.

Mr Vivian had kissed her.

Chapter Four

November came to Kidderminster, damp and murky. Fog stalked the narrow streets like a large, predatory animal, padding on soft grey feet, swallowing the brief glimpse of daylight and trailing darkness like a blanket in its wake. The knocker-up came round long before dawn, jerking weary workers from a slumber that seemed barely to have begun to send them through the chilly gloom to factories, sheds and shops that were no more welcoming than the cold, bleak homes they had left.

Fanny Himley seemed to have shrunk during the past weeks, since Tom and Bessie had disappeared. Already thin, her body grew more wasted, her nose standing out sharply from sunken cheeks, her eyes mere hollows of hopelessness. She rose each morning, made the gruel that served them as breakfast, and went off to the bobbin-winding shed with scarcely a word. In the evening, she returned, bringing whatever she could afford for the family's supper, then sat staring into the few smouldering ashes that remained of the fire until fatigue drove her to her bed.

Rebecca, herself tired almost to death after a day spent at her father's loom, searched for something that might cheer her mother. When her father stopped work for a while, allowing her to go out for firing, or bread for their midday bait, she found people to talk to, picked up snippets of news and gossip that might for a while take that look of bleak despair from her mother's eyes. But her efforts brought her home more depressed than ever. It was clear that everyone believed that Tom and Bessie between them had murdered Jabez in cold blood. The story had grown in the telling: they had mutilated and dismembered him; they had cut off his head and rolled it around the shed like a giant marble; they had robbed him of clothes and money and left him naked and unrecognisable on the new carpet. The stories were told with relish, whispered behind hands as Rebecca passed. But care was always taken that she might hear, just enough to know what was being said.

She dared not tell her father what was being said, though she realised that he must be hearing the same tales. He came home from the tavern in a worse temper than usual, and his visits were shorter. At home, he was taciturn, barely speaking to Rebecca, and even when Fanny came home of an evening he scarcely roused himself from his silence to greet her.

The atmosphere in the cottage grew darker, colder, heavier. A nameless fear struck ice into Rebecca's heart. She lay awake at night, her legs aching and a pit of misery in her stomach, wondering where her brother and sister were now. She had seen little of Tom since his apprenticeship had begun, but he had always been there, someone to look up to and admire, someone who came home whenever he could and – since Sam Hooman had taken him as a half-weaver and begun to pay him a shilling or two a week – brought the occasional few lumps of toffee for herself and Bessie, a pennyworth of gin for Fanny or a jar of ale for William. She remembered his dark, gentle eyes, his slow smile, the way he would ruffle her hair and call her 'our kid'. He was the only one who had ever used her full name – Rebecca – rather than the shortened version.

And she missed Bessie, too. Her sister had told her more than once how she had seen Rebecca born, how she had helped the midwife to wash her, watched her first attempts at suckling. And she had been Bessie's baby as much as Fanny's, for Fanny had been ill after Rebecca was born, ill with a raging fever that took away her milk and threatened Rebecca's existence as well as her own. It was Bessie, finding a woman in the next street to wet-nurse the baby for part of the time, and sitting patiently for hours dipping a rag into a jug of milk and water for Rebecca to suck, who saved her life. And it was Bessie who played with her when she was not too tired, who sang her nursery rhymes and made her a doll out of a few ends of wool; and, when she came home from the carpet-shop, brought stories of the women and men who worked with her, and news of their brother Tom.

It was Bessie who had told her about the Pagnel cousins, Vivian and Francis. Bessie had blushed and giggled over the bold, dark eyes of Vivian, but it was the fair-haired Francis who had fascinated Rebecca, so that she begged to hear more of him and his gentleness, so different from her own experience.

The cottage was darker without Bessie's presence. And Rebecca, too young to know how to cope with loneliness, cried herself to sleep on many a night, and knew that her mother did the same.

'Mam,' she said one dank afternoon, when Fanny had come home early with no more work to do and William was out delivering his piece to the manufacturer, 'where d'you think our Bessie and Tom are now?'

Fanny turned her head, her eyes dull in their sockets. She brushed back lifeless grey hair from her forehead, and Rebecca saw the lines there, carved from

77

years of toil and hardship, engraved more deeply now by misery.

'Where are they?' she echoed. 'Don't ask me, Becky. I don't reckon as we shall ever know just what become of them. We'll never hear no more of 'em, never.'

Rebecca crossed the cold stone floor and knelt beside her mother, her arms around her waist.

'I'm sure they're all right, Mam. We'd have heard if they'd ever been caught. They must have got away.'

'Aye, but where to? And what would they do?' Fanny turned sombre eyes on her daughter, the only one of her children left to her now. 'You know what happens to folk who go out of their parish. They'll never be able to get relief. They can't get help. They're probably starving in some ditch . . . or worse.'

Rebecca could not imagine what might be worse than starving in a ditch, but she took a firm hold on herself and tightened her arms around her mother's thin body. 'They'll have got work. Tom's a good weaver now, and Bessie's handy at lots of things. And maybe they'll write a letter. Tom can write a bit.'

'And where are we going to get the money for letters?' Fanny asked wearily. 'We'd just have to refuse it – and never know what it said.'

'But at least we'd know they were alive,' Rebecca said quietly, and her mother nodded.

'I reckon that's right enough. But – oh, Becky, I'd dearly like to know just where they are and what's happening to them. My own children, hunted like animals . . . It's a terrible thing, terrible. And nobody knows what happened that night. Not that it's hard to guess – there's many a draw-girl found herself in the family way after a night in the carpet-shop. And I reckon our Tom went in and caught Jabez at it, and that's the plain truth of it.'

'I know, Mam.' Rebecca laid her cheek against the dry skin of her mother's. 'But they never meant to kill Jabez – we know that. They couldn't. Not Tom and Bessie.'

Fanny was silent. What Rebecca said was true, she was certain. But what use was the truth, when you were nothing but a weaver's family, poor and friendless? If Tom and Bessie were caught, the truth – whatever it was – would be of no help to them. Justice was rough; they would be found guilty and hanged, side by side, for all to see.

'I'll not have you working in the carpet-shop,' she said suddenly. 'I've told your father that, time and again. It's service for you, when you're a bit older, and I'll draw for him if he can't get nobody else. But it's not going to happen to you, what happened to our Bess.'

Rebecca did not answer. She had no desire to go into the carpet-shop, but she had little faith in her mother's power to defy William. And he had said as often as she that no daughter of his would go into service. 'We're weavers,' he declared, 'and independent like all weavers should be. Becky won't go into the carpet-shop, right enough – she'll stay here and draw for me, and that's good enough. And I'll not hear another word about it.'

And Fanny, knowing the strength of his arm, would be silent. But there would come a day, they all knew, when William would be no longer able to weave. And what then?

With no experience of service, and only her years as her father's draw-girl behind her, there would be nothing but the carpet-shop left for Rebecca.

* * *

It was cold on the outside of the coach, too cold to sleep. But Bess was so weary that, chilled as she was, she dozed against Tom's arm and knew little of the long journey. She was aware of the constant rattling of the wheels, of her bones being shaken in her skin like sticks in a sack, of the clatter of the horses' hooves and the noise of the other passengers as they muttered, sang or cursed. But she saw little of the scenery through which they passed, did not notice the villages or the farms and barely took note of the inns where they stopped to rest at night, sleeping in the cheapest accommodation. When Tom handed her a mug of ale, she drank it; when he put a slab of bread and cheese into her hand, she ate it. She visited the privy or went behind a bush like the other passengers, and hardly knew that she had felt the need. She moved as if she were in a dream, a trance of shock in which she saw nothing but Jabez, lying on the bright new carpet with a wound in his throat like a scarlet, malevolent grin.

'You'll have to buck up, Bess,' Tom told her at last. 'We're coming to London, see? We'll have to be getting down soon, and we got to find that address Mr Vivian give us. We mustn't waste time – it's coming into afternoon already.'

Bessie roused herself and looked about her. Already there was an impression of bustle that was different, busier and more urgent, than any day in Kidderminster. Traffic filled the streets; carts and carriages clattered along the cobbles, their noise ringing in the narrow ways, bouncing off the walls of the shops and houses crammed on either side. People thronged the pavements: warmly clad women stared into the shop windows while others, poorly attired, cringed in doorways; well-dressed men stalked importantly about on business, ignoring the beggars who whined in the gutter; ragged children scurried to and fro, either running errands or looking for them. Their voices added to the clamour of the traffic, and Bessie put her hands over her ears and stared about, half afraid of this new and busy place.

The coach stopped and the passengers began to disembark. Tom jumped down to the pavement and helped Bessie climb down beside him. They stood for a moment, undecided what to do next.

Bessie drew closer to Tom's side. 'Have you got the address Mr Vivian give us?'

'Aye.' He took out the packet. 'But we'll have to ask. This is a big place, Bess, bigger'n Kidder. I dunno where this James Street might be.' He looked about for someone to ask, but the coach had already disappeared into a yard and the other passengers dispersed. As they hesitated, people brushed past without even appearing to notice them, except to curse because they were blocking the way. Bessie moved hastily, closer to the building where they had stopped, and stared with wide, apprehensive eyes at the hurrying crowds. All appeared preoccupied, busy about their own concerns; not one of them looked ready to stop and help two bewildered travellers.

'Tom,' she said, 'let's move away from here. I don't like it. Let's get ourselves something to eat and drink – there's a tavern over there. Then we can think what to do, and maybe there'll be someone we can ask.'

Tom hesitated. He had been reluctant to spend any of the money Vivian had given them, except on the barest essentials, but it was now several hours since they had eaten and he was as hungry as Bess. He nodded and, cautiously avoiding the traffic, led the way across the road to the public house.

Inside, the crowd was as noisy as in the street. Bessie stared about her as Tom went to buy drinks. Where did all these people work? Or were they, in the words of the weavers, 'playing' – unemployed, buying oblivion with their last few pence? She found a seat in a corner and sat down, hoping to remain unnoticed.

A few men were playing dice at a table near by. They glanced at her, their eyes moving over her in a way that Bess, without quite knowing why, found disturbing. For a moment, she thought of Jabez and of the horror she and Tom had left behind them . . . She looked away quickly and met the eyes of a woman occupying a seat on her other side, a glass and a bottle on the table before her.

The woman nodded. She was in middle age, Bessie thought, and had a face like a fox, sharp and pointed with little eyes that gleamed, but she was respectably dressed in a plain black dress and shawl. She looked Bessie up and down and touched the glass in front of her.

'You look tired, love.' Her voice was coarse but not unpleasant, though the accent was strange to Bessie. 'Why don't yer have a drink? I can spare a drop and there's a glass here you can use.' She poured some gin as she spoke and held it out. 'Here, take it. It's little enough to help a fellow-human being that looks as if she might be a bit down on her luck.'

Bessie felt tears moisten her eyes. Kindness was something she hadn't looked for in here. It seemed churlish to refuse the woman's offer – and besides, she really did need to drink something. She took the glass and sipped; the gin tasted raw and fiery and burned the back of her mouth, but it warmed her body and made her feel better.

'You are down on your luck, aren't yer, love?' the woman asked. 'Yes, I thought so. I seen you in here before, haven't I? I never forget a face, and yours is unusual – prettier'n most.'

Bessie shook her head. 'I've only just got to London – I never been here before.'

'Really? Well, I could ha' sworn . . . you got just the look of a girl used to live around these parts, real pretty she was, name of Jenny. Perhaps you're related – sister, or cousin or something? Now you mention it, of course I can tell you're not from hereabouts. Up north somewhere, I daresay.'

'Kidderminster,' Bessie said doubtfully, unsure as to whether this was north or not. 'I come on the coach.'

'On the *coach*? Well, you can't be as down as I thought. So what are you doing in here? Casing a new market, are yer?'

Bessie stared uncomprehendingly and the woman laughed. 'You *are* a country cousin, aren't yer! Don't you know what I'm talkin' about? Well, I can tell you this, it's a good job you fell in with me. Nice, well-brought up girl like you, you could have fallen in with some real bad lots, wanderin' round here on your own. But your Auntie Sal'll look after you, never you fear. Now – you'll be lookin' for somewhere to stay, and that's just where I can help.'

'Oh, no,' Bessie said, following her words with some difficulty. 'I've got somewhere to stay – that's when we find out where it is. You see—'

'We? You mean you ain't on yer own?'

'No, my brother's with me. That's him, getting us some food. We've got an address our – someone we know at home gave us. We're going to stay there until Mr – our friend comes. Then he'll find us work.' She ended a little doubtfully. Mr Vivian had never actually said what they were to do in London, or made any promises regarding work. In fact, he'd told Tom to find himself employment. But as far as she was concerned, he seemed to have his own plans, and Bessie hadn't had time to think what those might be.

Perhaps he knew of some grand house that might take her into service. Or a milliner who might want an apprentice – Bessie had always fancied herself at making hats. And she knew that Mr Vivian visited London quite frequently, on business for his father. He must know all kinds of well-to-do people here.

'And did this – friend of yours give you the fare for the coach as well?' Sal spoke delicately, as if probing a tender wound.

'Oh, yes. We couldn't have come otherwise – Tom and me, we don't have no money ourselves.' Bessie looked anxiously over towards the bar, where Tom was now in the middle of a crowd of men. 'I hope he's got enough to pay for our dinner. I'm scrammed.'

'Have another drop of gin. It'll do you good.' Sal poured another inch or two into the glass. 'It's all right, love. I told you, I'm not too hard up to help a girl down on her luck. I bin there meself a time or two.' She nodded and raised her glass, her sharp eyes surveying Bess over its rim. 'So you're all fixed up for tonight, are yer?'

'Well, I hope so – if we can find the place. We've got the address, but we don't know London at all, you see – we're scared of getting lost, and we don't know how far it might be.'

'Well, I can help you there. Ain't no one knows London like old Sal Preston. Haven't I lived here ever since I was born? I should think I know it!' Sal laughed, her coarse voice turning to a cough. She took another drink and wiped her eyes. 'I told you, girl, you're lucky you fell in with me. Innocent young thing like you – why, anything could happen if you asked the wrong person. Wake up tomorrow murdered in some dark alleyway, you could, yes and yer brother, too, big as he is.' She looked solemnly at Bess. 'This is London, not – where was it you said you come from? There's some funny people about, just looking for easy pickings.'

To her relief, Bessie saw that Tom was making his way across the crowded room with two tankards clutched in one hand and a large plate in the other. 'Oh, Tom, thank goodness you've come. I was afraid you wouldn't have enough money . . . I been talking to this person, telling her about the place we're supposed to be staying. She says she'll know where it is – lived in London all her life.'

'Ah, that's right,' Sal said cheerfully as Tom set the food and drink down on the table. 'Now, you two get that inside you – that's some good victuals you've got there, cold meats and pickles, they'll put new heart into you and then we can go wherever it is you've got this room fixed up for you. You did say there was a room? Let's see the address, I'll tell you where it is in a jiff.'

Tom looked at her, then at Bess. His mouth was pursed with doubt and she felt suddenly impatient with him.

'Well, what's wrong, Tom? What are you looking like that for?'

He flushed and looked down at the plate, and Sal laughed her hoarse cackle.

'Oh, I can tell you what's wrong with him! He don't trust old Sal, that's what it is – and why should he? An ugly old woman, picked up in a tavern – no, you shouldn't go trusting the first one you meets. But suppose I'd been the tenth, eh – you'd have trusted me then. Because you'd have knowed the other nine first, wouldn't yer? And you'd have knowed I was all right.' She gave them a triumphant look and sat back in her chair. 'So what's the difference if you trusts me to begin with? Not that it matters to me either way,' she added, making as if to get up. 'Lord knows, I was just offering a bit o' help out of the kindness of me heart, seeing as your sister here looked so down in the mouth and I can't abide seeing a pretty girl look mis'able. But if you can manage without me—'

'Oh, please don't go!' Bessie reached out and grasped her sleeve. 'Tom, don't look like that. Mrs Preston wants to help us – she knows London. We got to ask someone!'

Tom ate a piece of meat, frowning as he chewed it. He glanced quickly at Sal, then at Bessie.

'All right, Bess. I can see that. I just don't know as I like strangers knowing all our business, that's all—'

'Tom, I haven't—'

'An' quite right too,' Sal broke in. 'Keep a close mouth, that's what I say, then you can't get into no trouble. Now, I shan't ask no questions and you don't have to tell me no lies – that's a fair bargain, ain't it? Just tell me the address you got to find, and I'll help you if I can, and then we'll just say goodbye and you can be on yer way. You oughter be soon, anyway – getting dark, it is, and as I told your sister here, you don't want to be wanderin' about after dusk, not these foggy nights.'

'Show her the packet, Tom,' Bessie urged. 'Go on – we got to ask *someone*. Just because it's someone *I* found, and not you—'

'It int that,' Tom said sharply, and fished in the

pocket of his jacket. He dragged out the package, now looking dog-eared and grimy. 'Here, then, this is it, and that's the address. James Street, see? Now, if you can just tell us where that is, and how far we got to walk, we needn't bother you no further—'

'James Street?' Sal said, and took the package from him, peering at it in the dim light. 'Well, now that ain't so easy, is it? If it'd bin Regent Street, or Oxford Street, or Haymarket, why, anyone could have told you the way. But *James* Street . . .'

'Why, what's wrong with that?' Tom demanded. 'It exists, don't it?'

'Oh, it exists, all right. It just depends which one is is you want. See, there's three James Streets that I know of – and none of 'em's near here. I don't reckon you could reach one of 'em inside an hour, and then if it turns out to be the wrong 'un . . .' She shook her head and screwed up her mouth. 'No, if I'd knowed it was James Street you was lookin' for, I reckon I'd have told you to find yourselves a night's lodging hereabouts and leave it till tomorrow. That'd be the best thing you could do – specially with this pretty young sister of yours lookin' so bone-weary.'

Bessie stared at her, then turned her eyes to Tom. 'An hour!' she said. 'An hour through streets we don't know, with dark coming on – and then we might find out it's wrong when we do get there. Oh, Tom!'

He looked irritated. 'Well, what d'you reckon we can do? We can't afford lodgings – there's only enough money left to buy us a few meals while I find work. I don't see as there's aught else we *can* do.'

Bessie laid down her fork and rested her head on one hand. She felt suddenly overcome with weariness. The thought of trudging endlessly through streets that were filled with uncaring people, footpads or worse, ready to attack and strip her and Tom of even the little they had, ready to leave them for dead in some stinking alley, brought with it a black despair that washed over her and left her weak and close to tears. Yet, as Tom said, what choice had they?

For a moment she wished they had never left Kidderminster. And then the image of Jabez and his dreadful wound rose before her eyes and she groaned aloud.

'She's worn out, poor lamb,' Sal said. 'Here, love, have another drop of gin. It'll put heart into yer for that long walk . . . She'll never manage it, you know,' she said, addressing Tom. 'She's fit to drop.'

'I know.' He spoke dejectedly. 'But what else can we do?'

There was a moment's pause. Then Sal said, 'You could both come and stop along of me.'

Bess raised her head. Across the table, Tom was staring at Sal. 'Stop with you? But—'

'I got room. I run a bit of a lodging house. Rooms to let, that sort o' thing. I've got a few girls - respectable working girls - living permanent, but there's a few rooms for travellers and such as comes regular. I don't generally let out to strangers. But - you an' your sister - well, I've taken a fancy to the pair of yer, if the truth be known. And besides, as I said to - Bess, is it? I heard you call her that - I likes to give a bit of help where I can. So - if you've a mind to, you can stop along of me tonight and then tomorrow you can go and find this James Street.'

'But we haven't got the money—' Tom began.

'I told you, this is just a helping hand. You can pay me back later if you've a mind. What's one night, after all? Well—' Sal shrugged and began once more to rise to her feet '—take it or leave it. The offer's there, an' made in good faith, but if you'd rather tramp the streets—'

'Oh, no, please!' Once more, Bessie gripped her sleeve. 'Don't go. Tom, we can't go looking for that place tonight. Let's go with Sal. We'll never find anyone else to take us in. And I'm so tired. I don't think I can go on any longer.' Tears of exhaustion spilled out of her eyes and she saw Tom struggle for a moment, then give in. He lifted both hands from the table and let them fall again.

'All right, Bess. We'll stop the one night. But that's all. Tomorrow I'll find James Street and this Mrs—' he peered at the envelope again '—Markham, and then I'll find a job. And I reckon you'd better do that too. Mr Vivian'll have forgotten all about us by now, likely. I reckon it were just a bit of fun for him, getting us away from Kidder like that.'

'Oh, he won't forget us.' A different memory came into Bessie's mind; the memory of Vivian Pagnel, gripping her hard against him and kissing her with a cruel, exciting mouth. 'He'll find us.'

'Well, if you've made up your minds we'd better be goin',' Sal said. 'I got my girls to see to. They're popular girls, all of 'em – never an evening goes by without them bringing friends back for a bit of a party, and I likes to be there to see things are kept respectable. But you don't need to worry yourselves about that – you can go straight to yer own room and sleep. There won't be no noise to keep you awake.'

The food was finished, the gin and the ale drunk. As she stood up, Bessie was aware of a light-headedness that made her sway. The lights of the tavern blurred and swung before her eyes; she put out a hand to steady herself and lifted the other to her head.

Tom's face came close to hers, big and swollen, his eyes huge; then receded, becoming little more than a point of light in a sudden darkness. She felt sick and gulped.

'Here, take a hold of her arm.' Sal's grating voice sounded close to her ear. 'Let's get her out in the fresh air – she'll feel better then. Good job I live near by . . . that's it, love, just let us help you . . . there, we're outside now, soon be there. A nice comfortable bed, that's what you want, my duck . . .' The voice went on as they stumbled through the dark streets, Bessie held firmly between her brother and their benefactress. She staggered along the rough cobbles, tripping and catching her toes, quite unaware of which direction they were taking. At last she found herself being propelled gently through a door and then up some stairs. Firm hands pressed down on her shoulders and she sank on to a soft bed.

'That's it.' She was being covered now by something rough but warm; a blanket, drawn up to her chin where it scratched her skin gently. 'She'll sleep now,' Sal's voice said. 'She'll sleep till morning. And so will you – over here, see, on this pallet. You'll be all right, the pair of you. Just stay here now, and don't you worry about no noise you might hear – I told you, my girls has a party near every night, but it's all quite respectable.' Her voice faded. 'Quite respectable . . . quite respectable . . . respectable . . . respectable . . .'

Bessie did not lift her head until late next morning. Afterwards, she was never sure what was dream and what reality. That scream she heard, cutting through the darkness; the shrill laughter; the cackling that might have been in the next room; the hoarse voices of

90

men and the groans that might have come from the throat of someone in some strange agony. They all sounded real, but they were all entwined inextricably with her dreams; with those terrible visions of Jabez, lying on the carpet with his throat cut; of herself and Tom side by side on the gallows; of their bodies lying stripped and mutilated in some dark London alley.

It was a long time before the dreams left her, but at last she slid into oblivion, a welcome darkness that embraced her like a faithful lover. And then, for many hours, she heard nothing more.

She was in her coffin, dead and waiting to be buried. It was all over. The hanging had been done, the crowd gone home and now the prison bell was tolling her age. She counted. Ten . . . eleven . . . twelve . . . no, that wasn't right. And if she were dead, how was it she could still hear? Did you go on hearing and thinking after all, when you'd died?

Bessie opened her eyes with difficulty. The lids seemed heavy, as if someone had weighted them down. They did that when you were dead, didn't they? With pennies? She lifted a heavy arm and dragged her hand across her face, but there was nothing there. And at last she could see a dim yellow light and a face that hovered over her, first too big for a face, then too small; too close and then too far away.

'Ah, so you've woken up at last, duck.' The voice was hoarse and faintly familiar. 'Thought you was goin' to sleep the clock round twice, so I did. Well, you'll be wanting some victuals. A nice bowl of soup and a sup of ale, that'll soon put yer right.'

Bessie stared. The face had settled down now to a normal size and distance; a thin, sharp face with a few yellowing teeth and a foxy nose. Slowly, memory swam back. The hanging had been a dream. She wasn't in her coffin, but in a narrow box bed. The room was one she had never seen before, small with dirty walls and a window blocked with sacking instead of glass. It was lit by a guttering candle. And the face belonged to . . . to . . .

'Don't yer know me? It's old Sal – Sal Preston. Met in the public, didn't we, and you come home with me for the night – you and yer brother. It's all right – he's still about. Just gone out for a bit, that's all, but he'll be back.' A strong hand pushed Bessie back on to the bed as she tried to get up. 'Here – you get this down yer. It'll put heart into yer.'

Bessie found herself sitting up, with a bowl of soup steaming between her hands. She looked at it and realised that it smelt good – and she was hungry. She lifted it to her mouth and sipped. It was hot, but not too hot; she felt its heat snaking down inside her, warming her whole body.

'Ain't that the ticket?' Sal said, watching her. 'I knew you'd be ready for it. Here, have a bite o' bread along with it. That's it. You're empty, that's your trouble. You'll be right as a trivet when you gets that inside yer.'

Bessie gulped down the food and then drank the ale. She lay back against the pillow, and admitted that she did indeed feel better.

'Where's Tom?' she asked. 'You said he'd gone out. What time is it?'

'Time? Oh, we don't take too much account of time here, but I reckon I just heard the church clock give noon. As for your brother – what a nice, well-set up young blade he is, to be sure – he went off with that address you had, looking for James Street. I told him, there's more than one in London, so he'll have some walking to do if he don't get the right one first go. And if you're feeling up to it now, duck, we'll have to get going ourselves.'

'Go? Where are we going? To James Street, to find Tom?'

Sal clucked her tongue. 'Now, what use would that be, when we don't even know which one he's gone to first? No, we got to go to another house I've got, a few streets away. This room's taken for tonight, you see, one of my regulars, and the maid'll be wanting to come in and clean it. I likes my place kept tidy and respectable, as you can see. But there's room for you and your brother at my other place, stay as long as you like.'

'But we won't need to,' Bessie said. 'Once Tom's found the place we're supposed to be going to, we'll have a room there.'

Sal shrugged. 'Well, it's up to you. But I've knowed other girls come to London from the country with an address they've bin give, and it don't always work out so easy. Anyway, I've told your brother to go to the other house now – for all we know, he could be there waitin' this very minute.'

Bessie scrambled out of the bed. Sal could well be right – it was after twelve now, and if Tom had left early that morning he could have found the address and be back, waiting impatiently for her to arrive. She felt a small tremor of excitement. Kidderminster seemed very far away – they were in London now, beyond the reach of those who had pursued them, and a new life was about to begin.

'That's the ticket,' Sal said as they set out into the murky day. 'A good sleep and a bit of a brush-up works wonders. And you've got a lovely skin – all that fresh country air, I reckon. Pretty hair, too.'

She walked Bessie briskly through the streets, taking her along busy thoroughfares filled with hurrying people, past shops and stalls filled with goods that dazzled Bessie's eyes, through narrow backstreets littered with rubbish and into alleyways that were no more than slits between the buildings, dark and noisome.

'Don't lose me, mind,' Sal told Bessie. 'I don't reckon you'd ever find your way back.' Her eyes watched Bessie sharply, and when Bessie shook her head and agreed that she would be completely lost without her guide, she nodded as if satisfied.

'Well, it's not far now. And we might find your brother already waitin'. If not, you can wait comfortable for him. I've got some more girls living there – nice girls, you'll like 'em. They'll make a pet of you, if I knows anything.'

They stopped outside a tall, narrow house with steps up to the door. Sal took Bessie by the elbow and gave her a gentle push.

'This is it. Up them steps. Don't be nervous, now. My girls won't be about just yet – and they don't interfere, we all minds our own business here. It's better that way, I always says. Go on in, love.' She pushed open the door.

Bessie stepped inside. The hall was dark and smelt oddly – of cooking smells mixed with a strange, rich perfume she couldn't recognise. There was nobody about. She hesitated and glanced at Sal, who was closing the door behind them.

'It's all right, love. Just go up them stairs. The door on the right, that's your room. It's all ready for you.' She began to propel Bessie up the stairs.

Bessie tried to hang back. 'But Tom—'

'He ain't here yet, you can see that. Go on.' There

was an edge of impatience in Sal's voice and Bessie moved hastily. 'Here, I'll open the door for you.' She reached past and twisted the knob. 'Go on in, duck. There ain't nothing to be frightened of.'

Bessie hesitated and at that moment the next door opened and a girl came out. She was dressed showily, in a bright shawl over a dress that was lower in the neck than any Bess had ever seen. Her hair was loose and curly and her lips were brightly painted. She glanced curiously at Bessie.

'Is that you, Maud?' Sal's hand was on Bessie's back, urging her into the room. 'Goin' out, are yer? Well, have a good time, dearie. Maud's my best lodger, a very high-class girl. And she's got a very nice gentleman friend,' she confided as she pushed Bessie gently but firmly into the room and closed the door. 'Often sees him of an afternoon, she does, and sometimes she brings him back for a little talk. I don't say nothing – it's none of my business, and I know she's a respectable girl – so if you hears a man's voice, you'll know there's nothing to worry about. Now, you make yourself comfy in here, dearie, and wait for that brother of yours. I've got to go out for a while, but the maid will bring you something to eat and drink, and she'll tell your brother when he comes. All right, lovey?'

Bessie watched her go. She felt suddenly help- less – as if something were to happen to her that Sal knew perfectly well but chose not to explain. Her heart thumped with sudden apprehension and she went to the window.

Sal was hurrying up the street. She'd left Bessie alone in a strange house, where she knew nobody and nobody knew her. Trepidation fluttered like a bird in Bessie's breast, and she turned quickly and stared about the room.

It was small and shabbily furnished, with a bed along one wall, a small chest in one corner, a cupboard in another and a chair and rickety table. On the table was a bottle and two glasses. Bessie stared at it. *Two* glasses?

Her nervousness deepened to real fear. What – who was Sal Preston? Why had she taken such an interest in Bessie and Tom? Why had she taken them in – and sent Tom off that morning without Bessie's knowledge? And why had she brought Bessie here?

Had she really sent Tom to James Street? Had she really given him this address to come for Bessie?

And if she hadn't – if he returned to the first house, what would happen? Would he be told that Bess had gone out for a walk – never to return?

Bessie thought of the maze of streets and alleyways through which they had come. She would never find her way back, never.

Panic gripped her with cold, clammy hands. She ran to the door and jerked at the knob, but it refused to turn. The door was locked.

Bessie stared at it unbelievingly. She pulled and twisted until her fingers were sore; beat on the wooden panels until her fists were bruised, and shouted until she was hoarse. Nobody came. There was not even a sound to suggest that anyone else was in the house. Maud must have been the only girl in the house when they had arrived, and had not yet returned with her 'gentleman friend'.

She went back to the window and stared out. It was high above the street. There was no way of escape – but there were people down there. She waved and shouted, but nobody glanced up.

Should she break the glass? But the street was filled

with noise, the clatter of horses' hooves, the rattle of carts, the shouts and cries of hawkers and street vendors. Nobody would hear her.

Bessie gazed down. Then she turned away from the window and sank down on the chair, her head resting in her hands. Hopelessness washed over her, and she wondered how it had ever come about that she should end up here.

From Jabez's loom to a bawdy-house – for she had no doubt now that that was where she was – in London was a long way. Yet, it seemed now that she had travelled the journey in her sleep; she could remember so little of what had happened. Only a long, blurred dream of fear and horror, of being pursued, of hiding, of rattling through unknown miles by coach, of the noise and bustle, the confusion that was London.

And now this. A bare, cold room that was a prison cell.

And nobody knew where she was.

Chapter Five

The man grunted at last and lifted his heavy body away from her. Bessie lay still, afraid to move, bruised and sore from his attentions. She watched as he dragged on his trousers and a sob caught at her throat.

It seemed a very long time since that night in Kidderminster, when Jabez had forced her to work late. For the first time, she wondered what would have happened if Tom had not come into the carpet shop at that moment. She would be home now, and no worse off than any other draw-girl: worked to a deathly fatigue, raped regularly by her master, probably in the early stages of a pregnancy which would bring even more hardship and poverty; beaten and cursed by her father. But *home*. Safe. With no murder on her conscience, no bawd with her claws in her, no threat of more violent seductions like the one she had recently endured in this room.

At the memory, Bess shuddered. Jabez had been rough, but his attack had been spontaneous and quickly over. Sal Preston's 'gentleman' this afternoon had been calculatingly cruel, taking his pleasure from watching her fear. To such a man, an apparent virgin would be an extra delight. And until Bess could overcome her terror, Sal could go on selling her as a virgin to men who liked to believe they were the first to explore uncharted territory.

The man went out without another glance at her, and when Sal returned to the room, Bessie was lying on the bed, a crumpled, sobbing heap of dishevelled ruin.

'Now then, now then, you've no cause to take on like that,' the woman chided her as she moved about the squalid cell. 'Nothing's happened to you as don't happen to every girl at some time in her life. And I'd be surprised if it was the first time, eh?'

Bess broke into fresh sobs and made no reply. Her face was buried in the thin, grubby pillow.

'You don't know when you're well off, my girl.' Sal picked up the two glasses and sniffed. 'Hm. I see you didn't think yourself too high an' mighty for a little nip . . . And that was one of my nicest gentlemen. No rough trade in this house. He'd have treated you well – kind-hearted to a fault, he is. You ain't got nothing to complain of. Lots of girls has a much worse time than that.'

Bessie rolled over and stared up at the coarse face, its seams ingrained with dirt, its eyes bloodshot and rheumy. Why hadn't she seen these things before? Why hadn't she seen the calculating evil in those small eyes? Why hadn't she known that Sal Preston's apparent friendliness could not be real?

'An' you don't need to look at me like that,' Sal said sharply. 'If it hadn't ha' bin me, it woulda bin someone else, and you could have done a lot worse, let me tell you. Anyway, it's done now. And we got to have a talk, you an' me.'

'Where's my brother?' Bess asked in whisper. 'Where's Tom? I want Tom.'

'Tom? Now there's a well-set up young man. Yes . . . I bin thinking about Tom. Still lookin' for James Street, I reckon. And when he don't find it, why, I suppose he'll go back to my other house.'

'And they'll tell him where I am?' Bessie struggled

up on to her elbow. Her body ached; there were tender spots that she knew would turn into bruises. 'He'll come here for me then. He'll take me away.'

Sal looked at her, and Bess's heart sank at the coldness in those small, red-rimmed eyes.

'Why, no, my duck, he won't be taking you anywhere. He won't know where you are, will he? Nobody at that other house is going ter tell him anything. They won't know, see – they won't have seen you, none of 'em.' She smiled, a cold, cruel little smile. 'They knows better . . . And they won't know *this* address – oh, no. So unless I *tells* them to let on – why, how's he going to find yer?'

Bess felt cold and sick. Fear crept over her skin and thudded in her breast. From the street came the cries and shouts of street vendors, the rattle of carts and horses' hooves. All of London lay out there – huge and teeming, noisy and dirty. Filled with people going about their own business; filled with beggars and tarts, cripples and thieves. People who had no hope.

People like herself.

'It ain't no good piping yer eye,' Sal remarked. 'It's happened to plenty afore you, and it'll happen to plenty more. And if you've got any sense, you'll make the best of it. It ain't such a bad life, after all.' Her sharp eyes moved over the huddled figure. 'You've got a good enough body – young and firm, plenty of flesh, the men likes that. And you're the kind to enjoy it, too, I reckon, once you got over yer fancy ideas. They likes that as well. You got a lot to learn – I'll get Maud to have a talk with yer. A bit o' begging and whimpering don't go amiss, and you don't want to lay too still . . . but Maud'll tell yer. Yes, I reckon you could do very well.'

'But I don't want to!' Bess struggled up from the

bed and clawed frantically at Sal's skirt. 'I don't want to be a doxy! I never come to London for that. I got a friend, a gentleman friend, he's going to look after me, he'll be expecting me—'

'And you don't call yourself a dolly-mop!' Sal cackled loudly. 'What d'yer think you were going to do for him that's any different from what you'll do for *my* gentlemen? And how long d'you think it'd last anyway? I knows these "gentlemen friends" – all over yer for a few weeks and then some other gay girl comes along and it's out on yer neck. And then you'd be pleased enough to get taken into a respectable house like this, I can tell yer.' She came close to the bed and thrust her face close to Bessie's. 'Know what'd happen to you? You'd be walking the Haymarket, like hundreds of other girls. You'd be following soldiers and sailors, trying to get a room in a lodging house, you'd be going in the park in the bushes. *That's* what you'd be doing.' She moved away from Bessie's shrinking body, then turned and glanced down at her with contempt. 'Well, if that's what yer wants, go off out and try it. But you'll never see your brother again if you do, I can tell yer that. 'Cause the only way you're likely to find him is to stop along of me.'

Bessie stared at her. 'What d'you mean? I don't understand—'

Sal cackled again. 'Why, isn't he going to come back to my other house? And when he don't find you there, what's he going to do?'

'He'll look for me,' Bessie said, and knew as she said it what a hopeless task this would be.

'And where's he going to look – eh? London's a big place.' Sal moved to the window and gazed down at the thronged street. 'He'd never find yer, not without a big piece of luck. An' that don't happen often. Not to our sort. No, my duck, you'd be best off to stop here, along of me. And besides – I told yer, I got a few ideas about that brother o' yours.'

'About Tom?' Bessie felt a faint glimmer of hope, quickly dowsed. What ideas could a woman like Sal Preston have for Tom that could possibly be for his good?

'Ah. Like I said, he's a well-set up young feller. Handy in a bout of fisticuffs, I wouldn't wonder. Just the sort of young chap as I could do with round here, to help me out a bit. Just with general handiwork, you understand, and a bit of protection when some of the rougher gentlemen comes calling. I keeps a good, quiet house here,' she added quickly as Bessie drew in a breath, 'but you can't always tell, and some of the gentlemen, when they gets on the booze a bit, is liable to be a bit frisky. Now, your brother could be a help then, don't you reckon?'

Bess could not answer. Badly though she wanted to see Tom again, the thought of him in this house, sharing the degraded life that Sal intended for her, turned her already queasy stomach sick again.

'Please,' she whispered, 'please, why don't you let me go? What d'you want with me? There must be plenty of girls . . . plenty better'n me.'

Sal gave a short laugh. 'Let you go? Why, you're a good little property, you are. Fresh from the country – that's what the gentlemen likes, that's what they'll dig deep in their pockets to pay for. An' you can pass for a virgin four, five times easy. Specially if you ain't too keen . . .' She grinned, showing broken teeth. 'They'll pay over the odds for unused goods.' She watched as Bessie turned away, groaning, and her voice hardened. 'So don't even think of trying to get away, all right? You belongs here now. You owes me – for a night's lodging, if nothing else. Now – I bin here chattering long enough. There's work to be done. You needs some new clobber – I'll see what the other girls can spare. And evening's coming on – my gentlemen'll be arriving soon. Hungry?'

Bess shook her head. The thought of food turned her stomach afresh. But Sal pursed her lips.

'You got to eat. I'll send one of my girls out for a pie, that'll put heart into you. And then maybe I'll pick out a nice gentleman for you for later on, when you've had a bit of a rest. Someone as'll appreciate you.' She ignored Bess's terrified pleas and went to the door. 'And I warn you – you'd better behave yourself. No fancy tricks, see? Not if you wants to see that precious brother of yours again.'

The door closed behind her and Bessie, half off the bed, heard the key turn in the lock. Despairing, she sank back on the lumpy mattress and buried her face in her hands. Sobs shook her body, but there were no more tears in her and her throat was dry and aching.

She groaned and thought of her brother, trudging the streets searching in vain for the address Vivian had given them. Returning to the other house, only to find Bess vanished and nobody willing even to admit that she had ever been there. Oh Tom, Tom, what will you do? she asked desperately. And what would happen if you were to find me – how could you rescue me?

Kidderminster, the tiny cottage with William's clattering loom, Fanny's worn grey face, and her sister Rebecca, all seemed very far away now.

'I told you.' For the first time in her life, Fanny Himley faced her husband and defied him. 'I told you, our Becky's going into service. I'll not have her in this trade no longer. I'm taking her up to Pagnels' to see Mrs Hudd. She was head kitchenmaid when I was there, she'll remember me. She'll take our Becky, if there's a place for her.'

'Service!' William growled. 'I've never called any man master yet, and—'

'Oh, stop fooling yourself!' Fanny snapped, and both William and Rebecca stared at her with open mouths. 'All your life, you've told yourself nothing but make-believe,' she went on passionately. 'Calling yourself independent! Saying you're no man's slave! When all the time, you're as much a slave as any factory worker, sat at that loom day in, day out, working all the hours God sends for a few shillings a week. What independence do you have, when you must go to Pagnel's warehouse every week to buy the yarn and then get your piece back there by ten o'clock come fall day, or they'll not take it? And having to take their prices – if they decide to pay less, can you force them to do aught else? Is *that* your precious independence?' Her pale eyes flashed. 'Well, I've had enough of it. I've bin in service and it's hard, but at least you're fed and clothed and got a roof over your head. And you don't get into the kind of trouble our Bess has fallen into, and our Tom.'

Her voice quavered as she came to the thought of her other children but she remained standing, Rebecca's hand clutched tightly in hers, her mouth set with a determination she had never displayed before. William stared at her. His face darkened and he made a small movement, as if to strike his wife. But Fanny did not flinch, and he hesitated, nonplussed, then attacked with her own weapon.

'Not get into trouble?' he sneered. 'And how many young maids have found themselves with a bellyful of marrow pudding, put there by the master or one of the sons? Aye, and turned off without a character too, the minute the mistress finds out. That's better'n a weaver, is it? At least there's a chance of getting wed when it's one of your own sort.'

'That wouldn't happen to our Becky. She's a sensible girl – not flighty like Bess. And it's only the housemaids run into that risk – I'd have her in the kitchen.'

'Where there's boot boys and footmen and such,' William pointed out. 'And anyway, Becky works for *me* – there ain't no risk here. I dunno what all your fuss is about.'

'I want her out of the carpet trade, that's what.' Fanny spoke with a stubbornness Rebecca had never heard before. 'You knows very well that come another year or two you'll be wanting her down the factory, where she can earn more'n you can pay her. Same as Bessie.'

'And who's going to work for me then, if you take Becky away?'

William's voice was surly and Rebecca recognised that her mother had won, even though nobody was yet admitting it. She felt a quick, triumphant squeeze of Fanny's hand around her fingers.

'You can take on young Micky Gratton, he's coming up to eight and a bright enough youngster. You'd be looking for someone anyway, once you'd sent Becky off, like I said. You might as well start now. I've had a word with Marge Gratton and she's willing, and so's Sam.'

'You seem to have got it all fixed up, then. Don't I have no say in my own house any more?' William's voice was growing angry again, and Rebecca saw a new clenching of his big fists.

The tightening of Fanny's fingers showed that she had seen it, too, but her voice was steady as she answered him. 'I told you – I don't mean Becky to go into carpets. And you can have all the say you want – once she's gone.' Rebecca could feel her mother's body tremble. 'Beat me all you want to, Will Himley, it won't make no difference once our Becky's safe.'

'*No*!' Rebecca tore her hand from her mother's and jumped to stand between her parents. 'No, he won't hit you, Mam, he won't! I'll stay here—' she turned to her father, lifting her chin to look up into his dark, heavy face. 'I'll draw for you – I won't go into service – as long as you leave me Mam alone. I won't have you hitting her. She can't stand it – she's been through enough.'

'Becky!' Fanny gasped, and tried to draw her back, but Rebecca shrugged her hand away and faced her father, meeting his eyes with an expression as unyielding as his own, her own small fists clenched in unconscious imitation. He stared down at her, heavy brows drawn together, dark eyes snapping; and for a moment there was an almost uncanny likeness between the two, father and daughter. A likeness of personality, cracking in the small, shabby room, that was even more powerful than the physical likeness of dark eyes and brows, thick brown hair and sturdy, defiant stance.

'I'll stay here and draw for you,' Rebecca repeated. 'But you're not to hit me Mam – not any more.'

William's eyes narrowed. His jaw tensed and his big shoulders moved under the ragged shirt he wore for working. Behind her, Rebecca felt Fanny shiver and move closer, as if to protect her daughter. But again, she moved impatiently and tilted her head a little higher. And William, seeing the movement, lifted his brows and then, unbelievably, laughed.

'Well! It looks as if we've raised a firebrand! So you've spoken, have you, miss, and expect to be obeyed too by the sound of it.' He looked hard at her, and to her astonishment she saw a softening in the harsh lines of his face. 'Well, maybe there's some truth in it after all. Maybe you *would* be better off out of this.' He glanced round at the dark room with its flaking walls and rough stone floor covered with only a scrap of 'Kidderminster stuff'. 'All right – take her up to Pagnels' and see if they've a place for her. And I'll try young Gratton. His father's a good enough weaver, after all, and got enough childer to keep drawing for him for a good many years to come – he won't miss one.' He turned away, as if embarrassed by the incredulous joy in Fanny's face. 'And now I'm going for a drink. I suppose I can still do that without asking first?'

'Oh, Will,' Fanny said in a trembling voice. 'Will, you won't regret it – I'll see you never regret it—'

'I'd better not,' he said with a return to his old manner. 'Or you'll be the one to do the regretting. And hear this, young Becky – you're to behave yourself up there, if they take you, you understand? I'll have no more trouble brought to this house. It's bad enough with our Bess and Tom—'

'It wasn't their fault, Will!'

'Fault or not, I'll have no more of it!' His voice rising in a bellow of rage, he turned on Fanny like a bull. She shrank back, the defiance fled from her eyes. Will paused and looked at her, then at Rebecca. 'All right. You've had your say, both of you, and you've got your way. Becky goes to Pagnels'. And now I'm off out. I want to hear no more of it.' He thrust his way out of the door and into the cobbled street. The sounds of the street wafted in; the cries of children playing in the mud, of women gossiping, men laughing and arguing. And then the door swung shut and Rebecca and her mother were alone.

'Well,' Fanny said after a long pause, 'I never thought he'd take it that quiet. Becky, girl, we'd better get going afore he changes his mind and comes back. Come on – get your best pinny on and wash your face and hands. You got to look your best for Mrs Hudd.'

But Rebecca hesitated. 'Mam, are you sure? I don't like leaving you alone—'

'Look, I won't be any more alone than I was afore you lot started coming. And I'll be a lot happier for knowing you're safe and comfortable up at the house. It won't be easy for you, mind – Mrs Hudd'll make sure you work hard, and from what I hear Mrs Pagnel ain't an easy mistress. But you'll be out of carpets, and that's what I want. And it can't be no worse than it is here. Now – look sharp. I wouldn't put it past your father to come back and put a stop to it – and I want you out of the house before he gets the chance. And you know who'll get the brunt of it if he does.'

Rebecca hesitated no longer. She dipped her hands quickly in the bowl of water that stood on the rough wooden table, and smeared them over her face. Then she wrapped the clean white pinafore around her shabby dress and followed her mother out of the cottage.

They were both aware, as they walked through the narrow streets, of the curious glances that followed them. Three weeks had now passed since Jabez's death, three weeks since Bessie and Tom had disappeared. There had been no sign of either of them, nor any word. They could be, as William was convinced, dead in some ditch; or, as Fanny prayed, safe in some large town where they could find work and a decent room to live in, and start a new life.

'We'll hear from them one day,' she said over and over again, though whether to convince William or herself, Rebecca was never sure. 'Tom can write – he'll send us a letter. I've got the money saved, ready to pay the postage.' She had scraped and almost starved herself to gather enough to pay for a letter, and however much William might grumble at the waste of having such money put by, she refused to reveal where it was hidden.

In the past three weeks, Fanny had displayed an unsuspected core of strength. Frail as she was, and still afraid of the temper her husband could sometimes display, she was nevertheless prepared to defy him over her children – the ones who had gone from her, or the one who remained. It was as if a new, hidden energy had welled up in her at the thought of their danger; she was like a she-cat defending her kittens to her last breath, a doe rabbit turned suddenly fierce at the threat of a predator.

Rebecca had been surprised at her mother's determination that she should leave the carpet trade – and even more surprised that her father should give way. Neither of them had consulted her, nor did she expect it. But now, hurrying along beside her mother to the hill where the Pagnel house stood looking down over the growing town, she felt a tremor of excitement.

The Pagnel house – where Vivian Pagnel lived. And where his cousin Francis, whose description in

Bessie's tales had so enchanted her, must sometimes surely visit.

She turned to her mother. 'What'll it be like, being in service, Mam?'

'Well, I've told you that often enough. You never stopped pestering me for stories when you were little.'

'I know, but that was just stories. I want to know what it'll be *like*.'

Fanny looked down at her.

'What it's like? Well – it's hard work, make no mistake about that. Especially for you. You'll be put to scrubbing, I expect, scrubbing vegetables, scrubbing floors, scrubbing dirty dishes. That's a scullery-maid's job, and I reckon that's what Mrs Hudd'll take you as. You'll start early in the morning and finish late at night – if you're lucky. If they has a dinner-party, you'll be lucky to see your bed at all. And you'll be at everyone's beck and call, so don't think that if there's not much scrubbing to do you'll be let to put your feet up.' She paused. 'But you'll have three good meals a day if it's aught like it was in my day – and I reckon Annie Hudd'll keep that up – and you'll have a best black for church on Sundays, and you'll get a half day once a month to come home and tell me all about it. And if you work hard and behave yourself, you'll get on. Many's the scullerymaid as did what Annie Hudd did and rose to be cook or even house-keeper. And that's more'n you could ever say about the carpet trade.'

Rebecca was silent. It did sound as if it would be a hard life. But no harder than standing at her father's loom for hour after hour, her legs aching until she thought she could stand no longer, her arms wearied by the endlessly repetitive movements.

And Rebecca, like any other ten-year-old in

Kidderminster, knew already that life for her class was destined to be hard. Her childhood had been over for a long time; whatever work she did – and work must – it would be hard, tedious and probably unpleasant. Nothing she had seen so far had indicated that there would ever be anything different.

She had learned already that life was never fair.

'Well, she's a bit on the small side, but I reckon she'll do,' Annie Hudd said, looking Rebecca up and down critically. 'Girls always come a bit small at that age – she'll grow with a bit of feeding. And a lot of hard work.' She gave Rebecca a sharp look. 'I hope you don't think you're coming here for an easy life, miss.'

Rebecca shook her head and Fanny interposed quickly, 'She's used to hard work, Mrs Hudd. And I've told her about when I was here.'

'Aye, well, you were a good enough worker,' the housekeeper conceded. 'And she looks quiet enough. I like a quiet girl – biddable. Can't abide a sulky or insolent miss.' She examined Rebecca's face, rather as if she were judging a piece of meat. 'You're not a sulker, I hope? You've got the sort of mouth . . .'

'Becky never sulks. She's a good girl, Mrs Hudd. Been drawing for her father for this past two years – but I wants her in service, same as I was. It's a better life for a girl who's willing to work hard and get on.'

'Well, I'll see the mistress about her. It's her has the say-so, you understand – though of course she takes my advice over such matters. But I don't know as she'll be too keen, not after what's happened over that weaver down in Butts' carpet shop. She might think there's bad blood in the family.'

Fanny clasped her hands together. Her face was drawn into tight lines of anxiety.

'Please, Mrs Hudd. You know it int true. My Bess and Tom never meant that to happen – it must have been an accident. Gentle as a kitten, Tom is, and Bess – well, you can guess what that Gast did to her. That's why I want to get Becky out of the trade and into decent service. And I know you'll look after her.'

Mrs Hudd looked at her and nodded. 'Yes, I'd do that – I make sure all my girls keep themselves decent. And I've known you long enough, Fanny . . . All right, I'll put in a word for your Becky – but mind you behaves yourself, miss,' she said sharply to Rebecca. 'Mrs Pagnel won't stand no nonsense, and it's me as'll carry the can if you catches her eye for any reason.'

'I won't,' Rebecca promised breathlessly. She was somewhat overawed by the housekeeper. Mrs Hudd was tall and stately in her black bombazine gown, a bunch of keys fastened at her waist. In her broad hands rested the running of this great house, the organisation of a hierarchy of servants. Her eyes were as sharp as an eagle's, missing nothing, her jaw hard as a man's, her bearing as regal as that of any queen. Only Mrs Pagnel held authority over her and, if the truth were known, even she was secretly in awe of this majestic being.

Rebecca knew nothing of all this, but she sensed the power of the housekeeper. As her mother and Mrs Hudd talked, reminiscing over old times when they had worked together in this very house, she looked from under her lashes at the woman who held the strings of the Pagnel house in her fingers.

The contrast between the two women was unmistakable.

Fanny, even in her Sunday dress, was shabby. Annie Hudd, though dressed for work, wore quality fabrics: the bombazine for which Kidderminster had been famous, trimmed with black lace, exquisitely sewn. Her bosom swelled above a tightly corseted waist; her hands were plump and adorned with several rings.

Fanny's face, scrubbed for the occasion, was still grey and worn, the lines of weariness making her look older than she was. Her hands were wrinkled and thin, scored with the yarn she spent her life winding. Her hair hung grey and lank about her cheeks, sunken through loss of teeth. She looked old.

Annie Hudd, at almost the same age, could have been twenty years younger. She, too, bore the marks of hard work – they had been housemaids together, Rebecca knew. But where Fanny was cowed and submissive, Mrs Hudd wore a proud, even haughty aspect. The lines on her face were lines of confidence, of a calm belief in her authority. Nothing would go wrong in this household: Mrs Hudd would not allow it.

Fanny Himley was the victim of her own destiny; Annie Hudd was in charge of her life. Servant she might be, but her service was of a proud nature, and she would not easily be subdued.

In that moment, Rebecca knew that her own fate rested in the two small hands that lay so docilely in her lap – the hands that had wielded the sword and wire for her father, the hands that would scrub and polish for Annie Hudd.

She could follow her mother into a life of servitude and submission, a life ordered by other people – a housekeeper like Mrs Hudd, the other servants at whose beck and call she must be, to begin with at least; a husband, perhaps, overworked and bullying like her father, the children who would come and keep coming with marriage.

A life that wasn't hers at all. A life that belonged to others.

Or she could be like Annie Hudd. She could take charge of her own life. Work, yes, as she must – but always with a purpose. That of rising above whatever station she might hold at any time – rising, always rising, until she too could sit of an afternoon in silk bombazine with a bunch of keys at her waist, ordering the comings and goings of a household, answerable to no one but the mistress. And, in a subtle way which Rebecca only dimly suspected, holding sway over her too. And thus over the whole family.

It could be done. Mrs Hudd had worked her way up from a kitchenmaid. Rebecca Himley could do it too.

Her life would be *hers*. And no one else's.

Tom, walking the streets of London, felt as if he had stumbled into a nightmare.

He was accustomed to scenes of poverty in Kidderminster. The streets there were mean and narrow, many of the houses small and in a poor state. The people he knew lived in cramped conditions, often a whole family to one room, many of them in damp, unlit cellars. They often had no work and therefore no money for food or even water. He had himself made many journeys to a well or even a ditch some way from his father's cottage, carrying a bucket or pan to fill with rank green water. He had felt the gnawing pain of an empty stomach, the chill of a bitter wind through thin, tattered clothing.

Yet none of this had prepared him for what he saw

as he searched the streets of London for the address Vivian Pagnel had given to him.

There seemed no end to the maze of courtyards, alleyways and thoroughfares, all teeming with people and animals and littered with all manner of debris: dung and ordure from horses and dogs, household rubbish piled outside doors, rotting vegetables discarded from street-traders' carts, paper and mud and scraps of rag, all kicked and trodden by the hurrying feet of the people who all, it seemed to Tom, had somewhere to go and not enough time to get there. And all talking, shouting, calling to each other above the clatter of hooves and wheels, until his head reeled.

The wider roads were busy with carts and carriages, drawn by horses in every condition from starving and spavined to pampered and glossy. Men dragged hand-carts piled with goods: plump vegetables and glistening fresh meat, or scabby potatoes and rotting carrots; decent clothes fit for Sunday, or broken boots that only the poorest would buy. Children darted here and there, carrying jugs of ale or running other errands; some wielded brushes as they swept crossings, others stood at street corners selling matches, or vied to clean shoes or hold horses.

And there were women too. Sitting on steps or in corners, sometimes with a few scraps of clothing or chipped crockery around them for sale; more often with a hand held out in supplication for a penny or two from passers-by. And almost all with a dirty bottle beside them or tipped to their cracked lips. The 'mother's ruin' that Tom knew was their road to oblivion.

'Come on, love,' a wheedling voice said in his ear as he hesitated at a corner. 'You looks as if you could do with a bit of comfort on a cold day.'

Startled, he looked into the face of a girl not much older than Bessie and saw blue eyes, appealingly round, peeping through yellow curls. Lips rosier than Bessie's laughed at him, and he felt a rush of relief at being acknowledged. In the hurrying crowds, he had begun to think himself invisible.

'I'm looking for James Street,' he said quickly. 'D'you know where it is? Is it round here – I'm new to London and I'm a bit lost.'

Her eyes sharpened and she put up a hand to brush back the curls. 'New to London, are yer? Well, so you'll need someone to show yer around a bit. Look, I got a room near here – why don't we go an' have a bite o' summat? Yer not in any hurry to find this place, are yer?'

'Yes, I am.' Tom felt for the package with the letter Vivian had given him and what was left of the money. 'I've got to go to this address, and then I've got to go back and fetch my sister – she's waiting for me in a house near Portland Place.' He glanced up and caught the girl's eyes, narrowed now, fixed on the package. Suddenly uneasy, he folded it and slipped it back into his pocket. 'I've got to find it,' he repeated.

The girl looked at him speculatively. She ran a small pink tongue over her lips and he was suddenly aware of how pretty she was under the film of grime that seemed to hang in the London air. But there was something about her that struck cold, something in the hardness of those china-blue eyes, the set of that soft, pouting mouth.

'Come home with me,' she said persuasively. 'Yer looks cold and hungry. We can get a pie at the stall an' I'll make yer a gin and hot water. I've got a friend there, he knows London like the back of his hand. He'll be able to tell yer where this James Street is.'

117

Tom hesitated. It was true that he was cold and hungry; he was tired too. Weary from tramping the streets, from finding himself lost in alleyways and yards, from feeling more and more bewildered as he stared up at street names that were never the right one. The thought of a pie and a hot drink, the thought of rest – and, more than anything, the thought of actually being directed to the street he had sought for so long – was almost overwhelmingly appealing.

'Come on,' the girl said, and took his hand. He felt her small nails scratch lightly on the inside of his wrist. 'It's on'y a step.' She tugged gently and Tom gave in and allowed himself to be drawn along the crowded street. It couldn't do any harm, he told himself. He needed to eat and drink, to rest for a while. And Bessie was all right where she was, in Sal Preston's house.

'My name's Dolly,' the girl confided as she hurried him along. 'What's yours? We might's well be friends.'

'Tom. Tom Himley.'

'And you've on'y just come to London? Where are yer from, then? The country?'

'Kidderminster,' he said, but she shook her head as if she had never heard of it. 'Where they makes carpets,' he added.

'Coo-er. Carpets.' She giggled as if he had said something funny. 'Well, we don't have no fine stuff like that around here. Look, there's the pie-stall – get us a couple, will yer? An' I'll go on and tell my friend you're coming. It's that door over there, see?'

Tom bought two meat pies, realising as he did so how hungry he was. He wondered if Sal had given Bess anything to eat, and was sure she would have done. He paid for the pies and hurried after Dolly. It

118

was growing dark already. He hoped the right James Street wasn't too far away now.

'Here y'are, then.' Dolly was waiting at the door and reached out to take his hand again, tugging him inside. 'Coo, that smells good. Here – give us one, I'm starved. Come on – up here.'

Tom found himself in a narrow passageway, following her up steep stairs. It was almost dark; he stumbled on a broken step and almost fell against Dolly's plump body. She giggled again and said something he couldn't catch, and then opened a door at the top of the stairs.

The room was small, and not unlike the one he had left Bess in at Sal Preston's house. There was a bed, a chair and a washstand with a large china bowl and jug on it. A stale, fishy stench hung in the air.

Dolly went to the washstand and poured something from the jug into a cup. She handed it to Tom.

'It ain't hot – there's no fire. But it'll warm yer, just the same.' She watched as he drank and choked a little on the fiery liquid. 'Come on, yer must have had gin before. Good and strong – keep out the cold.' She took the cup from him and drained it. 'Want some more?'

Tom shook his head. He wasn't accustomed to gin – ale was the drink Sam Hooman allowed his apprentices. But the warmth spread through his body and he began to feel better. He changed his mind and nodded, and Dolly laughed and poured a second cup. She sat down on the bed and began to munch her pie.

After a moment she glanced up at Tom, standing awkwardly in the doorway, and made a patting gesture on the bed beside her.

'Come on, love, don't stand there like a stuffed duck. Sit down and eat your pie while it's hot. Do yer good – yer look proper clemmed. There – ain't that more cosy?' As Tom sat down, she moved slightly so that she was pressed against him and he felt the soft warmth of her body. 'Nice to be friendly, innit?'

'Yes.' He was beginning to feel strangely light-headed. 'But I got to find this place and get back to my sister. She'll be wondering—'

'Go on, a bit longer won't hurt. Yer bin walking about all day. Yer needs a bit of comfort.' She was rubbing gently against him now, her breasts large and soft against his arm. 'Why don't yer lay down for a bit, now you're here? My friend won't be long – he's just nipped out for a few minutes. When he comes back, he'll be able to tell yer where this place is and you'll be there in two ticks, see if yer ain't.'

Tom opened his mouth to protest, but the words wouldn't come. And she was right; he was tired. Bone-weary. And if she was right, if this friend of hers would be able to direct him to James Street, it did make more sense to wait. And maybe he could do with a bit of sleep too.

'Come on,' Dolly murmured and, slipping an arm round his back, pulled gently at his shoulders. 'I could do with a bit of a lay-down meself. And it's chilly in here – we'll keep each other warm, eh?'

Strange things were happening in Tom's head. A reeling, whistling sensation that made it difficult to stay upright. The noises of the street had faded and he could hear an insistent thumping that seemed to be inside his ears. He found himself lying on the bed. Dolly was beside him, warm and soft. The thumping increased and transferred itself. It was all over his body; all through him. He stirred and found a wet, open mouth against his.

'Come on, love,' Dolly murmured in his ear.

'Don't tell me you country boys don't know what it's all about. Yer knows what to do next . . . don't yer?'

It seemed a long time later when Tom finally stirred and raised himself on one elbow to stare about him.

His head was still thumping and he felt sick. He remembered Bess and groaned a little. What time was it? How long had he been away – and what had possessed him to come here?

The room was lit by the stub of a candle. Dolly was sitting in the chair, examining something on her lap. As his vision cleared, Tom saw that it was a packet. A letter.

The letter Vivian had given him.

He scrambled up on the bed and groaned again, holding his head with both hands. The room rocked a little, then steadied. Cautiously, he lifted his hands away from his head. Dolly was watching him now, her face oddly shadowed in the guttering light, her eyes narrowed and glittering.

'So you've woke up at last?' she said. 'It'll cost yer dear, that will. Yer bin here over an hour – I don't usually let my gentlemen have more'n a half. This ain't a posh hotel.'

'That's my letter,' Tom said, reaching out. 'You've been reading my letter.'

Dolly laughed and snatched it out of his reach. 'Don't be daft! I can't read. I bin saving it for my friend – *he* can read a bit.'

'Your friend. You said he could tell me where James Street is—'

'He could, I specs. If he feels like it.' She was watching him. 'But first, you an' me got a bit of business to settle, ain't we?'

'Business?'

'Look,' she said sharply, 'yer don't get what yer just had for nothing. It all costs money – and like I said, you've had twice as long as I usually gives. So it's on'y right to pay double, ain't it.'

'But I can't – I didn't mean—' Tom floundered desperately. His head felt thick and soft, his thoughts came as if through a layer of flannel. 'Look, I only came for—'

'Never mind what yer come for,' she said softly. 'Yer might on'y go in a shop for one thing, but if yer comes out with two yer pays, dontcher? And you're going to pay now. Or my friend'll know the reason why.' She got up suddenly and went to the door. 'Alf! The gentleman's acting up.'

Tom heard a sound from below, then heavy footsteps on the stairs. Suddenly afraid, he looked round for a weapon. There was none, except the jug on the table. He caught it up and Dolly gave a little scream and backed away.

'Look out, Alf! He's turning nasty.'

'Nasty, is he!' a deep voice growled from the landing. 'Well, we'll soon see who's nasty round here. Stand clear, Doll – I'm comin' in.'

The door crashed open and at the same time Tom threw the jug. It smashed against the door jamb and gin spattered over the face of the man who burst in, catching him by surprise. He staggered a little and Tom took advantage by leaping forward and grabbing the chair Dolly had been sitting on. Holding it up, with the legs pointing towards the burly figure of the man, he thrust his way towards the stairs.

'Here – stop that!' The man caught at the legs and twisted the chair, almost throwing Tom off balance. But he had the advantage now and forged steadily towards the top of the stairs, driving the man before him. He heard Dolly scream, felt a jerk as the other man's foot slipped from the top step, and then they were falling together, rolling and twisting, with the chair cracking and splintering between them, from the top of the stairs to the bottom.

'Oh! Oh! He's killing him – killing him. They're killing each other! Oh, help, help!' Dolly's screams echoed around the house and Tom, lying in a tangled heap at the bottom of the stairwell, heard doors opening and closing. But no one came to investigate; it seemed that, their initial curiosity satisfied, the other occupants of the house had decided it was best not to know what was happening. Only Dolly came scurrying down the stairs and tried, by the flickering light of the candle, to see if the two men were hurt.

'You've killed 'im,' she panted, jerking Tom roughly away from the body of the other man. 'An' look at my chair, all smashed up. That cost a lot, that chair . . . Alf, Alf, are yer all right? He hasn't killed yer, say he hasn't killed yer . . .' She dragged Tom away and he stood up shakily, relieved to find that none of his bones seemed likely to give way. He stared down at the face of the man he had forced down the stairs. Had he really killed him? There was blood on the heavy features . . . His stomach turned.

Dolly bent over the still figure. She looked up at Tom and there was hatred in her blue eyes. Her face, twisted and distorted, looked suddenly years older than Bess's.

'If you've killed 'im—' she began, and there was no mistaking the venom in her tone. 'I'll have the law on yer, so I will,' she said. 'You'll swing for this, swelp me God.'

Tom stared at her. For a moment, he was no longer in the dark, stinking hall but in a carpet shop miles away, back in Kidderminster. The girl on the floor staring up at him was his sister Bessie, and the figure on the ground was that of Jabez Gast, his throat cut in a gaping, grinning wound that spouted scarlet blood.

Panic tore at his breast, kicked into his legs. He leapt over the two on the floor and hurled himself through the door. His feet burned with terror, running their only relief, and he fled down the dark, narrow streets, through the alleyways, round corners, in and out of yards, and at last into a wider, brighter thoroughfare where shops spilled light on to the road and people strolled or scurried, laughed or begged. He bumped into men who cursed him, women who screamed or cackled, but he dared not stop. In imagination, he saw the watchmen pursuing him, sticks and bludgeons waving and ready to beat him to the ground. He saw soldiers with pikes and muskets and sabres, marching to cut him down or shoot him. He saw the prison walls closing about him and he saw the hangman with his black hood, fastening the rope about his neck.

He did not stop until he found the river in his way and the black waters brought him to a panting, sobbing pause. For a moment, it seemed this was the only, the inevitable way out. He looked at the water and thought how easy it would be, and how quick. The smooth, dark water closing over his head. The oblivion that it seemed everyone sought, one way or another.

And then he thought of Bess. Waiting somewhere in London for him to come back to her. Alone, and trusting him to protect her.

After a long time, he turned away from the river and walked slowly back into the heart of the city. All he wanted to do now was find Bess. And then—?

Tom had no idea. The letter that Vivian Pagnel had given him was in Dolly's room, where he could no longer go, even if he knew where it was. And the money was with it.

He and Bess were penniless now. And, except for Sal Preston, friendless.

But Sal had given him the wrong directions for James Street. And Tom was beginning to wonder now whether anyone in this teeming and uncaring city could be called friend.

Chapter Six

'So,' Mrs Atkins said, standing with arms akimbo, 'you're the new kitchenmaid, are you? You're a bit small.'

Rebecca, feeling that this must somehow be her fault, ducked her head in agreement.

'Still, I daresay you'll grow,' the cook went on, but rather as if she doubted it. 'Anyway, you can reach the sink, that's the main thing. And you don't have to be tall to scrub floors. Now – let's see what you can do. Ever been in a kitchen before?'

Rebecca shook her head and looked about her. The kitchen was nothing like the downstairs room of her father's cottage, where her mother did what little cooking she could manage on an open fire in a small grate. It was like a cavern; a huge underground room, with dim corners and shadows where the light of the oil lamps could not penetrate. A big iron range stood along one wall, with a dresser near by, its shelves ranged with pans, crockery and copper moulds. In the middle of the room stood a big scrubbed table. The floor was of stone, with wooden duckboards running along beside the table for the cook to stand on.

'Well, don't stand there like a stuffed doll,' Mrs Atkins said sharply. 'You're not here on holiday. There's a lot to do here, what with Mr Vivian getting wed soon . . . Now – can you scrub?' She led the way through a door leading into a large room furnished with two sinks connected by long benches. More duckboards stood before the sinks, and there were two large coppers in the corner with steam issuing from them and a smell of boiling vegetables and cloths. The only window was high in the wall, near the ceiling, and the walls were running with moisture.

'This is the scullery, where you'll be working most of the time. See, you've got good big sinks to work at, and there's always plenty of hot water so long as you keep the coppers boiling. Soda's here, and you ask me when you need more soap. There's a good brush and a scourer, and cloths for wiping and drying. Do the china in this wooden sink so it doesn't get chipped, and put the plates in this rack on the wall – that's everyday china, mind, the best stuff goes into the press in the dining room. And when you're not washing dishes, you can be helping me get the vegetables ready. But first thing each morning, directly the oddjob's finished lighting the range, you do the floors and get your boilers going, so you'll need to be about early – can you wake yourself up?'

Rebecca nodded. 'I get up early for my Dad. I've been drawing for him since I was eight.'

'Yes, Mrs Hudd told me he was a carpet weaver. Well, you should be used to work, then. Now, you've seen the mistress, haven't you?'

'Yes, Mrs Atkins.' Rebecca had been taken upstairs to meet Mrs Pagnel as soon as her mother and Mrs Hudd had finished talking together. She had stood in the drawing room, overwhelmed by its grandeur, gazing down at the carpet and marvelling at its texture and colours, so much finer than anything her father had ever woven, and listened as Mrs Pagnel questioned Fanny. Was Rebecca quiet, well behaved and industrious? Would she work hard and not answer back when her elders and betters chastised her? And her sister . . . Of course, Mrs Pagnel knew what had happened in the carpet shop. Fanny must not be surprised if she had doubts . . . Was there any other evidence of bad blood in the family? Was Rebecca likely to display any signs of temper?

'No, madam, there's never been anything like that. Her father and me, we've both led quiet lives, just doing our work and minding our own business. And Bessie, she was always a good girl, and Tom, he wouldn't hurt a fly. I don't know what happened that night, madam, nobody does, but it must have been an accident, they would never—'

'Very well, very well.' Mrs Pagnel lifted a languid hand to stop Fanny's tearful flow. 'I can see you believe it, and Rebecca certainly seems a quiet enough child . . . Well, I'm prepared to give her a chance. Mrs Hudd speaks well of you, and I accept her opinion. But mark this, child—' she paused and Rebecca lifted her head and met a pair of sharp blue eyes '—I shall expect *extra good* reports of your behaviour from Mrs Hudd and Mrs Atkins. Not many ladies would take a girl from a family such as yours into their homes. You're very fortunate that I have a generous nature. See that you don't abuse it.'

The interview was at an end. Rebecca and her mother bobbed clumsy curtsies and followed Mrs Hudd from the room. They went downstairs, through the door leading to the basement and into a different world.

And now Rebecca was a part of that world, her mother gone tearfully home and a strange woman standing with her hands on broad hips, giving her orders she barely understood. Around them, other servants were bustling to and fro, tradesmen were knocking at the kitchen door and bells tinkled from a row that hung above the door leading to the house.

Mrs Atkins went to a chest in one corner and took out a coarse apron.

'Here, wrap this round yourself, though what you've got on's hardly worth taking care of. That your only frock?'

'Yes, Mrs Atkins. It's my Sunday one.'

'Your Sunday one? Well, you'd better wear it for work from now on, the mistress won't want to see you going to church in that of a Sunday. I'll see if we've got anything might fit you – otherwise you'll have to have something made next time the sewing woman comes. You'll be given an allowance for uniform. Now – we've wasted enough time. There's work to be done.' She pushed Rebecca towards the scullery. 'Start on those dishes, and be quick – we'll want some of them for luncheon, and there's the carrots to scrape and get started . . . Well, don't stand there gawping, miss! Get on with it.'

Rebecca went into the scullery and gazed at the pile of crockery. Already it was higher than when Mrs Atkins had first brought her in here. And as she stood there, a kitchenmaid brushed past her with more plates and dumped them on the table before turning to stare at her.

'You the new scullerymaid? Well, let's hope you're better'n the last. *She* weren't no good at all – smashed more'n she washed.' She gave a short laugh. 'Well – you'll know *me* again, won't you? My name's Polly, if you're interested, and I'm over you, see, you got to do what I says. What's your name?'

'Rebecca. Rebecca Himley.'

'Rebecca?' The girl gave a hoot of laughter. 'My, we are smart! Int Becky good enough, then? Here—' her eyes sharpened '—did you say Himley? Wasn't it your brother and sister did for that old weaver down

130

Butts' shop? What did they do, d'you know? I heard they cut his head right off—'

'Well, they didn't, then.' Rebecca turned sharply towards the sink. 'And I don't want to talk about it. How do I get the hot water out of this copper?'

'With a pan, how d'you think?' Polly watched as Rebecca poured the steaming water into the sink. 'Here, there's no need to take umbrage. I didn't mean nothing.' Her face softened a little and became more friendly. 'I got a brother meself. I wouldn't like to see him in trouble . . . Anyway, I got to go now. You're sleeping in our room, aren't you?'

'Am I?' Rebecca had not yet been shown where she was to sleep. Looking at the pile of crockery she was expected to wash and thinking of the other jobs that had been mentioned as well, she doubted whether she would ever find time to sleep anyway.

'Up in the attics,' Polly said. 'We all sleep up there. Roasts in summer, freezes in winter, but it's a bed. I'll show you later. We might have some fun.'

Rebecca looked at her. Polly's face was friendly, her eyes bright and her grin infectious.

Fun? Would it really be possible to have fun here? And what sort of fun would it be?

Rebecca's ideas of 'fun' were hazy. Apart from her father playing with her on his knee when she was a baby, and some games long ago with Tom and Bessie, or out in the street with other children, fun had not figured largely in her life. She had certainly not envisaged having any here, in this great cavern of a kitchen.

Left alone, she began to wash the pile of dishes. It seemed to grow as she worked, so that the more she washed the more there were, and she wondered if she would ever come to the end.

She would, though. She would come to the end.

131

And she'd get out of this scullery and into the kitchen; yes, and out of that too and into the housekeeper's room.

Further than that, it did not occur to her to look.

Above stairs, all was bustle in preparation for Vivian's wedding.

'There's so much to do,' Isabella sighed. 'And so little time in which to do it. Six months' engagement is really rather short, Jeremiah.'

'Long enough,' her husband grunted. 'It's time Vivian settled down. He's shown signs of becoming wild lately . . . all these visits to London—'

'But they're for the business. You sent him there to meet people to learn about other aspects—'

'Oh, certainly, certainly. But I've suspected of late that he's made more visits than might be strictly necessary, and perhaps stayed overlong . . . Well, he's young and young men must be young men. But I want to see him settled now, and taking a proper interest in his inheritance. Francis, now—'

'Francis is no more than a boy,' Isabella said sharply. 'And I really do think that it's unnecessary to have him living here once he leaves school. He can learn the business just as well from his own home.'

'And I think it *is* necessary. Francis needs to be with carpetmakers, not scholars, if he's to be of any use. I can't see why you should suddenly begin to raise objections now, Isabella – this has been arranged for a long time. Francis leaves school at Christmas and comes here, to live and to work. It will be good for him to listen to conversation between me and Vivian, and to be part of the family. Geoffrey and Enid are in complete agreement over this.'

'Naturally – a growing boy's an expensive luxury.

Especially when he isn't even of one's own blood.'

Jeremiah gave her a cold look. 'That remark is unworthy of you, Isabella. Geoffrey and Enid have always looked on Francis as their own son, and still do. They simply want what is best for his future.'

'Which is coming to live here.'

'I think so, yes,' Jeremiah said in a tone which warned her that further argument would be likely to rouse his temper. Isabella hesitated, glanced at him and subsided.

'Well, husband, you'd better let me know which room he is to occupy and I'll have that refurbished as well as the others. The men might as well do them all together.'

Jeremiah frowned.

'Others? What others? What are you talking about now?'

Isabella smiled. 'Why, Jeremiah dearest, you must realise that almost the whole house needs attention with Vivian's wedding so near.'

'But Maria's not being married from here. The reception will be held in her home – and the expense is John Henwick's, thank the Lord. And he can afford it well enough – the ironmasters are prosperous. Why should we need to do anything here?'

'Really, Jeremiah. My Dorset relatives will be coming to stay – a good many of them, I don't wonder, they'll want to see Vivian married – so the guest bedrooms must be redecorated. They're barely fit to be seen at present. And then Vivian and Maria are coming to live here until their own new home is ready, as you well know, so their rooms must be refurbished. And we'll need to hold several dinner parties for our friends and relatives in Kidderminster, so the dining room and drawing room must be cleaned and polished and new chaircovers made. And—'

'Why not build a new house and have done with it? Clearly, we've been living in a hovel all these years and I've never noticed it.' He looked around the room, at the square of finest carpet woven in his own factory, at the thick curtains hanging at the windows, the polished wood of the breakfast table and the gleaming china they were using. 'If all this is good enough for us, why shouldn't it be good enough for our guests?'

Isabella was silent for a moment. Then she said quietly, 'Have you forgotten, Jeremiah, that our guests will be members of my own family – and Vivian's? Do you wish me to be ashamed of the man I allowed to become his father? Especially as you have been unable to father your own heir.'

Jeremiah's face darkened. He stared at her for a moment. Then he dropped his napkin on the table and stood up.

'Very well, Isabella. Make your arrangements. I suppose there will be new clothes needed, for yourself and the girls, as well as all this refurbishment?'

Isabella smiled again.

'But of course. You know that both Sarah and Isabel are to attend the bride. And as mother of the bridegroom, I must have something especially fine for the wedding day, as well as some new gowns for the dinner parties. I'll arrange for the dressmaker to come as soon as possible – she'll need to bring several girls to help her—'

'All, no doubt, needing beds to sleep in, a workroom, meals and God knows what else—'

'Really, Jeremiah! Your language. Yes, of course they'll need all those things. One must treat servants properly.'

'Well, if it must be done, I suppose it must. But see that Francis doesn't get forgotten in all this. I want that boy to be treated as part of the family. A large, pleasant room – he shouldn't be shut away in some cupboard. I have hopes of that boy, Isabella, high hopes, and I don't wish to see him treated as if he were a poor relation.'

'Of course not, Jeremiah,' Isabella replied demurely, and lifted her face for his kiss as he departed. But after he had gone, and the room was silent, she murmured aloud: 'But dearest, he *isn't* a relation – even a *poor* relation.' And her face changed, hardened. 'So why . . . ?'

But there had never been any answer to that question. Jeremiah had always had a fondness for Francis and she had learned that it must be accepted – so long as it did not interfere with her plans for Vivian.

And since Jeremiah had, on their marriage, agreed to adopt Vivian as his legal heir, there did not seem to be much real risk of that.

All the same . . . the idea of Francis living here at Pagnel House was not one she enjoyed.

Francis himself found his feelings about the arrangement mixed.

'I know it's the sensible thing to do,' he said to Enid as they sorted through his bedroom in the crooked house in Church Row. 'Apprentices do go to live in the master's house – and I suppose that's what I'm to be, a kind of apprentice. But it will seem very strange, being away from home.'

Enid turned away and busied herself with some shirts, shaking them out and refolding them. After a moment, she said, 'Pagnel House will be your home now, Francis.'

135

'No,' he said, 'this will always be my home, with you and Father. How could anywhere else mean so much.' He touched her shoulder. 'Will you miss me, Mother?'

Enid turned swiftly and threw her arms around him. As he looked down into her face, he saw that there were tears in her eyes, and he held her against him. 'Mother . . .'

'Oh, Francis,' she said, muffling her voice against his jacket, 'do you know that to a woman that's the most beautiful name in the world, and that to hear her son using it is the most beautiful sound . . . Of course I'll miss you. But you have to begin your own life now. You're almost a man. It's right for you to leave home now, and you won't be so very far away. Just a step. And it's a fine chance for you.' She paused for a moment, then added quietly, 'Your Uncle Jeremiah is very fond of you. And you're very fortunate to have such an uncle. Not all men would do as he's doing, considering—' She hesitated.

'Considering that I'm not really his nephew at all? Or even your son?' Francis said quietly. 'I know. Though to me, you and Father are my parents as truly as if you had actually given me birth. You've given me everything else, after all. But for my uncle – yes, it's different. And it's kind of him to give me the opportunity to learn the business. All the same . . . I'm not sure I'm fitted for that kind of life, Mother. Business . . . it frightens me a little. And Vivian is so clever, he knows so much—'

'You'll find your place,' she said with confidence. 'You don't have to try to be like your cousin Vivian. You have your own talents, Francis, as Vivian has his, and they may be different but they'll be just as valuable, you'll see. And they'll be discovered.'

'Well, I hope so, for I don't know what they are. And I'm sure Vivian doesn't believe I have any. He doesn't want me there, you know.'

'Well, it isn't his decision. Your uncle does want you, and that's all that matters.' Enid looked at Francis, frowning slightly. 'You mustn't let Vivian browbeat you. He likes to think himself very grand, but remember—' She stopped and turned away again. 'Francis, do you think it worth taking this shirt? It's almost worn through.'

'What? The shirt? Oh, yes, I'll take it – it's my favourite. I may as well get the last of the wear from it.' He took it from her and dropped it on the bed. 'Mother, what were you going to say?'

'Say? Why, nothing, dear. I was just asking you about your shirt—'

'No. Before that. About Vivian.' He held her shoulders and looked at her with searching blue eyes that were no longer those of a boy. 'What were you going to say about Vivian?'

'Why, only that Vivian is your Aunt Isabella's son by her first marriage, and that your uncle agreed to adopt him as his heir when they were married. Of course, he would have had to share the inheritance if they had ever had another son – but since only Sarah and Isabel have arrived, that's never arisen. But you know all this. I simply remembered that it's a subject neither Jeremiah nor Vivian likes to discuss, and I felt it better not to say any more on the subject. And we'll leave it there now, I think. It isn't seemly to gossip about our relatives – especially when you're going to become part of their household.'

'No, of course not, Mother,' he said, and they went back to their task without mentioning Vivian again.

It still wanted several weeks before Francis was due

137

to move into Pagnel House; first, he had to complete his schooling. But for the last two or three months it had become a custom for him to go to his uncle's house for dinner on Sunday afternoons. Here the conversation would turn frequently to the concerns of the factory, and he knew he was expected to listen and learn before venturing to make any comments of his own.

'Prosperity will soon return,' Vivian declared. 'We're beginning to recover from the Wars, and there are orders coming in from America. That's where our future lies, Father. We mustn't forget that. America's a growing country and they don't yet manufacture enough of their own goods – they can't, they're still too busy pushing back the frontiers. They'll look to us for their luxury goods for a long while to come. And when the moment's right—' he paused and his eyes gleamed.

'Well?' Jeremiah said impatiently. 'I suppose you'll be wanting to go and build a factory over there.' He laughed as if the notion were a good joke.

'Exactly,' Vivian said with perfect seriousness. 'We shall need to do just that, Father, if we're to maintain our position in carpet-making. I tell you—'

'Maintain our position? We're head and shoulders above any carpet manufacturer now – nobody can challenge that. Why should we need to go to America? So long as they send us orders we can fulfil here—'

'But they won't always.' Vivian spoke with certainty. '*Someone* will begin to make carpets in America, Father, and then the customers there won't want to pay shipping costs or wait while we receive their orders here, carry them out and then dispatch them on a long, slow journey. They'll order what they can see on the spot. And I intend to be there – taking their orders and selling them carpet.'

Jeremiah snorted, 'You're too ambitious by half! We're only just climbing out of a depression now – we've a long way to go before we can think of expanding, especially in another country. Still, ambition's no bad thing in a young man. I like to see it – provided it's kept under control.' He turned to Francis. 'And what about you, young man? Do you have any great ambitions?'

'Not to go to America,' Francis said, smiling. 'But – yes, I do have ambition, sir. I'd like to do well in some way. I'm looking forward to coming into the business.' He hesitated. 'I hope I won't disappoint you.'

'You'll not do that, provided you work hard and behave yourself.' Jeremiah rested his eyes on the face that was beginning now to lose the soft curves of boyhood and take on more clear-cut planes. 'So – you're looking forward to leaving home, are you, and coming here?'

'Not entirely,' Francis admitted. 'I'll be sorry to leave Mother and Father. But I'm ready to leave school and begin to make my own way, yes. And I know I'll learn more if I'm here.'

'I don't see that,' Vivian said grumblingly. 'You're only a step or two away at Church Row. You can be in the factories as quickly as we can, and if there's anything being discussed here that you need to know you can easily be summoned. Not that it's likely for several years yet – you know barely anything at present.'

'That's enough, Vivian,' Jeremiah said in a sharp voice. 'Francis has been too busy studying to give much attention to the business before now. He'll learn fast enough. And he'll learn more quickly if he's here, listening to us talk – provided what you have to say is worth listening to. All this chatter about America – that's just castles in the air. We'll be better off looking to our cousins across the Channel, and our dominions overseas.'

Vivian's highly coloured face darkened but he said nothing. He stared at his plate until his flush subsided a little, his mouth set mutinously. Francis felt his heart sink. He and Vivian had always had a rather distant relationship, with Vivian tolerating him, it seemed, only to patronise him. Now that Francis was about to move into the house, as well as coming into the business, Vivian's hostility had increased.

The meal over, Jeremiah went into the library to 'look over some papers' – which everyone knew meant to settle himself comfortably in a large armchair, with his feet on his desk, and snore. Vivian disappeared without any further word to his cousin, and Francis found himself at a loss to know what to do.

He wandered into the hall and stood for a moment gazing up at the pictures that hung there – huge, heavily framed landscapes of the looming mountains and brooding lakes of the north country. He was staring at them when his cousin Isabel emerged from the drawing room and came to stand beside him.

'Doesn't it seem strange that it's a part of England?' she remarked. 'It's so different from here – all that storm and menace.' She shivered a little. 'It's frightening – but exciting, too. I'd like to go there and see if it's really like that.'

Francis smiled. 'Perhaps you will, one day. Perhaps we'll go together. I'd enjoy that.'

'Would you really?' Her voice was light and quick,

and she looked up at him with bright eyes. 'I'd like it, too. We could go climbing in the mountains, amongst the rocks. Perhaps we could swim in the lakes.' She shivered pleasurably. 'They look cold, don't they – cold and menacing. But the sun must shine there sometimes.'

She had moved closer and he could feel the warmth of her body through the dress she wore. He looked down at her, surprised and a little uneasy. There was something in her voice – some undercurrent that he didn't recognise. It was the same quality that burned somewhere at the back of her eyes. Violet eyes, he noticed with a sudden tiny shock, and wondered why he'd always thought them blue.

'But Father never has time to take us away for a holiday,' Isabel went on sadly, looking back at the paintings. 'And Mother wouldn't go without him. And we could never go by ourselves.'

'Of course not,' Francis said, a little startled that she should even express such an idea. And then he glanced at her again and thought how pleasant it would be, to be in that wild countryside with Isabel. They had always been friends, ever since Isabel was a small child. He had always been drawn to her, delighting in her laughter and soft, undemanding warmth. And, later, she had taken a real interest in his pastimes – his butterfly collection, his drawing and painting, the fleeting enthusiasms of boyhood.

But she was growing up now. Almost fourteen years old, still in the schoolroom, yet unmistakably a woman. He glanced covertly at her small breasts and slender figure. A little too slender for fashion's taste, perhaps, but arousing pleasantly protective sensations in him. And her hair, rippling in loose sunlit waves almost to her waist . . . it would seem a crime, he thought, when the time came to put it up.

Isabel turned her head and looked up at him, her eyes wide as if in enquiry, and Francis became aware of his straying thoughts and felt his fair skin colour painfully. He turned away abruptly but Isabel laid her hand on his sleeve.

'Francis? Have I done something to offend you?'

He looked down at the hand, small, soft and narrow, felt the warmth of the slender fingers reaching through to his skin. 'Offend me? Of course not – how could you? I was just thinking—' He stopped, catching at the treacherous words before they could leave his lips, and started to move away. But Isabel tightened her fingers on his arm and her eyes burned into his.

'I know. You were thinking that we shouldn't be talking like this. About going away together.' Her voice was clear, without shame, and he felt his colour rise again. 'But we're friends, Francis, as well as family.' She sighed a little. 'It isn't always the same thing. And it *would* be pleasant. You know it would. We enjoy so many things together – why not a journey to the Lakes? And why not say so?'

He gazed at her. She made it all sound so reasonable – so possible. But it wasn't. In only one circumstance would such a holiday become possible – and as the thought entered his head, he felt himself veer away from it.

Aloud he said: 'We must try to make up a family party one day, Isabel. Perhaps when Vivian and Maria are married . . .' But he saw the disappointment like a shadow at the back of her eyes.

'It used to be so nice,' she said wistfully, 'when you took me fishing in the stream – do you remember? And collecting tadpoles from the pond. Mine hardly ever grew into frogs – there was just that one, Archibald. I still see him in the garden sometimes. At least, I tell myself it's him.' Her fingers were still on his sleeve. They slid down his arm and entwined themselves with his. 'Why does everything have to change, Francis? You're uncomfortable with me now. And soon we won't even be able to go walking together without a chaperone. It's all so silly.'

He looked at her helplessly. She was like a chrysalis, half child, half woman. He felt that she understood both more and less than he. He could go walking with her now, children together again as they climbed trees or poked long sticks into the pond to stir up the fish . . . and then, without warning, she would be a woman, with danger in those dark violet eyes.

'I have to go now,' she said sadly. 'Mother wants me to help her with her needlepoint. Shall I see you at supper?'

Francis shook his head. 'I have to go home now. But I shall be here during the week. And again next Sunday.'

'And after Christmas, all the time,' she said, but there was little joy in her voice. 'And I shall be shut away in the school room like a child . . .' She returned suddenly to her old, impulsive manner and exclaimed, 'Don't you think growing up is a *nuisance*, Francis? And it's for *ever*. There doesn't seem to be any escape.'

Francis laughed, glad of the release. 'It can't be all bad, Isabel. At least you're free to choose for yourself what you wish to do.'

She looked at him soberly. 'Do you really think so? For a man, perhaps . . . but not for a woman. And perhaps not even for all men. How much choice do you think you'll have, Francis?'

He opened his mouth to reply, but no words came. And as they stood looking at each other, the drawing room door opened and a querulous voice called her name.

'Yes, Mother, I'm coming,' Isabel called back without taking her eyes from Francis's face. Then she tilted her head slightly, lifted her eyebrows a fraction, moved one shoulder – and turned away. Her footsteps were light and quick as she crossed the polished wood floor. She went through the door without looking back.

Francis stood quite still. The short conversation had left him feeling bemused, as if someone had knocked him very hard on the head. So much had been said – or was it really so little? So much had been left unsaid.

It would not be long before Isabel was truly a woman. And he anticipated the day with pleasure – and with trepidation.

Rebecca was coming back from church when she saw Francis approaching her.

She knew who he was, of course. She had, it seemed, always known about Mr Francis, at least from the days when Bessie had come home from Albert Butts' carpet shop, talking about the two handsome young men who had watched her at Jabez's loom. Bessie had clearly favoured the dark, bold-eyed Mr Vivian with his air of confident arrogance, but Rebecca had been fascinated by the idea of fair-haired, blue-eyed Francis, who had always seemed to her to be like the prince in one of the fairytales her mother had told her when she was small. 'Oh yes, he's well enough,' Bessie would say carelessly when questioned. 'Handsome, but quiet. But Mr Vivian—' And her eyes would glow and her cheeks blush, and she would nudge her friend Nellie in the ribs and they'd both giggle and refuse to say any more.

When she had first come to work in the house, Rebecca had hoped there might be a chance of an occasional glimpse of Mr Francis. He didn't live there, though Mrs Atkins said he was going to, soon after Christmas, but he was a frequent visitor. Of course she rarely saw him, nor any of the folks 'upstairs'. Her work kept her confined to the kitchen or, even more, the scullery which she seemed to share with a perpetual pile of dirty dishes – the same ones, over and over again – replaced only by another recurrent pile of vegetables. Nobody but Mrs Atkins, Polly or the oddjob man or bootboy ever disturbed her in this dim, smelly lair.

But she had seen Mr Francis once or twice on the few occasions when she was released from the chains that bound her to the sink – the Sunday afternoons when she and the other maids were sent to church, and the moments when she escaped into the open air for a few minutes to take scraps to the heap. She had seen Francis once then, walking in the garden with his cousin Isabel. And she had spied him in the distance, striding with Vivian towards the carpet shop. And again, with some other boys from the grammar school, strolling easily and swinging his books on the end of a strap as they talked.

Now, when she saw him coming along the road towards her, her heart seemed to stop beating for a moment and then skipped and hurried to catch up with itself.

For once, she was alone. Mrs Atkins didn't normally allow the maids out of doors alone, and Mrs Hudd would certainly have disapproved, but Polly was indoors with a cold and the housemaid, Carrie, who was supposed to be with Rebecca, had slipped away to meet someone she referred to as her 'gentleman friend'. She did this every Sunday when they went to church, rejoining the other maids as they walked back again, her eyes bright and her cheeks flushed, and they would have to tell her what the sermon had been about so that she could answer Mrs Atkins' questions. It was a nuisance because it meant they had to listen extra carefully themselves, but they were bound in the camaraderie of their position and would never have dreamed of giving her away.

Today, she had not appeared as the service finished and Rebecca was walking slowly, unsure of what to do. If she and Carrie were late back, they would be in trouble – but if she went back without Carrie, the trouble would be much worse. Carrie would certainly be dismissed without a character, and Rebecca might well find herself dismissed with her. Even Polly would not escape.

Now she saw Francis coming towards her and her worry increased even as her heart leaped. He was, after all, from 'upstairs' and therefore one of *them*. Would he know she was not supposed to be out alone? Would he think it his business to inquire why? Would he even know she was a maid at Pagnel House? She glanced at him timidly as he drew nearer, prepared to hurry past, but he came to a halt in front of her and she was forced to stop.

'Hullo! Haven't I seen you before?' It was the first time she had heard his voice, except in the distance on those occasions when she had caught a glimpse of him with his friends or his cousin. 'You're a maid in my aunt's house, aren't you?'

'Yes, sir,' she said breathlessly. 'I work in the scullery.'

'The scullery?' It was as if it were a new concept to him. 'You mean you wash up and such?'

'Yes, sir, that's right.'

'But not all the time,' he said, looking at her very kindly. 'I mean, you must do other things.'

'I peel potatoes,' she said doubtfully, not sure of what he meant, and his brows drew together in a frown.

'You mean that's *all*? You don't do anything else?'

'It takes me all day, sir,' Rebecca answered with a touch of indignation. 'There's a lot of dishes to wash in a big house, and only Polly to help me a bit sometimes. And there's a lot of potatoes, too,' she added. 'And I have to do the floors first. I'm not lazy, sir.'

'No, of course not – I never intended to suggest that you were.' He seemed almost confused and she looked at him more directly, interested by the spectacle of one of the gentry at a loss. 'I meant, it seems such a hard life, doing nothing but wash dishes or peel vegetables. But you do come out, don't you? You have time off.'

'I have Sunday afternoons, for church. And I go to see my mother once a month for two hours.'

His eyes were on her and she met them with her own. They were a deep blue, deeper than the indigo dye used in the carpets her father wove. They brought a vitality to his pale face. His hair shimmered like gold in the pale winter sun.

'What's your name?' he asked suddenly.

'Rebecca, sir.'

'Rebecca. That's a nice name. Do they call you that?'

'No, sir. Most people call me Becky.'

147

'But you prefer Rebecca.' He smiled suddenly. 'I'll call you that. It suits you. Rebecca.' It lingered on his tongue like a caress and Rebecca felt her cheeks burn suddenly. 'Well, Rebecca, shouldn't you be getting back?'

'Yes, sir. I'll have to hurry or I'll be late.' She felt a return of her anxiety about Carrie. She couldn't linger much more; she would have to go back and take whatever trouble was coming. She saw Francis watching her and knew he was about to ask what was worrying her – and for a moment she struggled with an almost overpowering urge to tell him. He would understand, she felt sure, and do his best to help . . . But as they stared at each other, the words on their lips, she heard hurrying steps behind her and felt a surge of relief as she recognised Carrie's voice.

'Becky! Thank goodness you haven't gone back . . . I thought I was going to be late – oh! I'm sorry, sir, I didn't realise—'

'It's perfectly all right,' Francis said politely. 'I was just making sure that Rebecca was all right. You're one of my aunt's maids, too, aren't you?'

'Yes, sir.' She bobbed a curtsy and Rebecca realised she'd forgotten to do that. In fact, apart from calling Francis 'sir' she'd almost forgotten who he was – she'd talked to him as if they were equals. She looked to see if he'd realised it too and was angry – but he was smiling pleasantly, and she felt suddenly, instinctively, that they would always talk to each other as equals. And then the thought disappeared, dismissed as being too ridiculous to be given room in her mind.

'I was just held up for a minute, sir, talking to my old aunt,' Carrie was explaining glibly. 'I never meant to let Becky here walk home on her own – only my aunt's not well and I couldn't leave her. We'll be on our way now, sir, or we'll be late and Mrs Atkins will be angry.'

'Oh, of course – I mustn't cause you trouble.' He stood aside so that they could pass along the narrow footpath, and the two girls passed him and scurried round the corner. Out of sight, they stopped and Carrie doubled over.

'Got an awful stitch,' she explained breathlessly. 'Here – what were *you* up to, hobnobbing with Mr Francis on the street corner? You're a dark horse, Becky, and no mistake – and not much more than a baby at that!'

'I just met him and he stopped me,' Rebecca defended herself. 'I didn't even think he'd know who I was . . . He's nice, though. I like him better than Mr Vivian.'

'Do you?' Carrie looked at her queerly. 'Well, maybe that's just as well. Not that you'll ever have a chance with either of those two, stuck away in that scullery of yours. But I can tell you this – Mr Vivian's more exciting.'

'Exciting?' The word conveyed nothing to Rebecca. How could a man be *exciting*? Nor did the secret smile hovering about Carrie's lips tell her anything. And there was no time for further chatter – they would have to hurry as fast as they could now, to be back in time to escape Mrs Atkins' wrath.

But she carried the memory of her short conversation with Francis in her heart for the rest of that day, and slept with it held in her heart like a talisman. And when she looked out of the kitchen door at the azure of the sky just before dawn, or saw a salty blue flame flicker in the kitchen fire, or washed the best dinner plates with their border of deep blue, she thought of his eyes.

Their worlds were so far apart, he might have been on the moon. And on clear nights, up in the tiny attic room she shared with Polly, Rebecca would look at the moon and dream.

Chapter Seven

'Well, we're going up in the world and no mistake,' Polly declared, turning her back for Rebecca to fasten her buttons. 'Proper housemaids – new uniforms and all. I thought we'd never get out of that kitchen, didn't you?'

Rebecca remembered the years spent at the low sink in the dark little scullery, scrubbing at dishes, pans, vegetables – always scrubbing – and gave a heartfelt nod. 'I didn't mind it so much once I could help Mrs Atkins with the cooking. But it's better being in the house – not that it'll be any easier. We'll still have to work all the hours there are.'

'Oh, I know! And most of them afore breakfast too, seems to me. The family mustn't see us clearing out the fireplaces or dusting . . . Still, we'll get to see a bit of life, won't we. We'll see all the gentry coming in and out.' Polly held the candle stump up to the tiny window so that she could use it as a mirror while she set her new cap carefully on her head. 'And you never know, we might get up to be parlourmaids or personal maid to one of the young ladies. Miss Isabel's eighteen now – she'll be needing someone once Nanny goes. I wouldn't mind that job, doing her hair and laying out her dresses and such.' She sat on her narrow bed to pull on her shoes.

'Well, it's not going to be one of us.' Rebecca fastened the strings of her apron. 'By the time we're ready to be anything as grand as a personal maid, Mr Vivian's girls will be grown up – so you'd better be looking in that direction.'

Polly shivered. 'Oh, I don't know if I'd dare! Mr Vivian frightens me. The way he looks sometimes . . . He was watching me the other day when we had to help serve at table, I swear he was. I tell you, I wouldn't like to be caught on my own with him. And young Mrs Pagnel, she's a tartar, they say. One false step and you're out on the street with nothing.'

All the same, there was a glitter in Polly's eyes as she spoke about Vivian Pagnel. It reminded Rebecca of her sister Bessie; her eyes had brightened with the same excitement, her cheeks had flushed in the same feverish way.

It was an effect Vivian had on most of the servants, Rebecca knew; at almost thirty, he was even more handsome than he had been in youth, his boldness mellowed with authority, his arrogance deepened to a confident certainty of his own powers. He was just sufficiently heavier for his figure to have improved, filled out from its youthful awkwardness; his shoulders were broader, his chest deeper. Apart from that and from a stronger cast to his features, he showed no sign of age; his dark hair was neither receding nor turning to grey, and his ambition ran as high as ever. There were frequent arguments between him and Jeremiah, as the whole household knew, about the management of the carpet factory.

'Would *you* like to work for Mr Vivian?' Polly asked now, fastening her cuffs.

Rebecca considered. 'Well, it's not really working for him, is it? Maids work for the mistress of the house. And it's true Mrs Maria's said to be a tartar. I'm not sure I'd want to work for *her*. Our Mrs Pagnel's strict, but she's usually fair. I've heard Mrs Maria can be spiteful.'

'Yes, Annie that went to work for them a few

months back, she told me that. The first week, she kept finding sixpences under the mats. She thought they were just lost at first and put them on the mantelpiece, but when it kept on happening she told the housekeeper.'

'What happened?'

Polly laughed. 'Mrs Dobby pasted the sixpence to the floor – stuck it down real hard. "That'll show her we don't mean to be treated like thieves," she said. "Trying to catch us out. She can spend a few minutes trying to pick *this* one up." And next time Annie swept under the mat, the sixpence was gone and she never saw another one. But Mrs Maria didn't like it. She smashed a cup herself deliberate, and blamed Annie, and Annie had to pay out of her wages.'

'Poor Annie. And she hadn't done anything.'

'No. But what could she do, if she wanted to keep her position? Here—' Polly jumped up as the church clock began to toll five. 'Here, we'd better hurry – we've got all those fireplaces to do, and we mustn't be slack on our first morning, Mrs Hudd'll put us straight back in the scullery.'

Excited and scared by their new responsibilities, the two girls slipped out of the small bedroom they had shared ever since Rebecca had first come to Pagnels' over five years ago, and crept quietly down the stairs. The house was dark and Polly carried their candle stub with care, lighting the way down to the big kitchen where Jack, the oddjob, was already clearing the ashes from the range. The bootboy was kneeling in a corner with a row of boots and shoes before him and Susan, the head housemaid, was sitting at the table with a pot of tea in front of her.

'There you are,' she said as Rebecca and Polly

153

came in. 'You're two minutes late by the grandfather clock. I want you here in this kitchen before he begins to strike, not after. Now there's the fireplaces to do first – the drawing room, the breakfast room, the dining room, the library and the mistress's boudoir. I'll be coming round soon to make sure you've cleared and blackleaded them properly, so don't skimp. And the breakfast room fire must be lit and burning nice, ready for *them*.' She sighed and brushed a wisp of hair back from her forehead. 'And when you've done that, you must tidy the rooms and dust the furniture. Then there's hot water to be taken to the Family's bedrooms, and tea and bread and butter for the mistress and the young ladies. While they're getting up, there'll be breakfast to lay. They eat breakfast at eight-thirty prompt, so there's no time to lose – off you go now.'

She paused for breath, looking as exhausted as if she had just done, alone, all the work she had been describing. Then she shooed them out of the kitchen like sheep, giving them barely enough time to collect their brushes and dustpans, and Rebecca and Polly found themselves outside the kitchen door again and climbing the stairs from the basement to the main part of the house.

'Well, we're not going to have much time for gossiping, are we,' Polly observed. 'I'll do the drawing room and the dining room, shall I, and you do the library and boudoir. Here, this ain't going to be no picnic, you know.'

'Nothing ever is,' Rebecca said, and went softly along the passage to the library. Her heart was thumping a little. She had never been into this part of the house, except for that first day when her mother had brought her to ask for a job, and once last week when Susan had taken her and Polly over the house to explain their new duties. Now she was alone, tiptoeing through passages lit by the creeping dawn, her dustpan and brush in her hand and with only three hours to accomplish what sounded like an impossible amount of work.

And that, she knew, would be only the beginning of her day. As soon as the family were up and about, there would be the bedrooms to clean and tidy, beds to be made, laundry to be brought down to the kitchen and sorted out for the washerwoman to deal with. The dining table must be laid for midday dinner, and the meal served, then cleared away. After this, the kitchen dinner would be served – and then there might be an hour or two's respite, time to sit down and do a little mending perhaps, or just rest.

But all too soon it would be time for tea – possibly with visitors come to see the mistress or young ladies – and once that was over the flurry would begin again in the kitchen to prepare supper, with Mrs Atkins in full command as she kneaded dough, rolled pastry, slapped and sliced at meat or fish or poultry, mixed and beat and mashed until the muscles stood out on her powerful arms and the perspiration rolled from her red and shining face. And always, all the time, there was washing-up to be done, pans to be scrubbed, vegetables to clean and peel and chop.

'You know what a housemaid has to do,' Mrs Hudd had told her and Polly when she had offered them the jobs after Jenny and Beth left. The two sisters had been forever slightly behind time, scampering from one task to another. 'You've got to work quickly and quietly, and woe betide you if you're seen by one of the Family. Doesn't matter what state they've left the house in the night before, it's got to be just so when they get up in the morning, and they don't want to see the maids and their brushes and pails, so mind you don't let them.'

'And we used to hear tales of the brownies doing the work,' Polly remarked afterwards. 'You'd think it was like having a curse put on you, to be seen cleaning out a fireplace or dusting a table. They must know someone does it.'

'Well, so long as they don't know it's us. I don't want to get into trouble.'

Rebecca opened the library door and slipped inside. The curtains had been drawn and the early morning sun was slanting in, lighting up the rows of books that seemed to cover the walls and gleaming on the polished mahogany of the big table in the centre of the room. She advanced towards the fireplace.

'Hullo – it's Rebecca, isn't it? What are you doing in here? I thought you worked in the kitchen.'

Rebecca froze. Her heart gave a great lurch, seemed to hang for a moment in her breast, and then kicked back into life again. She turned her head and saw a young man lying on the big leather sofa by the window. His hair was bright in the golden light of the sun, and dark blue eyes – eyes she had imagined so often – glimmered like the sky outside.

'Mr Francis,' she stammered. 'I'm sorry – I didn't know anyone was here.' She looked helplessly at the fireplace, wondering what she was to do. If she didn't clear it out, ready to be lit later in the day, Susan would be angry – yet with Mr Francis here, how could she begin to scrape and brush and blacklead? 'I'm not a kitchen maid any more,' she said. 'Polly and me are housemaids now – we started

156

today. I've got to clear out the fireplaces.'

'Well, that's all right,' he said, 'you can carry on. I just got up early to do some reading. Just go on as if I weren't here.' He frowned a little. 'What's wrong? What are you waiting for?'

Rebecca felt the colour deepen in her cheeks. 'I'm not waiting for nothing, Mr Francis,' she said. 'It's just – well, we're supposed to have got all these jobs done afore you get up. And—'

'Well, it's not your fault if I get up early,' he said, sounding amused. 'And is it so very dreadful if you do the fireplace while I'm here?' He looked at her for a moment. 'Yes, I see that it is. But it doesn't matter if no one knows, surely. No harm will be done if I see you clear the fireplace.'

'No, sir, but—' Rebecca floundered for a moment. 'You see, this is my first day as a housemaid and Susan will be coming round to see how I'm managing, and if she finds me here with you—'

'Oh, I see. Well, I don't intend to be driven out by Susan, but I certainly don't want to cause you any trouble.' He smiled at her. 'Look, I'll go and sit in that chair over there, in the corner behind the bookshelves. You can get on with your work, I can get on with my reading and if Susan comes in she won't see me. How does that sound?'

'I think that would be all right,' Rebecca said after a moment's consideration, and he laughed.

'So solemn! All right, then, I'll hide.' He picked up his books and carried them over to the big chair in the corner and Rebecca, aware of how much time had already been lost, began to clear the ashes of the last night's fire.

But, anxious though she was about the head housemaid's wrath if she were to be late with any of her tasks, she could not forget the young man who was in the room with her, and her hand shook as she swept out ashes and applied blacklead to the dusty surround. When Susan came in, she was just laying fresh kindling, her job almost finished, but nevertheless she jumped guiltily as the door opened, and could not help a quick glance towards the corner.

'So there you are,' Susan said sharply. 'I thought you'd have finished here by now. Polly's got the dining room fire blazing already. No, you don't light this one yet – no one will be in the library until later. Just finish that quickly and get into the drawing room – goodness knows what they were doing in there last night, it looks a proper shambles. Well, don't just gape at me, girl – get on with it or you'll find yourself back in the scullery before you can say knife.'

She hurried out, leaving Rebecca gathering up her bucket of ashes and her dustpan and brush. Once again, she gave a quick glance towards the corner and this time saw Francis peeping round the back of his chair, his face red with laughter.

'My, what a tartar our Susan is,' he chuckled. 'And so meek and mild when she's waiting on us, too. Yes sir, no sir, three bags full sir . . . Is she a bully?' The mirth faded from his face as he stood up and came over to Rebecca. 'Are you treated well?'

'As well as anyone ever is,' Rebecca answered. She was feeling harassed, aware that she had still hardly begun her day's work and afraid that Susan might come back to see what was holding her up. 'Please, Mr Francis, let me pass. I've still got the other fireplaces to do, and if Susan knows I was in here with you—'

He looked down at her gravely. 'It's all right,

Rebecca. I won't make trouble for you. But you seem to have so much to do, and when I think how little—'

'I'm a servant,' Rebecca said, turning away. 'And servants *do* have a lot to do. That's all there is to it. At least it's better than what happened to my sister.'

'Your sister?' He frowned.

'I've got to go now,' Rebecca said desperately, and he stood aside. But as she passed him, he put out a hand and laid it on her arm.

'Do the fireplace in here again tomorrow,' he said quietly, and looked into her eyes.

Rebecca felt her colour rise again, almost painfully hot. She stared up at him, unable to look away for a moment; then she moved slightly and his hand fell from her sleeve.

'I'll have to go now, sir,' she muttered, and this time he did not detain her. And although she longed to look back from the door, she dared not do so.

She carried out the rest of her work in a daze and was reprimanded by Susan for laziness when she arrived back in the kitchen several minutes later than Polly.

As they toiled up the stairs with their heavy cans of hot water, Polly gave her a queer look.

'What's up with you?' she whispered. 'You look as if you'd been hit on the head.'

Rebecca smiled involuntarily. It was so exactly the way she felt – but she couldn't tell Polly that. 'I'm all right. It's just doing all this different work. I don't know how long anything's going to take, and I'm afraid of being late all the time.'

Polly nodded. 'It were easier standing at a sink, just scrubbing whatever were put in front of you. Still, this is more interesting. And I like being able to see the rooms and all. Whose hot water are you doing? Mr Francis's?' She giggled and dug her elbow in Rebecca's ribs. 'Lucky you! He ent Mr Vivian, but still he's a good-looker. Maybe he's just waking up now, eh?'

Rebecca did not answer. She hoped that Polly would not notice the flush on her cheeks – she seemed to have spent almost all her time this morning blushing. She knew, anyway, that Mr Francis would not be in his room, awake or asleep.

And about that, she could feel only relief.

Francis found the hot water in his room when he went to wash and dress for breakfast, and wondered which of the new housemaids had brought it. Rebecca, perhaps? Or the little dumpy one – Polly, was it? He washed his face, thinking of the brown eyes Rebecca had turned on him, the shining chestnut hair pushed under the stiff little cap, the waist that looked so small with the apron strings tied around it.

Stop it! he told himself with sudden anger. You're as bad as Vivian – always looking out for a new maid to seduce. But he knew that his feelings about Rebecca were not those that showed in Vivian's dark, acquisitive eyes when he wanted to bed a pretty young housemaid. They were more complex than that. He was interested in Rebecca herself. He wanted to get to know her. He doubted whether Vivian had ever wanted to get to know a woman in his life – even his wife.

But why should he want to get to know a young housemaid, a girl far removed from his own class, a girl he had spoken to less than three times in his life? What was there in those dark, rather brooding eyes,

160

in that full-lipped mouth and smooth, curving cheek, that drew him so? Why, ever since he had met her as a young scullerymaid, still a child, coming home from church, had he carried that face in his mind?

Francis shrugged into his jacket, took a quick glance in the mirror and went downstairs. Breakfast was a less formal meal in the Pagnel household – his aunt rarely put in an appearance, preferring to stay upstairs in her own room until the bustle of early morning was over – but his uncle still demanded a tidy appearance and his two cousins, Sarah and Isabel, would certainly be present. Although Sarah had recently begun to show her dissatisfaction with this arrangement and complained that she, too, would enjoy breakfast in bed.

'After all, I am a young lady now,' she was saying as Francis came into the breakfast room. 'Quite as busy as Mother, with all the visits I must make and so much to be done. It's different for Isabel, of course, she's still in the schoolroom. Good morning, Francis. Are you a little late, or did we start early?'

'My apologies,' Francis said, and slipped into his seat. Isabel, pushing a slice of bacon and an egg about her plate, gave him a swift, upward glance, inviting him to laugh, and his mouth twitched. His youngest cousin was almost as grown up as her elder sister but, unlike Sarah, had not lost her impish sense of mischief. He supposed that she would as soon as she left the schoolroom, where she declared she was heartily bored, and began the life of domesticity and making calls which seemed to be the destiny of all young women before marriage – and which, Isabel prophesied, would prove to be even more tedious.

'It isn't fair,' she would say passionately. 'Why should boys have all the fun? The older I grow, the

161

less I like it. Being a young lady sounds like a living death.'

'Isabel!' her mother would exclaim in outraged tones, whenever Isabel expressed such thoughts. 'The more you talk in that manner, the less grown up you seem. And if you think that boys have "fun" as you call it, you might like to think what sort of life they have to lead when they become men. Working, having to take responsibility for factories as well as families, knowing that so many livelihoods depend on them . . . You wouldn't enjoy that, miss, I'll warrant. No, you think yourself fortunate that you're a lady and able to live comfortably at home and have nothing to worry about.'

'Well, I don't think so,' Isabel retorted. 'I think it would be *fun* to be a man and manage a factory and earn money for my family. *Much* more fun than staying at home and arranging flowers and having to be polite to a lot of tabbies who have nothing better to do than make calls on other tabbies every afternoon.' And she would stab her needle at the embroidery she so much disliked, and pretend not to hear the tirade her mother poured about her ears.

Francis had heard such exchanges so often that he thought he would almost miss them when Isabel finally did grow up and forget her fancies – as he had no doubt that she would. Meanwhile, he enjoyed her rebelliousness and gave her a brief wink as he helped himself to eggs and bacon.

Sarah, twenty years old and engaged to be married, was already beginning to behave like a matron. She was constantly aware, and therefore constantly reminding others, of her new status as a prospective bride. Her time was very much taken up with preparing for her wedding in a few months' time, but she was also very concerned with the task of preparing Isabel for her important role as bridesmaid. Now, presiding in her mother's place at the breakfast table, she directed a disapproving frown in her sister's direction.

'Do eat your breakfast properly, Isabel. You're playing with your food like a child in the nursery. You're too thin as it is. No man likes a broom-handle, you know.'

'Then perhaps that's why I like to be one,' Isabel answered. 'I don't intend to marry, so it will save a lot of trouble if nobody wants to marry me.'

Sarah gave her a cold look.

'And now you're being even more childish. Of course you want to get married.'

'Why?'

'Because that's what a woman *does*,' Sarah said with exasperation. 'And I don't know why *you* find this so amusing, Francis. But then, you're as bad as Isabel is. You encourage her. You're both children, and I despair of you. Don't you, Father?'

'Eh?' Jeremiah looked up from his morning paper. 'What's the matter? You're not squabbling again at this hour in the morning, surely.'

Sarah gave him a look that was not unlike the one she had given her sister. 'Squabbling? Of course not – I'm merely trying to point out to Isabel that it's time she began to behave like a young lady instead of a hoyden. And Francis seems to find her amusing, which does not help in the least. I wish *you* would have a word with them, Father.'

Jeremiah laid his paper down and looked at his daughter as if she had asked him to cross the Sahara in a rowing-boat.

'I? But what do you want me to say? Isabel seems

very well as she is, and Francis is working hard – those new designs you showed me yesterday promise very well, Francis, by the way, but I'm not sure about the colours. The red seems rather bright. Oh, and I wanted to talk to you about the new yarn – do you really think it's strong enough? Vivian's enthusiastic, but you know how he catches at any new idea. He still talks of America, you know. I suppose one day we'll have to let him go and have a look, if nothing more.' He rose to his feet, his daughters forgotten. 'Finished your breakfast? I want to go early this morning – old Carpenter wants me to cast an eye over the ledgers and there are several other things needing attention . . .'

He was at the door, and Francis stood up quickly, giving Isabel a swift, apologetic glance. But her eyes were twinkling and there was a suppressed mirth in her voice as she bade him goodbye, and he felt his own mouth tug into a smile. He bowed to his other cousin.

'Forgive me, Sarah. My uncle wants me to go at once.'

'So I observe,' Sarah said tartly. 'It will absolve you both from an awkward situation – oh, I'm well aware of the fact that you and Isabel enjoy your little jokes at my expense, Francis. And that Father would do almost anything rather than reprimand his two favourites . . . Go along, do,' she added sharply as Francis hesitated. 'You mustn't keep him waiting.' She watched as he went to the door, and then redirected her attention to her sister. 'I've been meaning for some time to speak to you about your behaviour regarding Francis,' she said. 'It was all very well when we were all children, treating him as a brother. But now that we're grown up, you should cultivate more modesty.'

'Modesty. With Francis? But he lives with us!'

'Exactly. It's therefore all the more important that

you should be discreet. I've seen the way you look at him, Isabel – those little glances and smiles. If it were any other young man, I would say you were – well, to speak quite plainly – flirting with him. Fortunately, I know that you have no such intention – but others might not realise that and you could risk giving quite the wrong impression. I don't want people to think you forward, especially with my wedding so close. Edward's family are of very good class, as you know, and I don't wish them to think that we don't know how to behave, simply because our father is in Trade.'

Isabel sat through her sister's speech without moving. When Sarah fell silent at last, she raised her eyes and said innocently, 'Why should I have no intention of flirting with Francis, Sarah?'

'Why?' Sarah stared at her. Clearly she had expected almost any reply other than this. 'Well – because he's Francis, of course. Our cousin. And because he's lived here in this house for – how long now? Four years, five? It simply wouldn't be seemly.'

'Oh,' Isabel said, nodding. 'Seemly.'

Sarah gave her a sharp glance. 'I hope you're not making fun of me again, Isabel. I'm quite serious about this. Your behaviour at times is more like that of a – a—'

'Schoolgirl?' Isabel said helpfully. 'But I *am* a schoolgirl, Sarah. And I shall be until Christmas. But don't worry – by the time you're married, I shall be out of the schoolroom, with my hair up, and transformed into a young lady.' The smile that always seemed to be hovering at the corners of her mouth, pulled at her cheeks. 'I wouldn't dream of mortifying you in front of Edward's family.'

'I should hope not,' Sarah said, but there was still a lingering suspicion in her voice, and she watched with a frown as Isabel rose to her feet. 'You still haven't eaten all your breakfast,' she pointed out.

'No, I haven't, have I. But I daresay I'll be more than ready for luncheon.' Isabel whisked to the door. 'Don't work too hard this morning, Sarah. I know how tired you get, answering all those letters and preparing for your afternoon calls. And Mother will be down soon, too.' She flashed a bright smile at her sister and was gone.

Left alone, Sarah sat frowning at the littered breakfast table. She heard Isabel's quick steps flying up the stairs to the schoolroom. Then she picked up the little bell and rang it sharply.

'Oh, there you are, Rebecca,' she said when the maid came in. 'You may clear this away now. And then make sure the fire is good in Mrs Pagnel's boudoir. We shall be in there all morning. We have a great deal to do.'

'Yes, miss.' Rebecca began to load the breakfast dishes on to the tray. She had been nervous about coming into the breakfast room, but Francis was not here after all. He must already have gone out with his uncle.

She carried the tray down to the kitchen and took it into the scullery for the new little maid, Tilly.

'Here you are,' she said, dumping it on the bench. 'Here's your first lot for the day. And there'll be more before you've finished them, if I know anything about it.' She looked at the small face and felt a wash of sympathy. 'It's not so bad really,' she told the child comfortingly. 'At least you get fed properly.'

But there was no time to talk. She had been

working for four hours now with only a short time for breakfast, and the day was still in its infancy. Already, Susan was calling for her.

She straightened her back, gave Tilly a quick smile, and hurried back into the kitchen.

Vivian was late arriving at his stepfather's office.

'I would have thought you could manage to arrive on time,' Jeremiah grumbled. 'Your house is nearer than mine. Perhaps I should have built it in the yard for you – or would you still have found it too difficult to get out of bed in the morning?'

'I'm sorry, Father,' Vivian said smoothly. 'Maria was feeling unwell . . . I couldn't leave her.' He could feel his face tugged by the triumph in his heart, ruining his efforts to remain secretive. Maria had begged him not to tell anyone just yet. But he couldn't resist giving Jeremiah a challenging glance.

'Unwell?' Jeremiah lifted his head from the designs Francis had just placed in front of him, and stared. 'Do you mean—?'

'Another child, yes.' Well, why keep it secret after all? They'd know soon enough. He allowed his jubilation to show in his voice as well as his face. 'By Christmas, she thinks. And this time it will be a son.'

'I'm glad you can be so sure,' Jeremiah grunted, and then rose to shake Vivian by the hand. 'Well, it's wonderful news. And Maria – she's not really unwell? It's no more than usual?'

'Good God, no. She'll take care, of course, now that we know . . . but she's a strong girl, made for breeding.' He shot a glance at Francis. 'Well, what do you say, Frank? My fourth child on the way – and you haven't even picked out a wife. D'you intend to remain a bachelor for the rest of your life?'

'I congratulate you,' Francis said. 'It's good news.'

Vivian laughed. 'I think I embarrass you!' he exclaimed, clapping his cousin on the shoulder. 'Perhaps I'm too fecund for your taste. But it's a good thing to have a quiverful of arrows – even if some of them have to be daughters, eh, Father?'

Jeremiah smiled wryly. 'Let us hope they will not all be daughters, Vivian. That's one thing we can't order to suit ourselves. And now . . . if you could give your attention to what Francis has been showing me. I think these designs are his best yet. You've certainly discovered where your talents lie, Francis. If we can produce these, we shall do very well. But they're complex – what do you think?'

'Oh, they look pretty enough,' Vivian said carelessly. 'I daresay we can manage. Of course, drawing an attractive picture isn't exactly a talent—'

'Is it not?' Jeremiah gave him a cold look. 'I think it is, Vivian. And to draw a picture, or a design, that can be woven as a carpet, with all the limitations and difficulties we face, is a talent we cannot afford to denigrate. Our business, our whole livelihood depends upon the design – make no mistake about that. We're fortunate to have a designer like Francis in the family.'

'Well, of course, I never meant to imply otherwise,' Vivian muttered. 'And they are good designs, I agree. This one in particular . . .' He bent closer, his finger tracing the colours. 'Yes . . . but have you thought about the weave? How many knots do you envisage for this? It needs to be very close.'

'Certainly,' Francis agreed. 'And should be one of our best carpets, once we've got it right. I think we should turn over the whole of one shop to the production – we'll need to produce it in quantity, it's going to be popular in all the best houses. Butts', perhaps . . .' He went on explaining to Jeremiah and Vivian how he thought the designs should be used, what quality yarn should be employed and where they should begin to display it.

Vivian watched as he talked. He saw how Francis's face flushed with enthusiasm, heard how his voice grew both quicker and firmer, watched the light in his eyes and the gestures he made with his hands. He felt the triumph of his own achievement dim and lessen as Jeremiah nodded and answered, and knew that his father's pride in Francis was more real than his apparent pleasure when he had congratulated Vivian a few moments ago.

A surge of jealous anger filled Vivian's heart. He looked at the designs and knew that he dared not disparage them. But he longed to do something – anything – to take that complacent smile from his cousin's lips, and to direct that pride on his father's face to himself instead.

'I don't understand why you're so worried,' Maria said when he went home for luncheon. She was looking better now, the colour back in her cheeks, and attacked her food as though she were starving. Yet tomorrow morning she would be wan and pale again, complaining of feeling sick and unable to face even the cup of tea brought by the maid. It had been the same with the other three babies, lasting for several weeks into each pregnancy.

Now, hungry after her morning's fast, she helped herself to cold meat and boiled potatoes. 'Francis is only a cousin. You're the son.'

'Stepson,' Vivian reminded her. It was a fact not

often mentioned, but it was a fact all the same.

'But you're his heir. He's made his will in your favour. The business will be yours, and our son's.'

Vivian looked at her broodingly. 'And what if we never have a son? We've three daughters already—'

'Then it's all the more likely that this child will be a boy.' Maria rested her hands on her stomach, still plump from the previous births. 'It must be.'

Vivian said nothing. He wanted to share her certainty, but doubt nagged him. Before his father and cousin, he was cock-a-hoop, boasting his confidence. But when he saw that look on his stepfather's face and heard the pride in his voice as he discussed Francis's designs, his heart grew cold and heavy. Suppose the coming child were not a boy? Suppose he never fathered a son – only an increasing brood of daughters? Who would be the heir then – himself or Francis?

He knew that when his mother – widowed and already the mother of two daughters and a baby son – had married Jeremiah, the marriage contract had stipulated that, failing any sons to be born to them both, Vivian was to be Jeremiah's heir. And Jeremiah had indeed always treated Vivian as his son, and hidden any disappointment that he might have felt when Isabella produced only two more daughters before her childbearing came to an end.

But he had also displayed a fondness for Francis, the adopted son of his brother Geoffrey. A fondness which had increased as the years went by and had, in Vivian's view, become immoderate since Francis had moved into Pagnel House. A move that Vivian had always thought unnecessary and now saw as a threat.

He wished that he had done as his mother had wanted, and stayed at Pagnel House instead of moving into his own home. There would have been plenty of room, and as the babies came along the household would have revolved around his family, gradually ousting Vivian's sisters from the centre of attention and leaving no room for Francis at all. Francis would have had to return to his father's house in Church Row and thus been safely out of Jeremiah's eye, except in the factory. And there, Vivian might have had some control over events.

As it was, Vivian was the one who went to a different home each evening, while Francis went back to Pagnel House with Jeremiah, ate dinner with him, sat talking in the evening and met him at breakfast each morning.

Francis was becoming more of a son to Jeremiah than Vivian. And a jealous fear gnawed at Vivian's heart when he watched them together.

He looked again at Maria. If this child were indeed a boy, all his troubles might be solved. He might not be Jeremiah's true grandson, but Isabella would see to it that he was treated as such. To him, eventually, would pass the business and all its wealth – which Vivian intended to increase substantially, once he had control. And Francis would be left on the fringe, a valuable designer no doubt, but nothing more. As he should be, for he was no Pagnel.

Vivian chose to forget the fact that no Pagnel blood ran in his veins either.

'You're not listening to me, Vivian,' Maria complained. 'I was telling you how much I would like to visit Sarah this afternoon. Can you drive me to the house when you go back to the factory? I would like a little female society, and Sarah's wedding plans are so interesting.'

Sarah, Vivian thought. Another one who could

soon begin to produce children – sons. Sons who would be indeed of Jeremiah's blood. Could the inheritance go that way instead? Could Sarah, even more than Francis, be the threat he dreaded?

And even if not, there was Isabel . . .

'Well, there's no need to look as if I'd asked you for the moon,' Maria said pettishly. 'I only want to be driven to your father's house. But if it's too much trouble . . .' Her lips began to quiver and Vivian hastened to reassure her. Maria must not be upset in her present condition. She had almost lost the last baby through an attack of hysterics, and if it were to happen with this one – the one who might be a boy . . .

'Don't cry, my love,' he said, getting up to go to the other side of the table and take her in his arms. 'Of course it isn't any trouble. I'll take you willingly, and collect you whenever you wish. I'm afraid I was thinking of something else. Something quite unimportant.' He held her close, his cheek on her hair. Women needed such a lot of care. He hoped desperately that this baby would be a boy. Then they need worry no more. No doubt Maria would have more children, but they wouldn't matter so much. And he would not need to take such care of her.

He stirred restlessly. Life was a cage, from which he escaped only on his journeys to London, where he had taken care to set up his own private amusement. And even that had not been easy, in the early days.

He still felt angry when he thought of that girl Bessie and her brother, who had taken his money and his help – and then vanished. He'd been looking forward to possessing Bessie's ripe little body; to having the two of them in his power.

He had been naïve, supposing that they would ever

go to the address he'd given them. Since then, he had grown wiser. But he often wondered what had happened to them.

It would be the worse for them if he ever ran across them again, he reflected, as he held Maria to him and waited for her tears to subside. Nobody gulled Vivian Pagnel. Not now.

Chapter Eight

As autumn brought a sharpness to the air and touched the trees with flame, the preparations for Sarah's wedding gathered pace. The air was filled with plans, with discussions about wedding dresses, trousseaus, the wedding breakfast. Jeremiah ordered a new carpet, specially designed by Francis, to be made for the young couple's new home; and the bridegroom's father, an ironmaster from Dudley, gave over part of his works to making an elaborate wrought iron fence and large gates for their garden.

'Edward's taking me to France for a holiday when we're married,' Sarah told Isabel proudly. 'We're travelling on the new steamship – the *Rob Roy*. It takes under three hours to make the crossing. We shan't go until the spring, though – it will be too cold in January. And I'm happy to spend our first few months in our own home.'

Isabel nodded and tried to repress a yawn. She had sat through so many of Sarah's eulogies about her coming wedding, and she was bored almost to screaming point by the endless discussions, the poring over pictures and patterns, the interminable fittings for dresses – both Sarah's and her own. And she saw no end to it: with Sarah married and her own schooldays over, it would fall to her to fill the gap left by her elder sister. She would be expected to do what Sarah did now – occupy her days with flower-arranging and embroidery, making and receiving calls, sitting in clothes that were restricting and uncomfortable while her mother's friends filled the air with inconsequential chatter.

With only a few weeks to go before her governess finally left, she was seldom able to go to the schoolroom, which had become a haven in her mind. Each morning, when she rose from the breakfast table to go upstairs, something would prevent her. 'Oh, Isabel, *would* you be an angel and help me with my letters this morning?' Sarah would ask, but more as if it were an order than a request. Or: 'Don't forget I have a fitting at ten. There's really hardly enough time to make all the clothes I shall need, and they *must* make a start on my wedding dress this week.'

'But you don't need me for a fitting,' Isabel protested, and at once earned herself a frown from her sister.

'Of course I do. I must have someone there. It's so tedious, with no one to talk to.'

'But Miss Smith and I were hoping—'

'Really,' Sarah said with an edge of impatience in her voice, 'whatever you and your governess were planning can hardly compare with my wedding. It's not as if your education is ever going to be of any use to you – you're not a boy. I've always thought Father was mistaken in letting you go on for so long – *I* was glad to finish with lessons as soon as possible. Anyway, you've only a few weeks to go now – there can't be anything essential for you to do at this stage.'

Isabel was silent. She could not tell Sarah about the reading she and Miss Smith were doing together, the worlds they were exploring. Her sister, so wrapped up in her own concerns, would never understand – would be more likely to go straight to their mother and tell her that Miss Smith was warping Isabel's mind and must be dismissed immediately. And then even the occasional haven of the schoolroom would be denied to her.

'Why do we have to grow up?' she asked Francis one Sunday morning as they walked back from church a little behind the rest of the family.

Francis smiled. They had had this conversation before and he still did not know the answer to Isabel's complaints. 'I think most women seem quite happy with their lot,' he hazarded. 'Perhaps you'll feel differently soon and enjoy being free of lessons and able to please yourself.'

Isabel gave him a withering look. 'You're as likely to see pigs fly past the window as find *me* being happy embroidering tablecloths and gossiping with those silly women Mother calls on . . . Francis, I want to *do* something. I want to work. I *like* working . . . I wouldn't even mind working in the carpet shop. At least I'd be doing something useful.'

'You wouldn't. Not if you saw what it was like in there.' Jeremiah had never allowed his daughters into any of the carpet shops, with their noisy looms, coarse-mouthed workers and stinking cauldrons filled with size and urine. 'You have no need to envy the girls who work there – they have hard lives. Isabel, it's foolish to go on hankering after a different life. What could you do, after all? There's nothing for women to do – not women of our class. And you wouldn't really want to be a governess, would you, trying to teach other people's spoilt brats and patronised by your employers.'

'I suppose not.' Isabel sounded unwilling to admit it, then spoke with energy and fire, so that her mother glanced back reprovingly. 'But, Francis, why *should* there be nothing for women? Oh, perhaps many do enjoy a life of idleness and pleasure – though what

177

pleasure there is in sitting at home all day, I don't know, to me it's simply tedious – but there must be others like me, who have brains and would like to use them, who must be *able* to do something useful. Why should we be denied?'

Francis shrugged helplessly. 'I don't know, Isabel. But I do know that there's nothing you can do to prevent yourself from growing up.' He glanced at her, recognising that she was becoming a beautiful woman. 'It won't be so bad, you know,' he said gently. 'There are a good many compensations.'

'I suppose you mean marriage,' Isabel said in a tone of deep scorn. 'Well, I've seen enough of Sarah's wedding to know that I shan't be interested in *that*. All this fuss about gowns and hats and who must be invited and what we must eat . . . And it will be no better afterwards. There's the grand new house to be planned, all the furniture and carpets, the china and glass. And then I suppose there'll be *babies*.'

Francis laughed. 'I expect so. Some more little nieces and nephews. Though you haven't any nephews yet, have you? Perhaps by then, Maria . . .'

'I hope so,' Isabel said. 'If Maria doesn't have a son this time, I think Vivian will begin to hate her. And that's marriage.' She was silent for a moment, then turned to him. 'Francis, the only man I could ever think of marrying would be you. Imagine what times we could have together! We could have our own house with a big, wild garden with trees we could climb and a pond where we could catch tadpoles – wouldn't it be heavenly?' She looked up at him, her eyes wide. 'Shall we, Francis? Shall we escape from all of them?'

Francis gazed down at her. Her words were artless, childish, and could be taken at face value. But did she really mean them that way? Was even Isabel still as childish as she sounded – or was there something deeper, some subtle undercurrent running through her words? Was she in fact more adult that she pretended – or perhaps was willing to admit even to herself?

There was something in her face, in the direct glance of eyes that were yet shadowed, that stirred uneasy feelings in him. He saw her beauty, felt her allure, and was tempted for a moment to treat her suggestion seriously and turn it into his own proposal. Why not, after all? Hadn't he and Isabel always been friends? What better basis than that could there be for marriage? And she was old enough – almost eighteen. A woman, in spite of her protestations. And almost quivering now with a fire that was very attractive.

But side by side with this sudden urge was a reluctance, almost a distaste. Isabel was too close. He had known her all her life. It would be like marrying his sister.

He took refuge in laughter.

'Yes, let's do that,' he said, smiling. 'We'll build a tree-house and live in it, shall we? And go for long voyages in a raft on the pond. It'll be fun – though a little cold at this time of the year. Perhaps next summer.'

Isabel stared at him and he saw her eyes change and knew that he had hurt her. So there really had been some serious intent in her words – even if she hadn't known it herself. And now she felt spurned and mortified, and it was his fault.

'Come along, Isabel,' he said gently, taking her arm. 'We're being left behind. Don't worry about growing up. It won't be so bad. And perhaps you will find something useful to do with your life. Women have before.' He cast about in his mind and could think of no one to use as an example. 'Look at Queen Elizabeth,' he said at last, rather lamely.

Isabel laughed then, a higher, shriller laugh than normal but a laugh all the same. 'Well, that's a great comfort to me,' she said, walking on rather fast. 'All I need to do is be born a princess. How careless of me not to have seen that before.'

She strode on quickly and Francis hurried to keep up with her. He sought for something to say to mend the breach that appeared to have opened between them, but could find nothing. In silence, they caught up with the rest of the family and Isabel began to talk quickly and with apparent enthusiasm about the dress she was to wear as bridal attendant at Sarah's wedding.

'Rose pink,' she said in tones of deep satisfaction. 'My very favourite colour. I'm really looking forward to it. Weddings are so exciting – don't you think so, Francis?'

But she did not look at him and he felt a pang of sadness. He knew that during that short walk, something important had happened.

Isabel had, in spite of all her words, become a woman.

It was now understood between Rebecca and Polly that the library was Rebecca's responsibility.

Each morning, her heart quaking, she slipped in through the big door and was met by Francis. Usually, he was stretched out on the big sofa, reading, but he always put down his book to sit beside the fireplace to watch and talk to her as she worked.

Their talk ranged widely, but mostly concerned

their own lives. Francis would tell her about his home, his schooldays, his work; in return, answering his questions with some diffidence, Rebecca would describe her own home and childhood, touching only lightly on the poverty and hardships which were so different from his own experiences. Like her parents, she was too proud to complain about her lot. And she knew that her life had been much improved since coming to work at Pagnel House. Her mother had been right – three meals a day and a good Sunday dress were worth a great deal of hard work.

Why should he want to talk to her – a servant? Rebecca, scurrying through her work for the rest of the day, puzzled over the question but could find no answer. After a while, she gave up and simply allowed herself to look forward to their brief, early-morning meetings. She became adept at clearing the fireplaces quickly, so that she could finish the others first and give herself as much time as possible in the library. She always made sure that she left the library the moment the grandfather clock in the hall began to strike six.

During the second week, she was shocked to find the ashes already swept into a neat pile and the fire laid with fresh kindling.

'Oh, Mr Francis – you shouldn't have done that.' She was overwhelmed, disturbed. Nobody had ever voluntarily done her work for her – everyone always had too much of their own. And for Francis to kneel down and sweep up ashes for her . . . She looked at him, almost afraid because she did not understand.

'Why not? It gives us more time to talk.'

'But it's my job. And suppose Susan should come in and find me not working.' She was really distressed. It was almost as if the world had suddenly shifted on its axis.

'Well, you've got the blackleading to do, and she'd just think how quick you were.' He smiled at her. 'Don't look so frightened, Rebecca. I'm not going to hurt you. I just enjoy talking with you for a few minutes each day.'

Rebecca took the blacklead and brush out of her box. 'I still don't think you should do my work for me,' she said uneasily. 'Someone might find out, somehow, and it'd be me as got into trouble. You can't lose your position here, Mr Francis. I can. And I can't afford to be turned away without a character. The mistress was good to take me in, what with my sister and everything.'

'Your sister?' He looked at her, frowning a little. 'Why, what did she do?'

'She didn't do nothing – anything,' Rebecca amended, remembering the training the butler had given her. To rise up in the world, you had to be able to speak properly, and she had asked him to help her get rid of the local dialect that would keep her from the position she desired. 'It's what people thought she did. It's a long time ago now – before I come – *came* here. It was old Jabez Gast, in Butts' shop.'

'Jabez Gast? Oh, yes – I remember. He was killed, wasn't he? By his draw-girl.' Francis looked at her in surprise. 'Was that your sister?'

'She didn't kill him.' Rebecca rubbed vigorously. 'He – well, she didn't kill him.' She felt embarrassed. She knew now what had happened between Bessie and Jabez, but it wasn't something you could say outright, not to a young gentleman like Mr Francis.

'Did he attack her?' Francis asked quietly.

'I suppose you'd call it that. Yes. He did. And my brother Tom came in and caught him.'

'So it was your brother—'

182

'*No*. Neither of them killed him.' Rebecca sat back on her heels, remembering the shock and pain of that morning. She remembered the watchman coming, remembered peeping out at him from behind her mother's skirts, felt again the fear in the room, and shivered. 'It was an accident – only nobody would ever have believed that, so they had to run away.' She hesitated, wondering why she was telling him all this. It was a secret between her parents and herself.

'You can trust me,' Francis said, watching her. 'I shan't give away any secrets. Did your brother and sister get safely away? I never heard of them being caught.'

'No, they weren't caught.' She stared at the brush in her hand. 'Someone gave them some money – Tom never said who – and they went to London. They're still there, frightened to come home I think. Bessie's got work in a house, domestic work like this I suppose, and Tom does all sorts of jobs – handyman kind of things. It's a shame – he was a good weaver.'

'But they write to you?'

'Not often,' Rebecca said with a glance at him. 'Folk like us can't afford letters much. We had to save up to get the one Tom wrote telling us they were all right. Now he just sends an empty envelope and Mam tells the postman she hasn't got the money. That way, we know they're still all right.'

'But suppose there was a letter inside one day? Suppose they *weren't* all right and had written to tell you? You'd never know.'

Rebecca shrugged. 'Well, there wouldn't be anything we could do about it anyway.' She caught the expression on his face and said with unexpected energy, 'It's no good looking like that, Mr Francis. That's how things are for people like us. What can we do about anything? Bessie and Tom never killed that old man, but it weren't no good staying in Kidder to say so. And now they're in London, there's nothing we can do to help them. Any more than they can help us.' She rubbed viciously at the black surround of the fireplace.

'Do you need help?' Francis asked after a moment. 'Is there something wrong – with your parents, perhaps? Other brothers or sisters? Is there anything I could do?'

'I haven't got no other brothers or sisters,' Rebecca muttered. 'There's only me, and me mam and dad. And I only have one afternoon a fortnight to go and see them.'

'And is something wrong? Are they ill? Out of work?'

She laid down her brush and looked at him. 'Mr Francis. You don't want to know all this. It's not your business. We're different from you, folks like us. We have to take what life hands us. It's no good worrying about it. We just have to do our best.'

He gazed at her. 'You make it sound as if we live in two different worlds.'

'Well,' Rebecca said, rubbing again, 'don't we?'

Francis sighed and lay back in his chair, looking at the ceiling. Then he sat up again and said with a controlled energy, 'Rebecca. Tell me what's wrong with your parents. Please.'

Rebecca stopped rubbing and looked at him. To her dismay, she felt tears sting her eyes. She looked down at the hearth. She wanted to speak, but couldn't.

'Trust me, Rebecca,' Francis said again, very gently, as a tear splashed on to the dusty slate.

'It's my dad,' she said at last. 'He's not been well

for a while. He's got a sort of growth.' Her throat was thick and aching. 'He can't do much work now, he gets so tired. And Mam has to help him so she can't go to work proper – she goes washing and that, to earn what money she can.'

There was a long silence. Then Francis put his hand on her shoulder. It felt warm and comforting and strong. And there was something else: a kind of thrill, a tingle that ran down through her body, spreading through her limbs, aching almost into the soles of her feet and the palms of her hands. She wanted to lay her cheek on the warm fingers and rest there, knowing that here was someone who could lift the burden from her shoulders and carry it for her.

'Has your father seen a doctor?'

She nodded. 'He went to the new dispensary up in Blackwell Street. They said—' her voice faltered '—they said they couldn't do anything for him. It'll just go on . . . getting bigger.' Tears were running down her cheeks now. 'And it hurts him so much. He don't say much, but you can see it. And Mam looks so tired. And there's nothing I can do. I give them my wages, but it int enough.' She lifted her hands and let them drop. Then she said, with a note of bitterness that seldom sounded in her voice, 'They've never had nothing, my mam and dad. Never had anywhere nice to live, never had enough to eat or proper clothes to wear or good shoes for their feet. They've never had a day out in the fields, just walking in the sun; and they had to watch all their children but us three die when they were still babies.' She looked at Francis, her eyes shadowed with the hardship that had been handed down to her through all the generations. 'It's the same for all poor folk, Mr Francis. And it int fair. We hurt, just like rich folk do. We get tired and sick and sad, just the same as you. And we work hard. We work all the hours God sends, and then the rest. We has time off to sleep and eat, and not much else, while our *betters* sit in good chairs, full of rich food and wonder what to do with theirselves. Why does it have to be like that, Mr Francis? Why?'

She stopped, feeling the heat in her face, and lifted her hand to brush back a lock of hair that had escaped from its pins and swung across her cheek. Her fingers came away wet and she realised that there were tears streaming from her eyes.

Abruptly, she turned away to the fireplace, but Francis leaned forward and laid his hands on her shoulders, gently turning her to face him. She tried to resist, but his fingers tightened and he held her with a firmness she had not expected. She looked up into his eyes and saw there a warmth and compassion that brought a fresh ache to her throat.

'I don't know why it has to be like that, Rebecca,' he said quietly. 'And you're right – it isn't fair. People shouldn't have to live like your parents have, like so many thousands of others do. There ought to be enough for all to share – enough food, enough good houses, enough medical care. Maybe one day there will.'

'There won't,' she said hopelessly. 'Not while folk like us are kept down. We can't even read, most of us. There's no schooling – how can we ever get better? And the rich aren't going to help us – why should they? We might not want to work for 'em then. And look what happened up in Manchester two years back. Those soldiers just rode at women and children and cut 'em to bits with their swords.'

'Peterloo. I know. But I don't know what the solution is, Rebecca. Perhaps you're right, and there should be education for everybody. But that won't help people like your father, now.' He hesitated. 'Would you like me to speak to my aunt about him?'

'No!' she exclaimed, startled, then spoke more quietly. 'No, please don't do that, Mr Francis. It wouldn't be right. She'd think I was taking advantage, and so would the others below stairs. And no one can do anything. That's what Dr Bradley, at the dispensary, said. That kind of growth, no one can do anything about.'

He looked at her helplessly. 'But isn't there *any-thing* I can do?'

'No, Mr Francis. There's nothing.'

They stayed there, silent in their own thoughts, for a moment or two. Then the grandfather clock, out in the hall, began the whirring sound it always made just before striking. Rebecca leapt to her feet as if she had been scalded.

'That's six o'clock! I'll have to go – and I haven't even finished the blackleading properly.' She gathered up her things and piled them back into her box, trembling. 'What Susan will say if she comes in and sees it, I don't know . . . Please, Mr Francis, you shouldn't be here when I come in the mornings. If anyone knew . . . I'd be in terrible trouble, I really would.'

'No one's going to know,' Francis said, watching her. 'Rebecca, don't look so afraid. Nothing is going to happen to you.' He rose as she stood up, clutching her box of brushes and pans, her face still damp from her tears and streaked with soot and ash where she had brushed her hand across it. She lifted her face to him, and saw his expression change as he gazed down at her. There was an odd softening, a darkening of his eyes . . . Rebecca felt a tremor low down in her stomach and as the warmth flooded into her cheeks she turned swiftly away.

'I'll have to go now,' she murmured, and almost ran for the door.

When she reached it and looked back, Francis was standing before the hearth, still watching her. Still with that strange expression on his face; an expression which haunted her through the rest of the day.

'Women are strange creatures,' Vivian declared, stretching out his long legs and lighting a cigar. 'I probably understand them better than most – and even I wouldn't pretend to know what goes on in their pretty heads most of the time. Why, even my own wife can baffle me on occasion, and there's nobody more simple than dear Maria.'

Francis watched him. He never felt quite easy with Vivian, but they were forced to work together and the undercurrent of hostility which he sensed had never wholly surfaced. And it was certain that there was no greater authority on women than his handsome cousin.

He had accepted their invitation to supper, knowing that Maria's condition now precluded any company outside the family, and was glad enough to escape the constant wedding talk that pervaded the Pagnel house. Jeremiah had put his foot down over a repetition of the amount of redecoration that had gone on before Vivian's wedding, but there was still a good deal of upheaval taking place. And Isabel did not seem to have recovered from the annoyance Francis had evidently caused her during their walk home from church a week or two ago. He could feel her eyes, fixed reproachfully on him as he sat opposite her, and he could not think what he should do to put matters right between them. He was not even sure what was wrong. It was disconcertingly unlike Isabel to behave in this manner. Until now, they had always been able to tease each other out of any minor sulks, but now something had come between them and made their old easy friendship impossible.

'I don't know what it is she wants of me,' he said now. 'She behaves so oddly. At one moment, things are as they've always been and she's as friendly and comfortable as when we were children. And then, without my even knowing what's caused it, she's changed. Become withdrawn and irritable. It seems there's nothing I can do or say that will be right. It's almost as if she dislikes me. And yet at other times – she seems almost as if she's – well, forming an attachment to me. But that's even more nonsensical.'

A broad grin spread itself across Vivian's face. He lay back in his chair and laughed. Francis stared at him, baffled and slightly annoyed.

'I don't really see what is so amusing about all this,' he said stiffly. 'I'm fond of Isabel – very fond of her. If she's upset about something, naturally I'd like to put things right, if I can. Is that really a matter for mirth?'

'Not to you,' Vivian said, wiping his eyes. 'But then you're such an innocent still. How old are you now, Francis? Twenty-two? It was your twenty-first birthday we celebrated last year, wasn't it? And yet you might be still in the schoolroom.' He sat up, still smiling. 'Isabel's growing up. Becoming a woman – and a handsome one, too. She's beginning to think of what all pretty young women think of. Love – whatever that is – and marriage. Naturally, she's looking around her. And the first eligible man her glance happens to fall on is you. It's not surprising, really.' He began to laugh again. 'She thinks she's in love with you. It's all right, Frank – it won't last. These early infatuations never do. It'll be the baker's boy or the new curate next week. Girls like Isabel, who have spent their childhood wishing they were boys, are the worst of all. In love a dozen times before they marry some suitable young man who will take them off their long-suffering father's hands.' His smile grew rueful as he thought of his own nursery full of daughters. 'And a damned expense right up to the happy day. I daresay Father's feeling the draught now, with Sarah demanding a trousseau fit for a queen and God knows what besides. Take my advice, Frank – have sons. Let some other man foot the bill.'

But Francis did not respond to his banter. He was frowning.

'But Isabel can't really be in love with me. That's ridiculous, Vivian. We've always been such friends.' He broke off in annoyance. 'Vivian, this *isn't* amusing. Please stop laughing. I came to you for advice. And help, for it seems I need both. What am I to do?'

'Do? Why, nothing.' Vivian was still chuckling. 'Don't look so appalled, Frank. I've told you, she'll get over it. After all, you've no intention of marrying her, have you?'

'No!' The vehemence of Francis's reply startled himself. He stopped, wondering why the idea caused such an aversion in him. Isabel was pretty, lively, interesting and he had known and liked her all her life. A marriage between them might even be approved by their families – they were not true cousins, after all, and he was already working for her father. Yet . . . there was something in his heart that told him it would not do.

He caught Vivian's surprised look and shook his head. 'No,' he said more quietly. 'Of course I've no intention of marrying Isabel. She's like a sister to me.'

'Well, that's all right, then. All you have to do is wait for her to grow up a little more and meet some other young men. Which she'll assuredly do, in the near future. After all, she's almost out of the schoolroom. Mother will make it her business to see that Isabel has plenty of chances, and once Sarah's married she'll have time on her hands which she'll be only too happy to devote to Issy. You've really nothing to worry about, Francis.' He leaned forward and lifted the decanter from the low table between them. 'Here – have another glass of port and take that worried frown from your face.'

'You were talking with Francis for a long time, dearest,' Maria said later, as they prepared for bed.

Vivian began to smile again. 'I know. The poor fool's worried about Isabel. She's growing up at last and sees Frank as a future husband. I've told him there's nothing to worry about, but he's still gone off looking as if he bears the weight of the world on his shoulders.'

Maria stopped unbuttoning the loose petticoat that covered her burgeoning stomach and stared at him. 'I hope you're right.'

'Well, of course I am. Issy will be infatuated half a dozen times before she's married, and that will probably be to someone Mother has chosen for her – just like Sarah. And it won't be Francis.' He suddenly registered the odd note in her voice and turned to look at her. 'Why – you don't think—'

'Isabel is a very strong-minded girl. If she sets her

heart on a marriage . . .' Maria came over to him and laid her hands on his arms. 'Your father's very fond of Francis. He may welcome an opportunity to bring him closer into the family. And if Francis becomes Isabel's husband—'

'His children will be Father's grandchildren,' Vivian said slowly. 'And if we have no sons . . .' His gaze dropped to her stomach and he laid his hand on it and pressed hard. 'But we *are* going to have sons, Maria. This is just the first. The first of many.' He took no notice of the fearful expression which crossed her face. 'Feel that – he's kicking. It *must* be a boy, with a kick like that.'

Maria said nothing. She turned away and continued with her preparations for bed. Vivian went across to the washstand and sluiced his face and hands. He felt triumphant, certain of himself and his future. And he was still laughing inside as he thought of Francis, so horrified at the thought of Isabel's being in love with him.

Nevertheless, as he settled himself in bed beside Maria and blew out the candle, he was conscious of a small, niggling voice inside his head which whispered uncomfortable questions. Questions about what would happen if Maria did not produce a son; if Francis did indeed marry Isabel; if Vivian himself were to grow old with no heir to inherit the business from him.

Damn! It was all Maria's fault for raising the possibility. And in spite of her bulk and her condition, he turned and caught her against him and proceeded to punish her in the way that he had made his own; regretting only that this time it could not possibly result in a son.

*　　*　　*

'But the family's in poverty, Aunt Isabella,' Francis said pleadingly. 'I've talked with the maid – Rebecca. She tells me the mother has to take in washing and her father has a growth of some kind that's killing him—'

'Please, Francis,' his aunt protested, turning her face aside, 'not so soon after breakfast. I must beg you—'

'No, Aunt,' he said insistently, '*I* must beg *you*. I know you're kind-hearted – look at the work you do for the Missionary Society. But these are our own people – our own workers. William Himley has made carpet for us, his children worked in one of our factories—'

'And look what they did there!' Isabella interrupted. Her face was flushed with anger. 'I must ask you, Francis, to think what you are saying, what you are asking. It was the Himley brother and sister who murdered – brutally murdered – one of our best weavers. One of *Vivian's* best weavers. Most women would not have countenanced another of the family working under their roof. What risks might I have taken in employing that maid – Rebecca, is it? Yet I did so out of sheer kindness of heart. I do not think that there is anything else I could be expected to do.'

Francis waited a moment. He thought of Rebecca, so modest, so hardworking and conscientious. So . . . gentle.

'Aunt Isabella, they're starving in that cottage,' he said at last, quietly. 'They can't earn enough to keep them alive. And although Rebecca gives them all she can, it isn't enough. Please – won't you do something to help them?'

But as he spoke the last words, the door opened and Sarah rushed in, a pile of cream silk spilling from her arms, her face rosy and flushed, alight with pleasure.

'Mamma, look! The materials have arrived. Isn't this one perfect? I must have it made up immediately. And the hats, you must see the hats.' She caught at her mother's hand and tugged her towards the door, noticing Francis for the first time. 'Oh, hello, Francis. What are you doing here? Shouldn't you be at the factory with Papa?' She glanced at their faces. 'You weren't discussing anything important, were you?'

'No,' Isabella said, allowing herself to be led from the room. 'Nothing important at all.'

The cottage was just as it had always been: too cold in winter, too hot in summer. The brick floor was red with loose dust, left unswept so that when the door opened the draught blew it into swirls that settled on the rough table and the two old chairs, and dulled the colours of the carpet that William was working on now, so slowly and painfully.

'He'll never finish it in time for fall day,' Fanny said when Rebecca went over to the loom and stood fingering the yarns and bobbins. 'But what can I say? It's all he's got left – that and a drink in the tavern.' She began to cry; a weary, defeated weeping that tore at Rebecca's heart. She moved back to her mother and crouched beside her, her hands covering the thin, worn fingers, splashed with tears, and remembered all the other times when she had done just this, comforting her mother as she wept for Bessie and Tom, as she cried when William had stamped out to spend their last few coppers at the tavern. And now he was too frail, too ill and weary himself, to grumble or lose his temper with the woman who had stayed by his side through so much hardship. He was little more than a shadow and death itself could not be far away.

Yet he still struggled on with his work. He had been

194

to the warehouse and collected his bobbins and yarn, he had sat at his loom and forced himself, through pain Rebecca could not begin to imagine, to carry out the work that was all he had ever known; to produce carpet that he would never walk on, for the feet of those who had never known hardship such as he had endured since he was born.

Rebecca felt a wave of rage shake her body. She thought again of the conversation she had had with Francis. Why *should* so many people live like this, when others grew fat, clothed in fine silks, shimmering with rich jewels? Why should men like her father have to work their lives away, with nothing but poverty to show at the end of it, while others lived only for pleasure and then complained that their lives were empty?

She thought of Sarah Pagnel, fussing about her wedding, demanding this and that finery, declaring that she could not live without the latest style of hat or furniture for her new home. She thought of Mrs Pagnel, served breakfast in bed, rising only to lie on a couch and issue orders during the morning, being dressed by her maid in the afternoon to go languidly out and pay calls – and yet there was nothing wrong with her, nothing at all. All the servants knew that. 'She just likes to think it makes her more interesting,' Rose, her maid, said savagely when Mrs Pagnel had kept her up past midnight yet again after a dinner party. 'She can stay up late enough when there's company here, yes, and be pleasant about it, too. But it's me that has to suffer her tantrums when it's all over and she's bored again.'

And Fanny Himley, who had never had breakfast in bed in her life – who rarely ate breakfast anyway, more than a cup of water and a crust of bread, and whose bed was a pile of sacking and an old blanket or two in the corner of the room – had to go out at five each morning to the bobbin sheds, or drag herself around to the big houses to do their weekly wash for them, or find whatever work she could do at home so that she could care for William during his worst moments and draw for him when he felt strong enough to sit at his loom.

And nobody to help them but Rebecca, with one afternoon off a fortnight and only a few shillings to give them, together with whatever Mrs Atkins could spare from the kitchen.

'I've brought you some eggs today, Mam,' she said encouragingly. 'You could give Father one for his tea. And have one yourself. It'll put strength into you.' She caressed the thin fingers, noticing how loose the skin was now over the bones. 'And there was some cake left over from the kitchen tea yesterday, Mrs Atkins said I could bring that, too. And I've a shawl Susan gave me – the mistress gave Rose a new one, so Rose passed hers on to Susan. It's warm, look. It will keep you cosy in winter.'

'I'll be in the poorhouse, come winter,' Fanny said drearily, but Rebecca shook her hands gently.

'You mustn't say that. Look, I'll put the eggs up here on the shelf. If Father comes home soon I'll cook them for you before I go. Hullo – what's this?' She lifted down a small bag and looked at it in surprise. 'Money! Where did this come from, Mam?'

'That?' Fanny seemed almost uninterested. 'Why, your friend brought that. The young man from the house. He said we were to get the doctor, but Will says it's too late for that. He says he'd rather enjoy himself in The Anchor with his mates. And I don't blame him. What's the use of doctors to folk like us, tell me that.'

But Rebecca was shaking her head. 'I don't understand, Mam. What young man? I don't know any—' She paused and stared down at her mother's bent head, at the grey hair so thin that the scalp showed through it. 'You don't mean Mr Francis?'

'I don't know who he was, he never said. Just said he wanted to help.' A mirthless smile twisted her lips. 'I don't think he'd ever bin in a weaver's cottage afore. Seemed a bit surprised. I felt like telling him they were all like this – what did he expect?'

Rebecca stared at her, then looked at the money in her hand. There was enough here to pay for several doctor's bills. Or enough food to nourish both her parents for several weeks. For warm clothes for the winter, for boots, for a new blanket to cover them during the bitter nights.

'I'll take this money, Mam,' she said. 'There are a lot of things you need – I'll get them for you. I'll leave a bit for Dad, to buy his drink in the tavern. He don't get much else, I know. But we can't let him spend it all there.'

'Why not?' Fanny said. 'He'll kill hisself all the quicker and be well out of it. And I'll go into the workhouse and be fed and kept, with nothing to do all day but sit in the sun. And maybe one day our Tom and Bess will come back and fetch me out of it and take me back to London with them. They've a grand house there by now, I'll be bound. It's just a matter of saving for the fare.'

Rebecca looked at her with pity. Fanny was as close to death as William, her body wasted almost to nothing, prey to any illness that might strike at her. What use, indeed, was it to buy warm clothing for a winter she might never see? What use to cover the body against a cold that would come most bitterly in the grave?

She knelt down again beside her mother.

'I'll buy food with it, Mam,' she said softly, laying her cheek against the thin, dried skin of her mother's. 'I'll buy food and kindling to keep you both warm. And Dad can have some for his ale.' She heard the church clock strike and knew she dared not stay much longer. 'I'll go now and fetch it back here directly. And I'll come again, soon as I can.'

She hurried to the nearest shop, returning with a bowl of steaming broth, a loaf of bread and wood for the fire. And when she had stirred the sticks to a blaze, seen her mother sip the broth and set some eggs to cook for her father's meal, she left, looking back with an ache in her heart.

Fanny had barely stirred during the entire visit. She had taken the soup like a child, almost without interest. Even now, she did not raise her head to look up. She was, quite simply, too tired.

Rebecca went out and walked slowly away along the cobbles, slimy with refuse and dirt. She felt a heavy weight deep inside her breast. She knew quite well that when she came again, in a fortnight's time, neither Fanny nor William might still be alive.

Chapter Nine

Francis had taken to rising even earlier than usual and going straight to the library where, as quickly and quietly as possible, he cleared the ashes from the fireplace and swept them into a neat pile. He could not do any more, much as he wanted to, until Rebecca arrived with her box and pail. And then he knew she would not allow him to do her work. But it was something, a token.

Increasingly, he wanted to lift the burden from Rebecca's shoulders, to take the sadness from her face and the weariness from her body. He had seen the bright flash of her eyes; he knew that inside the deferential housemaid was a very different person. He wanted to meet that person, talk with her, learn to know her. And these early morning meetings in the library were his only opportunity.

Rebecca, too, was keen to learn – though he knew that she did not yet suspect just what they were learning together. Instead, she had confessed one day that she could not read or write. Francis saw this as a chance to keep her with him, to ensure that their early morning meetings would continue. He gave her a brief lesson each day and, slowly, she was learning her letters like any child in a schoolroom. And Francis, bending over the paper with her, found himself enjoying the role of tutor.

This morning, his heart was beating rather quickly. Yesterday had been Rebecca's free afternoon, the afternoon when she was allowed a few hours to go to visit her mother. She would have learned of his own visit. And, unaccountably, he felt apprehensive.

Suppose she were offended? Poor people were often proud, easily offended by 'charity'. Yet how could she, knowing the conditions her parents endured, take offence?

All the same, when the library door opened his heart jumped. And as Rebecca slipped into the room in her normal quiet fashion and stood looking at him, he found it difficult to know what to say.

'I went to see my mam and dad yesterday,' Rebecca said, kneeling at the fireplace. She began to scoop the cinders into her pail and sift the ashes. 'Mam says a man went to see her and gave her money.' She looked at him squarely. 'Why would anyone want to do that?'

Francis shifted in his chair. 'I supposed he felt it was needed.' Please, please don't let her take offence. 'Wasn't it?'

'Oh, yes. It's needed all right. But why should someone well-to-do – like yourself, Mr Francis – do that for folk he'd never met? Why them?' She met his eyes with a steady look. 'It was you, wasn't it, Mr Francis? You went after I'd told you about how bad they were.' He nodded, still unsure, and she said in a low voice, 'It were good of you, Mr Francis. Thank you.'

'You don't have to thank me, Rebecca,' Francis said, relieved. 'It was little enough to do.' He hesitated. 'Seeing how your parents lived – it came as a shock . . .'

'I can believe that,' Rebecca said with an unexpected tartness. 'Folk of your sort don't go down that way much. Why should you know how we live?'

Francis flinched. 'Yes, you're right. We don't

200

know – we don't care, not enough. Or that's how it must seem. But I'm sure more people would care, if only they did know.'

'And are you going to tell 'em?'

'I'd like to,' he said quietly. 'I'd like to put it right. There are a lot of things in the world that need putting right, Rebecca. But one man can't do it alone.'

Rebecca sighed. 'No. And there's more important things than my mam and dad and thousands like 'em . . . I know, Mr Francis. You don't need to tell me. Though what's more important than folks starving and dying, I don't know. I suppose it depends what folks they are.'

Francis watched her silently. She spoke without bitterness, as though it were natural for poor people to accept their lot without complaint. And yet there had been a hint of rebellion in her earlier words. Deep down, he knew, she resented the difference between master and servant.

'Is there anything more I can do for your parents, Rebecca?' he asked.

She sat back on her heels and looked up at him. Once again, he was struck by the velvety darkness of her brown eyes, the sheen of her tightly drawn-back hair. Her lips were full and sensuous, belying the modest demeanour she had been taught. What would she be like, he thought, with that hair falling loose, the generous mouth smiling, the eyes alight with laughter and love . . . ? Shocked by his thoughts, he pushed them aside. But he could not prevent the sudden kick of his heart or the stirring somewhere deep in his body.

'There's not much anyone can do for them now,' she said hopelessly. 'Me dad's dying on his feet. He's still trying to weave . . . but I don't see him finishing the piece he's working on now. And Mam's drawing for him when he can sit at the loom, and taking in washing and doing rough cleaning for other folk – whatever she can find. And what food they can scrape for, she gives to him. There's naught but skin over her bones now. I tried to get her to eat yesterday, some bits and pieces Mrs Atkins let me take from the kitchen – but she couldn't manage more'n a bite, says she can't seem to stomach it. And Dad's living on ale.' Her voice, dry and difficult as if forced through a throat swollen with repressed tears, broke and she bent her head suddenly, lifting her hands to her face. 'They're both dying,' she said through a gasp of misery, 'and there's naught anyone can do about it.'

Francis slid out of his chair and knelt beside her. He took her in his arms, drawing her head against his shoulder, and brought one hand up to stroke her hair, fingers trembling. He laid his cheek gently on the top of her head and felt her quiver like a frightened animal in his arms.

'It's all right, Rebecca,' he murmured. 'Don't worry – don't worry about anything. Just stay quiet for a few moments . . . there.' He soothed her as he would a frightened and unhappy child, and felt a great protectiveness well up in him as he wrapped his arms more closely about her slender body. The thudding of her heart vibrated through his own body, and he felt a deep, burning indignation that a girl so young – younger than his cousin Isabel – should bear such burdens. A sister and brother lost in London, afraid to come home; a father dying of some malignant disease; a mother starving herself to keep him in the ale that was his only comfort . . . How could life be so unfair? So cruel?

Rebecca stayed in his arms, sobs shuddering

through her, and he held her close. He could feel her bones, fragile as a bird's, through the chill of her shivering flesh and he wanted suddenly to lift her in his arms and sweep her away, away from the library, away from the house, away from the town where they were both known, to some strange and undiscovered place where they would no longer be master and servant but simply two people, a man and a woman, free to behave with each other as they most desired . . .

Rebecca moved suddenly and looked up at him, her eyes wide and startled as if she had divined his thoughts. Shaken by the direction they had taken, he loosed his hold and she drew back, real fear in her eyes now.

'Mr Francis – I—'

With sudden dismay, he realised what she was thinking and words tumbled from his mouth in an effort to reassure her.

'Rebecca – it's all right, don't look like that. I'm not going to hurt you – I'm not going to do anything.' God, how could he explain? Housemaids were used to being pursued and even seduced by the men of a household – Vivian wouldn't have hesitated for a moment to take advantage of the situation. But Francis had never done so; nor, heated though he was by her nearness, did he want to now. His feelings were far more complex . . .

He shook his head as if trying to clear his muddled thoughts. 'Rebecca, you've nothing to fear from me. I'm your friend. I want to help you and your parents – and I'm not looking for anything in return.' He paused. Had he said too much? Not enough? 'Do you understand me?'

She nodded slowly, but her eyes were still wary.

'I simply wanted to give you some comfort,' he said quietly. 'I feel you need it, Rebecca. Don't refuse me the – the privilege.'

He chose the word as a substitute for 'pleasure', afraid that she might misconstrue his meaning. But as he said it, he realised that it was a far more accurate description of his feelings. To hold her in his arms, even for a moment, was more than a pleasure. It *was* a privilege.

Her eyes were very dark. They looked at him a moment more, then were hidden by her heavy lids. She turned away and picked up her brush.

'I'd best get on with this.' She began to sweep. 'Mr Francis . . . it *was* good of you to give them the money. And it'll make their days a bit easier. But it won't do any more than that.' She was looking at her work, but she turned her head again and looked him full in the face with eyes that smouldered with angry grief. 'They're going to die – both of them. And thousands of others the same. Because there's nothing in the world for folk like us except work, to keep us alive. And once that goes . . .'

'There's nothing. Yes. I understand that, Rebecca.'

'There's always the workhouse, of course,' she went on, still sweeping. 'But have you ever been inside that place?'

'No,' he admitted, and felt ashamed that he had not.

'I haven't, either. But I've met folks that have. I've seen them.' She said no more, but to Francis it was as clear as if she had spent an hour describing to him the misery of such a place. He looked at her, crouched over her work, and felt a wave of almost unbearable agony: pity, mixed with anger and distress, and some other emotion, deeper and more painful than either of these, which he could not name. He looked at her bent head, at the slender white neck which supported the shining head, and knew a shock of desire. He wanted to take her in his arms again, hold her to his heart as he had done a few moments ago, kiss that vulnerable neck. He wanted to turn her face up to his and close those great, drowning eyes with his lips; he wanted to lay his mouth on hers . . .

Abruptly, almost angrily, he came to his feet. Rebecca jumped and looked up at him, her eyes as soft and startled as a deer's, and he cursed himself. Was there nothing he could do this morning without frightening her? And he wanted to do just the opposite . . . but no, he must not begin to think like that again. He turned away and walked to the window, knowing that she was watching him, knowing she must be disturbed by his odd behaviour, yet unable to reassure her.

'Mr Francis,' she said from somewhere behind him, 'is there something I've done wro—'

'For God's sake!' he cried, wheeling. 'Stop calling me that! Stop calling me *Mr Francis* all the time. Can't you see—' He stopped. Of course she couldn't see – he didn't even know himself what he meant. He didn't understand these strange, conflicting emotions that wrenched at his breast. They were like no experience he had ever had before. He didn't even like them – yet he knew that he would treasure them later. Just as he had done every morning, every day, when he had met Rebecca in the library before anyone else was up.

But they had never been as strong as this before. Never shaken him as he had been shaken this morning – ever since he had first touched her, first taken her in his arms.

He was aware of Rebecca staring at him, her face white, her eyes huge and almost black.

'I'm sorry,' he muttered and then, unable to help

himself, took two long strides across the room to kneel before her. His arms went around her as if without his volition; he caught her against him and buried his face in her neck, holding her head against his to prevent any escape. He groaned against the soft skin and kissed it.

'Rebecca, I'm sorry. Forgive me. I just—' He felt her tremble against him and thrust her away as swiftly as he had drawn her against him. 'I don't know what's come over me this morning,' he muttered. 'I think I'd better go.' He stood up and looked down at her. 'Don't look at me like that – please. I've told you – you've nothing to fear from me.' And, before he could succumb to the desire to lift her from her position on the floor, before he could clasp her again, he turned and strode from the room.

Bemused, Rebecca stayed where she was for several long, breathless minutes. Then, moving as stiffly as if she were an old woman, she turned and picked up her brush and began again to do her work.

Sarah's wedding took place just before Christmas, and when it was over the whole household breathed a sigh of relief. The preparations had swept through the house like a hurricane, catching up everything that lay in their path and whisking it into a turmoil that had everyone reeling.

'Is this house ever going to be back to normal?' Jeremiah asked as he hunted yet again for papers that had been tidied away. 'I thought I gave orders that my desk was to be left untouched. Yet someone has pushed all these letters in – letters not even addressed to me – and I can't find anything. Who's been meddling?'

'The letters are mine, Jeremiah,' Isabella said,

taking them from him. 'I had to put them in your desk – mine has been filled with invitation cards, replies and letters concerning the wedding. These are ordinary correspondence. And all you have to do to find your own papers is to look. They're all there, just as they were. Nobody has disturbed them.'

'No, simply buried them,' he grumbled. 'Well, now that Sarah is safely married and in her own home, I suppose we can hope to return to our own lives again. If we can remember what they were before all this began.'

'Don't complain so much,' his wife said, drifting over to the mantelpiece and fiddling with the ornaments. 'You know you were proud of Sarah on her wedding day. She looked extremely beautiful. And she's made a good match.' She frowned a little. 'I wish I could be as hopeful about Isabel.'

'Isabel? Why, she's scarcely more than a child – you're surely not thinking of marrying her off yet?'

'She's almost eighteen, Jeremiah. Fully marriageable, although she makes no effort in that direction.' Isabella sighed. 'I worry about that child. She seems to have no idea of the importance of taking trouble with herself. She seems happier wearing her old gowns, the ones she kept for the schoolroom, than dressing in the new fashions. And she doesn't appear to have any understanding of how a young lady should comport herself. There are times when she's a real hoyden. Why, only yesterday I saw her running across the garden with Francis as though they were both still children. Yet a few days ago they were squabbling. I really think you should have a talk with that young man. It simply isn't suitable.'

'Oh, I think you're over-anxious,' Jeremiah said

absently, sorting through his papers. 'Isabel and Francis have always been close – why shouldn't they have a little fun?'

'But they have no right to be close,' Isabella said sharply. 'They aren't even cousins. And it is unsuitable – quite unsuitable. It could cause quite a scandal and ruin Isabel's chances of marriage, should anyone outside the family happen to see them behaving so freely together.'

'Nonsense—'

'It isn't nonsense! No, I think that now that Sarah is settled, we should concern ourselves very much with our youngest daughter. I have been looking around for a husband for her. She'll need someone who can control her, someone with a firm hand.' Isabella pursed her lips. 'An older man, perhaps.'

Jeremiah stopped what he was doing and stared at her. A sudden picture rose in his mind, of himself driving to the church with his younger daughter at his side, dressed in all her wedding finery – and going to a husband perhaps as old as himself. A man who was past his first youth, who would take her because he needed a wife, who would exercise that firm hand Isabella spoke of and tame her – if she could be tamed. Who would subdue that lively personality, dim the light in her eyes and drive the laughter from her lips.

'Isabel does not need to marry well,' he said, slamming the lid of his desk and taking a bundle of papers over to the table. 'She does not need to marry at all – unless and until she wishes. Forget your machinations for a while, wife, and be glad that she is happy as she is. There will be a husband for her, but I would like him to be one of her own choosing – not ours.'

Isabella opened her mouth, and then closed it again. The look on Jeremiah's face was implacable, his dark eyes hard as he fixed them on her face. She hesitated, then shrugged slightly and turned away.

'As you wish, husband. You are, after all, master in your own home. But I trust that you will not live to regret your decision. No woman likes to be an old maid, and Isabel may not thank you for this. However—' She gathered up her skirts and walked to the door '—I am sure you know best. And now I am going to have my rest. All this discussion has left me feeling quite fatigued.'

She left the room, her back straight and dignified. Jeremiah watched her go. Then, with a sigh, he turned back to his papers.

Isabella was not the only person concerned about her daughter's future.

Vivian, the father of yet another baby girl, had been observing the relationship between his sister and cousin with increasing disquiet. And when his mother spoke to him about her worries, he listened with all the attention and agreement that she had wanted from her husband.

'Of course it isn't suitable,' he declared when they had admired the new baby and retired from Maria's boudoir to his own drawing room. 'Francis must be made to understand that he's jeopardising Isabel's future by allowing her to behave so freely with him. As a matter of fact, Mother, he has spoken to me about this – he seemed uneasy about the situation himself. But he seems also to think that he can continue to be Isabel's friend, as if they were still children. He doesn't appear to understand the risks. In some ways, he's still very much a boy. I suppose it's growing up with Uncle Geoffrey, who's hardly worldly.'

'No, indeed.' Isabella looked at him hopefully. 'You understand so much, Vivian – will you speak to him? He may take notice of you. All he seems to want to discuss when he sees me is the problems of one of my housemaids, if you please.'

'One of your housemaids? Why, what interest does Francis have in the servants?'

'Well may you ask! I confess I find it difficult to understand that young man. We all know about the living conditions of the working classes – squalid, depraved, drunken as they are.' Isabella spoke with distaste. 'But they are not a subject for drawing room conversation – and I apologise for bringing up the subject in your drawing room, dear Vivian. If we were not alone, I would never think of doing so. But Francis sees nothing wrong in drawing such things to my attention, and even demanding help. As if I did not do quite enough already.'

'You certainly do more than enough,' Vivian said warmly. 'But tell me – what exactly has Francis being saying? And what does this housemaid have to do with him?'

'That I should like to know too, but he doesn't see fit to explain to me how he comes to know so much about her. I've questioned both Susan and Mrs Atkins, and both say there's nothing to complain of in her behaviour, she does her work well and gives no trouble – but I've warned them to watch her closely. I want no trouble with maids in my house.' Isabella paused to allow her indignation to subside before continuing. 'The girl is the sister of the two who were involved with that murder down in Butts' carpet shop – you may recall it, Vivian, I don't choose to dwell on such unpleasantness – and now, as one might expect, the parents are virtually destitute and looking to her for help.' She took a small square of lace from her sleeve and dabbed her nose with it. 'Really, it's all quite disagreeable, and what Francis expects *me* to do about it I cannot—'

'Just a moment, Mother,' Vivian interrupted. 'You say one of your maids is the sister of the two who killed the weaver – Jabez Gast?'

'So I believe. Your memory is remarkably good – it must be five or six years ago now. But of course, the Butts' carpet shop is yours, isn't it? Your father settled it on you as a twenty-first birthday gift. So you have reason to remember them, since they robbed you of one of your best men.'

'I have reason indeed,' Vivian said grimly. 'And which of the housemaids is this girl, their sister? How long has she been working for you?'

'Oh, almost ever since it happened. That's what I mean, you see,' Isabella said, not noticing Vivian's reaction. 'I've done more than anyone could reasonably expect of me. I've taken her in – she was no more than a child, far too young to be of any real use, but you know my soft heart, Vivian. And Mrs Hudd assured me that the mother was of good character – she worked here years ago as a maid herself. Even so, not many mistresses would have done as I did and given her a place. Why, I doubt if she earned her place here for a good year, she was so small when she came. I believe she started as a scullerymaid, and should have thought herself fortunate.'

'So she's been in the house for several years. And now she's a housemaid. I must have seen her. What's her name, mother? Is she the plump one with the saucy eyes?'

'Vivian, really!' But the admonishment was only fleeting and softened by her glance. 'No, Rebecca is dark and rather thin. Certainly not saucy – in fact she seems pleasantly modest, but there's a look in her eyes on occasion . . . I would not entirely trust her, Vivian, and that's the truth. She makes me . . . uneasy.'

'Rebecca,' Vivian said musingly. 'And she's been in the house since before I married Maria. Well, well, well.' He sat thoughtfully for a few minutes. 'And what does Francis ask you to do?'

'Why, help her parents. The father's mortally ill, evidently, and the mother having to support and care for him. But really, Vivian, what is so different about their story? There must be thousands in like case – why should they be singled out for help? Especially after what happened. If they'd brought their children up to be God-fearing Christians, that terrible business with the weaver would never have happened and they would have had another daughter and a son to help them now. But it's no use telling them that, of course – they've barely heard of Christianity, people like that. And Francis is so sentimental, he can't see the ugly truth.' She paused. 'But why are we discussing this? It's Francis and Isabel I wanted to talk to you about.'

'And quite rightly so,' Vivian declared. 'I'll speak to him at the earliest opportunity, Mother. He sounds thoroughly confused to me, but I'll soon set him on the right path.' He pulled in his upper lip and frowned again. 'Have you thought that it might be a good thing if Francis were to take a little trip away somewhere for a while?'

'A trip away?'

'Yes – why not? I could take him to London with me, it's time he understood that side of the business.

And then he'd be away from both Isabel and this housemaid. Two quite unsuitable attachments.' He smiled at her. 'Two problems solved. A good solution?'

'It would be, indeed.' Isabella gazed at her son. 'I knew you were the right person to talk to, Vivian. You see things the right way – you understand my problems. You're a great comfort to me, my dear.'

'I'm glad.' He gave her a warm smile and then came over to kiss her cheek. 'Leave it to me, Mother. And don't worry about either Francis or Isabel any more. Now – tell me all about Sarah's new house.'

They talked for another half-hour, until Isabella declared that it was time for her to go. Vivian went to call the carriage for her. He tucked her in with furs and rugs, kissed her again and watched as she was driven away. Then he went back into the house, his face thoughtful.

So . . . there was definitely an attachment of some kind between Francis and Isabel, sufficiently strong to worry his mother. In which case, it must worry him as well. Isabel was a strong-minded young woman, and the apple of her father's eye, the spoiled youngest child. If she had set her sights on their cousin, she might well get her own way – whatever Francis felt about it now. He was fond enough of her to think it a good match. There was a real risk there. And with this latest child turning out to be yet another daughter . . .

The situation with the housemaid was interesting, but little more. Most young men formed some kind of liaison with a maid or two, if not more – in Vivian's view, that was what pretty young housemaids were for. All the same, it might be turned to good account. A little scandal wouldn't come amiss. She would be a good card to keep up his sleeve, anyway.

Vivian determined to look out for the housemaid next time he went to his mother's house. He hadn't forgotten that she was the sister of Bessie and Tom Himley. He would like very much to know just what had happened to those two. And to the money he had given them.

During the last few tumultuous weeks before Sarah's wedding, Rebecca had little opportunity to visit her parents.

Her anxiety showed on her face, bringing lines of worry to her forehead and a tremble to her full lips. More than once she forgot some small task and Polly quickly did it for her, or accepted blame when Susan or Mrs Hudd began to scold. But eventually she took matters into her own hands.

'It int Rebecca's fault,' she explained when Mrs Atkins complained that the housemaid's box had not been put away in its proper place and that cinders had been left in the pail instead of being returned to the fireplace. 'She's worried sick about her mam and dad. And she haven't had a chance to go and see them for nigh on three weeks now.'

'Is her father still poorly, then?' the cook asked, rolling pastry on the big wooden table.

'You might as well ask if he's still alive,' Polly said. 'He'll never be anything but poorly while he draws breath. Becky told me she didn't expect to see him again, and that was last time she went. He could be dead now, for all she'd know.'

'Well, it's no easier for the rest of us,' Mrs Atkins said sharply. 'I haven't had my time off either, what with this wedding and Christmas and all. Still, she could slip home for half an hour in the evening, when the family's had their supper, if that'd be any help. It might ease her mind a bit to see them.' She wiped flour from her hands and went to the larder. 'Look, there's a few eggs here, she could take those. And a bit of cold meat, and some potatoes. Little enough, but I can't go giving away the mistress's food to all and sundry.' She put the food into a basket and left it in a corner. 'You tell her she can go this evening. But she'll have to finish her jobs first, mind. Nobody else is going to do her work for her.'

'No, of course not. Thanks, Mrs Atkins – she'll be that pleased.' Polly finished putting away the brooms she had been using. 'I know she's been fretting.'

'Well, let's hope she'll do her work a bit better once she's seen 'em.' The cook cut out a large circle of pastry and laid it in a pie-dish. 'And now give young Ruth a hand with those apples, she's been paring them long enough and I wants 'em for the pie. It's got to go in the oven now or it'll never be cooked in time.'

Polly did as she was told, humming cheerfully as she helped the little scullerymaid with her work. She was looking forward to giving Rebecca the news – although she was well aware of the fact that nothing could cheer her friend up. The situation with Fanny and William was too grim, too desperate, for anyone to gain comfort from seeing them. But at least it would lift the burden of guilt, for a while anyway.

Polly's own parents had died years ago, in circumstances not so very different. In her experience it was something most people had to endure, watching the family sicken and being unable to help them. Death was commonplace.

All the same, it hurt. Just because you knew only a few of your babies would grow up, it didn't mean you weren't going to suffer when they died. And knowing that your parents were too exhausted, too weakened by years of toil, poor food and bad working conditions, to be able to resist disease, didn't mean that you could watch their pain and not suffer along with them.

But pain, hunger and suffering were the lot of the poor. It would never change.

It was dark and cold as Rebecca hurried along the street, on her way back from the cottage. Sleet lashed against her face, blending with the tears that already wet her cheeks. A thin wind knifed between the buildings, slicing through the shawl she had gathered around her and numbing her bare fingers. She slipped on the icy cobbles, almost fell and then gave a gasp of surprise and fear as she felt strong arms catch and hold her.

'It's all right.' The voice was one she knew, but it didn't lessen her fear. 'Don't struggle so, my pretty little bird,' it went on smoothly. 'I'm not going to hurt you. It's Rebecca, isn't it?'

'Yes,' she whispered, straining her eyes to see through the darkness. 'Mr – Mr Vivian?'

He chuckled. 'Who else? I've been waiting for you – you've been out, haven't you? Does your mistress know?'

'No.' Rebecca shook her head. 'Please, Mr Vivian – please don't tell her. It'd get Mrs Atkins into trouble, too. I've only slipped out to see my mam and dad – they're both sick and I haven't had any time off for near a month.'

'All right, spare me the tears,' he growled, and pulled her into the shelter of a nearby building. He held her firmly against his side and she realised that he was fumbling with a key. She stiffened in fear. What did he intend to do? The answer was all too plain and she trembled against his arm.

216

'Please, Mr Vivian, I must get back—'

'Not until we've had a little talk. And I don't intend to have it out here, in this weather.' He had the door open now and thrust her inside. Terrified, Rebecca staggered and almost fell; but this time he made no effort to save her. He closed the door and a moment later the darkness was pierced by the light of a lantern. He held it up and looked closely at her face.

'Yes, you're an attractive little piece,' he said coolly. 'Not a bit like your sister, though, are you?'

Rebecca stared at him. A deeper cold than that caused by the weather seemed to invade her body and spread through her bones. 'My . . . sister, sir?'

'Don't pretend with me!' he said sharply. 'We both know about your sister – Bessie, was it? – and your brother Tom. They killed my best weaver between them and then escaped.' He bent closer, holding the lantern frighteningly near to her face. 'Where did they go, hey? What happened to them? Don't tell me you don't know.'

Rebecca shook her head. Why was Mr Vivian interested in her brother and sister? Why had he taken the trouble to find out that she was out that evening, that she would be coming back along that street – why had he waited for her?

She thought of the scene she had left in her parents' cottage – William, lying on the pile of straw and rags in one corner, barely warmed by the few coals that smouldered on the hearth, Fanny crouched beside him, feeding him gruel that he could hardly swallow. The money that Francis had left them had almost gone; William's loom, the symbol of the independence he held so dear, had been sold; and the cottage was empty of any other furniture.

'It's the workhouse for us now,' Fanny had told

Rebecca. 'There's naught left. I just hope he can slip away quiet afore they comes for us. It'd kill him, ending up there.'

Rebecca saw no irony in her mother's words. She understood the fierce independence that made her father want to die in his own home, poor as it was.

'I've brought a few things,' she said and took them from the basket. 'Try to get him to take some milk, Mam, and an egg. It'll do him good.'

'Nothing will do him good now,' Fanny said, and she looked at the food with empty eyes. 'You might as well say goodbye to him now, girl, for he'll not see many more days.'

Rebecca bent over her father. She looked at his grey, wasted face, at the body that had once been so tall and strong and now lay curled like a baby, thin and frail, the knees drawn up to the chin, the head ducked down into the bony chest. The gruel that Fanny was feeding him dribbled from his mouth and he made small lapping movements with his lips. His eyes were closed.

'Dad,' she said in a low voice. 'Dad, can you hear me? It's Becky. Becky, your little girl.'

He made no answer, but she thought she saw the eyelid flicker slightly. She felt for his hand and held it, shocked by the coldness of the skin that hung so loosely around the bones.

'Remember when I used to draw for you?' she said. 'Remember how we'd work together, day after day – remember the carpet we made together?'

She waited anxiously for a reply. There was no movement in the hand that she held in hers. She stroked the dry fingers, thinking of the way they had moved, swiftly and surely, amongst the bobbins and yarns, the way he had manipulated the shuttle, the rapidity with which he had worked.

A faint, rasping rattle sounded in the scrawny throat and she bent closer. His mouth worked; a few gasps came from his lips and spittle drooled between his gums. Rebecca bent closer, her heart aching.

'Bess,' he muttered at last. 'Bess . . . our Bess . . .'

'She's coming soon, Dad,' Rebecca said softly. 'She hasn't forgotten you. She's coming. And Tom.' He would never live to know that they could not come home again, ever. 'Tom and Bess will be here soon.'

'Tom,' he whispered. 'Tom and Bess . . . And our Becky, she's a good girl.' She realised that he did not know who she was, didn't even know she was there. 'Ah, a good girl. A good . . .' His voice trailed away and his eyelids fluttered again and then closed. For a moment, she thought he had gone, but he was breathing still, light and shallow breaths. When she touched his chest, she could feel the fluttering of his heart.

'I'll have to go now, Mam,' she said, realising how long she had been here.

'Ah. I know.'

'I wish I could stay,' Rebecca said wretchedly. 'I hate leaving you here, like this. Look, I'll try to get out again tomorrow. I'll tell Cook – Mrs Hudd – they'll let me come, I'm sure. And maybe Mr Francis will help again.' She quivered a little at the thought of asking him for help. Since that morning in the library when he had held her, she had not seen him. He had not come to the library again, and she was unhappily certain that he had regretted his own behaviour and been shocked by hers. To approach him now would take a good deal of courage . . . but if there were any chance at all that he might help, she must do it.

'It's all right, girl,' Fanny said. 'It's summat we all have to go through and your dad's near the end of the road now. Don't you lose your place over it. You go on, now, and don't forget to thank Mrs Atkins for the eggs and that.'

'No, Mam, I won't.' Rebecca stood up, then bent to give her mother a kiss. She had looked once more at the figure that lay huddled so small and frail on the tumbled sacks, and then turned and stumbled to the door.

After all that, it was too much to bear when she was caught by Vivian and dragged into the dark, empty warehouse. She stared at him in the light of the lantern, wondering again just what was his purpose in bringing her here. Why should he be so interested in Bessie and Tom? And, suddenly, she was tired of it all, sick of the poverty and despair, sick of the glossy, well-fed faces of the wealthy and prosperous. Sick of the life that had condemned her to slave as her mother and father had slaved, and for what purpose? For what end? So that Vivian and his like could grow ever plumper, ever sleeker – and she and her fellow-servants end their days as paupers, too poor even to die with dignity?

'Well, then, tell me what you want,' she said and her voice was ragged with anger, weariness and a reck-less misery. 'Do whatever it is you want to do, and then let me go.' Her eyes were haunted shadows under the lantern's unsteady light. 'There's nothing you can do that could make things worse,' she said and believed it. 'And nothing you can do to Bessie nei-ther – though what she's got to do with you, I don't understand. You didn't even know her.'

She looked up at him and remembered Bessie's giggling remarks when she'd first gone to work at Butts' carpet shop, the way she'd rolled her eyes and bridled as she described Mr Vivian, the handsome young owner. The way she'd sighed and blushed and twined her hair into curls; the way she'd hurried to work on the chance that he might be there.

'You *didn't* know her,' she said slowly, 'did you?'

Chapter Ten

'You didn't know my sister,' Rebecca repeated. 'Why should you? She was just a draw-girl – no interest to you.'

Vivian laughed and she flinched at the sound. There was a harshness to it, a hint of cruelty. 'You think so? Many's the draw-girl I've enjoyed knowing – though your sister wasn't one of them, as it happens. Though she would have been . . .' He set his lantern down on a box, then gripped Rebecca's shawl, jerking her closer to him, and glared down into her white face. 'That girl owes me something,' he growled through his teeth. 'Money, if nothing more. And I never forget a debt. Now – where is she?'

'Bessie owes *you* money?' Rebecca stared at him, bewildered. 'But – how can she? Why would you give her money?' She tried to imagine and shook her head. 'She didn't even get her wages for that week,' she said at last.

Vivian laughed again, louder than before. 'Wages? You think she should have been paid wages for killing my weaver?'

'No, but – she *didn't* kill him. It was an accident.' She saw the look in his eyes and stopped, knowing that whatever happened she must not let him know where Bessie and Tom were. He had a grudge against them, it was plain – and it was well known that Mr Vivian's grudges were always paid for.

'So you know where they are,' he said softly, and twisted his hand in her shawl so that it tightened around her shoulders. One edge bit into her neck. 'Tell me.'

Rebecca shook her head. 'I don't. Nobody knows. They just disappeared that night and—'

'And you never heard another word.' His voice was still soft, disbelieving. Rebecca's glance dropped. 'Tell me the truth!'

'It is the truth, sir,' she said desperately. 'Please – please, Mr Vivian, let me go. I'm going to be terribly late and Mrs Hudd will be angry – she'll never let me out again. Please.'

'Just what are you doing out this late anyway?' he asked, diverted for a moment. 'I thought the maids were only allowed an afternoon a fortnight? Are you sure Mrs Hudd even knows you're out?'

'Yes, sir, she does, she gave me permission. My father's dying and I haven't been able to visit him and my mam with all the wedding – and if I'm late back, she won't let me go again.' She lifted her hand and tried to pull her shawl from his grasp. '*Please*, Mr Vivian.'

Vivian shook his head. 'Oh no, my pretty one – you don't get away that easily.' His eyes moved over her. 'In fact, it might be worth my while to keep you here a little longer . . . after we've finished this little bit of business. You're a handsome little piece, with those big brown eyes and that mouth . . . and your hair coming loose the way it is.' He lifted his free hand and stroked her head, pulling at the curls that had escaped from their pins. 'Hmmm . . . yes, this could be quite rewarding. I wonder why I've never noticed you before.'

Rebecca struggled frantically. 'Mr Vivian – please—'

'They all say that, at one stage or another,' he

observed as if to a third person. 'Often at every stage
. . . Well, we'll think about it. I haven't overmuch
time myself, tonight. And I think you'd pay for taking a little time.' A smile curved in his dark face.
'Meanwhile – that brother and sister of yours. The
murderers.'

'No! They're not murderers.' She shook her head
violently. 'They didn't kill Jabez deliberately. It was
an accident – he attacked Bess and Tom came in and
fought him. It was Jabez who picked up the wire –
they don't even know how it happened, but there was
nothing they could do—' She felt Vivian's grip tighten
and stumbled into silence, staring at him with wide
eyes. 'Let me go!'

'Let you go? After what you've just said?' The
shawl was cutting into her neck now, its edge almost
as sharp as the wire that had killed Jabez. 'You *do*
know where they are. Tell me.' He shook her hard.
'*Tell me!*'

She shook her head. 'I don't understand. Why do
you want to know? What was our Bess to you? How
could she owe you money?'

'You don't need to know that. Just believe me. She
owes me money – she and your brother. A tidy sum,
too. And I mean to have it back – or payment in kind,
I don't much care which.' His eyes glittered in the
lantern light. 'Now – tell me where they are. And
don't pretend any more, or it'll be the worse for you.'

'I don't *know*,' Rebecca repeated. 'We did have a
letter – but it was years ago. And it didn't give us any
address. London, that's all we knew.' She lifted her
shoulders. 'I can't tell you any more than that, Mr
Vivian, no matter what you do to me.' And I wouldn't
if I could, she added silently.

He looked down at her and she met his eyes

steadily. Her own were wet with tears of pain and misery, and she could feel the drops on her cheeks. But she did not look away and after a few moments he grunted.

'Very well. You don't know where they are – I'll accept that. In which case—' the hand he held against her head slid down to stroke her throat, and she shivered. '—you'll probably be willing to pay their debts yourself . . . won't you.'

'But I don't have any money.' Anger welled up in her. 'I give all I earn to my mam. I told you – my father's dying, they need it, I can't—'

'I'm not concerned with money.' His face was very near, his breath hot on her cheek. 'Payment in kind will do very well.' She felt his fingers tighten on her throat and drew in her breath. 'It's what your sister would have given me in any case,' he muttered, and pushed his mouth against hers.

Furiously she struggled against him, trying to wrench her mouth away, twisting and turning in his grasp. But he only gripped his arms more tightly about her, crushing her against his big, muscular body, and she knew that she had no hope against him. His mouth was bruising her lips, his teeth nipping the soft flesh, his tongue thrust against hers like a living animal with its own energy, its own strength. Disgust matched her anger and she found new strength of her own to fight against him; but he only laughed deep in his throat and held her more firmly.

'So you're a fighter, my pretty one,' he muttered, his teeth scraping her mouth. 'Well, I enjoy a battle myself – and I *always* win.' One hand slid round her waist, pushing her shawl aside, and fastened around her breast. 'Yes, you're a nice little handful. I can understand Cousin Francis's interest.' He laughed as

226

Rebecca gasped again. 'You didn't know I knew about that, did you? You probably thought no one knew. But when a man starts to take an interest in a housemaid's family problems – well, there's only one deduction to be made. I take it he's done nothing about it, yet?'

'I don't know what you mean.' Rebecca stopped struggling to take in this new idea. 'Mr Francis and me – there's nothing, he's never touched—' She stopped abruptly, remembering that last morning in the library, the last time she had seen Francis alone, when he had held her in his arms. But so gently, so tenderly, so unlike the way in which Mr Vivian was holding her now. New tears came to her eyes as she thought of him, of the difference between the two men.

Vivian laughed. 'So! But he hasn't taken you yet, is that it? Well, it'll be an added pleasure to go where he hasn't yet trod. Will you tell him, I wonder? Or shall it be a secret between us?' He bent his head to hers again and Rebecca jerked back. 'Stop that, wench,' he growled. 'There's nothing you can do about this. I've had as many women as you've had hot dinners, and some of them have had to be forced a bit at first. It makes no difference in the end – I'll enjoy it, even if you don't. But it's much better fun if you enjoy it, too.'

Rebecca felt his lips on hers again, hot and wet, and rage blazed up within her. Why should he think he had the right to treat her like this? She would *not* let him have his way – not without a struggle. The thought of him, the feel of him, filled her with repugnance; it was as if slugs were crawling over her, creeping into every part of her body, seeking out every crevice, searching amongst her most secret places to

227

sully the soul that she could not hide. She must fight – and fight to the end. Vivian might win, but he would not leave unmarked.

With a strength that she had not been aware that she possessed, she twisted again in Vivian's harsh grasp. Her elbow caught him in the ribs and he grunted and slackened his grip momentarily. But it was long enough for Rebecca to pull back a little, long enough for her to lift her arms and thrust them against his chest, long enough for her to raise one knee and jab it hard against his body. Instantly, she felt him jerk away from her, exclaiming with sudden pain. She barely heard his obscenity as she jabbed again, making the same effective contact, and when Vivian dropped away from her she followed it up with a kick on his shin. Her boot met his leg with a satisfying crack and Vivian swore again.

'You little bitch! You vicious little bitch! You're as wild as your murderess of a sister.' He reached for her again but Rebecca dodged out of his way, fumbling along the wall for the warehouse door. 'You realise you could lose your position over this,' he snarled, and she felt his finger brush against her in the darkness. 'My mother would turn you into the street as soon as look at you. Housemaids like you are two a penny—'

'Let her, then!' Rebecca panted as she shrank away from him. Where was the door? 'I'll be glad to be out of the house and away from you—' She barely knew what she was saying, but at that moment the bleakness of life with no position, no roof over her head, seemed preferable to a life sharing a roof with Vivian Pagnel. 'Let her turn me away.'

Vivian paused. He was still clearly in pain, his voice muffled and cracked when he spoke again. But he had regained a little of his menace and her skin crept as she heard his words.

'On second thoughts, it might be more interesting to keep you about,' he muttered, and she could feel him coming closer. 'I've waited a long time for payment from that sister of yours – and if I can't have her, you'll do as well.' He reached out again and Rebecca twisted away and found the door at last. 'Don't think you can escape me,' he said as she dragged it open. 'I know where you are – I can find you any time. And I will, you little vixen . . . You'll regret what you did tonight, believe me. You'll regret it as long as you live . . .'

Rebecca flung him one last glance of loathing and scuttled past into the icy darkness. Her only concern now was to get back to Pagnel House, back to the safe warmth of the kitchen where Polly and the others would be wondering where she was. Whether they would believe that she had been attacked by some unknown assailant – for she could never tell them what had really happened – she did not know. But she could feel blood on her lips and a stinging on her face, and she knew that there must be bruises on her body.

And whether they believed her or not, there would be work to do, chores to carry out that would soothe her with their familiarity and prevent her, for a while at least, from dwelling on what had happened. Later, with luck, she would be too exhausted to do more than fall into bed and sleep.

But eventually, the memories must return to haunt her. The memories of Vivian Pagnel's hot lips against hers, his arms hard about her, his fingers cruel on her breast and throat. The memories of her mother, sitting so patiently beside the shrunken body of her dying husband. And the questions.

* * *

Francis woke early, as usual. He lit his candle and lay staring at the ceiling and resisting, as had also become usual, the impulse to get up and go down to the library.

He had acquired the habit of early rising from Geoffrey and continued it when he had come to Pagnel House. There was little time for reading once the family day had begun. Jeremiah liked to discuss the business with him – indeed, Francis suspected that this was the real reason why his uncle had insisted that he move in with them; with Vivian married and about to move into his own home, Jeremiah would have been surrounded by women. And if Jeremiah were not there, Isabella would fill the air with chatter about fashions, calls and domestic matters which she would discuss with endless enthusiasm with Sarah. Now Sarah had gone too and, with only Isabel left, the conversation was more petulant, with attention being continually drawn to Isabel's faults and comparison made with her sister's virtues.

'I do wish you would find a more becoming style for your hair, dear,' Isabella would remark. 'It looks so plain, drawn back in that way. You ought to have curls – don't you agree, Jeremiah? And couldn't you wear a more attractive gown during the day? That one is positively dowdy.'

'It's good enough to wear at home – and I've only had it for a few months, anyway. You liked it well enough when it was new.'

'Yes, but fashions change so quickly and those sleeves were never the best feature of that one.' Isabella moved her playing cards around the table. Playing Patience seemed to be her only comfort these days. 'And where are you going now? I'd hoped we could have a game together.'

'I want to do some reading.' Isabel, halfway to the door, glanced at Francis. 'There was a book you were telling me about – I hoped you would come and show me where it is.'

'Reading!' Isabella said before Francis could reply. 'I'd have thought you'd be thankful to finish with that, once you were out of the schoolroom. Yet you seem to do more than ever these days. Oh well, run along if you must. You'll be poor company anyway. Your mind always seems to be somewhere else. I don't understand it. Your sister was never like this.'

'But I'm not Sarah, am I,' Isabel muttered when she and Francis were outside the door. 'I'm Isabel – a very poor substitute. Do *you* ever feel you're being used at a stopgap for someone else, Francis?'

He glanced at her, surprised by the bitterness in her tone. 'Sometimes, yes. But I know Vivian's of more importance to my aunt than I am – it's only natural. He's her son.'

'And she never stops reminding you of the fact.' Isabel led the way along the passage to the library and opened the door. They went inside and Francis looked involuntarily at the fireplace, almost as if he expected to see Rebecca kneeling there. But there was nobody; only a brightly burning coal fire to prove that someone had been in the room recently. He wondered which of the housemaids it had been.

He had found Rebecca's face increasingly in his mind lately. Even before the morning when he had taken her in his arms and tried to give her comfort, only to find himself swept by an almost overwhelming desire for her, she had crept into his thoughts at unexpected moments. A glimpse of her about the house had been enough to distract him from his business; the sight of her coming into a room with a bucket of coals and kneeling to sweep the hearth would dry the words on his lips. When she helped Susan at table during a dinner party, he found her presence almost unbearable, and he would compare the flushed, laughing faces of the female guests with her quiet deportment and wonder why it was that someone so clearly a lady should be born in poverty while those who would never be anything but vulgar should consider themselves her betters.

There were times when Francis wondered why it was that a simple housemaid should exert such a powerful attraction over him. Why should her quiet presence, her unassuming manners, mean so much more to him than the flirtatious glances and the confident prattle of the young ladies who visited the house? Why should her slender figure, dressed only in a plain uniform, please him more than the frills and laces of the dresses he saw daily amongst his aunt's friends?

It had little, he thought, to do with Rebecca's looks, much as these delighted him. Her quiet eyes told of a quiet mind, her firm mouth would twitch into a smile that went to his heart, to sudden laughter that brought light to his life. There was strength in her, an integrity that called to something in himself. There was something he could not define; something that matched his soul.

Isabel crossed to a chair and sank down in it, staring into the fire. She looked up at Francis and smiled.

'Why don't you sit down? Let's be quiet together for a while.'

Francis hesitated. 'Didn't you want me to show you a book?'

'Oh, Francis, don't be so simple. Of course I didn't. I just wanted to get away from Mother for a while – and to be alone with you.' Some of the old mischief glinted in her eyes. 'What a good thing we're cousins. Otherwise we wouldn't be trusted to be alone like this.'

Francis shifted uneasily. 'Isabel, I'm not sure—'

'Oh, don't be pompous.' She stared at him, her eyes very wide and violet in the firelight. 'You're as bad as Vivian. Do you know what he said to me the other day? That he doesn't think we should be such friends! As if we could stop, just like that.' She stood up suddenly and came close. 'We'll always be friends, Francis, won't we?'

'Of course we will.' He wanted to move away but dared not, for fear of hurting her. 'We'll always be friends,' he repeated.

'And perhaps more than friends?' Her voice was barely more than a whisper. She laid her hand on his sleeve and lifted her face. 'Francis . . . do you remember the conversation we had on our way home from church one Sunday morning?'

He looked down at her. He remembered clearly – all too clearly. But he shook his head. 'We've had so many conversations—'

Isabel's eyes darkened with anger and she gave his arm a little slap. 'But not like that one! Francis, don't pretend with me. You know quite well what I mean. We talked about marrying – about having our own home, where we could live as we pleased without others interfering—'

'*You* talked about it,' Francis said uncomfortably. 'I thought it was just make-believe.'

'Perhaps it was – at first.' A shadow crossed her face. 'But when I'd said it – when I thought about it – it seemed real to me. And since then – I've thought about it more and more.' She slid her hand down to his wrist and gripped it with strong, slender fingers. 'Francis, it would be ideal. We know each other well – we've always been friends. We could be happy together, I know it. And what else is there for me? Marriage to some man Mother thinks "suitable" – some elderly widower, probably, whom I'll hate. Or else a lifetime of embroidery and cards and silly, *silly* conversation about nothing. I should go mad, Francis.'

Her voice throbbed. She gazed up at him with wide eyes and, as she spoke, reached up to lay her other hand on his shoulder. He felt her fingers cool against his neck, and then she was drawing his head down to hers, rising on her toes to touch her lips against his.

Francis drew in a quick breath. He was aware of the scent of her, rising to encompass him, musky and potent in his nostrils. He felt the softness of her breasts pressing against his body, the slenderness of her waist as his hands moved automatically to hold her. Her hair was like silk against his cheek and her mouth whispered over his.

For a full minute, she clung to him, moving her body against his and seeking his mouth with an urgency that shook him. She trembled in his arms and he heard a faint whimper deep in her throat.

Francis felt a dark, warm flood of sensation flow through his body. His senses leapt to match her urgency. He gripped her against him – and then, coming swiftly in the wake of that initial response, he was shaken by a revulsion of feeling so deep and sharp that he dropped his arms and stepped quickly back. Only a deeper desire, that she must not be hurt, prevented him from thrusting her away. As it was, the look in her eyes as she opened them and fixed them on her face, cut straight to his heart.

'Francis—'

'No,' he said as she moved towards him again. 'No, Isabel, don't. It's not possible between us. It can't be – ever.'

'But why not? Because we're cousins? But there's no—'

'It isn't simply that.' He looked at her, wondering whether to tell her the truth. Wouldn't she see it as an even more powerful advantage to her cause? 'And we aren't cousins, Isabel – not truly. You know that. My father and mother – they're not my parents. They adopted me as a baby, took me for their own. Whoever I am, I'm not your cousin.'

'Then there's no reason—' she began eagerly, just as he had feared. But he shook his head again.

'There is, Isabel. I don't know what it is – but there can't be what you want between us. I want you as my friend – but nothing more.' He stopped, knowing how this must be hurting her. 'I'm sorry, Isabel,' he said and, moved by a deep pity, a desire to comfort her, stepped forward to take her in his arms again.

At that moment, he heard the door open. But Isabel ignored it. She flung herself against him, pressing her body against his with a fervour that almost had him staggering. He caught at her waist to steady them both, and she lifted her face to his again and kissed him with small, frantic kisses. Desperately, Francis held her away from him. He turned his head towards the door, fearing to see his uncle or aunt, knowing that if he and Isabel were caught in this compromising position they would certainly be forced to marry.

But the door was already closing behind a quiet figure. And as he looked, he saw the dark material of a housemaid's uniform, with the white bow of an apron tied around a narrow waist.

Rebecca.

235

The news came just after breakfast, on a bitter February morning with snow falling steadily on icy roads. The kitchen range was giving trouble and Billy and Oddjob were dismantling it, sooty pieces scattered over the floor. Mrs Atkins was nearly hysterical, Susan in one of her worst tempers and even Mrs Hudd's usual composure shaken. Whenever the kitchen door opened, an icy draught screamed through the big, cold basement.

'Oh, who's that now?' Susan snapped as there was yet another knock. 'Polly, see who it is – and *don't* keep the door open, it's like the Arctic in here already. Billy, if you make any more mess with all that soot I'll pack my bags and go. Well, Polly, what is it? Don't just stand there, girl – open your mouth and tell us.'

There was a brief silence. Rebecca, helping Mrs Atkins peel vegetables they couldn't yet cook, turned to look at her. With one glance at Polly's face, she knew.

She dropped her knife on the table and left her work.

'It's me dad, isn't it.'

Polly nodded. 'A boy just brought the news. He died in the night. I – I'm sorry, Becky.'

Rebecca shook her head. 'We knew it was coming. I just don't know how he held out so long. The past few weeks have been bad, for him and me mam.' She looked uncertainly at Susan. 'She'll be needing me . . .'

'And we don't, I suppose!' Susan looked exasperated. 'Well, I suppose you'll have to go. You'd better ask Mrs Hudd – I can't take responsibility, not this morning. Billy, *will* you be careful brushing up that soot? There's more soot in here than there is snow outside and I don't know which is worse.' She turned away and Rebecca wiped her hands and went quickly out of the kitchen to the housekeeper's room. She knocked on the door.

'Your father?' Mrs Hudd repeated, when she had told her the news. 'Well, of course you must go, child. Poor Fanny – she'll need you, especially as your brother and sister . . . You'll let them know, of course?'

Rebecca shook her head. 'I don't know if they're still at the address they gave us – we haven't heard for a long time. I could write, I suppose. I can a bit.' She blushed a little, remembering those early mornings in the library with Francis. 'But they can't come back, anyway.'

'No, I know. Your poor mother – she's had a lot to bear.' Mrs Hudd, a strict housekeeper, could usually be relied upon to be kind when necessary. Otherwise, Rebecca reflected, she would never have agreed to take on the sister of a supposed murderer as kitchenmaid. 'Well, you go at once and see how she is and what she needs. I'm sure we can help a little, between us. And tell Mrs Atkins I said you were to have some bits and pieces from the larder. She'll know what to let you have.'

'Thank you, Mrs Hudd.' Rebecca bobbed her head and returned to the kitchen. Billy and Oddjob were putting the range back together and Polly and the scullerymaid were busy sweeping up the soot. Mrs Atkins, a little calmer now, listened to her request.

'It would happen today,' she grumbled, as if William had died simply in order to cause her even more inconvenience. 'Still, if her ladyship says so, I suppose you must go. Yes, take some things from the larder. And don't linger all day, taking advantage . . .

Here.' She went over to the dresser and pulled open a drawer. 'Take this shawl – it's bitter out there and I don't want you going down with a chill. It's bad enough as things are, I don't want one of my house-maids ill as well.'

Rebecca accepted the shawl gratefully, realising that it was Mrs Atkins' way of belying her sharp tongue and showing sympathy. She gathered a few eggs, some milk and a crust of bread from the larder and packed them into a basket. Then she opened the kitchen door and slipped out into the snow.

The cold air struck at her lungs. Snow swirled through the air, covering her face, feathering into her eyes and mouth, creeping into the folds of the shawl. It lay deep upon the ground; already the footprints of the boy who had brought the news of her father's death were filled. A heavy silence lay like a blanket over the town. There were few people about and those who had ventured out hurried along, their faces buried in heavy wrappings.

Rebecca's boots slipped and slithered on the treach-erous cobbles. Underneath the fresh snow, they were covered with a thick layer of ice and it was almost impossible to keep a steady foothold. She put one hand up to the wall beside her and stepped carefully down the steep road leading from the house into the town.

Only now was she beginning to realise just what had happened.

Her father had died. Died. She tasted the word in her mind, turning it this way and that. It was so final. There was no escape from it, nowhere to hide from its meaning. Something that had been in her life since the moment of birth had gone, and gone for ever. There was no calling it back.

Rebecca's father had never been an easy man. Often bad-tempered, sometimes drunk, he had been a dominating presence in the small cottage when she was very young. But there had been other moments, too, moments when he had come home from the tavern no more than pleasantly mellow, when he had taken her on his knee and jiggled her up and down, pretending to be a horse; when he had drawn her against his broad chest and wrapped big, warm arms around her so that she had felt sheltered and safe.

And when Bessie had stopped drawing for him to go and work in Butts' shop, leaving Rebecca to spend her days alone with her father, they had slowly established a strange rapport. Always taciturn, William had never had much to say, yet an understanding had grown between them, a sympathy and affection that had never existed between him and his other children. Occasionally, at the end of a wearying day, he would give her an approving glance from his dark eyes, or nod and touch her shoulder. That was all. But Rebecca had always felt a glow of pleasure at his small acknowledgement, more than she would have known from the most fulsome praise.

As she had grown older, he had talked to her. He talked about weaving, about independence, about unions. He told her how men had suffered for the right to strike, how it was their only weapon yet one of such power that employers everywhere were afraid of it. 'They'll fight it all the way,' he said, his dark eyes burning as he worked. 'But it'll come, Becky, it'll come. Once working men band together and stand firm, nobody will be able to browbeat them any longer. But there's a long road to tread afore that happens.'

Rebecca had listened, hardly able to believe in such

a vision of the future. But her own feelings chimed with his. Hadn't she understood from childhood that life wasn't fair? Hadn't she always felt that there must be something someone could do to make it so?

And whenever she had gone home to visit her parents since leaving home for Pagnel House, he had been there. Working at his loom, with Fanny or some neighbour's child drawing for him, but never failing to give her that dark, searching glance, the look that asked if all was well with her. Never speaking much, yet communicating with her all the same, in his own difficult way.

And now gone. After months of change while the big body shrivelled, became a husk that needed to be fed and cleaned like a baby, and the powerful voice that had bellowed at her or grunted a sparing approval had died to a papery whisper. Watching him, it had seemed impossible that he could go on living; daily, Rebecca had expected the summons that had come this morning. But now that he had indeed gone, she felt a gap as cold and shocking as if his death had been totally unexpected.

Lost in her thoughts, Rebecca had forgotten to watch her step on the icy footpath. She slipped and skidded, catching at a bush to save herself. At the same moment, a figure loomed up suddenly in the driving snow. Startled, Rebecca stumbled again and almost fell. She was caught in a pair of strong arms, and then held.

'*Rebecca.*'

Rebecca peered up through the swirling flakes.

'Mr Francis! I'm sorry – I never saw you—' She was burningly aware of his arms about her. 'It's all right, I can stand. It's just so icy—'

'Don't worry, Rebecca.' He went on holding her,

not tightly but firmly, warmly. 'I won't let you fall. But where are you going on such a nasty morning?' He bent to look closely at her. 'Are those tears on your cheeks? Why, they're like little icicles. What's wrong?'

Rebecca sniffed and rubbed her nose. 'It's nothing, Mr Francis. I – I'm just going to see my mam. She – she—'

His hands tightened. 'Are things worse? Your father—?'

'He died in the night,' Rebecca said tonelessly, and he drew her against him. The warmth of his body radiated through her thin clothes and, unable to resist any longer, she gave a little sigh and rested against his chest.

'I'm sorry,' he said quietly. 'I'm very sorry.'

'Oh, we knew it was going to happen,' Rebecca said in a muffled voice. 'I'm glad, really – it was awful for him, just lying there like that. But all the same—' her voice broke '—he was my dad, and now—'

'And now he's dead. I know. It's over, and there's nothing you can do any more.' Francis's voice was warm, as warm as his body and the arms he still kept around her. 'Are you going to see your mother now? I'll come with you.'

'Oh, no,' Rebecca protested, but he turned and, keeping her arm firmly in his, began to walk along the street.

'Of course I'll come with you. You can't go there all alone – there'll be things your mother needs, things I can help with. And it's too bad a morning for you to be out by yourself. You could fall and break a leg, and who would help you?'

There were certainly very few people about, and Rebecca was glad of Francis's company as well as of the strength of the arm that clasped hers against his side. Together they made better progress than when she was alone and before long they entered the maze of tiny backstreets that led to the row of weavers' cottages where she had been born.

There were people about here, shovelling snow away from their doors, making trips to the well and coming back with buckets carried in frozen fingers, searching along the banks of ditches for a few sticks to use as kindling. Outside the Himley cottage was a small group of people who ceased their whispering and turned to stare as Rebecca and Francis appeared.

'It's young Becky,' someone muttered, and a woman stepped forward, her sharp eyes on Francis while she addressed Rebecca.

'Your mam's in a bad way, Becky. She won't leave him – don't seem to understand what's happened. You'd better get in there quick.'

The knot of people cleared a path for her and, with a swift, scared glance at Francis, Rebecca hurried through past them. He followed her, bending his head to duck through the low doorway, and they stood for a moment just inside, letting their eyes grow accustomed to the dimness.

Fanny was crouching in the corner, bent over the pallet with its huddle of old sacking which had formed a bed for as long as Rebecca could remember. Her head was buried in her folded arms, so that she looked like no more than a bundle of old clothes herself. And from the bundle came a low, keening sound that chilled Rebecca's bones.

'Mam!' She went forward and knelt by the shivering figure. 'Mam, it's me – Rebecca. Oh, Mam . . .'

She tried to take her mother in her arms, but the

trembling body shrank away as if it had been struck. Dismayed, Rebecca looked up at Francis and then tried again to gather her mother close.

'Mam. Don't be frightened. It's me – Becky, your Becky. You know me.' She spoke gently, as if to a sick child, and realised with a stab of fear that this was just what her mother was like – a sick child. Shaking and afraid, bewildered by the blows that life had dealt her, unable to face any more. 'Mam, look at me.'

She slipped one hand under her mother's chin and raised it, trying to make the blurred eyes meet hers. But they slid away, as if Fanny were afraid to look at her, afraid even to acknowledge that she was there, and Rebecca felt an aching pity grow and spread through her body. Ignoring Fanny's resistance, she hugged her close, trying to transmit her own tenuous warmth to those frozen bones.

Fanny shuddered in her arms. Her body was even more wasted than before; it was like holding a sack of firewood. Her skin was so dry, it almost crackled; her hair, brushing against Rebecca's cheek, was the texture of old hay. She was cold, even to Rebecca's touch, and Rebecca realised that she probably could not talk. Her lips and tongue were just too cold to move.

She looked up at Francis again, agony in her eyes. 'She's frozen.'

'Hold her – just keep holding her.' He bent and wrapped Rebecca's shawl around the two of them, enclosing them in a cocoon of wool, and then took up the blanket that covered William's body. 'It's doing him no good now,' he said almost roughly, in response to Rebecca's involuntary gasp of protest. 'I'll get a fire going.'

But there was no kindling, nothing at all in the bare

little cottage that could be burnt. He hesitated a moment, then went outside. Rebecca could hear him questioning the neighbours. Then the voices faded.

She held her mother close. Fanny was shivering now, great waves of uncontrollable shudders that seemed to sweep across her body like an ague. Her face was buried in Rebecca's shoulder as if she were afraid to expose herself to the world, even the tiny world of her own cottage. Her skeletal fingers dug into Rebecca's arm and clung there, like the claws of a bird on the bars of a cage.

Rebecca sat very still, trying to warm her mother's body with her own. Cold as she was, she knew that she had not reached the dangerous level of chill that Fanny had. People had died – did die, every winter – through nothing more than growing too cold. And it was the old, the sick and the very young who were most in peril.

She looked around the room. It was almost bereft of any kind of furnishing now; there was nothing apart from the rough bed on which William's body lay, an old pan standing in the hearth and a cracked cup and plate with a few utensils beside them. No chairs, no cupboards, no form of lighting other than a stump of candle in a saucer; no bucket for carrying water. How had her mother been managing? Had she been creeping to the well, or to the frozen ditches, with nothing more than a cup?

The money that she and Francis had brought had been spent, it was clear, but on what? And Rebecca knew that she did not need to ask that question. It had gone on firewood to keep William warm, on food for William, food that must be bought already cooked once the firewood had run out. And probably a good deal of it had been spent on the ale that was all he

244

could swallow in the last few weeks, and the gin that was all that Fanny could stomach.

I ought to have done more, Rebecca thought remorsefully. She knew she should have asked Francis for more money. He would have given it gladly, had he realised it was needed; she should not have expected him to understand that money went quickly on food and warmth, both taken so much for granted in his comfortable world. But her foolish, stubborn pride had prevented her, and this was the result.

She had given her mother all her wages, brought food from the Pagnels' larder when Mrs Atkins had allowed it, had collected sticks on her way to the cottage.

If only Tom and Bessie had been here . . . One child was not enough. And she understood why people had so many children, knowing that many of them would die before they grew out of babyhood. If only a few grew up, they might be enough to keep you from the workhouse; from a death like this.

She let her eyes come at last to rest on her father's body, exposed now that Francis had removed the blanket that had covered it. It was quite unrecognisable as her father. Shrunken, misshapen by the muscular spasms he had suffered in those last few weeks, he lay curled on his side. His hair was thin and white, the scalp showing through to look peculiarly naked. The flesh of his cheeks had fallen away, leaving his face thin with a nose that stood out razor-sharp, like a beak, and his mouth was drawn in like a purse with the strings pulled tight.

And he smelt. He smelt of the pungent odours of a body that had released its last excretions. He smelt of decay, as if he had not been able to wait for death before beginning to rot. He smelt of dirt and mould and despair.

Rebecca was shaken by a sudden anger, a fury that heated her blood and surged through her body. She thought of all the people who would die in this way through the bitter winter, all those who had already done so. She thought of her mother, quivering in her arms like a damaged child, starved and chilled probably beyond rescue, ready for death herself. She thought of babies, born into the world only to suffer.

And she thought of people like the Pagnels, wealthy and prosperous, well fed, sleek, warmly and richly clad. Sarah, with her expensive wedding finery; Vivian, with his horses and his grand cigars, who thought that housemaids were there for his enjoyment and never saw them as people at all. Even Francis, who could toy with her in the mornings by the library hearth and then embrace his cousin Isabel before the very same fire.

Rebecca had not seen him alone since that evening when she had gone into the library to replenish the coals and seen the two of them together. But the sight had burned itself into her mind; through all her toils, all her worries, she had been unable to forget it.

Even now, surrounded by death, the memory was like a weight in her heart. And when Francis returned, she looked up at him with a sadness that darkened her eyes and brought a quiver to her lips.

'Rebecca,' he said, dropping to his knees beside her, 'don't look like that. Please, my dearest, don't look like that . . .'

Chapter Eleven

Getting Fanny through the snowy streets was an anxious, perilous business. Frail and weakened by her ordeal, she could scarcely walk and, even with Rebecca's shawl wrapped around her thin body, she shook with cold. She clung to Rebecca's hand yet seemed not to notice Francis, who was holding them both in the circle of his arm. Her eyes barely opened, even when her feet slipped on the icy cobbles, and she mumbled incessantly and incoherently as if to someone else, someone not present yet who walked with them; a shadowy, ghostly presence.

'She don't seem to be with us at all,' Rebecca said unhappily. 'It's as if she's in another world. Mam. Mam – it's Becky. Say something to me, Mam, please. You know your Becky, don't you?' She felt her eyes stung by tears and swallowed the lump in her throat.

'She's shocked by all that she's been through,' Francis said with compassion. 'Don't bother her, Rebecca. It may be happier for her to be as she is.'

'She wants our Bess,' Rebecca said. 'She keeps asking for her, her and Tom. She thinks they're still at home. She thinks she's cooking supper for them.'

'She'll be better in a while,' Francis said gently. 'When we've got her into the warm and she's had some food. She needs some of Mrs Atkins' soup. That'll put heart into her.'

'I hope it'll be all right, taking her back with us. I'm nervous about it. Suppose Mrs Hudd won't allow it.

Or the mistress – I don't think Mam would live through another walk like this.' Rebecca shivered in the searing wind and drew her mother closer. 'She's failing now. I can feel it.' She tried to beat down her panic, but its edge was in her voice. She bit her lips, turning her face away from Francis in an effort to hide her despair.

'It's not much further now. We can keep her going that far.' She wondered if he were really as confident as he sounded. 'I promise you, once we get your mother inside, warm and dry, with some hot soup inside her, I'll make sure it's all right. I'll see my aunt straightaway.'

They started up the last steep slope. Fanny was stumbling at every step now, her legs moving slowly, reluctantly, almost as if she had ceased to care; as if she longed to cast herself down into the snow and die there in peace. Terrified, Rebecca urged her on, holding her up in arms that shook with cold, her fingers numb on the fragile body. 'Only a little way now, Mam,' she repeated over and over again. 'Only a little way. Try – please try, for your Becky's sake, please.'

But it seemed that Fanny was too weak to try for anyone's sake, least of all her own. Her legs crumpled under her; she gave a little moan and collapsed in the soft snow. Huddled there, she looked no more than a heap of old clothes cast off by some tramp or gypsy who had come by a better suit. And when Rebecca bent to her, there was no sign of life in the thin, grey face. 'She's gone – she's gone after Father,' Rebecca whispered, and turned a grief-stricken face up to Francis.

'Here,' said Francis, lifting Fanny in his arms, 'I'll carry her the rest of the way. She's not dead, Rebecca, she's just very cold and tired. She needs warmth, and it isn't far now. Poor woman – she's as light as a baby.'

'The kitchen range was out this morning,' Rebecca said as he began to stride on up the hill. 'Mrs Atkins was in a terrible taking over it. If it's not put right—'

'There are other rooms with fires.' He glanced down at her from the corners of his eyes. 'The library, for instance.'

Rebecca felt a blush sear her cheeks, its heat stinging against the biting cold of the wind. She glanced away quickly, looking down at her boots that were almost hidden by the depth of the snow.

'I've missed you the last few weeks,' Francis said quietly.

'I do the fireplace every day.'

'I know. I've kept away – deliberately. I didn't want to hurt you, Rebecca. But it hasn't been easy.' He paused and when he spoke again his voice was almost too low for her to hear. 'I wanted to come and see you – every day. I wanted to talk to you.'

She thought she caught a faint whisper of some further words, but they were lost in the wind and she could not be sure. And neither could she answer. What was there to say? That she'd missed him, too? That each morning, as she opened the library door, her heart had thudded with the hope that he might be there, and had sunk when she found that he was not? That the pain of glimpsing him in Isabel's arms was as sharp now as it had been on that evening when she'd gone to replenish the fire and discovered them together?

'It's best we don't, Mr Francis,' she said at last. She had been waiting every day for the announcement of an engagement between Francis and his cousin. To continue their brief morning meetings would, she knew, only bring fresh pain. Yet the thought that he might have been missing her, thinking of her, set her heart leaping.

But there was no time now to think of such things. They were going carefully down the steps to the kitchen door of Pagnel House, and as the snow swirled more fiercely than ever about them Rebecca felt her fears returning. Suppose she were ordered to take her mother away? Suppose Mrs Atkins would not even allow her inside the kitchen? She knew that if Fanny were not given warmth and nourishment soon, she would die . . . if she were not already dead.

'Open the door, Rebecca,' Francis said quietly. 'And don't worry.'

She gave him a last doubtful glance and set her fingers on the handle. The door swung inwards and the comforting warmth flowed out to meet them. At least they'd got the range lit, she thought thankfully, and stepped into the great, cavernous room. If only her mother could rest here for a while. If only she could stay.

'*There* you are.' Mrs Atkins was standing at the kitchen table, rolling pastry as if her life depended on it. She raised a red harassed face to look at Rebecca. 'Well, come in, girl, and shut the door, you're letting all the cold in. Who's that with you – why, it's Mr Francis! Whatever have you been doing? What's that you've got in your arms, sir?'

'It's Mam,' Rebecca said as Francis came slowly into the kitchen and stood with Fanny still huddled in his arms, no bigger than a child. 'She's that poorly, Mrs Atkins. And she'd no food, nor any firing, not even a bed fit to lie on. Mr Francis said we must bring her back here. She's so cold, Mrs Atkins – please, can she sit by the fire a while? Otherwise I'm afraid she'll die.' She looked at the shrunken face and whispered, almost inaudibly, 'That's if she's not dead already.'

'Well, I don't know.' The cook was flustered. She glanced at the other servants who had come crowding around, staring at the crumpled figure and making sounds of pity. 'I'm sure I don't know. The mistress—'

'I'll speak to my aunt,' Francis said again. He moved over to the range and set Fanny down in the big chair normally occupied by the butler when he was in the kitchen. 'She'll be warmer here, near the fire, but I think she ought to have some blankets round her. And some soup, Mrs Atkins, if you've any hot. Can you see to that, please? Polly – can you find me some blankets, quickly?'

Polly hesitated. 'I'll have to ask Mrs Hudd, she's in charge of all that—'

'Then go and ask her.' His voice was pleasant but there was no doubting his authority; it was clear that he meant to be obeyed. Polly glanced at the cook, who lifted her palms. She slipped out of the door.

'The soup?' Francis said to Mrs Atkins, still in that pleasant tone which brooked no argument. 'Is there any hot?'

'Why, yes sir, I was just getting it ready for the Family's lunch.' She turned and took a bowl from the dresser, spooning soup into it from the pan which simmered on top of the range. 'Here, girl, you'd better feed her – I've got work to do, I'm all behind as it is. I'm sorry, Mr Francis, and I don't wish to be stingy – heaven knows, poor Fanny Himley looks as if she could do with a spot of good nourishment inside her – but it's the Family's victuals, when all's said and done, and I don't know what the mistress—'

'I've told you, I'll talk to your mistress.' For the

first time, there was an edge of impatience in Francis's voice. 'Now – where's the girl with those blankets?'

Rebecca knelt beside the big chair and eased her mother's head into a better position. Fanny's eyes were closed and Rebecca feared again that she had already died. But when she slipped her hand inside the ragged shawl, she could feel the faint flutter of her heart, and fresh hope surged through her. She held a spoonful of soup to the blue lips and whispered encouragingly. Whether Fanny could hear or not, she didn't know, but it seemed there was nothing else she could do.

The lips were barely parted. Despairing, knowing that warmth and nourishment were vital, Rebecca tilted the spoon a little. Soup ran down her mother's chin, but surely some had slipped in through the slightly open mouth. She tried again, then a third time. Surely there had been a tiny flicker of reaction then? A minute movement, almost like that of a newborn baby forming its lips ready to suck? Her heart beating quickly, she wiped her mother's chin and held up a fourth spoonful, and this time there was a definite response.

She heard a movement behind her and turned to find Francis, Polly and Mrs Hudd. Polly's arms were filled with blankets and Mrs Hudd moved forward to lift Fanny in the chair while they were wrapped around her. A pillow was placed behind her head and Rebecca gave the housekeeper a grateful look.

'There, that's better,' Mrs Hudd said. 'She looks more comfortable now, at least . . . Poor Fan. To come to this . . . Not that she ever had much, poor girl. It's a hard life for women.'

'And for men, too,' Rebecca said. 'My dad died in terrible pain.'

'And women live with it.' Mrs Hudd had never, to anyone's knowledge, had any children, nor did she ever mention a Mr Hudd, but no doubt she had seen and heard enough about it. 'Well, let's hope the mistress will let us keep her here until she's strong enough to go home. Have you arranged the funeral?'

Rebecca shook her head. 'We didn't have time. Mr Francis said we must get Mam back here at once. We left a neighbour with the – with Dad.' She felt the sudden threat of tears; in all the anxiety, she had almost forgotten her father. She half rose to her feet. 'I ought to see to it—'

'I'll do that.' Francis laid his hand on her shoulder. 'You look after your mother. And I'll see my aunt as well. Don't worry about any of it. I'll go at once.' His fingers tightened in a brief squeeze and then he turned away. She looked after him, her heart filled with words she could not say, aware of the eyes that watched so curiously. Then she turned back to her mother.

'I wouldn't give her too much now,' Mrs Hudd advised as she began to spoon up the soup again. 'If she's as half-starved as she looks, she'll not be able to take much at a time. Give her some more in half an hour or so . . .'

The rest of the servants returned to their tasks. They murmured amongst themselves, their voices subdued. Without saying anything about it, they took over Rebecca's chores for the rest of that day and she stayed beside her mother, keeping the frail body warm, willing her to keep her hold on life. Every now and then she gave her some more soup, thankful when she could see that it was being taken, knowing that it must do good. And she felt a deep, increasing gratitude towards the people she had lived and worked with for the past six years.

With them, she had shared work and leisure – more of the former than the latter, but they had had their good times, their small parties, their laughter and song. With them, she had risen early to patter about the house so that the Family never saw the rough work being done; with them she had watched the life above stairs; with them, she had shared a fatigue that seemed as if it could never be assuaged, as she laboured from dawn until long after darkness had fallen; with them she had shared her life.

And now they were sharing her sorrow. They were her family, as much as the trembling bundle of bones in the chair by which she knelt. As much as William, lying dead in the bare and icy cottage on the edge of the town. As much as Bessie and Tom, far away in London.

If Fanny died, they would be all the family she had.

'Keep the woman *here*?' Isabella sat upright in her chair and stared at her nephew. 'Francis, is this a jest?'

'No, of course not.' Francis moved uneasily. His aunt was not reacting as he had hoped she would. 'I'm perfectly serious. Aunt, the woman has just lost her husband and she's near death herself. It was bitterly cold in the cottage, and there was nothing there, nothing to keep her warm, nothing to eat or drink. I would have taken her to my own mother, but you know several of the boys in the school are ill with a fever – she's up night and day nursing them. It was impossible to leave her – we had to bring her here—'

'Really, this is all quite beyond me,' Isabella said coldly. 'I fail to understand any of it. What were you doing there at all, Francis – in that part of the town?

Don't you realise the risks you run? Disease is rife in those parts—'

'And it's easy to see why.' He bit his lip, annoyed with himself for letting his anger show.

'Please, Francis, don't interrupt me in that uncouth way. I don't know what's come over you this morning. Is it the cold that's got into your brain? Are you feverish? I really think you ought to see Dr Cully—'

'If anyone needs a doctor, it is not I,' Francis said tightly. 'It's that poor soul in the kitchen. Aunt, I am not asking that you should see her or do anything for her yourself—'

'I should hope not, indeed!'

'—only let her stay for a few days, until she's recovered enough to go back to her own home. A bed somewhere, a cup of hot soup, a meal or two—'

'All available in the workhouse, which is where she should be. Why do you imagine such places are built and maintained? The poor are adequately cared for, Francis, and interference with the system can only do harm. Why, suppose it becomes known that we took such a woman in? We'd have every beggar and vagabond for miles around coming to our doorstep.'

'But this is a woman who used to work here, Aunt. One of your own maids. And her daughter is your maid now. Doesn't that count for something?'

'I fail to see any reason why it should. We paid her well while she was here and if she chose to leave in order to marry a common weaver and live a life of penury, that was her affair. As for the daughter, she's a good enough housemaid but no better than a hundred others. She certainly doesn't warrant any special treatment.' Isabella's eyes narrowed. 'I should like to know just why she was able to go jaunting about the streets at such an hour in the morning – and I still do not understand how you came to be with her, Francis.'

Francis sighed. The conversation was not going at all well. He had presented his case – Fanny's case – badly to begin with, and made matters worse by allowing himself to be drawn into argument. But he had been so disturbed by what he had seen that morning, so desperate to help Rebecca and her mother, that it had never occurred to him that there could be any other point of view.

'Aunt, she received a message to say that her father had died. She was given permission to go to her mother. And I met her in the street and could do nothing else but accompany her. Have you any idea what it's like out there, Aunt?' He glanced at the window, at the snowflakes hurling themselves against the glass as the blizzard raged more fiercely than ever. 'I couldn't let a young girl like that go alone, and on such an errand, too.'

'One would imagine,' Isabella said, her tone as icy as the weather, 'that this housemaid was a young lady, gently brought up, who needed protection. But the very fact that she was out alone should indicate to you, Francis, that she is nothing of the sort. She's a *maid*. One of the lower classes. Such a girl does not need the protection of a gentleman. She would have been perfectly capable of finding her own way. By doing what you have done, you've given her ideas above her station and there's no knowing what trouble might ensue.'

'There'll be no trouble,' Francis said wearily. 'Rebecca is not the sort of girl to make trouble of any kind.'

'Indeed? You seem to know her extremely well.' Isabella's eyes narrowed suspiciously, but before either of them could say any more the door opened and Isabel came in. She looked at them both, her eyebrows lifting as she caught the tension in the atmosphere. After only a slight hesitation, she crossed the room to stand at Francis's side, looking up into his face.

'What's happened? You look anxious.'

'Francis is trying to play the philanthropist,' Isabella said tartly before he could answer. 'He has been out on the streets this morning, collecting the dying to bring back here and save. Apparently we are to form some sort of luxury workhouse for the dependants of housemaids.'

Francis felt his skin colour a deep, angry red. Isabel stared at her mother, then turned back to look at him again, a frown on her brow.

'Whatever is all this about, Francis? What does Mother mean?'

'I went with one of the housemaids to visit her mother this morning,' he said tautly. 'Her father died last night and the mother was frozen and starving. If we had left her there, she would have died. So—'

'Instead of taking her to the workhouse, where she ought to be, Francis brought the woman here,' Isabella cut in. 'Apparently she is in the kitchen at this very moment, being fed and pampered as if she were royalty—'

'A cup of soup which she is almost too ill to swallow, and a blanket to wrap around her frozen body.' Francis made no attempt now to hide his anger. 'And this is supposed to be a Christian household!'

There was a long silence. Isabella's face whitened. Francis stared at her, then looked down at his feet. There would be no chance now for the starving woman downstairs. She would be turned out into the snow, sent either to the workhouse or back to the bleak, cold cottage. In either case, he was sure that she would die.

She would probably die anyway. But at least in the kitchen, amongst the servants who were worked so hard yet were not too busy to show compassion, with her daughter beside her, she would die knowing that someone cared.

He felt Isabel's hand on his sleeve and glanced down at her. Her face was soft, her eyes tender, and he felt a wave of gratitude.

'You will apologise for that remark,' Isabella said at last. 'And I repeat what I said just now – I think you must be ill. This behaviour is most uncharacteristic – I shall speak to your uncle.' Her voice shook with anger. 'I always did think it was a mistake to have you living here. It's given you inflated ideas of your position. You seem to imagine you have the right to speak and act as if you were a son of the house. Let me remind you that you are not – nor ever will be.'

Francis stared at her and opened his mouth, but before he could speak Isabel moved closer and tightened her hand on his sleeve. She lifted her head and he saw the colour like flags in her cheeks.

'But there is no reason at all why Francis should not behave like a son of the house,' she said clearly. 'After all, when he and I are married—'

Isabella's shock matched Francis's own. '*Married*? What are you talking about, child? Has this madness spread to you as well?'

'Isabel—' Francis began, but she gave him such a brilliant smile that he fell silent.

'Francis hasn't actually asked me yet,' she said to her mother. 'I expect he wants to speak to Father first.

258

But I'm sure he means to – don't you, my love? – and then he will have as much right here as anyone. As much as Vivian.'

'He will not!' Isabella said furiously. 'Vivian is your father's heir – nothing will change that. So if you imagine you will inherit the business, Francis, or any part of it—'

'I don't. I don't think anything of the kind. Aunt – Isabel – I must tell you—'

'I know we weren't going to say anything yet,' Isabel cut in quickly. 'It's no time at all since Sarah's wedding, after all. But it's better for everyone to know the situation, don't you agree? And I *want* everyone to know. I want to be engaged.' She smiled and dimpled at him. 'I'm sorry, my love. I know I say too much. I've always been scolded for that.'

'And with good reason,' her mother said grimly. 'Now let me understand. Just what has been happening between the two of you?' Her eyes were fixed on Francis, sharp and bright as swords. 'I hope you have behaved as a gentleman should? Though it seems clear that you have not.'

'Aunt Isabella,' Francis said desperately, 'I assure you, I've never even dreamed—'

'But I have,' Isabel said sweetly. 'I dream of you all the time, Francis. I dream about that evening when we were in the library together – you remember? Oh—' she closed her eyes for a moment '—it was so delightful, wasn't it? I knew then, didn't you?'

'In the library?' Isabella too closed her eyes. She opened them again. 'Francis, have you compromised my daughter?'

He shook his head, unable to speak. What was Isabel doing – was this some sort of game, some horrible joke? Did she want him to be turned away,

259

thrown out of the house that had become a home, his livelihood lost to him? But she was looking at him now with eyes that shone with love and he knew, with a sinking heart, that she had seen an opportunity and was grasping it with both hands. He had not responded to her as she had wanted. He had not returned her kisses, though she was unaware of the strange revulsion that gripped him whenever she talked of love and marriage. And now she was trying to force him into an impossible position.

He felt a wave of anger. But there was nothing he could say or do about it. Denial would make him appear even more dishonourable.

'It seems that this situation has gone further than I believed,' Isabella said at last. 'I knew that the two of you were becoming closer than was desirable. I even discussed it with Vivian, and he agreed. But with all the business of Sarah's wedding . . .' She looked at her daughter. 'I've been foolish,' she said harshly. 'I believed that you could be trusted to behave as a young lady should, with modesty and decorum. Obviously, I was wrong.' She rose from her chair and stared coldly at them both. 'I shall speak to your father as soon as he is home for dinner. Meanwhile, you will go to your room, Isabel, and stay there until you are told to come out. Polly will bring you a tray. As for you—' she turned to Francis '—I think you had better not be here when my husband comes home. Go to your room or the library, wherever you wish, but keep out of my sight. You'll be called when we have decided what is to happen.'

Isabel, her head held high, left the room, turning at the door to give Francis a glance of triumph. He looked back miserably. What had she done – to him, to his life? But there was still nothing he could say.

His aunt would never believe now that he had not compromised his cousin. Isabel had maneouvred him very neatly into a corner.

Yet in spite of his initial anger, he could not find it in his heart to hate her for this. She truly loved him - he was sure of it. He had seen it in her eyes, heard it in her voice, felt it in the soft touch of her hand. It was not her fault that he could not return her love, nor that she was unaware of his feelings. No, the fault lay in him, that he had not made them clear. But he had never dreamed that she would go this far. He had hoped - believed - that her attachment would fade, become no more than the affection that had always existed between them. He had trusted that time would work for him.

'You may go, Francis,' his aunt said, her voice as freezing as the storm outside. 'I have no more to say to you now.'

Francis bowed his head. He felt that he should say something - make some sort of apology. But there was nothing that would not be taken either as offence or an admission of guilt. He hesitated, gave up and walked quickly from the room.

Go where you like, she had said. To his room, to the library - anywhere, so long as it was out of her sight. He paused outside the door, wondering unhappily which to choose, and then remembered Rebecca and her mother. Well, at least his aunt appeared to have forgotten them.

He turned and went straight to the green baize door that led to the staff quarters and kitchen.

'Francis and Isabel?' Jeremiah repeated. 'But that's impossible!'

'I agree - but it seems to have happened.' Isabella

sat ramrod-straight in her chair by the fire. She had ordered dinner to be delayed by half an hour – which suited Mrs Atkins, after the turmoil of the morning – and asked that Jeremiah should come to the drawing room, where they could talk privately. Vivian, who had accompanied his stepfather home, came too at his mother's request.

'I don't know what has happened between them, nor do I wish to,' Isabella said distastefully. 'But it seems quite clear that we have been remiss in letting them grow so close. They've been given far too much freedom – allowed to wander alone at will, permitted to sit in the same room without a chaperone. Isabel has always seemed such a child, uninterested in adult affairs – clearly, she is nothing more than a scheming and deceitful hussy. And as for Francis – well, I was never happy about his coming to live here. It always seemed unnecessary. And now he has abused our hospitality, and they'll have to be married. It's a great pity. Isabel could have made a good marriage.'

'Married!' Jeremiah said. 'But – no, that's impossible, my dear. Out of the question.'

'I wish I could agree with you,' his wife replied. 'But the matter is out of our hands. Isabel herself admits there has been impropriety. We can do nothing but arrange a wedding as quickly as possible.'

'No.' Jeremiah stood up and moved to the window, staring out at the snow which filled the air. 'No, Isabella. We shall do nothing of the sort. Francis and Isabel will not be married, and that's an end to it.'

'But the situation – husband, we can do nothing else. There is a definite understanding between them – I cannot imagine why we've not noticed it before—'

'Why you've not noticed it, you mean.' He turned

swiftly. 'You are at home all day with Isabel. You've seen her, talked with her far more than I have. Why have *you* not noticed this attachment? Why could you not put a stop to it before it properly began?'

'Oh, I knew you would blame me,' Isabella said resentfully. 'Let me remind you, Jeremiah, it was not I who brought Francis into this house. Let me remind you, too, that we know very little about him – about his own parentage. A foundling from nowhere – who knows what bad blood runs through his veins? No, if your brother and his wife wished to take him in, that was their affair, but there was never any reason for us to count him one of *our* family.' She paused, then added in a tone of deep bitterness, 'And now we shall be forced to do so. Oh, why did this have to happen – just when everything was going so well?'

Vivian stepped forward and laid his hand on his mother's shoulder. 'Mother, don't distress yourself. It can't be so bad. So far, this is all between ourselves – need it go any further? None of us wants this marriage – why should Isabel and Francis have their way, through their own misbehaviour and convention's demands? If this attachment hasn't gone too far, it's not too late. Francis can be sent away – I'll take him to London with me. I've been planning to do so anyway. Or Isabel can visit Maria for a while, or perhaps some of my relatives in Dorset. She'll soon meet some other young man and forget Francis, and nobody but us ever need know what happened.'

'But we *don't* know what happened,' Isabella wailed, and Jeremiah strode quickly across the room.

'We soon shall,' he said grimly. 'I'll see Francis at once and find out just what's been going on. He'll tell me the truth, I'm sure. As for bad blood . . .' he hesitated . . . 'I'm sure you need have no fears.

263

Geoffrey and Edith have brought him up to be as honourable as any gentleman.'

'So I see,' she said bitterly, and turned to her son. 'Vivian – do you really suppose this dreadful situation can be saved? What should we do?'

'I've already told you what we should do about Isabel. And as for Francis – he needs a good horse-whipping,' Vivian said with a touch of relish in his voice. 'I'll be glad to help, Father. Isabel's my youngest sister – I've always had a special affection for her.'

Jeremiah shot him a suspicious glance but said no more. He jerked open the door and stamped out. They heard his footsteps going up the stairs towards Francis's room.

Isabella looked up at her son and lifted her hand in appeal. He caught it in his own.

'Don't worry, Mother,' he said softly. 'Everything will be all right. Why, it might even turn out to be for the best in the end. Isabel wed to some suitable husband – an older man, I think, to curb her spirit – and Francis discredited and out of the way.' His smile showed his teeth. 'I think this morning's work may turn out to be quite profitable after all.'

Isabella looked at him doubtfully. But his smile was so confident, his manner so jaunty, that after a moment or two she relaxed and smiled in return.

'I'm sure you're right, Vivian my dear,' she said. 'You really are such a comfort to me. And now let's go and have dinner. It's such a dreadful day out there – you must be hungry.'

She rose and they left the room together. As Francis had supposed, all thoughts of Fanny Himley had quite left her mind.

* * *

It had become clear to Francis quite quickly that his presence in the kitchen was not only an embarrassment but a hindrance. Owing to the problems with the range, which had put Mrs Atkins's day severely out of joint – only partially redeemed by Isabella's sudden order to delay dinner – and Rebecca's work being shared by the other servants, the kitchen was an even busier place than usual. And, large as it was, it seemed full of people, all bustling with purpose. There was no room for anyone without a job to do.

Francis stood helplessly for a moment, then went over to Rebecca who was sitting on a small stool beside her mother. He bent and she looked up at him. Her eyes were filled with tears.

'Is she no better?' he whispered.

Rebecca shook her head. 'I can't tell. She's warm now – see, she's a better colour. But she won't open her eyes or speak, and she won't even take soup now. It – it's as if she don't want to live, Mr Francis. It's as if she's given up.'

He looked down at her. She was white with fear and shock, her normally tidy hair escaping from its pins and curling round her face. He longed suddenly to twist those curls around his fingers, to place his hands on either side of that pale oval face and warm the trembling lips with his own. Was this, he thought suddenly, the reason for his feelings about Isabel? Was this why he couldn't love his adopted cousin – because he was in love, instead, with a housemaid?

He pushed the thought away and looked at Fanny Himley, who was lying huddled in the big chair, in almost exactly the position she had been in when he last saw her. She looked very far away, as if she were nearer to death than to life. Perhaps she had indeed given up; perhaps life had no more meaning for her now that her husband and children had all gone. And could she be blamed, he thought with grim anger, when one considered the life she had been forced to live?

'You'd better go, Mr Francis,' Rebecca said quietly. 'There's nothing you can do here.'

'I wish there were,' he answered, feeling the wretchedness in his heart. 'But at least I can make the arrangements about your father. I'll do that, Rebecca. You must have been worrying about it.' He hesitated. 'Would – would you come to the library later on? Say at about five? Then I can tell you what's been done.'

She glanced at her mother, then nodded. 'I'll come. If I can.' There was a movement from the huddled figure, a long, low groan, and she leaned over at once, holding the wrinkled hands, touching the papery cheek. 'Mam? Can you hear me, Mam? It's Becky. Open your eyes – it's Becky.'

Francis waited for a moment, but Rebecca did not turn back to him. He left her and went out of the kitchen. He would do as he had promised, and make the arrangements, whatever they might be, for William's funeral. And then, he hoped, have a few moments alone with her in the library.

He no longer deluded himself as to why he wanted to see Rebecca, why he wanted to be with her. But he knew that it must go no further than it already had. She was out of his reach. And he would not do as his cousin Vivian would do, as many men would do without hesitation. He did not see serving maids as easy game. Rebecca, least of all.

For a few moments, he had forgotten Isabel. But now, seeing Jeremiah standing on the stairs and waiting

266

for him, the memory of the scene in his aunt's drawing room came back in full force. He felt the scarlet colour flood into his face and stopped.

'Yes,' Jeremiah said with a grimness Francis had never before heard in his voice, 'you may well look discomfited. I want to speak to you, my boy. Into the library – now.' He fell back to allow Francis to precede him, then followed close behind. 'We'll forget dinner. This is going to take some time, I fancy.'

Someone – Polly, perhaps – had stoked up the library fire so that it burned brightly. The room was warm, a welcoming contrast with the wintry scene outside. The heavy velvet curtains kept out draughts and a lamp, standing on the big table where Jeremiah often held discussions with the two young men, gave out a mellow glow. It was very different from the chilly aspect it had in the early mornings, before Rebecca had cleared out the hearth.

Jeremiah took up his position on the hearth, his back to the fire. He stood with legs apart, imposingly big in the flickering light, and motioned Francis to stand before him. The two men faced each other.

'Well?' Jeremiah said at last. 'I imagine you know what this is about.'

Francis nodded. 'My supposed liaison with Isabel.'

'Supposed? There seems to be precious little *supposed* about it – why, the girl herself admits to an attachment and has hinted at worse. If that's true . . .' His face darkened and he made an involuntary movement, then seemed to take a grip on himself. 'Well? What d'you have to say? I've always been a fair man, Francis. I'll listen – but take care. I want the truth, not lies.'

Francis shook his head and spread out his hands. 'I

267

don't know what to say, Uncle. I was as surprised as Aunt Isabella when Isabel said what she did. Uncle, believe me, I've never mentioned marriage – never thought of it—'

'But Isabel clearly has. Now, I know my daughter, she's given to fancies and whims – no one understands that better than I. I could quite believe that she's read more into a word or a glance than you ever intended.' Jeremiah looked at Francis. 'Can you tell me – honestly – that it's no more than that? That there's never been any – any physical contact between you? You've never – er – touched her in any way?'

Why, he wants me to say that, Francis thought. He wants me to say there's never been anything – so that we can all go back to where we were a few hours ago.

But he could not say that. Partly because it wasn't true. And partly because Isabel would deny it. Isabel, he realised with a sick feeling, would admit to anything to get what she wanted – and she wanted marriage, at any cost. Whether she had actually counted the cost of this folly, he had no idea. As a child, Isabel had been inclined to commit her sins without even considering the consequences. Had she grown up at all?

'Francis?'

He shook his head slowly. 'I can't say that, Uncle. We did kiss once – in this very room. Isabel was so – she clearly wanted it. I could not refuse.' He bent his head unhappily. 'I knew it was wrong, but—' He stopped abruptly. He could not tell Jeremiah how shamelessly his daughter had behaved, throwing herself at him, making it impossible to reject her. 'Uncle, I can't say more without touching my cousin's honour. Please – don't ask me to.'

Jeremiah stared at him. His face was suffused with dark colour. For a moment, Francis thought his uncle was about to strike him. Then he turned away, laid his arm along the mantelpiece and sank his head on it.

'My God,' he said thickly, 'what did I do to deserve this?'

There was a long, painful silence. Francis stared at the broad back and longed to touch it, to lay his hands on the heavy shoulders, to offer comfort. But what comfort could he possibly offer to the man whose daughter he had compromised, whose honour he had besmirched? Perhaps, he thought wretchedly, it would be better if he simply went away, left the library, packed a bag and went back to his parents. But would they want him? And none of it would solve this problem.

Oh, Isabel, why did you have to do it? Why did you have to say what you did?

At last Jeremiah turned round. Francis looked at him and felt a shock. His uncle seemed to have aged ten years in those few minutes.

Racked with guilt, Francis stepped forward.

'Uncle, I never intended – it was quite innocent, I swear I never – Uncle, I'll do anything – I'll marry Isabel tomorrow if that's what you wish. I'll try my best to make her happy. I'll be a good husband—' Even as he spoke, he could feel the same repugnance, the same revulsion against taking Isabel in his arms in any but the most brotherly way, but he was forced to ignore it. His words swept on until Jeremiah, with a bellow like that of a bull in pain, a roar that shook the library walls, stopped him in mid-speech.

'No! *No*! It's impossible – it can't be. You can never marry Isabel, never. Whatever you've done – however you've compromised her – you can never, never marry her. Is that clear? Is that understood?'

Francis stared at him. His uncle's face was distorted with passion, dark with emotion. His words came thickly from a throat that seemed riven by pain. His chest heaved and his clenched fists shook the air between them.

Shocked, Francis took a step back and the movement seemed to restore Jeremiah to the present; he blinked for a moment, as if he had returned from some distant time, then slowly lowered his raised hands.

'Do you understand?' he repeated, more quietly now but with a thread of intensity running like iron through his voice. 'You can never marry my daughter.'

'Yes, I understand,' Francis said quietly. 'But I don't understand why. You speak as if there's some reason against our marriage – some secret that nobody else knows.' And as he spoke the words, he saw his uncle's face change and knew that somehow he had hit close upon the truth.

Jeremiah looked at him, long and hard. Then he sighed heavily. His body sagged, his fists unclenched. He turned away, as if the sight of the young man before him were too much to bear.

'Very well, Francis. I can see you have to know. And perhaps you should have known long ago. If I had been honest with you, we would not be standing here now. You would never have allowed that minx of a daughter of mine to make up to you – oh yes, I believe that's what happened. I know you both, you see – both, very well.' He paused, as if choosing his words, then settled for the simplest there were. 'You can never marry Isabel, Francis, because she is not your cousin. Because she's closer to you than that. She—' he struggled for a moment, then allowed the words finally to pass his lips '—Francis, Isabel is your sister. Your half-sister. And may God forgive me for my sins.'

Francis felt a cold hand pass down his spine. He stood rigid, unable for a moment to take in the sense of what he had just been told. Isabel his sister? No.

But when he looked into Jeremiah's eyes he could no longer doubt the truth.

'I'm your father, Francis,' Jeremiah said quietly, and put out his hand. 'And whatever God may think of all this . . . can *you* forgive me?'

Chapter Twelve

'Can you forgive me?'

The words seemed to hang in the air, vibrating through the silence of the library. Francis heard them ring in his head, repeating themselves over and over again as the blood throbbed hotly through his brain. *Forgive me . . . forgive me . . . forgive me . . .* He shook his head blindly and saw his uncle's - *father's?* - hands held out towards him, palms upwards in supplication.

'Francis?'

Jeremiah's voice was dry, little more than a cracked whisper. Francis looked at him and was struck to the heart by the sight of this man, so massive, so imposing - a man known to all Kidderminster, with the probability of becoming Mayor within the next year or two - asking forgiveness for something that had happened over twenty years ago.

Forgiveness? But how could there be forgiveness, when the truth was still so largely hidden? When there were so many questions still to be answered?

He shook his head slowly. 'I don't know what to say. There are so many things . . . I don't even know what to call you any more,' he said helplessly. 'Until a few minutes ago, you were my uncle - and only an adoptive uncle. As far as I knew, there was no blood relationship between us at all. Now, I find that there is - and of the closest kind.' He spread his own hands. 'What can I say? How can I forgive you when I know nothing of the truth?'

Jeremiah stared at him, then nodded and lowered himself slowly into one of the heavy armchairs. His big shoulders were stooped, his head bowed. The lines on his face were suddenly deeper.

'You're quite right,' he said. 'How can I expect your forgiveness when you know so little – perhaps even less when you know it all. But you have the right to know, and the right to choose whether to forgive.' He looked up at Francis and indicated the chair opposite. 'Please. We may as well be comfortable.'

Francis moved to the chair and sat down, facing Jeremiah. His heart was racing. He stared at the older man's face, trying to read its expression, trying to deduce whether there were any likeness to himself in those familiar features. He had never before even wondered whether there might be any resemblance between him and the Pagnels; having been told from a very early age that he had been adopted as a baby by Geoffrey and Enid, it had never occurred to him that there might be. Now, he began to wonder.

But – no, there was nothing to mark him as Jeremiah's son. No likeness at all between them. In fact, Jeremiah's dark, heavy features could not have been more in contrast with the slightly delicate fairness that Francis had always had since a baby. Vivian – no blood relation at all – was more like Jeremiah.

Vivian . . . With a sudden thump of his heart, Francis remembered the man he had always thought of as his cousin, who must in fact be – what? His step-brother? Or could no kinship at all be claimed, Francis himself being outside the family – unacknowledged. He was a bastard after all, he thought with sudden cold realisation.

'You've nothing to say,' Jeremiah said at last, heavily. 'Are you hating me?'

'Hating you?' Francis stared at him, then shook his head again. 'Unc – Fath – I don't know *what* to think. My mind – it won't take it all in. First Isabel – then this.' He raised a hand to rub across his face. 'It's as if the whole world had suddenly started turning the other way.'

'I'm sorry. I never intended that you should find out in this manner. In fact—'

'You never intended that I should find out at all.' Francis heard a quiver of emotion in his voice and recognised it as anger. 'I was never to know – that's the truth, isn't it? I was never to know that you were my father. Or—' He paused and stared at Jeremiah, then added slowly, 'or who was my mother. Who was she? You must tell me now. You must tell me everything.'

He could feel his body begin to shake as emotions and desires he had never suspected came flooding to the surface. His mother, his father – ever since he was a small child, playing in the nursery of the schoolmaster's house in Church Row, he had known that Geoffrey and Enid were not his true parents. They had believed it right that he should know this, but they had always parried any questions he might ask about his true parents. He had grown up believing that nobody knew the truth – that he was a foundling, perhaps, abandoned by some desperate girl. And as he had grown out of the childhood fantasies he had woven about the mystery, he had almost forgotten the matter. Geoffrey and Enid had been parents to him in every way except one, and he was happy to think of them in that way.

And now it was all changed. Geoffrey and Enid were his uncle and aunt. Jeremiah was his true father. And his mother . . . ? Again, he felt his body tremble.

275

'You must tell me everything,' he repeated, and looked Jeremiah in the eye.

Jeremiah sighed. 'I shall, Francis. As I said, you have the right to know. But hear this first – there was never any blame attached to your mother. You must never, never think ill of her. Of me, yes, since I am a man and should have protected her. And you'll never know the remorse I suffered over what happened . . .' His voice failed for a moment. 'Perhaps you will hate me, Francis, when you know it all. And perhaps I shall not blame you if you do.'

There was a long silence. Francis got up and stirred the fire. Outside, it was growing dark. The short day was almost over. He lit a taper in the flames and set it to the lamp. The glow illuminated his father's face, softening the harsh lines.

'Tell me,' he said again, and sat down.

Jeremiah stared into the fire for a moment, then seemed to gather himself together and took a deep breath. He spoke as if to the flames themselves, without looking at Francis, but nevertheless every word was addressed directly to his son.

'It was not long after Isabella and I were married. Isabella's first marriage, as you know, left her widowed with three children. She was mistress of the house, of course, and Edith and Jane were in the schoolroom, Vivian in the nursery. I had agreed to adopt Vivian as my heir even if we should have sons of our own.' He shot Francis a quick glance. 'It was part of the marriage settlement. Isabella brought a considerable sum of money to my business and it was only right that Vivian should inherit. Otherwise, she would have taken her fortune elsewhere. She was simply protecting the interests of her only son, and any others would have been adequately provided for. As it

276

turned out, we had only daughters – Sarah and Isabel.'

'But not for several years,' Francis said quietly.

'No. Our marriage was not easy to begin with. I suspected then – and I do still – that Isabella had already made up her mind to have no more children, and she took the most obvious measures to guard against them. And I would not force her.' His face twisted a little, as if with remembered pain. 'It was many years . . . In the meantime, I did what I could. And then Mary came to the house.'

Francis felt his heart give a quick leap. 'Mary?'

'She was a governess. We seemed to have new governesses then as often as the weather changed. None of them any use, as far as I could see, and none at all comely. But Mary . . . Mary was different.' He stared into the fire. 'Tall, slender but womanly, modest enough yet with a spark in her eye. Not as fair as you – her hair was a richer gold – yet you have a look of her at times. A trick of turning your head, a way of glancing up suddenly – you remind me very much of her.'

Francis felt a sudden ache in his heart for the mother he had never known. It was a new and unexpected sensation. Until now, apart from those childish fantasies in which he had imagined her to be a beautiful princess or grand lady, he had rarely wondered about the woman who had actually borne him. Now, suddenly, she was taking shape in his mind. A real woman, who had lived and breathed – and loved. And he looked at the man sitting near the fire and thought: This was the man she loved. This is my father.

And still it was almost impossible to believe.

Jeremiah stirred himself out of a deep silence. He

277

glanced at Francis, letting his eyes move over the fair hair, the sensitive features, and nodded slightly.

'Yes – you remind me of her. More and more, as you approach the age she was. About twenty-three, when she came here first. A vicar's daughter, poor since her father had died leaving a large family to cope for itself, but she'd had a good enough education. She'd been governess to one of Isabella's friends in Dorset and came with high references. And it looked as if she might stay. The girls liked her as much as they would ever like any governess – they treated her abominably at first, but she knew just how to handle them and within a few weeks they adored her.' He paused, then added quietly. 'And so did I.' He fell silent again.

Francis waited, knowing that this was no time for asking questions. Jeremiah had begun his story and would complete it in his own way, his own time. Clearly, it was painful for him to talk of the young woman who had come to teach his stepdaughters and stayed to love him. And Francis had no doubt that Jeremiah had loved her, too; the quality of his voice, the strange softness in his heavy face, told all that was necessary.

'It didn't begin at once,' Jeremiah said at last. 'Though I knew the moment I saw her that here was a woman I could love – I was not many years older than she and had married an older woman, a widow, for her fortune. Oh, there was never any doubt about that and it was common enough – the match was advantageous to us both. But it did not satisfy me as a man. Marriage, it seems, rarely does.

'But I couldn't approach her – not at once. If she had been bold and flirtatious herself, it might have been easier. But then I wouldn't have loved her – it was Mary's modesty that attracted me so much. And she never gave me any hint by so much as a word or a glance that there was any hope for me. She concealed her feelings with such success that we might never have known had it not been for a Christmas gathering several months after she came to the house. The children wanted to play games, and arranged a system of forfeits. One of them was a kiss . . .' Jeremiah looked up and met Francis's eyes. 'I paid my due to Mary and we both knew that it could not stop there. We kissed again, later, where no one could see. Even then, we didn't make the final commitment at once. It was well into the New Year before I went to her room for the first time.'

Darkness filled the corners of the big room. The lamplight made a pool of yellow light on the table, its edges merging with the glow of the fire. Outside, the wind had died down, its howl no longer sounding in the chimney.

'We loved each other through the rest of the winter and into the spring,' Jeremiah said at last. 'And then, one day, she came to me and told me that she was expecting a child.'

Francis imagined the scene. Mary, tall and slender, with rich golden hair, giving her lover the news they must both have dreaded throughout their liaison. He thought of Jeremiah, a young man then, deeply in love with the beautiful governess; of Isabella, rich in her own right, the marriage settlement firmly tying her money to herself and her son. The fear and the shame, the desperation.

'What did you do?' He could not hold back the question. His voice was tense as he contemplated the effect of the news. What had they done? And where was Mary now?

'We thought of everything,' Jeremiah said with a great weariness in his tone. 'We thought of leaving together – going abroad, perhaps. But without Isabella, I had nothing. Her property was, in law, mine as soon as we married – but her family had been careful to ensure that I could never take it from the business or from Vivian. I was virtually a pauper. And Mary was equally poor. Leaving was impossible. And if it had become known that we had been lovers, or that she was carrying my child, it would have spelt disaster for us both. There seemed to be no way out. It's not a state of affairs that can be hidden for long.'

He stopped again, and this time Francis remained silent. After a few minutes, the deep, aching voice continued.

'I was desperate, and Mary must have been too, although she remained calm. She said she would go away, alone somewhere – to one of her sisters, perhaps, in the country. But that wouldn't do either. The scandal would leak out and it would take no time at all to connect her with me. Eventually, she said she would go somewhere far away, where nobody knew either of us. I could pay to keep her comfortably until the baby was born. But that brought a fresh problem.' He gave Francis one of his quick glances. 'Until then I had not quite realised the full truth – that we were bringing another person into the world. Someone who would depend on us for everything – someone we owed a duty, if nothing more. And when I did realise it, I knew that this was someone else I would love. My own flesh and blood. My son, or daughter. I could not let you go to strangers, as had seemed to be the only solution. And neither could Mary. Yet, it would be impossible to acknowledge you as mine. Again, we did not know what we could do.'

280

Francis watched him. All his life he had known this man, thinking of him as an uncle, half awed by his massiveness, half afraid of his big, booming voice, his brusque manner. Since coming to live in Jeremiah's house, he had grown to know him better and to lose his childish fears. Jeremiah had treated him as an adult, a person of worth whose carpet designs were as valuable to the business as Vivian's acumen in selling the finished product. Now, he realised that he had also been treated as a son.

He was seeing a different side of Jeremiah now. In place of the strong, forceful businessman was a young husband in love with the governess, unsure and afraid, facing the disastrous consequences of his love. Somewhere in that bulky body, these two men came together. And few people knew it. Only Mary – wherever she was now – and, he realised suddenly, his own foster parents, Geoffrey and Enid.

As if Francis had spoken the names aloud, Jeremiah glanced up and nodded.

'You know what we did in the end. I went to my brother Geoffrey and asked his advice – indeed, I asked for his help. We had never been close as brothers, but there was no enmity between us – it was merely that we were so different. And I knew I could trust him. What I didn't know was that he and Enid had been longing for a child of their own ever since they had married, and had only recently come to the conclusion that they were never to have any. Geoffrey asked my permission to speak to Enid, and her answer came without hesitation. They would be more than willing to take the child and bring it up as their own – if only Mary could bring herself to give it up.'

'What a terrible decision,' Francis said softly.

'It was. For Mary would have to go away. She had

281

to leave Pagnels' and it wasn't likely that she would be able to come back. We were forced to part from each other – and she would be forced to lose her child. But it would have been impossible, you understand, for her to bring you up alone. Impossible for her, and for you. Illegitimacy would have marked you for life.'

Francis nodded. He could understand the terrible, heart-rending dilemma that had faced his parents – and he could understand the course they had at last taken. But . . . what had happened to his mother?

'She went away to friends of Geoffrey's who could be relied upon to be discreet – though they never knew the full truth. I was able to make sure that she lacked nothing, and for that I shall always be grateful.' His voice had dropped and Francis leant forward, afraid to miss a single word. He knew that his father would be unable to repeat his words; they seemed to come from his dry throat like small sounds of pain. 'She waited there for you to be born, while I waited here and Geoffrey and Enid waited with me. Never a day passed without one or the other calling in, to see if there had been any news. And then, at last, the message came.'

He stopped again as if it were impossible to go on. Francis waited, his heart beating so hard that he felt his father must hear it. He clenched his hands on the arms of the chair.

'A son. A fine, healthy son. But Mary . . .'

In that moment, Francis knew the truth and knew that he didn't want to hear it. The pain in his father's voice pierced his heart and caught at his throat. He felt the hot sting of tears in his eyes.

'Mary died a day later,' Jeremiah said at last, his words little more than a breath on the quiet air. 'She lived to see you, for a few moments, and to name you. They said it was quite peaceful, in the end.'

In the kitchen, Rebecca had stopped spooning soup into Fanny's mouth. The grey lips would not part, the throat refused to swallow; the last few drops oozed out from one corner and dribbled slowly down the sagging chin. The sunken chest rose and fell very slightly, as if living were now too much effort.

'She's going,' Mrs Hudd said quietly, coming to look at the body that was so frail it looked no more than a heap of rags. 'Poor Fanny.'

Rebecca's eyes blurred. She set down the bowl and spoon and took Fanny's hands in both her own. The fingers were dry and cold, as if the warmth of life had already left the body. They were limp in her hands, thin and fleshless as a bundle of sticks, with no response to indicate that her mother knew that Rebecca was there.

'I don't know what I should have done,' Rebecca said sadly. 'I couldn't leave her there – it was so cold, she had no food in the house, and Dad—' Her voice broke and the tears brimmed over and slid down her cheeks. 'I should have done more – helped – but—'

'There was nothing you could do,' the housekeeper said, laying her hand on Rebecca's shoulder. 'You gave them all the wages you earned, you took food whenever you could. What more could you have done?' She leaned over and touched Fanny's cheek. 'She's never warmed up since you got her here. She's given up, child. Let her go.'

'Oh, Mam . . . Mam . . .' Rebecca wept, cradling the frail hands in hers. But the dying woman gave no sign of hearing her. The faint breaths continued for a few moments, then stopped. Rebecca drew in her own breath.

With a long, shuddering sigh, Fanny opened her eyes. She looked directly at Rebecca, as Rebecca had looked at her in the moment of her birth. Eyes aged before their time gazed for a brief space into eyes that were young and dark and living. And then the papery lids fell, the last breath was exhaled and Fanny's chin dropped to reveal almost entirely toothless gums.

'She's gone,' Mrs Hudd said. 'Well, she's peaceful now.'

Rebecca nodded. She held her mother's hands for a little longer, then kissed the spindly fingers and folded them across the thin breast. Then she stood up, slowly and stiffly, and bent to kiss her mother's wasted cheek.

'What must I do now?'

'She'll have to be laid out,' Mrs Atkins said, coming over from the table. The other servants had withdrawn a little and stood at the other end of the kitchen looking sober. 'And the mistress will have to be told. Didn't Mr Francis say he was going to make it right with her?'

Rebecca nodded. 'But that was before dinner. And he hasn't come back.'

'Mr Pagnel and Mr Francis didn't take dinner,' Mrs Atkins said. 'The mistress ordered it to be put back and then they went off to the library and she had hers with Mr Vivian. Nobody knows what's going on, but it sounded as if the mistress was in a fair taking about something. And Miss Isabel is up in her room and wouldn't open her door for anything.'

They stared at each other. What could have happened to cause such a family disturbance?

'It can't be aught to do with Mam,' Rebecca said at last, and the housekeeper shook her head.

'I don't see how it can be. Not to cause all that

bother. Well, someone will have to do something. I'd better go and see her myself. Rebecca, you'd better come with me in case she wants to see you, too.'

Rebecca took another glance at her mother, lying peacefully now, and then turned reluctantly. She had no wish to face her mistress now; the tears were still wet on her cheeks. With no time yet to grieve for her father, she was faced with the loss of her mother. Isabella, who had probably never grieved for anybody, was the last person she wanted to encounter.

What had happened to Francis? she thought as she followed Mrs Hudd up the stairs. He had promised to return, yet she had seen no more of him and he was evidently too concerned with a business discussion with his uncle to think about her now. No doubt he had forgotten about her and about Fanny as soon as he had left the kitchen. And why not? Why should he concern himself with the troubles of a housemaid? Had he not done enough already?

At the top of the stairs, Mrs Hudd turned and gave Rebecca a critical glance.

'You look like a dog's dinner,' she said. 'You'd better slip up to your bedroom and tidy up a bit – brush your hair and put a clean cap and apron on. And be quick, the mistress won't want to be kept waiting.'

'No, Mrs Hudd.' Rebecca ran quickly back down to the basement and took the back stairs up to her room – it would never do to be seen in the house looking like this. She was well aware of the fact that she looked untidy and dishevelled – since getting up that morning, she had trudged through the snow to her mother's cottage, struggled back with Fanny supported between herself and Francis, and sat for the rest of the morning trying to restore the failing body.

Her cap was crooked, her hair unfastened, her apron wet and grubby. The mistress would certainly be angry if she appeared looking like this.

Back in the room she shared with Polly, she hastily washed her hands and face in water that was almost frozen in the can, then brushed her hair and found a clean cap and apron. A few minutes later, she was running down the attic stairs again. She reached the main house and slowed to a walk. It would be permissible to use the main stairs now, since she looked tidy again and was on her way to see the mistress.

On the landing above the first floor, where the drawing room and library were, she paused. A door was opening somewhere below.

Rebecca hesitated. She heard footsteps, a low voice which she recognised as Mr Pagnel's. He was coming out of the library and someone was with him.

She remembered what Mrs Atkins had said. Mr Pagnel and Mr Francis had not taken dinner. They had gone instead to the library and nobody had seen them since.

Rebecca felt her heart thump. She looked down and saw Mr Pagnel moving along the carpeted passage. He disappeared into the drawing room.

Perhaps Mr Francis wasn't with him after all? She began to descend.

As she reached the bottom stair, she was aware of a movement. She stopped again, her heart jerking, and looked towards the library door.

Francis stood there, perfectly still. He leaned against the door jamb, one arm supporting his body as if he were overwhelmingly weary. Or, thought Rebecca with an insight born of her own experiences, as if he had just been given a great shock.

The fair head lifted and the dark blue eyes met hers.

He made a slight movement towards her and Rebecca found herself responding. She turned her body in his direction, her hands outstretched, palms upwards. Her breath came quickly; her skin tingled.

'Rebecca . . .' Francis said, and with one swift step, he took her in his arms.

Mrs Hudd's eyebrows rose when she came out of the drawing room to find Francis waiting with Rebecca.

'Is there something you want, Mr Francis? I can send for Polly – the mistress wants to see Rebecca.'

'Nothing, thank you, Mrs Hudd. But I promised to talk to my aunt—' he stumbled over the word '—about Rebecca's mother. I did, but now I understand that Mrs Himley has died and I think I should speak to her again.'

Mrs Hudd looked at him doubtfully, but moved back through the door. Rebecca heard her murmur something, and then felt Francis's hand clasp hers firmly and quickly before he preceded her into the room. Quivering a little, she followed.

Isabella sat stiffly on her chair. Jeremiah stood by the heavily curtained window. Rebecca saw his face change as she and Francis entered, and wondered at the cause of it. Suddenly, she was afraid. Had she done a terrible wrong by bringing her mother here? Was she about to be dismissed?

Yet there was no anger in Jeremiah's expression.

Rebecca looked again at her mistress. Isabella Pagnel's face was cold and severe, but oddly absent, as if she had greater matters on her mind than the aberrations of a housemaid.

'This is Rebecca, madam,' Mrs Hudd said unnecessarily, and stepped aside. Francis, too, moved away slightly and Rebecca was left standing alone, momentarily isolated in the big room. She made a bob and stood with eyes downcast, staring at the carpet. She remembered her father weaving this pattern . . . The tears came to her eyes again, hot and stinging.

'Well, Rebecca,' Isabella said coldly, 'what do you have to say for yourself?'

Rebecca hesitated. She stared at the carpet. Her father might have woven this very piece, sitting at his loom for hour after hour, day after day. Probably her mother had drawn for him. She lifted her head and looked around the room, contrasting its warmth and comfort with the cold bareness of the cottage where her parents had lived and her father died. She looked at Isabella Pagnel, plump and pampered, whose idea of a day's work was discussing meals with Mrs Atkins, and thought of the frail bundle of bones that had once been her mother.

'I'm sorry, ma'am,' she said quietly. 'My father died in the night and my mother was ill too. I couldn't leave her there. I didn't know what else to do. I brought her here so that she could be warm and perhaps have something to eat.'

'I see. You consider it your right to bring sick people to my home, to warm them by my fire, nourish them with my food? Did it not occur to you—?'

'Aunt Isabella, please.' Francis stepped forward. 'Rebecca didn't do this alone. I was with her when she found her mother. It was by my suggestion that we brought Mrs Himley here, and I came to tell you immediately—'

'*Tell* me!' Isabella interrupted. Her face was pale and there were red spots on her normally sallow cheeks. 'Tell me, indeed. Do I have no position in this house? Am I mistress here, or not? Perhaps you would like to take over the housekeeping completely,

288

Francis. You seem to be on sufficiently familiar terms with my servants.'

Rebecca looked at her in astonishment. She had never heard Isabella speak so passionately; her anger usually displayed itself in icy sarcasm. It was as if she had some other cause for anger with Francis, something that was burning inside her and needed an outlet. Rebecca remembered the talk in the kitchen, that there had been some kind of family upheaval that had resulted in Miss Isabel being sent to her room and Mr Pagnel and Mr Francis being closeted together in the library and not even eating dinner. And she thought of the way Francis had caught her in his arms only a few moments ago; the sudden urgency of his lips on hers, the sense she had had of some deep need within him.

What did it all mean? What was happening?

But she had no time to wonder further. Francis was speaking again, his voice low with controlled anger.

'Please, Aunt Isabella! Of course I don't wish to usurp you. But please try to understand – there was no time to decide anything else. Mrs Himley was clearly ill and in distress. She needed help, and who else was there to give it? We couldn't leave her there, alone with her dead husband and dying herself. You know she has died now?'

'I do, and in my kitchen, too,' Isabella said distastefully. 'And now I suppose we must have a laying-out and all the accompanying disturbance. And am I to pay for a funeral too?'

'Aunt, *please*.' Through her tears, Rebecca caught his quick glance at her face. 'Rebecca has just lost both her parents – this is no way to talk before her—'

'And am I now to be told how to conduct myself in my own drawing room?' Isabella was on her feet, her eyes flashing. She wheeled towards Jeremiah. 'Do you hear this, husband? Do you hear the way this boy speaks to me? Do you mean to stand by and condone his behaviour?'

Jeremiah came quickly away from the window. He gave Rebecca a swift glance from his dark eyes; they lingered a little more on Francis. Then he turned to his wife and placed his hand on her shoulder.

'Sit down, Isabella. It's been a trying day for you. Why don't you rest, and let me deal with this?'

'But the servants – it's my task to manage—'

'And you do it excellently, my love. But you're exhausted now, and no wonder. And there really is no cause for you to be upset by this sad business.' He turned to Francis. 'I understand your decision to bring the poor woman here. You did the best you could do, in the circumstances. I feel sure that if your aunt were not overtired and upset already, she would have been only too glad that you did so – after all, my dear,' he added, turning back to his wife, 'don't we all know how much care you give to the poor, how you help their charities and work as an overseer of the workhouse? Nobody can accuse you of being hard-hearted. Now—' He turned back to Francis '—I suggest that you complete the task you began, and see to the disposal of the remains. No doubt Rebecca herself will be glad of your help in this – do I understand your father has died too? Well, then, you have much to do. Mrs Hudd, can you release Rebecca from her tasks for the rest of the day?'

'We've managed without her so far, sir,' Mrs Hudd said dryly.

'Then let her do this. And then, my dear wife, I suggest we forget all about this sad incident. We have other matters to concern us.' He nodded at Mrs

Hudd. 'Thank you, Mrs Hudd. Mr Francis will come with you now and make all the necessary arrangements. And if you could send up a tray of tea? I'm sure my wife would like some refreshment, after all this distress.'

Mrs Hudd motioned to Rebecca to leave the room, and then followed her. After a moment, Francis too came out and followed them down the stairs. Just outside the kitchen door, he touched Rebecca's arm. She stopped. Mrs Hudd went into the kitchen and they stood alone in the dim passage.

'I'll arrange everything,' Francis said quietly. 'Don't worry any more. Your mother will have to be removed, of course. Perhaps you might like her to be taken back to your cottage, to be with your father for this last night? And then they can be buried together as soon as it can be arranged. Will you be happy with that?'

She looked up at him, her eyes filled with tears. He was watching her with a strange expression on his face, a darkness in his eyes that turned her heart over. She gave a little gasp, but could not look away.

'Rebecca . . . I must see you. I must talk to you . . .'

'No,' she whispered. 'No, Mr Francis – you mustn't talk to me like this. We mustn't . . .'

'*Yes.*' He gripped her shoulders with both hands and she felt the tremor pass from his fingers into her own body. She shivered and knew that he sensed it. His fingers tightened.

'Yes, we must,' he said. 'We have to talk to each other – to find out just what's happening between us. You feel it too, don't you. *Don't* you, Rebecca?'

She tried to meet his eye and deny it, but could not. Slowly, she nodded her head.

'But there can't be anything between us, Mr

Francis. There can't. You must know that. I'm just a housemaid and you're – you're—'

'You don't know what I am,' Francis said grimly. 'I'm not what you think – that's certain. I'm not even what *I* thought. But that makes no difference. Between us, there's—'

'There's nothing between us, nothing,' Rebecca said desperately. 'Mr Francis, we hear things below stairs. We see things. And everyone's saying how you're going to be engaged to Miss Isabel. So how can you say there's something happening between you and me? It can't. Nothing can. Ever.'

Francis dropped his hands from her shoulders and stared at her. 'They're saying that? Then hear this, Rebecca. There is not, nor ever will be, any possibility of my marrying Isabel. Never. Do you hear me? Do you understand me?' The intensity in his voice, the burning in his eyes, were almost frightening. Rebecca stared up at him, her heart thumping.

'Yes, I hear you. But—'

'Then believe it,' he said quietly, and reached out for her again. But before his fingers could touch her, there was a sound at the kitchen door. And when it opened, Francis and Rebecca were standing well apart, and Rebecca had her back to him.

'There you are,' Mrs Hudd said. 'Well, I've given orders that you're not to be disturbed from whatever you want to do today, Rebecca – not that there's much left of the day, it's almost six now. Mr Francis, they've taken the body into the small scullery and I'd be glad if it could be removed as soon as possible. It's not healthy, having a dead body in a kitchen.' She looked at Rebecca's white face. 'I'm sorry, my dear, to be so blunt but there it is. She shouldn't have been here at all, and you know it.'

'And it's entirely my doing that she is,' Francis said at once. 'Don't worry, Mrs Hudd. I'll see to everything.' He gave Rebecca a last glance. 'Find something warm to wear and come with me,' he said, and she bowed her head and followed him.

'And now I hope you're satisfied,' Isabella said to her husband. 'You've humiliated me in front of my own servants and undermined my authority. A good day's work which took you only minutes to achieve.'

'Don't be silly, my dear. I've done nothing of the sort. And I've relieved you of an unpleasant responsibility—'

'Responsibility! It was by no wish of mine that a pauper was brought to die in my kitchen! Francis should have had more sense. She was almost certainly diseased – goodness knows what filth she brought with her. I shall be afraid to eat anything cooked in that kitchen until it's been thoroughly cleansed and fumigated.'

'Then perhaps you had better go away for a while,' Jeremiah suggested. 'To Vivian's house – I'm sure he and Maria would be glad to have you, and you can enjoy pampering your granddaughters. You could take Isabel with you, too – which would get her away from Francis for a while and give her a chance to forget this obsession she has for him.'

Isabella stared at him. She opened her mouth indignantly, then seemed to think better of it.

'It is a solution, I suppose,' she said grudgingly. 'When Vivian went back to the factory after dinner he suggested that I might take Isabel away for a while. And the weather is too bad for us to travel far. But I think it is Francis who should be leaving – not Isabel.' She looked at him. 'Did the boy admit to

293

anything, Jeremiah? Had any real impropriety taken place?'

'None at all,' Jeremiah said swiftly. 'And Francis assured me – though without once casting the slightest doubt on Isabel's own honour – that he never intended to make any advance towards her. He does not wish to marry her, I am convinced of that. The feeling is entirely on her side and came with as much of a shock to him as it did to us.'

'Then we must part them and keep them apart until she recovers from her fancies,' Isabella said firmly. 'You are right, husband – a period away from this house will do her good. She can help Maria with the children – that will keep her occupied. And I shall be able to forget the dreadful things that have taken place here today.' She shuddered theatrically. 'A dead body in my own kitchen – why, it does not bear thinking about.'

'Then don't think about it any more. Francis will deal with everything. And I'm quite sure you need fear nothing tonight. Mrs Atkins is a most careful cook – she won't have allowed any risk to our health.'

'All the same,' Isabella said, 'I think I would like to go to Vivian's as soon as it can be arranged.'

'I'll send a message to him at once,' Jeremiah said. 'He will expect you tomorrow, I'm sure. And now – will you tell Isabel, or shall I? Shall I have her called down?'

'No. I'll go to her room and speak to her there. Let us hope that the past few hours have given her time to consider her foolish behaviour.' Isabella rose to her feet. 'In any case, I intend to tolerate no more of her hysterics. I never had trouble of this kind with my other daughters – I do not intend the youngest to defeat me.'

Jeremiah watched her go. He moved over to the

window and lifted the heavy velvet curtain to peer out into the dark, snowy night. He thought of all that had happened during the day, of the truth he had been forced to reveal to Francis.

Francis. His son. For the first time in over twenty years, he was able to let the words move in his mind. For all that time, ever since the motherless boy had been brought home to Kidderminster and handed to Geoffrey and Enid to bring up as their own, he had never allowed himself to think of Francis as his son. Always, he had been forced to remind himself that he was no more than a nephew . . . and not even of his blood.

Explaining this to Francis had been painful, as though he were rejecting him all over again. And he had known that he must make it clear that the truth must remain a secret between the two of them, that Vivian would remain his heir. But that Francis was his true son was something he could deny to himself no longer. He could look at him and see recognition in the eyes that looked back. He could look at him and remember Mary.

Jeremiah turned away from the window. He walked slowly, heavily, across the room and came to a stop before the fire. He rested his arm on the mantelpiece and stared down into the flames.

He thought about Mary, the woman he had loved deeply, passionately, wholly. The woman he had condemned to death with that love.

And for only the second time since Francis's birth, he allowed his grief to flood into his heart. And allowed the tears to fall.

Chapter Thirteen

Isabel stayed in her room all afternoon. She was not, as she had often been as a child, locked in; but she was too proud to come out. When her mother was ready to treat her as an adult, she must come and tell her so. Until then, Isabel would remain in her room as if she were indeed the naughty little girl her mother seemed to think her.

Over and over again, she re-enacted the scene in the drawing room in her head. The sudden moment when she had stepped forward and made that surprising announcement about herself and Francis. Yes – she had surprised herself, too. It had not been in her mind to make any declaration before Francis had made his. But she had begun lately to feel a disquiet about Francis's feelings for her. She was not quite as sure as she would have liked to be that he returned the passion she felt for him. And her mother's remark, designed as it was to humiliate him, had stung her into action.

When Francis and I are married . . . The words repeated themselves in her head, a litany that she had sung to herself many times before but never spoken aloud. Words that still surprised her, for hadn't she declared often enough that she would never marry, that the state was abhorrent to her? Yet with Francis, it would be different. Their marriage would not be arranged to suit two families financially, as her sister Sarah's had been, nor to bring breeding to the line as in Vivian's case. Theirs would be an alliance between two people already friends, two people who could laugh and play as if they were still children, ignoring the tedious concerns that seemed to beset most married people. Their home would be an extension of the tree-house they had played in as children, their family no more trouble than the cluster of toy animals they had dragged up the tree with them.

Did Francis feel the same? The question had tormented her through many sleepless nights. He was still her friend, she was sure of that. But did he share her views on love and marriage – that both could be a simple continuation of a childhood friendship, a happy, comfortable relationship that ignored both passion and convention, in which she could feel safe?

Safe . . . The word was a strange one. What did she have to fear, after all, in marriage, in adult life? Yet there was something dark and sinister about it. Something that hovered at the edges of her mind like a nameless shadow.

It had been there when she was in the library with Francis, feeling that sudden desire to be in his arms, that sudden need to be close to him. It had frightened her a little, yet she had known that she was safe with him. There was that word again – *safe*. What did it mean? And what was the fear that kept her from the idea of marriage with another man, yet was absent when she was with Francis?

It had been the same urgency that had driven her to make that declaration. She had seen, with a quick surge of frightened amusement, the shock that it had been to both Francis and her mother. And she had been terrified that he would deny it, reveal her for a liar and a wanton, and tell Isabella that there had never been any understanding between them, that he neither loved Isabel nor wished to marry her. If he had done that, Isabel thought, she would have wanted the earth to open beneath her. She would have wanted to disappear for good.

But he had done nothing of the kind. And that, surely, must mean that he loved her, too – that he wanted to marry her – that he had been keeping his own feelings under restraint, behaving as a gentleman should, and perhaps had even been afraid that he would not be considered a worthy suitor anyway.

Well, he would have to be considered now. They might well *have* to be married, for fear of what impropriety they might have committed.

Isabel began to feel excited. She sat in a chair, watching the snow fall against the window, waiting as the afternoon drew slowly into evening. Soon, someone would come to say that her parents wanted to see her downstairs. Soon, she would know what had been decided.

But what else could be decided? In Isabel's mind, there was no possibility of dispute. She must – she *would* – be permitted to marry Francis.

But the darkening afternoon brought with it a growing unease. What could they be talking about, down there? Why was it taking so long? She had heard her father and Vivian come in, Polly had brought her dinner on a tray, and an hour or so later she had heard the front door slam. Looking down from her window, she had seen Vivian going out alone, presumably back to the factory. Her father seemed to have stayed at home and she guessed that he and her mother were discussing the marriage between her and Francis. Possibly they were even discussing it with Francis himself. No doubt her father would be angry that Francis had not spoken to him first, but that would soon settle down. They must be arranging settlements and things – Isabel was vague about the details but recalled long discussion between her father and Sarah's husband when their marriage was being arranged. How dreadfully tedious for poor Francis, she thought with a moment's sympathy. But men didn't mind that kind of thing, did they? They even seemed to enjoy it.

Isabel got up and moved restlessly around the room. She looked at the tray Polly had brought; she had touched little of the food and now it was cold and unappetising. She broke off a small piece of cheese and put it in her mouth. It tasted dry and musty and she had difficulty in swallowing it. Her body was tense, her heart racing. She felt very slightly light-headed.

It was fully dark, and had been for some time, when Isabel heard at last footsteps on the stairs. She started up, wondering if she were dreaming – her head felt muzzy, as if she had been asleep. Then, fighting an impulse to leap to her feet and face whoever was coming to her, she leaned back and rested her head on the back of the chair.

The door opened. Her mother came in, carrying a candle. She looked at Isabel and went to the wash-stand, lighting the candle that had been placed there that morning by the maid, and setting her own beside it. The room was filled with flickering light and shadows.

'Well, miss,' she said, taking the chair beside the bed, 'you have certainly done your best to create trouble, have you not?'

Isabel stared at her. It was not the greeting she had expected, but perhaps her mother was still angry over the scene she had caused. Isabella had never particularly liked Francis, it was true – she had tolerated him as a child and had been against his coming to live in the house. But surely now that he and Isabel were to be married . . .

'I didn't mean to cause trouble, Mother. I would not have said anything at all, but—'

'But you were impulsive, as usual. You spoke without thinking, just as you have always done. Indeed, I sometimes wonder whether you think at all. Your tongue does not appear to be connected with your brain in the same way as other people's.'

Isabel flushed. 'Mother—'

Isabella lifted her hand. 'Please. I did not come here to argue, nor even to discuss. I simply wish to tell you what is to be done. Then I shall go. Polly will be with you soon, to help you pack.'

'*Pack*?'

'Certainly. You did not imagine you would be permitted to stay here, did you? To create fresh scandal? It's your good fortune that there does not seem to have been any yet – but scandal there will certainly be, if you and Francis remain in the house together. And since your father refuses to send him away—' Isabella's voice tightened '—then it must be you. And I shall come with you. There is no better chaperone than a girl's own mother, after all.'

Isabel's hands tightened on the arms of her chair. 'But where are we going?'

'Only to Vivian's, for the time being. The weather is too bad for us to contemplate going to Dorset, which I would have chosen to do. But you'll be kept busy enough at Vivian's, helping with the little girls. You'll soon forget this nonsense.' She rose to her feet. 'Well, that's all I came to say. You'll be ready to leave first thing in the morning. Meanwhile, you'll stay in your room. There is to be no idea of leaving it, you

301

understand? And no attempts made to see your cousin. I hope I've made myself clear about that.'

'But—' Isabel stood up, her eyes wide and frightened. 'Mother, you can't mean this. You can't take me away – away from Francis. I won't go!' She moved closer, laid her hand on her mother's sleeve. 'Mother – are you saying I can't marry Francis? Are you really saying that?'

Isabella slapped her hand away as if its touch revolted her. 'Of course I'm saying that, you silly child! This idea is quite out of the question – impossible. Marry Francis! I never heard of such a thing. And when you come to your senses, you'll agree with me, Isabel. You'll see that it's no more than a foolish whim, a childish fancy. You'll thank me then for what I'm doing now.'

'I won't! Never!' Isabel faced her mother, her body trembling. 'I'll hate you for ever if you do this to me, Mother. Yes, and Francis too – I'll hate you both. I shall never marry anyone if I can't marry Francis. Do you hear me? I shall *never* marry. Never.'

'Then you'll be an even more foolish girl than I take you for,' Isabella said coldly. She went to the washstand and lifted her candle. 'You'll be an old maid, and there's no pleasure in that, I can assure you. But that won't happen, Isabel. You'll forget Francis and marry someone else – quite happily, I think, in about a year from now. Just wait and see if I'm not right. Meanwhile—' she glanced around the room '—you may take out the things you want to have packed and Polly will come and help you soon. And be ready immediately after breakfast tomorrow.'

She glided from the room, leaving Isabel standing alone, shaking with anger and fear, unable to believe what had happened. Not to be allowed to marry

Francis! To be sent away – only to Vivian's it was true, but it might as well be a hundred miles away. To be kept from him; to be forced into marriage with some other man.

No. No. She would not do it. She could *not* be forced.

There was a tap on the door. Polly entered with a fresh tray of food. She set it down on the low table and clucked with disapproval as she saw that the first had been left untouched.

'Miss Isabel, you must eat something,' she said. 'You'll starve. You'll starve yourself to death.'

'Yes,' Isabel said, staring at the two trays of food, the fresh one as repellent to her as the stale. 'Yes, I shall, shan't I . . .'

The funeral of her mother and father was something Rebecca tried as quickly as possible to forget. Even though Francis insisted that she allow him to make the arrangements – which enabled him to give them a 'decent' though plain funeral, rather than the pauper's burial they had always feared – Rebecca still found it a painful experience. Never had she missed Tom and Bessie so much as on that raw morning when she stood under the lowering sky and watched the coffins being lowered into their chilly grave. Never had she felt quite so alone.

Yet she was not alone. Mrs Hudd was there, to pay her last respects to Fanny, the housemaid she had known years ago. Polly was there, her arm around Rebecca's waist as they left the church. There were others, too – weavers who had drunk and 'played' with William, neighbours who had helped and been helped by Fanny, the women she had worked with in the bobbin-winding shop. But there was nobody of her own, no kith, no kin.

But Francis was there. Tall, pale and sombre in his black clothes and tall hat, yet with a warmth in his eyes as they rested on Rebecca. She could feel them throughout the brief service; she could feel them as they left the church and walked slowly down the path. At the gateway, she turned and looked up at him.

'Thank you, Mr Francis,' she said gravely, and held out her hand. 'It was good of you to come. It was good of you to do so much.'

Francis took her hand in his. She felt his strength and warmth and her skin prickled. Her cheeks were suddenly hot.

'I'm glad I was able to do it,' he said quietly. 'I'd do more, if I could.'

Rebecca was conscious suddenly of the eyes of Mrs Hudd and Polly and withdrew her hand. She gave him a swift, upward glance and then made a quick bob before turning back to them. Together, they walked back through the town and up the hill to Pagnel House.

'What'll you do now?' Polly asked. 'Can you get in touch with your brother and sister?'

Rebecca shrugged. 'I've got an address, but it was a long time ago they were there. Maybe they've moved on – I don't know. I can try.'

'Write them a letter,' Polly suggested. 'Your Tom can read, can't he? Didn't he write to your mam once?'

Rebecca nodded. But she had little hope of being able to contact Tom and Bessie again. It was a long time since their last envelope had arrived and been sent away again. Perhaps it had, at last, contained a letter. Perhaps it had contained news they needed to know. Perhaps one of them had been ill – had even died.

All manner of things might have happened to them in London. They might both have perished, unknown and unmourned, in the city that had swallowed them.

She might as well consider herself entirely alone.

'Well, that's over,' Mrs Hudd declared, taking off her shawl and jacket as they came back into the kitchen. 'A cup of tea if you've got one handy, Mrs Atkins, we're all chilled to the marrow. And then you two girls can get back into your uniforms as quick as maybe – there's plenty to be done.'

'Oh, not for Becky, Mrs Hudd, surely,' Polly protested. 'She's had a bad time these past few days – can't she be excused? I'll do her fires for her.'

'And how many times have you already done that?' Mrs Hudd demanded. 'And the others, too – why, even Susan's done Rebecca's work for her. No, she's got to start again some time and it might as well be now. It won't help her to mope about with nothing to do, anyway – set her brooding, that will, and that does nobody any good.'

'It's all right, Polly,' Rebecca said. 'I'd rather do my work. Mrs Hudd's right – I'll only start thinking if I've got nothing to do. And there's nothing but sad thoughts now, it seems.'

Polly looked at her with concern, then gave her arm a squeeze. 'Well, you just say if you're tired or want to go and have a cry,' she said. 'I shan't mind. I know when my mam died, I kept on crying, couldn't seem to help myself somehow.'

'And quite right too,' Mrs Hudd said briskly. 'A girl's mother's a special person – it's a hard thing if you can't shed a few tears for her. But that don't mean you can't sweep a few floors and mend a few fires at the same time. And that's what you'd better do first – I'll be bound the upstairs fires want seeing to. Drink your tea quickly now, the pair of you.'

Rebecca took her coal scuttle and went upstairs. It was almost dark – although the evenings were drawing out now, the bad weather had closed in again after a brief thaw and the heavy-bellied clouds threatened more snow. She hurried along the passages, shivering, and went to the drawing room first. There was nobody there but the fire was low; she replenished it, did the same in the dining room, and then came to the library.

As soon as she turned the knob on the door, she knew there was someone in the room. She hesitated, her heart hammering. Was it Francis? He had said he must see her . . . and this was the place where they most often met. But she dared not tarry. Mrs Hudd and Susan would be expecting her back in the kitchen, ready for her next chore . . . Briefly, she wondered if it would not be better to return now, and leave the library fire to Polly.

But even as the thought passed through her mind, she was inside the room and drawing the door closed behind her.

She looked around, half afraid. The room was lit by a single lamp, set in the middle of the table, and by the glow of the fire. And near the fire, in the big armchair where Francis would so often sit, lay a sprawling figure.

Rebecca approached slowly. And then drew back.

The man in the chair stirred. His eyes glinted in the dull red light. His teeth gleamed as he smiled. He sat up.

'Why, Rebecca – so it's you. How fortunate.'

Rebecca gasped and backed away, but Vivian was on his feet now and moving swiftly past her to block her exit. Her heart jerked. Ever since he had threatened her in the warehouse, she had known that he meant to have her. She had known it would not be easy to avoid him, for even though he no longer lived in Pagnel House he was constantly in and out, and as the son of the house was free to go where he pleased.

The thought of being dragged into his arms, forced to endure his kisses, his hands on her body, brought a shudder to Rebecca's spine. But surely he would not dare to attack her here, in his father's library . . .

Vivian smiled mockingly. 'Did you come to add some coals to the fire, sweet Rebecca? Well, do so, then. We don't want it to go out, do we? It's a cold day.'

Cautiously, Rebecca did as she was told, kneeling in front of the hearth and taking one lump of coal at a time in her tongs. She was aware of Vivian moving nearer as she did so, until he was standing so close that she could not stand up without brushing against him. She stayed where she was, praying that he might move away. But he did not; indeed, she could feel that he had inched a little closer.

She was quite still, determined not to give him the satisfaction he sought.

'Stand up, Rebecca,' Vivian said softly. 'Stand up and look at me. Let's see what you look like, with that pretty hair loose – I'll wager you've loosened it for other men.'

'No—' she began indignantly, but he bent and raised her easily by her elbows, keeping her between himself and the fireplace so that she was trapped by his body. She could feel his heat against her breasts, his quick breath on her face. She tensed her muscles and tried to use her fists against his chest, but he laughed and tightened his fingers so that they bit painfully into the nerves of her elbows.

'Still the protesting maiden! Well, I'll enjoy it all the more. And as well here, by this fire so delightfully replenished as anywhere else.' His tone hardened. 'I told you, miss, that you would pay your sister's debts for her. And she owes me many, I warn you.'

He looked down at her for a moment, his eyes glinting cruelly. Then he turned quickly away.

'We'll have the door locked, I think. I wouldn't want young Poll to walk in, looking for you. Nor my mother . . .' He was at the door, stretching out his hand towards the key. Rebecca cast a quick glance around the room, but there was no escape. Hardly knowing what she did, she picked up the poker and held it like a weapon. Vivian saw her movement and laughed.

'That won't serve you, my pretty young firebrand! What good will it do if you break my skull with that? No more than it did for your sister to cut Jabez Gast's throat. And this time there'll be no one to help you get away.' He stayed by the door, still laughing at her, but his tone was vicious as he continued. 'Yes, I helped your brother and sister to get away, I hid them and gave them money and an address to go to. And what did they do? They took it and fled – and were never seen again. They were going to be useful to me in London – your brother as a servant and your sister as a bedfellow. They were to be there for me whenever I needed them. And what happened? They stole my money and disappeared. That's a debt they owe me – a debt you're going to pay.' His hand dropped away from the door and he came back to her, his eyes glittering in the low light. 'And you'll start paying now.'

Rebecca backed away, raising the poker in her hand. 'Don't you come near me – I'll use this, I swear I will!'

His harsh laugh sounded again. 'Why, she really means it. She'd kill for her honour.' His hand shot out and gripped her wrist, the strong fingers sending an almost paralysing bolt of pain through her hands, so that she was forced to drop her weapon. Before she could escape, he caught her in strong, hard arms and assaulted her mouth with his.

She twisted in his arms, wrenching her head aside, but she could not escape that cruel grip, nor those searching lips. She felt his teeth in her soft flesh and cried out, but the cries never left her throat. And she heard Vivian's chuckle, deep in his chest, and knew that he was indeed enjoying her fear, and that her struggles were inflaming the dark passion that was driving him on.

His tongue was now forcing its way into her mouth, a powerful intruder that brought a threat of a further, even more intimate, invasion. Rebecca felt his hands on her body, his fingers fumbling with her skirts. Anger flared inside her. She knew she must get away, but she knew also that she wanted to punish this man for his arrogant cruelty, his careless violation.

Sharply, she brought her teeth together, feeling the softness of living flesh between them, the sudden recoil of the squirming muscle of his tongue. As Vivian grunted and jerked back his head, she tasted blood and turned away, sickened, to spit it out.

Vivian recovered and, swearing, reached for her again. But she was back at the fireplace, the poker hastily snatched up again into one hand, the coal scuttle in the other, facing him with flashing eyes, and he hesitated.

The doorknob rattled. There was a squeal of hinges. Vivian dropped his arms at once, and she heard a muttered curse. Distracted by his own words, he had forgotten, after all, to lock it.

Jeremiah Pagnel came into the room. He looked at

Vivian and then at Rebecca. She looked down at the floor, thankful that the dim light hid the scarlet colour in her face.

'So there you are, Vivian,' Jeremiah said. 'I've been looking for you . . . Francis and I have something to discuss. Those new patterns – he's got an idea he thinks will be better.' He turned and beckoned. 'Come in, Francis, Vivian's here. We can talk about it now.'

Rebecca seized her chance to slip out of the room. She hardly dared lift her head as she went through the door. But Francis was there, just outside, and she could not prevent herself from looking up and meeting his eyes.

She saw his glance move over her burning face, saw it rest on her parted lips. His eyes narrowed and he looked past her, at his cousin who stood straddle-legged on the hearth. Rebecca caught her breath and slipped past him.

But as she went, she heard a breath of a whisper – a whisper that sounded like the one word 'Tomorrow . . .' And she carried it in her heart through the rest of the day.

Rebecca slept little that night. Her mind was in turmoil. So much had happened during the past few days – the deaths of her parents, the funeral, the strength and comfort of Francis's presence and finally the shock of Vivian's assault. She tossed and turned in her narrow bed, the events mingling in her mind until she scarcely knew whether she was awake or dreaming. Twice she dozed and then woke with a start, once imagining Francis's arms around her, once convinced that Vivian's dark, handsome face was close to hers in the darkness.

At last she gave up trying to sleep and lay staring into the darkness. She could hear Polly's light breathing in the other bed, and envied her. Nothing much seemed to ruffle Polly; she sailed through her life with a saucy smile on her lips and seemed to get a lot of fun one way and another. The highlights of her day were the moments when the various tradesmen came to the kitchen door. Milkman, fishman, butcher's boy – they all knew Polly, all had a cheeky remark to make when she came to the door, and Polly always had a quick answer for them. Any one of them, Rebecca knew, would have been glad to get Polly to meet them on her afternoon off, but Polly would only toss her head and laugh.

'I've got better fish to fry,' she would say with a sidelong glance.

But she was not concerned about Polly now. Her mind was too busy with her own worries and griefs. The sadness of her parents' deaths haunted her. Why did people have to live and die like that, with so little joy to help them through their lives? Why were so many lives dragged out in poverty, with the threat of disease and death a constant companion? Why was it all so unequal – the poor so grindingly poor, the rich so carelessly rich?

It was so unfair. And even for those like herself and Polly, there was little security. At any moment, Isabella Pagnel could for no reason at all turn her and Polly out into the snow with only a week's wages and no character to help them find another position. They could be forced to wander the streets, reduced to no more than beggars, scraping a living in the most degrading manner. And it could happen to any of them. They lived at the mercy of their employers.

She turned on her side, staring at the pale square of

the window, and remembered those terrifying moments in the library. She had known, as all the maids knew, that Mr Vivian was to be avoided if you didn't want to find yourself trapped in some dark corner with your skirts up. And she'd known too that it was only a matter of time before he remembered his promise to make Rebecca pay Bessie's 'debts' for her.

It was common enough, after all – maidservants were considered fair game by the gentlemen, young and old, in many houses. In Pagnel House they were luckier than most. Mr Pagnel never so much as glanced at a maidservant and Mr Francis was too shy. But when Mr Vivian's bold eyes rested on a young housemaid, it was certain that he intended to pursue her. And not many girls were determined enough to resist. Some of them didn't even want to.

'Why should they?' Polly had enquired once as she and Rebecca scrubbed potatoes together in the scullery. 'A girl could do a lot worse than Mr Vivian – he's young and handsome, and generous too if a girl pleases him.' And then she'd stopped suddenly and given Rebecca a quick, sideways glance before going to pour the dirty water away in the corner of the yard.

Rebecca said nothing. She had suspected for some time that Polly had been one of those who did not resist. She had seen a secretive glimmer in her friend's eyes and noticed Polly's suppressed excitement when Vivian had been in the house. But she had never asked questions, even when Polly had dropped hints. It was something that she didn't want to know.

She wondered again about her sister, Bessie. Could she really have been helped to escape by Vivian? Could it really be true that he had given her and Tom money for the journey, that he'd intended to use them as servants – and worse – on his visits to London? Rebecca remembered Bessie's remarks about Vivian when she had first gone to work at the carpet shop. She had always had her eye on him. It looked as if she had been successful. But if so – why avoid him? Why vanish once she was in London?

Perhaps Tom had influenced her. He had always been straitlaced, looking down his nose at Bessie's giggling chatter about the men she worked with. And he had defended her against Jabez. Perhaps the idea of risking a hanging, only for Bess to sell herself to Vivian Pagnel, had been too much for him.

At last Rebecca's thoughts came to Francis. He had been so strong, she was not sure how she would have managed to cope with the last few days if Francis had not been there to help her, there with her in the cottage, to bring Fanny back to the house, to arrange the funeral and be beside her at the graveside. She had come to rely on him, knowing that she could do so without imposing, knowing that he expected and welcomed it. Knowing that he wanted her to rely on him – turn to him.

There was a strange comfort in the thought of Francis. And, alongside it, a tingling excitement that frightened her a little but was so pleasurable that she could not turn away from it. Instead, finding which thoughts brought it most strongly to her heart – the thought of her arm in Francis's as he supported her through the snowy streets, or his eyes on her when no one else could see – she held them in her mind and let the tingling grow. What harm was there in that, after all? It could hurt nobody. And it was the only comfort she had now.

His whisper came into her mind again. *'Tomorrow . . .'*

313

She was aware suddenly that the darkness was beginning to give way to a cold, bright light. She got up and looked out of the window.

The sky had cleared and a full moon rode high above the town. The snow lay like a soft, feathery quilt over the roofs and gleamed in narrow streets, hiding the litter and dirt to bring an impression of bright cleanliness that was entirely false.

As false as the life so many people lived, she thought bitterly. Bright and clean on the surface; hiding a seething mass of dirt and misery underneath.

The church clock struck and Rebecca realised that in only half an hour she and Polly would be beginning their working day. There was no use in going back to bed now. She might as well dress by the light of the moon and start work early. There were still tasks left undone from yesterday, and it would please Mrs Hudd and Susan if she were to make an effort to finish them today.

Quickly and quietly, she dressed and slipped out of the room, leaving Polly fast asleep. She went down to the kitchen where Oddjob and Billy had finished stoking the range, and felt the teapot.

'Ah, there's a cup there if you want it,' Oddjob said. 'About early, ain't you?'

'I couldn't sleep.' Rebecca poured a cup of tea and drank it, then collected up her box and cinder pail. 'I'll start doing the fireplaces. Tell Polly when she comes down, will you?'

In the house, she hesitated. The library? Her skin prickled and she turned towards the drawing room. Perhaps Polly would do the library fire . . .

But this was silly. There would be nobody in the library now. Vivian had gone home last night and Francis – Francis had not been to the library recently.

He preferred to stay in bed on these cold mornings, and Rebecca could not blame him. Indeed, she was thankful for the respite.

It would be perfectly safe to go to the library.

She turned back at the drawing room door and trod softly along the passage to the library door. As usual, it was closed. She turned the knob and went in.

The light of her lantern mingled with a light already there. Halfway through the door before she realised it, Rebecca drew quickly back. But it was too late.

'Come in, Rebecca,' Francis said quietly. 'I've been waiting for you.'

Rebecca set her lamp on the table and came slowly forward to stand her box and cinder pail on the hearth. Francis watched her from behind the chair in which he normally sat. He stood with his hands on the back, gripping it as if he were afraid it might escape. His eyes were dark and watchful.

'Rebecca. You know we have to talk.'

'There's nothing for us to talk about,' she whispered, not daring to move closer to him. 'I'm just a housemaid. And you're engaged to Miss Isa—'

'Rebecca, I've already told you that there's no question of any engagement between me and Miss Isabel.' With a swift movement, he came round the chair and caught her wrist. She gave a little cry and tried to pull away, but his grip was strong and he drew her near him. He held her hand against his breast and laid his other arm around her shoulders. His eyes were dark as the night sky, the pupils glowing with a light as brilliant as the full moon. Rebecca quivered. She gazed up at him, her eyes wide and lips slightly parted.

'Mr Francis—'

'Francis,' he muttered, and his lips brushed hers.

'No "Mr" between us, Rebecca, please. Call me Francis.' He waited a moment and then repeated with urgency throbbing through his voice. 'Please, Rebecca. Use my name.'

'I – can't.'

'Yes. You can. *Please*.'

His lips were touching hers now and she felt their trembling. Suddenly, the differences between them disappeared. It no longer mattered that she was only a housemaid, that his aunt was her mistress. They were a man and a woman together, shaken by the desires that raged between them; desires Rebecca had never allowed herself to recognise but understood now with all the natural intuition of any human being. She lifted herself on her toes, pressing against Francis's body, raising her arms to wind them about his neck. She felt his hand move slowly, caressingly, down her back and shivered; in response, she opened her mouth against his, letting her lips soften against his seeking tongue and replying with her own.

The kiss seemed to go on into eternity. Rebecca, her eyes closed, swayed in Francis's arms. She felt the length of him against her, the warmth of one hand supporting her shoulders while the other stroked gently down her spine. Her body shook, her fingers twined in his hair and she whimpered deep in her throat. Time was forgotten.

At last, reluctantly, Francis finished the kiss and drew his lips away. He looked down at her and Rebecca opened her eyes to find him gazing down at her.

'Oh, Francis . . .' she murmured, and laid her head against his shoulder.

She felt his quiver of pleasure. 'Rebecca, if you knew how that sounds to me. To hear you use my name with no "Mr" to remind us—'

Rebecca jumped and tried to pull away. 'Mr Francis – I'd forgotten – we mustn't do this—'

He gripped her hard against him. 'No! Don't spoil it. You called me Francis – you kissed me. I'd swear you felt the same way as I do. Don't spoil that, Rebecca, I beg you. Forget again. Forget who we are, where we are – forget everything but that I love you . . . and tell me that you love me. Please.'

His lips were on hers again and she could not resist him. She let her head fall back under the pressure of his mouth and felt his hand supporting her neck, his fingers in her hair. All the emotion of the past few days rose up in her, all the fear and pain were calmed and eased, the longing assuaged; and it all drew together in this soaring desire, concentrated in the feeling Francis roused in her, in her need of him and her knowledge of the need he had of her.

He drew her down into the big chair and they lay there together, softly entwined. Rebecca sighed and moved against him, wanting to feel him closer.

'I love you, Rebecca.'

She lifted her head, gazing into his face. Love? Was this what she felt, this tremulous fluttering, this aching need to be with him . . . was this what he felt for her?

Love? Between a young gentleman and a house-maid?

'But—'

'Ssh.' He laid his fingers on her lips. 'No "buts", my love. Let's just be happy for a while. We'll think of "but" later.'

They lay quietly together, Francis moving his fingertips slowly and tenderly over the curves of Rebecca's body. She quivered in his arms, half afraid of the sensations he was waking in her. A tingling in

317

her stomach, a prickling of her skin, an ache that spread itself through her limbs, throbbing in her palms, curling her toes. A warm desire that glowed in her loins and made her want him to explore more, further – and a tremulous fear of the unknown that made her want him to stop.

'The fire,' she murmured at last. 'I'll have to see to the fire.'

'I suppose so.' He loosened his arms and she sat up in his lap, looking at him with wonder. Was she really here, curled up in the arms of Francis Pagnel, feeling herself loved and warm under his indigo eyes? Was she really still plain Rebecca Himley, housemaid and weaver's daughter? Or had some change overtaken her during the past half-hour, and was she now someone entirely different, a being from some exotic and far-off land?

'You came early this morning,' he said as she knelt to do her work.

'I couldn't sleep. So much has happened.'

'I know.' His hand rested lightly on her shoulder and she shivered. 'I couldn't sleep either, Rebecca. Your face kept coming into my mind . . . your eyes, so big and dark, your mouth, the little smile you give when you're afraid you shouldn't be smiling but can't help it – and the way you smile when you're not afraid at all. Smile at me now, Rebecca.'

She turned and her lips parted and widened. He stared at her and then caught her in his arms and buried his face in her dark, glossy hair.

'Rebecca, I love you. All these months, I've loved you, though I scarcely knew it to begin with. You flew into my heart as softly as a butterfly and you've stayed there ever since. And I shall never let you go.'

He held her for a moment, and then gently put her

away from him. 'I hate to see you work like this, Rebecca,' he said quietly. 'But there must be no trouble for you. There's enough disturbance in this house at present. But w 'll talk about that later . . . tomorrow, perhaps. Till then, know that I love you – and that I'll never, never do anything to hurt you.'

Rebecca looked at him uncomprehendingly, then turned back to her work, her heart beating quickly. What did he mean? The house had been disturbed, she knew – something to do with Miss Isabel, though none of the servants seemed to know quite what. But how did it affect herself and Francis? Rebecca had no illusions about the kind of liaison that was likely between a housemaid and one of the young gentlemen of the house. A secret one, carried on at odd moments in secluded corners, with perhaps the occasional night-time visit to his room . . . nothing more. And likely to end in shame and disgrace – dismissal and its dreadful consequences.

She had vowed that it would never happen to her. She had meant never to fall prey to the folly of so many girls she had known, hungry for love, vulnerable and unwary.

And now here she was, deeply in love, ready to risk anything for the man who sat so close to her now, whose lips had burned like fire on hers, who had set a seal on her heart. As foolish as any frivolous serving maid, as reckless as any coquette.

But Francis's words, and his tone, had implied that he did not want such a liaison – that this meant more to him than that. He had said he loved her. The difference between his intentions and those of his cousin Vivian was as wide as the ocean.

Rebecca turned back to the fireplace and swept vigorously. Love, he had said. Love. And even though

319

she could not believe it would ever come true, the word was like a song in her heart. A song she carried for the rest of that cold February day.

Chapter Fourteen

The sudden thaw brought its own problems. Streets that had been thick with ice and snow became quagmires, or sent rushing torrents to sweep debris into cottage doorways and leave a thick coating of slime on stone floors. The bitter cold became a raw, sullen dampness that seeped in through every crack and made fires burn dully. Winter diseases that seemed to have been driven off by the dry cold returned, and the factories and shops found themselves short of workers.

'Just when we've taken that large order from Haisemore Court, too,' Jeremiah fretted as he and the two young men walked around the largest of the Pagnel loom shops. 'Another dozen men off this morning, and half of those who are here are suffering from colds and fever. This will set us back weeks.'

'Nonsense, Father.' Vivian paused beside one of the looms, his eye apparently on the pattern that emerged from the heddles, but in fact appraising the young draw-girl who stood operating the wire. 'Once the men come back they'll be glad to work extra time to earn the money they've lost through being sick. Their so-called Friendly Societies may help with the odd few pence, but not many of them will support a family of squalling brats while their father lies in bed. And there are plenty of unemployed we can take in their place if they do decide to be tardy.'

Francis looked at his cousin. Vivian had filled out lately and showed signs of becoming corpulent in future years, but he was still handsome, his black curls showing no sign of grey. As Francis watched, the draw-girl glanced up and caught Vivian's dark eyes on her; he saw the colour rise in her cheeks before she turned hastily back to her work. A small smile tugged at Vivian's lips and he looked at Francis and grinned.

'They're a buxom lot, these wenches,' he observed as the three men walked on. 'Willing enough, too, many of 'em. How many have you had, Frank?'

Francis felt his own face redden. He shot a quick look at Jeremiah, but his uncle – he still found it difficult to think of him as father – was a few yards ahead and out of earshot. Vivian laughed.

'Don't tell me you haven't sampled the wares! Really, Frank, you're simply not true. How old are you – twenty-two? Have you *never* had a woman? I can't believe that.'

The heat was painful in Francis's cheeks. He shook his head and shrugged. There had been a girl – one of the maids at school, who had made it clear that she had an eye for him. Eventually, nervous and excited, he had found himself alone with her and snatched a kiss, thinking that was enough. But the maid had other ideas; she'd guided his hands and used her own, giggling all the while, and Francis had found himself swept away on a tide of adolescent frenzy. It had been all over in less than five minutes; then they heard footsteps approaching, the maid had pulled away from him, pushed down her skirts and vanished with a pile of linen. And Francis, breathing hard, his heart pounding, had hidden in a corner until the master had walked by.

For several nights after that, he lay awake in a fever of reminiscence and longing. He had prowled the corridors, hoping to find the maid alone again, unable to believe that she was avoiding him. But at mealtimes, when she served him, her eyes were turned demurely away and the small touches she had contrived to give him before were missing. And when he heard smothered giggling from a dark corner one evening, and caught a glimpse of her back vanishing through a doorway only seconds before one of the other boys emerged, looking flushed and rather sheepish, he knew that she was no longer interested in him. He had been initiated and would now have to find his own sport.

But somehow he had never wanted to. The encounter had left him feeling soiled and he was not eager to repeat it. Until he had first met Rebecca, no woman had ever roused any real interest in him.

Now his mind was filled with thoughts of her, his heart ached with a yearning he had never felt for the school maid. But mixed with his feelings was a distaste for the kind of liaison he knew Vivian would have embarked on without hesitation. He could not treat Rebecca as if she were some common slut.

Rebecca had a quality that lifted her out of her class, set her in a class of her own. He thought of her eyes, which could flash with fire yet melt to a gentle warmth; her mouth, so firm yet soft when she gave him her smile; her skin which seemed lit by the luminous glow of her personality. All her physical attributes, which told of the person within, the person he would delight in taking a lifetime to learn to know . . . He could not sully all this; he could not take her, use her and then toss her aside. What he felt for her demanded more than that.

He wanted to spend his life with her. He wanted to marry her.

Vivian was watching him curiously. He repeated his question.

'Have you really never had a woman, Frank?'

Francis hesitated, then laughed. 'Of course I have! But I don't make a hobby of it, like you do. Quite honestly, I'd rather spend the evening sketching and designing – it's less trouble in the long run and might even produce something useful.'

'Oh, I'm sure *I* produce something useful by my "hobby" as you call it, too,' Vivian said slyly. 'Quite a few new little draw-boys and girls. Someone has to keep the labour force going, Frank.'

'I would have thought the weavers themselves were capable of doing that.' Francis felt fresh distaste at Vivian's words. Did he offer to support these 'new draw-boys and girls' through their babyhood? Did he help their unfortunate mothers, some of them barely more than children themselves? Or was he merely boasting?

'Well, you're a real Mrs Grundy,' Vivian observed. 'Too good to enjoy yourself and too selfish to allow other people their pleasures. I do give these girls their own pleasure, you know. Provided they don't fight too much – and most of 'em don't.'

Francis walked quickly on. He caught up with Jeremiah by the last loom and stood with him, watching the new pattern take shape. It was a recent design and one he was pleased with.

'But we need something new,' he said thoughtfully. 'This design – it's good enough. But it's the same kind of pattern as we've been using for years now. We ought to be thinking of fresh ideas.'

'Well, you're the designer,' Jeremiah said. 'I can't see what's wrong with this myself. It's bright, you've made good use of the five colours and it's already popular with our customers. What more can we ask?'

'A new method,' Francis said. 'Something that will

enable us to be more versatile. Something that will make it possible to use more colours and more intricate patterns – or at least to use the whole of the yarn in the front of the pile, rather than so much colour being buried in the back where nobody ever sees it. Have you ever thought of the waste? And there must be ways to produce carpets faster and more efficiently. Suppose we could power the looms by steam – think what a difference that would make.'

'Steam?' Jeremiah said. 'No, Francis, you're talking wildly – carpet-making is a handcraft, it'll never employ steam power. Greater efficiency is highly desirable, I agree – but it won't come through steam.'

'I'm not so sure. I think it will come. Other industries are using steam – you can even cross the Atlantic now by steamship. But in any case, there ought to be ways we can adapt the looms or at least the method by which the pattern is woven. Just think, if we could produce a finer carpet, more quickly and efficiently than our competitors, needing fewer weavers for each piece—'

'It sounds like Utopia,' Vivian said, joining them. 'We could employ fewer men. I agree, Francis – such a method would greatly increase our profits. But what do you have in mind?'

'I'm not sure that I have anything specific in mind. And I wasn't thinking of increasing profits at the expense of our weavers. But there must be some way . . .' Francis frowned as he watched the weaver working his loom. 'The way the yarn's formed into the pattern. And the backing – I've heard mention of jute being used. That would make a strong backing, cheaper, too, than wool.'

'That wouldn't make it easier to use new designs or speed up production,' Jeremiah said. 'But I agree, it could make a cheaper carpet with the same pile. And by doing that, if we could increase our market, we could expand and make more carpets, using the same workforce.' He directed a severe glance at Vivian. 'Better than laying off valuable weavers for other manufacturers to employ, surely.'

Vivian inclined his head. 'Certainly, Father, if you've no objection to spending money on new buildings – our existing ones are full as it is. It would be a considerable speculation, and as yet – if I understand aright – we've no real basis for supposing it will ever come about.'

'No, it's all castles in the air at present – unless Francis can produce a brilliant idea.' Jeremiah led the way out of the loom shop and they picked their way across the puddle-strewn yard to the dyehouse. 'How are the womenfolk settling down with you and Maria, Vivian?'

Vivian shrugged. 'As well as might be expected. Mother's besotted with the baby, of course. By the way, we've finally settled on a name for her – we're going to call her Lucy. Maria's fancy, of course – I hadn't really considered any more girls' names.' He frowned.

'And Isabel?' Francis asked quietly.

Vivian gave a short laugh. 'Oh, Isabel's still refusing food. The silly girl's getting quite pale and thin. I can't imagine why she's worked herself into such a state over you, Frank. She's known you since she was in her cradle. Why, she's been almost a sister to you.'

Francis felt the colour touch his face again. 'I've never encouraged her, I assure you. I've never wanted to be more than a – a friend. A—'

'A brother,' Vivian said helpfully, and Francis shot

him a quick, half-guilty glance. Did Vivian know the truth? Did he suspect? He looked at Jeremiah but there was no flicker of acknowledgement in the eyes that looked back at him. Surely Jeremiah had not told Vivian . . .

'Well, I don't know why she's fixed her ideas on me,' he said at last. 'I wish she wouldn't. I wish she would do as my aunt wishes and find some other man to please her.'

'Well, we're doing our best,' Vivian said heartily. 'Maria's arranging several parties in her honour – young people, friends of hers that she grew up with. She'll soon forget you, Frank.'

'It'll do her good to mix with other young people,' Jeremiah said abruptly. 'Vivian, I want to talk to Bressler about the new indigo dye. He's going to need extra vats to get it into white and then back to blue. I'm not sure it will be worth it.'

'Oh, I'm sure it will, Uncle,' Francis said at once. 'Let me come with you – I'd like to hear what Bressler has to say. But we ought to use that dye – it's a fine, strong colour. I planned to use it in my new designs. And if we don't use it, and Broom or Brintons do—'

'I'll take myself back to the office, then,' Vivian said, turning his steps in the opposite direction. 'I've some work to do before I go to London tomorrow.' He glanced sideways at Francis. 'You really should come with me, you know. There's a good deal for you to learn in London. At the very least, you ought to be looking at the work of other designers.'

'Yes, perhaps you should, Francis.' Jeremiah rubbed a hand over his chin. 'It would do you good to have a change of scene, after all. It's been a long winter for us all.'

Francis moved uneasily. He did not want to leave

Kidderminster now, not with all the revelations of recent weeks weighing on his mind. Isabel's passion for him had disturbed him more than he wanted to admit; in spite of his disclaimer, he felt that he must be responsible, that he ought to have seen the change in her and in some way prevented it. And to discover that Jeremiah was his natural father had been a shock from which he had still not recovered. He had not even begun to consider the implications: his relationship with Vivian, his position in the family, the business. It seemed easier to go on thinking of them all as if nothing had changed. After all, so far as the rest of them were concerned, nothing had.

And then there was Rebecca. Rebecca, whose calm presence had refreshed him through the early summer mornings, whose warmth had comforted him – and who had turned to him in her own need. When had he first begun to love her? During those soft dawns when she had come to the library each morning, to sweep and dust and polish? When he had gone with the money to the hovel where she had been born and seen for himself the conditions in which people lived and died, here in Kidderminster? Or had it been long ago, when he had met her coming home from church one Sunday afternoon, barely more than a child, so small – she had told him once – that she'd had to stand on a box at the scullery sink to do her work?

It hurt him now to think of the hardships she had endured in only sixteen years of life, the long working hours which had begun when she was only eight years old, the sadness of losing her brother and sister, the loneliness she must be feeling now. And he knew that he could not leave her now; not until they had talked, until he had reassured her that his love for her was real.

What he could do about it, he didn't yet know. But he knew that there was more talking to be done between himself and Jeremiah. Perhaps he could tell his father the truth; perhaps he, with his own experience of love, would be able to help them.

'He never will,' Rebecca said positively. 'Why should he? He's the master. He won't want to see his nephew marry a servant. And Mrs Pagnel wouldn't like it at all.'

Francis couldn't deny that. He looked down at Rebecca, lying snuggled in his arms in the big chair, and wondered whether he should tell her the truth about Jeremiah. He was not quite sure why he didn't; he loved her, he trusted her, why should he not share with her this secret? Perhaps it was because he had only learned it himself recently, and wasn't yet used to the idea of being Jeremiah Pagnel's son; perhaps he needed time before he could tell anyone else.

'Well, whether they like it or not, I mean to marry you,' he said now. 'I never thought I could feel like this about anyone, Rebecca – and I'm not going to let you go now. We belong together. I love you.'

'And I love you, Francis,' she said, still a little shyly. She was still not accustomed to the strange, heady freedom of being able to treat him as an equal – a man who loved her as much as she loved him, who allowed her to speak and behave just as she pleased. So far, she had barely taken any advantage of this new freedom, beyond returning his kisses with an inexperienced tenderness that was growing now to a passion that startled her. The feelings that surged inside her when Francis touched her hand or stroked her neck were far beyond the mild stirring she had known when the new butcher's boy had winked at her one morning. And she had never expected to know such longings when he wasn't with her, such a deep yearning as she lay in bed at night and relived their short meetings in the library.

It was still their main meeting-place, but both were looking forward to Rebecca's next afternoon off, when they had planned to meet outside the town and walk in the woods together. 'Nobody will see us at this time of year,' Francis had said when he suggested the idea. 'And we must find somewhere where we can be alone, my darling. You're always afraid of someone coming in and finding us here.'

'And so would you be, if you were afraid of losing your position,' Rebecca said a little tartly. 'It's easy for you, Francis – gentlemen are expected to have fun with the maids. It's not so easy for the maids, when they find themselves dismissed without a character. What do you suppose they do then? Where can they go?'

'Rebecca, you surely don't think I'm having "fun" with you? I love you – I wouldn't do anything to harm you. You do believe that, don't you?' Francis put his fingers under her chin and held her face up, searching her eyes with anxious intensity. She returned his look seriously for a moment, then smiled.

'No, of course I don't think that. I believe you. But – there's many a maid's thought the same and finished in the gutter for it. It's not easy,' she repeated. 'It's one law for the rich and another for the poor. And when it comes to a question between the two, it's always the poor girl that gets the blame.'

Her voice was soft and warm when she began to speak, but a bitterness she could not control crept into her last words. She felt Francis tighten his arms around her, and laid her face against his shoulder. Why did she always grow so angry when she thought of the injustices between rich and poor? It had always been the same. And it was not Francis's fault.

'I know,' he said quietly, his lips moving in her hair. 'It's very unfair. But nothing can be done about it, Rebecca. It's the way of the world, and always has been. All we can do – those of us who have the means – is try to reduce the suffering as much as possible. There's nothing else.'

Rebecca sat up and looked at him. Her eyes were dark, burning with the fire that had smouldered within her ever since, as a small child, she had seen her mother's work wasted and known that it meant hunger for herself and the rest of her family.

'Nothing?' she said. 'Don't you be too sure of that, Francis Pagnel. People are getting tired of being downtrodden. Look at that revolution they had in France. Lords and ladies – *royalty* – with their heads chopped off. Look at the bread riots a few years ago. The Luddites, smashing machines. The unions – the old Friendly Societies – they're going to get more and more powerful. There'll be strikes – what can the employers do if all the men refuse to work? And when the Parliament's properly reformed, with working men getting the vote and a secret ballot, we might begin to get a bit of justice. Then we'll see who's really got power.'

Francis looked at her in surprise. 'You obviously feel very strongly about all this. And you seem so well informed. Does this kind of talk go on down in the servants' quarters?'

'No, not much. Mrs Hudd wouldn't allow it – nor Mrs Atkins. My dad used to talk to me a bit, when we were working. He and his mates, they were very keen on independence but they could see a time coming when all weavers would have to work in factories, and they'd need unions then to protect them.'

'Well, he might have been right,' Francis said thoughtfully. 'My uncle is just enough to his workers, I believe – but other employers may not be. Even so, I can't believe that strikes will help. Men who go on strike will simply be locked out, and others taken on in their place. There are always plenty of men looking for work.'

'But not all skilled weavers and such. And the more men you employ, the harder it would be to replace them. You'd need to get them all working the looms right. And it's not just the weavers – there are the colour rooms, the yarn rooms, the dye house and all the rest. Where would you find dyers who knew just how to set the colours you use? And how would you be sure *they* all wouldn't go on strike as well?'

Francis stared at her. Her eyes were smouldering, her voice low and urgent. He had never seen such passion in any woman – yet this was a housemaid, uneducated and ignorant, or so many people would have said. A housemaid, talking more sense than he'd heard in a long while.

'Do you really think all this will happen?' he asked at last.

Rebecca shrugged. 'If the manufacturers don't act fairly, yes.' She gave him a look so direct that he flinched. 'And your uncle's not much better than the rest, fair though you think he is. Are his workers any better paid than others? Do they eat meat more than once or twice a week? Do their children grow up stronger and healthier? Do they have better homes, a fire to cook over every night, warm beds to sleep in?' She paused and gathered control over her trembling voice. 'You saw how my mam and dad lived, Francis. There's plenty living the same. We couldn't afford a fire every night – we used to share with our neighbours. Three or four cottages together, and everyone would take the few sticks they could gather from the poll willows to a different house each evening. They'd cook their bit of soup or few potatoes together. That meant the cottages got warmed only one night in four. The rest of the time, they shivered. And we didn't have no warm beds to go to, either. You saw the sacks and stuff my dad died on.'

'I did,' Francis said soberly. 'And I know you're right, Rebecca. None of the carpet workers is paid enough. No one, in any industry, is paid enough to live warmly and comfortably. But—' He hesitated and Rebecca broke in bitterly.

'Oh, I know what they say. If the poor have too much money, they'll only waste it in the tavern. If they have better homes to live in, they'll turn 'em into hovels same as before. If they have good clothes, they'll be rags in a fortnight. I know all that. And you know what my dad used to say to that?' Her eyes burned into his. 'He used to say – "Ah, and if folk were paid well, the manufacturers wouldn't have so much money. They couldn't eat so much fine food, or get their womenfolk up in jewels and velvet and lace. They couldn't live in such fine houses." And he was right. But you could still live quite well, Francis, even if you did share it with us.'

Francis held her body against him, trying to soothe the trembling. She was bringing thoughts to his mind that he had never had before, pointing out truths that his uncle – *father* – and cousin had never considered. As long as the men and women arrived for work each day and carried out their tasks efficiently, nobody had ever wondered about the rest of their lives. And although a few voices were beginning to mutter now about improved conditions, most of the manufacturers took little notice.

He must speak to Jeremiah. And to Vivian – but he had less hope of sympathy there. Vivian had shown himself so many times to be cold and calculating, even callous where his own interests were threatened.

And he would, one day, inherit the business. Francis felt a chill of unease, and made up his mind to speak to Jeremiah as soon as possible.

'I must go now,' Rebecca said in a low voice, and he brought his attention back to the girl in his arms. Did she know what she had done? Did she really understand – or was she simply repeating the things her father had told her?

He looked gravely down at her and thought what a fine wife she would make. Strong, yet soft and feminine. Able to think and talk, rather than merely chatter. A staunch friend and helpmeet, as well as a warm and tender lover.

Emotion swelled up in him and he caught her against him and kissed her with an urgency that surpassed even that which he had felt before. He felt her gasp and then her joyous response. For a long moment they lay together in the big chair, in total, close accord.

Then, slowly and reluctantly, Rebecca withdrew herself from his arms. She lifted herself away and stood looking down at him.

'I love you, Rebecca,' Francis said, rising to his feet and taking her face between his hands.

'And I love you,' she said. And her voice was low and serious; as if she were making him a promise.

Then she gathered up her box and cinder pail, turned and left the library.

Francis walked over to the window and stared out. In the garden, the grass was showing green after its long submersion under the snow. A patch of snowdrops held up brave white heads in a corner. The tips of bulbs had already begun to push through the wet earth.

He wanted very badly to marry Rebecca. But would his uncle – his *father* – ever agree? And if not, what would happen then?

He thought of leaving Kidderminster, taking Rebecca with him to start a new life somewhere, penniless and unskilled except in his drawing. And who knew how much use that would be to him?

Could he do that? Could he reduce her once more to the poverty she had escaped when she came here? She worked hard and long at Pagnel House, but she was sheltered, fed and clothed, she had friends amongst the other servants. If he took her away . . .

There must be a way, he thought, staring out at the pale sunshine. Because he couldn't live without Rebecca by his side.

And for the first time, he began to understand Isabel.

Isabel was, as Vivian had said, still refusing to eat.

But it was not so much a refusal as a total inability. The sight of a table laden with dishes sickened her. The aroma of a steaming roast, the scent of meat and potatoes and vegetables, turned her stomach. The knowledge that she was being watched by the whole family as she tried to force herself to eat, brought her close to fainting.

'You're just being foolish,' her mother said crossly as Isabel sent yet another plate away from the table untouched. 'You think that by doing this you'll force us to give you your own way. Well, you won't succeed so you may as well give up. You'll make yourself ill if you continue in this childish fashion.'

Isabel said nothing. She already felt ill. Her body felt hollow, her stomach ached, but the thought of forcing food into it made her shudder. The gnawing pain inside her had nothing to do with ordinary hunger; it was a hunger for something she had been cruelly denied. A hunger for love.

'Why can't I marry Francis?' she asked over and over again. 'We're not even true cousins – there can't be any reason against it. And I love him.'

'Well, he doesn't love you,' Isabella said bluntly. 'Or he would have asked your father for your hand before you even knew of his intentions, as a gentleman should. Not that Francis has ever been raised as a gentleman,' she added with a caustic note in her voice. 'A schoolmaster is hardly a gentleman, and Enid's not much better – she has no idea how to dress or behave in company, no conversation at all. All she can think of is her husband and *art*, if you please. Not at all suitable for a lady.'

Isabel was silent. She had always been fond of her uncle and aunt, and wished that she could see them now, to talk to them and find out what they thought about the situation. They had brought Francis up as their son, after all. Surely they would be on her side.

The thought stayed in her mind all day, and the next morning, when her mother had left to pay some calls, she put on her outdoor clothes and slipped quietly out. There was nobody to see her go – Maria was still in bed and the servants were busy with their chores. It would be some time before she was missed, and she might even be able to get back without anyone's being the wiser.

She picked her way through the streets, keeping the hem of her skirt away from mud and litter. It was a long walk to the schoolmaster's house in Church Row – longer than she'd realised. But the air was warmer today, with a tremulous sunshine touching her face, and she felt better for being outside. She had kept inside for too long.

At last she arrived at the old, wood-beamed house where Geoffrey and Enid Pagnel lived. She knocked on the door and after a few minutes it was opened by the little maid who was Enid's only help.

'Isabel!' Enid cried as the maid showed her in. 'My dear, whatever are you doing here? You look tired out – so thin and pale. They didn't tell me you were ill. Come and sit by the fire – Jenny, bring Miss Pagnel some tea.'

Isabel slipped off her cloak and sat down, shivering. She seemed always to feel cold these days. She held her hands out to the blaze and Enid caught them in her own, holding them to warm them.

'You're fading away,' she said in concern. 'Isabel, what's been happening to you?'

'Don't you know? Haven't they told you? I've been taken away from home because I want to marry Francis.' Isabel turned huge eyes on her aunt, and her thin body shuddered. 'That's all I've done – fallen in love with Francis. But apparently it's wrong, and now I'm treated like a prisoner. Why? Why is it so terrible, Aunt Enid? Why can't Francis and I marry?'

Enid gazed at her. Isabel saw the compassion in her eyes and felt her tense body relax a little. She did understand. She would help. Francis was her son, after all – or as good as – and she would want to see him happy.

Isabel could not believe that Francis did not love

337

her. That was a cruel fiction of her mother's. Enid wouldn't tell her such lies.

'My dear—' Enid began, and then broke off as Jenny brought in the tea. She waited as the girl set it on the table, then poured a cup and handed it to Isabel. Isabel took it, looked at it and set it aside.

'Drink it while it's hot,' Enid said gently, but Isabel shook her head. Drink did not affect her in the same way as food, but she still could take it only when she was really thirsty, just as she could only eat a few morsels when she was really hungry. But she had stopped being hungry now, so hardly needed to eat at all. It had become almost a challenge, to see how little she could eat and still survive. She felt quite triumphant when she could go to bed knowing that she had eaten almost nothing for another day.

'Please help me, Aunt Enid,' she said now. 'Please help me persuade them to let me marry Francis.'

Enid looked back helplessly. 'But, my dear – are you sure he wants to marry? Francis is very young – he may not feel ready—'

'But we love each other! Why should we have to wait? Men do marry young. And *I'm* not too young – I'm past eighteen. In another year or two people will say I'm on the shelf.'

'If that's all you're worried about, I'm sure—'

'It's not all I'm worried about! I didn't even *want* to get married – ever – until I realised that Francis was the only man for me. Please, Aunt Enid—' Isabel slipped from her chair and knelt at her aunt's knee, her fingers gripping Enid's hands '—please, you must believe me. If I don't marry Francis, I think I'll die. There'll be nothing to live for, anyway.'

Her eyes were glittering feverishly and Enid felt a chill run through her. There was no disbelieving

Isabel; it was plain that the child meant every word. And she was so thin, so white. It was easy to see that the situation was making her ill.

But marriage with Francis . . . it was impossible. And she remembered the day, over twenty-two years ago, when he had been brought to the schoolmaster's house, a tiny baby.

'Your brother's son,' she'd said softly to Geoffrey, taking the bundle in her arms and feeling a slow spread of warm, protective love. 'And now he's ours. He really is ours, Geoffrey? Jeremiah won't make any demands in future?'

'He's given me his promise.' Geoffrey stood beside her and touched the soft shawl with one finger, drawing it aside to look at the sleeping face. 'He'll do all he can for Francis, but he'll never demand to be acknowledged as his father. How could he?'

Enid had known this was true – Jeremiah would never be able to admit that Francis was his son. All the same, she hoped that there would be no difficulties caused by the unusual situation. She hoped that Jeremiah would be able to keep his promise, and forget that Francis was his son, treat him always as hers and Geoffrey's.

At that time, Isabel had not even been born. And when Enid had first seen her as a newborn baby in her mother's arms, there had been no sign of the difficulties that would come from the innocent friendship of two apparent cousins. Nobody had recognised the danger as the two children grew.

'My dear,' she said to Isabel now, and gentle though her voice was she knew that it must still strike like the knell of death into the girl's unhappy heart, 'my dear, I cannot help you. Marriage with Francis is something you must forget. Believe me. It can never,

never happen.' She paused, holding Isabel's hands tightly, looking into the stricken face. 'Drink your tea, my dear, and try to forget all this. Put it in the past. There really is nothing else you can do.'

There was a long, long silence.

'So even you won't help me,' Isabel breathed at last. 'There must be something very terrible about me, that nobody believes I'm fit to marry Francis. What is it? What do you all know about me that's too dreadful to say? What awful secret do you all know? That I'm going mad? That I carry the seed of some horrible illness? That I'm wicked in some way I never knew about?' She was on her feet, her voice rising hysterically as Enid leaped up and tried to calm her. 'No! No, no – leave me alone. Don't touch me. I'm not fit to be touched. I'm not fit to *live*!'

Snatching up her cloak, she turned and ran from the room. And by the time Enid, stumbling over the low table that stood between her and the door, reached the street, she had vanished. The gathering shadows had hidden her fleeing form.

Rebecca's free afternoon heralded the first real day of spring.

She and Francis walked slowly along a deserted woodland path. The other strollers had been left far behind and the air was filled with the singing of birds. The buds on the trees were already beginning to show a mist of green, and a few early primroses sprinkled yellow patches in the moss that covered the banks.

Rebecca felt Francis's fingertips on her wrist. He stretched his hand against hers, palm to palm, then interlaced his fingers with hers so that they were closely entwined. She looked up at him and smiled, feeling at once excited by his nearness, yet totally at ease.

'It's so peaceful here,' she said softly. 'I've never come so far into the woods before . . . You don't think anyone saw us together, do you, Francis?'

'I don't care if they did.' He stopped and drew her into his arms. 'Rebecca, when will you believe that I love you? When will you realise that I'm not ashamed of our love? Everyone will have to know some time. I want to marry you.'

Marry her . . . For a moment, she allowed her mind to play with the notion, imagining herself and Francis sharing a home, free to love each other, raising a family . . . Then she shook her head. 'It'll never do. Your aunt wouldn't hear of it, and I don't believe your uncle would either. He's going to be Mayor of Kidderminster soon, everyone says so. How could he have a nephew that marries a housemaid? He'd be a laughing stock.'

'He wouldn't. Why should people laugh at him?'

'Because he's your uncle,' Rebecca said quietly. 'And you're living in his house. They'd say you'd taken advantage of me. They'd say you'd taken leave of your senses. They'd pity Mr Pagnel for having a nephew like you, and it might even damage his business.' She looked up into his face, sighed a little and then stroked back his hair with both her hands. 'Just let us enjoy the love we can have now,' she whispered, and drew his face down to hers, closing her eyes and opening her lips for his kiss.

Francis's arms tightened around her. His lips were firm on hers, shaping them to his own. She felt his fingertips stroke gently down the length of her spine, and shivered at the sensuous touch. One of his hands cupped the back of her head, supporting her for the kiss as he explored deeper into her mouth; his tongue touched hers and she felt as if a cloud of tiny bubbles

341

had suddenly burst somewhere deep inside her. Her fingers moved in his hair and she felt his groan as it vibrated through his body.

'Rebecca . . . We must go. I can't be alone here with you – I can't trust myself . . .'

'I don't want you to trust yourself,' she whispered against his mouth. 'I want you to love me, Francis.'

He drew back his head and stared down into her eyes. His own were almost black, the sapphire colour no more than a brilliant rim around his widened pupils. His dark gold hair fell over his forehead and she brushed it back, smiling, wondering at her own confidence. Had she intended this when she agreed to come for a walk with him? Had she even considered it this afternoon, as she washed and dressed with such special care? Had she even thought of it as she walked along the deserted path and listened to the mating songs of the birds?

She could not answer those questions. She only knew that she had been tingling with a nervous excitement for days, that she had longed for this day as she had never longed for anything in her life. That she had a doomed feeling that this afternoon might be the last they could spend together, and that it mustn't be wasted.

'Rebecca . . .' he said, his eyes searching hers. 'Do you understand what you're saying?'

'I think so.' A flame smouldered deep in her velvety eyes. 'Francis, I'm not one of your well-brought-up young ladies who don't know what marriage means until the wedding night. Where I come from, there's not room to stay ignorant, and not many girls are still – well, pure – when they marry. Not many have the chance,' she added a little bitterly, thinking of her sister and all the other girls who had been exploited, if not raped, by their employers – weavers or gentle-men, they were all the same when it came to a girl at their mercy. 'I want you to be my first man, Francis. I don't think we'll ever be able to marry – but I shall always love you. And I want you to love me – now – just in case we never have the chance again.'

Francis took her hand in his and looked down at it, stroking the finger where a wedding ring would rest.

'Rebecca, I mean to marry you. And we shall have the chance again – many, many chances. I promise you that. I don't want to take advantage of you, like any man might do with a housemaid. I love you.'

'Then you wouldn't be taking advantage,' she said steadily, and then suddenly pressed herself against him with an urgency that brought a gasp from his throat. 'Francis, love me – please. I have this feel-ing – this feeling that something terrible's going to happen to us. Something will part us – and I don't want to go to my grave never having known your love. Please . . .'

He stared at her. 'Rebecca, don't talk like this. Graves! Terrible happenings – partings. None of those things are going to happen. We shall marry, I promise you. We shall grow old together. *Nothing* is going to stop that. I know it. I swear it.'

'Then it won't hurt if you love me now,' she said, and brought his lips down to hers again.

Francis held her close. She could feel the length of him against her, feel his heart pounding against her breast. She whimpered a little and moved in his arms, and knew that she had won.

With a low mutter, he lifted her and carried her away from the path, through the trees to a small clear-ing, where they were hidden from sight of any passers-by. He laid her gently on moss as thick as any carpet and looked down into her face.

'You're sure, Rebecca?'

She nodded slowly, her eyes fixed on his. He touched her face with a fingertip, drew it slowly and gently down her neck and into the fastening of her blouse. His hand covered her breast, barely touching it, and she closed her eyes and shivered.

'Rebecca . . .' he murmured, and stretched himself beside her, his lips once more on hers. 'Oh, my Rebecca . . .'

Jeremiah paced the library. His frown had etched itself deep into his brow. He glanced up impatiently at the window, then at the clock. It was growing dark outside. Where in God's name had the boy got to?

When the door opened, he was standing at the far end of the room, staring moodily at a row of books he had never opened. Yet someone had been reading them. He wondered who. Unlikely to be Vivian. Francis, then? Isabel?

The door opened and he swung round.

'Francis! There you are. I've been waiting for you.'

'I went for a walk.' Francis came in slowly and Jeremiah eyed him. He looked different, somehow. His colour a little high – that could be a result of his walk. An odd glimmer in his eyes. A subdued restlessness, as if he were suppressing some excitement.

Well, what Jeremiah had to tell him would soon override any excitements Kidderminster had to offer. Though whether Francis would be pleased by it or not, Jeremiah really was not sure. Francis never did react quite as he might be expected to do.

'What is it?' Francis asked, suddenly wary, and Jeremiah sighed. This was not going to be as easy as he had hoped. Something had happened to the boy – something beyond the shocks he had received lately, the revelations of Isabel's passion for him and the truth about his parentage. Something was going on there, and Jeremiah had no idea as to what it might be.

He wished for the thousandth time that he had been able to acknowledge Francis as his son, that he could have brought him up in his own home, that Francis could have been his heir. Instead, their relationship must remain for ever a secret, betrayed by not even the slightest hint. It was a loss that he realised more each day.

'I've some news for you,' he said at last, deciding to treat it as good news. Most young men would, indeed, have seen it that way. 'You're going to London with your – your cousin Vivian. I want you to see the business as it is there. I want you to stay for a while. Or perhaps go further afield – visit our wool suppliers in Yorkshire, take a look at some of the manufacturers there or in Scotland, take a look at Wilton. Perhaps even go across to Brussels to see what you can learn – we've had success with their methods, maybe they'll have new ideas that you may be able to spy out.'

Francis stared at him. 'London? Scotland? *Brussels*? But I shall be away for weeks. Why? Why do you want me to go away?'

Jeremiah shrugged. 'Oh, it won't be so long – a few months, perhaps – we'll see how you get along. We've decided—'

'A *few months*?' Francis interrupted, his face white. 'But Uncle – Father – I *can't* leave Kidderminster for that long. A few days, perhaps, a week or two – but no more than that. I simply can't.'

'Don't be foolish. Of course you can.' Jeremiah snapped his impatience. 'What is there so important in Kidderminster, for heaven's sake?'

Francis opened his mouth, then closed it again. Before parting from him after their ecstatic afternoon in the woods, Rebecca had begged him to give her a promise. 'Don't tell anyone that you want us to marry,' she had said. 'Please, Francis – please don't tell anyone.' And, reluctantly, he had taken her hands in his and given her the promise she wanted.

Could he break that promise now, less than an hour since it had been made?

Jeremiah stepped a little closer. He looked gravely into Francis's face.

'Listen to me, Francis. I want you to go on this trip. It will be good for you to see the business from that end. It will be good for you to mix with other people, to see how things are beyond Kidderminster. You've barely been out of the town in your life. You need to see fresh scenes, to meet different ideas. It will be good for you in every way. But—' He held up one hand to silence Francis's objections '—but there's another reason, too. Your . . . cousin Isabel.' He dropped his voice. 'Your . . . sister.'

'Isabel?' Francis said. 'What's wrong with Isabel? I thought she was recovering at Maria's. Vivian's talked of parties – young men—'

'None of which have done any good whatsoever,' Jeremiah said heavily. 'She sits at the parties like a ghost, refuses to talk to the young men and eats less every day. She has gone into a decline, Francis, and young women have been known to die of that. Her mother was angry at first – she saw this behaviour of Isabel's as a wilful rebellion, refused to allow any suggestion that Isabel might wed you after all. And now she can't – or won't – retract.' His look was wry. 'Not that it would be of any use if she did . . . But the two of them are as stubborn as each other.'

'Isabel – in a decline?' Francis sat down and Jeremiah looked down at him with compassion. Francis had never, he believed, done anything to bring about this terrible situation. He had never looked upon Isabel as anything but a friend. And now it seemed that she might die because of a love that he could not – *must* not – return.

'Today, she slipped out of the house and went to see Enid – your mother,' he said, acutely conscious of the inaccuracy of the term. 'It seemed that she hoped to enlist her aid. Enid, of course, could give nothing of the sort. She and Geoffrey are the only ones besides yourself who know the truth. When Isabel realised that she would get no help there, she ran away. She was found an hour later, collapsed and almost frozen to death in an alleyway. When she was brought home and undressed, Isabella saw how thin she had become and called the doctor. He says there is little that can be done for her. Her only hope is to forget you – and while you and she are still in the same town, living in the same family, she never will.'

'And there's no possibility of her going away?' Francis asked through dry lips.

Jeremiah shook his head. 'She's too ill, Francis. Too weak.'

Francis sat very still. Jeremiah watched him. The boy looked shaken, distressed beyond measure. If it had been possible, Jeremiah believed that he would have offered to marry Isabel, love or no love, simply to save her life. But there could be no question of that.

'I'll go to London,' Francis said at last. 'I'll stay as

347

long as you think it advisable. I only hope that it will help Isabel if I'm not here.'

He got up and went to the door, and Jeremiah watched him go. The door closed, leaving the older man alone with a weight he didn't understand, heavy on his heart.

It was as if he had dealt Francis almost as severe a blow as had been dealt to Isabel. Yet what was it that was so important to the boy that he did not want to leave Kidderminster?

Could he have loved Isabel more than he had realised – more than he had confessed? Was he in the grip of a passion that he knew now to be illicit and totally impossible?

Jeremiah sighed and sank into an armchair, staring at the fire. What kind of imbroglio had he begun, that day twenty-two years or more ago, when he had fallen in love with Mary?

How long would its effects linger?

Chapter Fifteen

London. The capital city of England. The hub – so Vivian declared – of everything that was important and pleasurable. And looking, on this early spring morning, at its best.

'I daresay you're surprised to see so much green,' Vivian observed as they clattered through the streets in the cab he had hired. 'London's full of parks – I suppose Hyde Park is the greatest of them. People walk there a good deal, and they have open-air meetings and so on. And of course, Rotten Row is the only place to be seen riding.'

'I don't expect to have much time for riding and taking the air,' Francis said. 'I've come to London to work and learn, and the sooner I do that the sooner I can go back to Kidderminster.'

'And what in God's name is so attractive about Kidder?' Vivian asked scornfully. 'A dirty provincial town with no style about it at all. If it weren't for the business, I can tell you, Maria and I would live in London all the time. There's so much more going on. Those are the Houses of Parliament. And there's Westminster Abbey – rather fine, don't you think? I expect you've seen pictures of it.'

'One or two,' Francis said dryly. Vivian seemed to imagine that he'd just crawled out a hole in the ground. 'We learned a little about English History at school. But it's good of you to take the trouble to complete my education.'

Vivian gave him a sharp glance and closed his

mouth. He looked studiedly out of the cab window until they arrived at their hotel. There, he was once again unable to suppress his eagerness to show superiority.

'The porter will take in the luggage. I've booked my usual rooms, and you'll have the one next door – we'll share the sitting room. The boy will show you where everything is, and Brown will unpack for you when he's dealt with my things.' Vivian turned to the manservant who had accompanied them. 'See that Mr Francis has everything he needs, Brown. I have to go out for a while – things to attend to.' He gave Francis a clap on the shoulder. 'Make yourself comfortable till I come back, Frank. We'll have dinner together.'

He sauntered out of the hotel and Francis watched him go. Vivian had never mentioned that he had business to attend to as soon as they arrived in London. What could it be that was important enough to warrant his immediate attention? And – since Francis was supposed to accompany him in order to learn as much as he could about the business – why had he gone alone?

The inescapable conclusion was that Vivian's business had nothing to do with carpets. And when he did not return for dinner and only appeared much later, when Francis had eaten alone in the restaurant and gone back to his room, he made no secret of what he had been doing.

'Hullo – in bed already?' He put his head round the door and then came in, tweaking the book from Francis's hand. 'I always knew you were a country bumpkin, Frank – how many other fellows of your age would go to bed early on their first night in London?' He threw himself down in an armchair and sprawled there. He looked slightly dishevelled and smelt of whisky. His face was red, his eyes a little wild. 'Couldn't you find yourself any entertainment? Don't tell me you've been stewing in here ever since this afternoon?'

'No, I went out for a walk. I went to Regent Street – it's very fine. And I looked at the shops in Oxford Street, and then walked in Hyde Park. You're right, it's a splendid place. Like a piece of countryside right in the middle of London.'

Vivian looked as gratified as if he had been personally responsible for the planning of the capital city. 'Well, I'm glad you approve. You didn't seem very happy when we arrived this afternoon. In fact, you haven't seemed happy about the whole trip. But there are better things to do than walk about looking at shops, Frank. Didn't any nice little doxies approach you?'

'One or two,' Francis said, and Vivian laughed.

'You sound disapproving. I take it you didn't like their terms.'

'I didn't like *them*. Dirty, sluttish and unattractive, all of them. I felt sorry for them, having to live by such a trade.'

'Oh, don't be such a prude. I agree, the ones you meet walking the streets during the day are probably downtrodden bawds who need to work all day to earn a crust. But in the evenings—' Vivian rolled his eyes lasciviously '—Frank, I'll tell you what I'll do. I'll take you to the Haymarket one evening and show you just what there is on offer. Or perhaps to Queen Street. That's where the French girls gather – and there's no woman better at the art of love than a Frenchwoman. An hour or so at the music hall, an intimate supper in one of the cafés, and then back to

351

the young lady's room. Choose the right one, and you can discover all kinds of delights – delights you'd never dream of in stuffy Kidderminster.' He grinned. 'We'll do it tomorrow, Frank – make a man of you, eh?'

Francis looked at him with distaste. He understood now why Vivian was always so eager to make these trips to London. Was that where he'd been this afternoon – sampling the delights of the Haymarket?

Vivian caught his look and laughed again. 'Don't tell me what you're thinking, Frank – I can read your mind. You're wondering what my business was this afternoon. Well, I'll tell you.' He leant forward. 'I don't need to go walking down the Haymarket or Regent Street,' he said in a confidential tone. 'I've got my entertainment nicely arranged – a pretty little piece with rooms in Gower Street. Found her a year or two ago and spend as much time as possible with her whenever I'm here. But I'm not averse to a night on the town with you, sampling the other pleasures available. Variety is the spice of life, after all. What do you say?'

'No, thank you. I'm really not interested, Vivian. I'd rather do what I came to do – look about to see what new fashions are developing in design and decoration, and learn anything I can about the business. The sooner I can do that, the sooner I can return to Kidderminster.'

'Return to Kidderminster – that's all you think about,' Vivian exclaimed in disgust. 'Frank, I'm beginning to think there must be something seriously amiss with you. This is *London* – and there's nobody to watch what you do or tell tales. You can enjoy yourself here, without prying eyes and ears – have a different woman every night, a dozen a night if you

352

have the capacity.' His laugh was coarse and Francis turned his head away from the strong smell of whisky. 'There's no need to be shy – any one of these wenches would be glad to show you the ropes if you're not certain.'

Francis coloured angrily. 'I don't need tuition, thank you.' He stopped, biting his lip as Vivian laughed again. 'I don't wish for the kind of experience you're suggesting,' he said coldly. 'It seems extremely unattractive to me – using women in that way—'

'Why, what other way is there to use them? That's what they're for.'

'Vivian, you're a married man—'

'So are most of the customers of these gay ladies. You don't imagine they demand proof of bachelorhood before offering their services, do you?'

'But what about Maria?'

'What about her? She has a comfortable home, servants, enough money to dress well and entertain. She has her daughters to dress up and play with like so many dolls.' A trace of bitterness crept into his tone. 'And I have no objection to cohabiting with her when I'm at home – though she doesn't have the knowledge or skill of my pretty little Amalie in Gower Street, nor would I wish her to. Quite unsuitable for a gently brought up girl. No, with Maria it's duty, and the hope that she may, eventually, manage to produce a son.'

Francis shook his head. He thought of Rebecca and the sweet, willing way in which she had given herself to him only a week ago. Since then he'd barely had the chance of a word alone with her; all he'd been able to do was to tell her about his trip to London and assure her again of his love. But he'd thought of her constantly. His mind had been filled with her face, so grave in repose, lighting like a starry sky with laughter and animation when she forgot her worries and became the carefree girl she ought to be. Her voice rang in his ears, low and musical even though still roughened by the accents of Kidderminster; and even those accents held a charm for him now. They were Rebecca, and everything about Rebecca was loved.

The thought of paying for the 'favours' of one of the ladies of Haymarket or Piccadilly turned his stomach sick. And Vivian's attitude, so callous towards his wife Maria, was even more repugnant. Francis liked Maria. She was not very intelligent, it was true, but perhaps that was just as well – a sharper mind might have seen through Vivian's glossy charm and realised just what kind of man he was. But she was friendly and amiable, and very fond of her children. And although she liked to dress in a way that showed off her small, pretty features and figure, she wasn't vain like his cousin Sarah. His *sister* Sarah, he amended with a small, cold shock.

He felt sorry for Maria, left at home while Vivian came to London to carouse with his Amalie. Did she suspect? Francis hoped not. There could be little enough happiness for her with Vivian as it was – she might as well be spared as much unhappiness as possible.

Vivian was watching him curiously.

'What is it, Frank? What's the great attraction back in Kidder? You can't really be uninterested in women. Is there someone at home?' His eyes narrowed suddenly. 'You're not actually carrying a torch for Isabel, are you? I understood that was entirely on her side.'

'It is,' Francis said, perhaps too quickly. The knowledge of Isabel's true relationship with him, explaining the reluctance he had felt to have any physical contact with her, brought a swift reaction. But Vivian lifted his head a little, almost like an animal scenting prey, and Francis realised that his attitude could be misconstrued.

'Is it really?' Vivian's tone expressed a sly disbelief. 'Well, well, well. So you did have your sights set on my little sister. And Father and Mother didn't like it – I suppose they've got someone rather more well-heeled in mind. Rather ungallant of you, though, to let poor Issy take all the blame, wasn't it?'

'I didn't – I've told you, I never did feel like that about Isabel. We were friends, nothing more – as far as I was aware. I'd no idea she was building up these fantasies in her mind—'

'Fantasies? Maria told me Isabel had confessed to a certain amount of lovemaking—'

'No!' Again, Francis knew his denial was too quick, too vehement. Conscious of Vivian's sceptical glance, he went on more quietly: 'There was a day in the library – she more or less threw herself at me, there was nothing I could do about it. But I did not take advantage, Vivian – you must believe me. And I never encouraged her.'

'Even though you must have been able to see the advantages of such a match? Come now, Francis, what do you think I am – a fool? You must have considered it. Unless—' his voice grew thoughtful '—unless you had some other reason for not wishing to marry my sister. And I can only think of one reason for that – or perhaps two,' he added in a different tone of voice. He looked hard and speculatively at Francis. 'Either there's some other lady who has a hold on your affections – and all I can say is, if there is you're a very dark horse indeed, Francis, since I've

355

never seen any sign of interest in any young woman in the Kidderminster area. You barely leave the house unless it's to visit your parents and I hardly think you'd meet anyone likely *there*. Or else . . .' His voice drifted into silence and he stared at Francis as if he were possessed of an entirely new idea. 'Well, I suppose that's quite possible . . .'

'What?' Francis said irritably. 'Look, Vivian, I'm tired. It was a long journey – I'm not used to spending several days jolting along in a coach – and I was just about to blow out my candle when you came in. If there's nothing else you need to say—'

'Oh, but there is,' Vivian said softly. 'And it won't take long. But it would account for your not being interested in the ladies of London.'

'What would? I don't know what you're talking about.'

'Don't you? I'll put it in a nutshell, then. What reason can *you* think of, Francis, why a man wouldn't be interested in women? Because he's more interested in men, of course. Is that why you're not interested, Francis? Because you can be accommodated in that way, too, you know. Nothing easier.'

Francis stared at him. His repugnance deepened to disgust.

'Get out of my room, Vivian,' he said in a trembling voice. 'Get out and leave me alone. And don't make any more suggestions to me – about men *or* women. I'm not interested in either. Do you hear me? Not *either*.'

Vivian looked at him with amusement, then hauled himself to his feet. He stood, swaying slightly, regarding Francis through half-closed lids.

'Of course you aren't, Francis,' he drawled. 'You're made of marble, aren't you? Or is it plaster?

A plaster saint, perhaps . . . Very well, I'll go now. I
need a good sleep after the evening I've just enjoyed.'
He went to the door, then looked back with a mocking
expression on his dark face. 'But remember this,
Francis – we're all human. None of us is immune.
You may set out to be a saint – but you're not. And
you'll find it out one day. Even plaster saints can have
feet of clay, and you're no exception. Better to discover it in the arms of some doxy you'll never see
again, than the daughter of one of Father's friends in
Kidderminster.' He laughed again and then went out,
slamming the door behind him.

Francis watched him go. Then he lay back on his
pillow and stared at the smoke-darkened ceiling.

Vivian's remarks left him feeling strangely uneasy.
The hints he had made, the insinuations were unpleasant enough – but there had been something else as
well. An undercurrent – almost a warning.

It was as if, quite unknowingly, Vivian had warned
him about possible trouble in his relationship with
Rebecca. And for the first time, Francis began to feel
that perhaps it was not going to be so easy, carrying
out his intention to marry his aunt's housemaid.

He blew out his candle and turned over. But, tired
though he was, it was a long time before he slept.

Pagnel House was eerily empty with only Jeremiah at
home. Isabel and her mother were still at Vivian's
house with Maria and the little girls. Isabel, the
rumour went, had gone even further into her decline
and there were fears for her life.

'Seen it before, I have,' Mrs Atkins declared as the
servants sat at their midday meal. 'There was a girl
like that at my last place. Lost her head over a young
man and went funny in the head. Never the same

again. Just faded away to nothing, she did.'

'And what happened when there was nothing left?' Billy asked cheekily. 'Did she just vanish away?'

Mrs Atkins gave him a stern glance. 'It's not funny. She died, of course. What else d'you expect when a growing girl stops eating? And there didn't seem to be nothing to be done about it, neither. It was as if she'd forgotten *how* to eat.'

'My friend Jenny, over at Mr Vivian's, says it's like Miss Isabel's frightened of food,' Polly remarked. 'Almost as if it's poison. She says it's pitiful to see her at mealtimes – and Mrs Pagnel gets that angry with her. She thinks it's all put on, deliberate.'

'Nobody'd starve themselves like that deliberate,' Mrs Atkins said, setting a huge pie on the table. 'Not in any house where I was cook, anyway. It's something else – something that happens when a girl's crossed in love. I've seen it before, I tell you.'

Rebecca ate her dinner in silence, thinking of Isabel. She felt a strange mixture of emotion regarding the other girl. She had never had very much to do with Isabel, but from what she'd seen of her she seemed a nice enough person. And the other servants seemed to like her too. They were all sorry for her now, and Rebecca couldn't help sharing their compassion.

Yet tangled with her pity was an anxious jealousy. Everyone knew by now that it was over Mr Francis that Isabel was pining away. That, too, was why he'd been sent away. He'd told Rebecca that he didn't want to go, assured her that he loved Rebecca herself and wanted to marry her, repeated over and over again that he had never loved – *could* never love – Isabel. And she believed him. But . . .

Rebecca could never rid herself of the knowledge

that their love was an impossible one. For Francis to announce any intention of marrying a housemaid would create a scandal that would ruin his uncle's chances of becoming Mayor of Kidderminster. Rebecca would be dismissed without a character and reduced to a poverty more dire even than that of her parents. And Francis would be disgraced and probably sent far away – to one of the new colonies, perhaps, in Australia or Canada.

A match with Isabel, out of the question though he'd told her it must be, would surely be more favoured than marriage so far below his station.

Rebecca thought of the afternoon when she and Francis had lain together on the moss. She thought of the way he had loosened her blouse so that her breasts tumbled into his hands, the way he had gazed at them and kissed them with such reverence; the gentleness of his fingers on her skin, the whisper-light caresses with which he had explored her trembling body.

She thought of the way he had kissed her quivering lips; his own firm, parting hers with tender insistence, opening and shaping her mouth to his. His tongue flicking lightly, so lightly, over the softness of her inner lips, touching her teeth, teasing her own tongue with the tiniest of quick, darting movements. And her response, seeking his mouth as he sought hers . . .

Rebecca felt the strange, almost violent tingle deep in her stomach, the tingle she had felt whenever she thought of those moments, whenever she thought of Francis and his body and hands and mouth on her. She closed her eyes and shivered.

'Here, are you all right, Becky?' Mrs Atkins demanded suddenly. 'You look real queer. You're not sickening for anything, I hope.'

'No.' Rebecca opened her eyes and looked around

at the faces watching her. 'No, I'm all right, Mrs Atkins.'

She went on with her meal, hardly listening to the chatter of the other servants. But she was aware of Polly's sharp eyes on her, and she was not surprised when her friend began to ask her own questions, as they got ready for bed.

'You did look a bit funny, down in the kitchen at dinner-time, Becky. You feel all right, don't you?'

'Of course I do.' Rebecca peeled off her stockings and hung them carefully over the back of the chair. 'It was just one of those shivers you get sometimes.'

'You'd tell me if there was anything wrong?' Polly persisted, unfastening her dress. 'I'm your friend, Becky – I'd help.'

'Polly, there's nothing wrong. Honestly.'

'Well, it's just that you've been acting a bit queer too these past few weeks. Getting up early and that – and you don't seem to have done any more than usual, even so. You've been almost late for prayers a time or two. I wonder sometimes what you do . . . And sometimes you're happy as a lark, and others you look as if you'd lost a shilling and found sixpence. And last Sunday evening – I couldn't get a word out of you nohow.'

'I'm sorry, Poll. It's all the things that have happened lately – Mam and Dad, you know. It's made me feel a bit funny.' She felt guilty, using her parents' deaths as an excuse, but it was half true, after all; she did still miss and grieve for them. But she knew that it wasn't the real reason for the odd behaviour Polly had noticed.

'Well, I suppose that's it,' Polly said dubiously. 'Mind, if you were to ask me, I'd say you were in love. But I don't see as it can be that – you never bother

360

with any of the tradesmen or errand boys that come to the door. And some of 'em are quite good-lookers. That butcher's boy's a real cheeky lad, and he's got an eye for you, I can see . . . It's not him, is it?' she asked with sudden anxiety. 'You haven't been meeting him on the sly?'

Rebecca laughed and shook her head. 'It isn't the butcher's boy,' she said. 'You can have him, Polly.'

'I didn't mean that,' Polly denied quickly, then caught Rebecca's eye and grinned. 'Well, perhaps I did. Now that Mr Vivian's away . . . and I don't suppose he'll be interested in me when he comes back from London.'

'Mr Vivian?' Rebecca paused as she climbed into bed. 'Polly – you haven't!'

'Why not? He's all right – generous, too. Gives me a sovereign now and then.' Polly slipped under her blankets, looking at Rebecca with a touch of defiance. 'You got to look after yourself in this world, Becky. Nobody else is going to do it for you. And so long as you gets something out of it and don't get caught for a kid, what do it matter?'

'But suppose you do get caught?' A coldness touched Rebecca's skin. 'How do you stop it, Polly?'

Polly shrugged. 'Just hope for the best. And *he* can do something about it – if he remembers. Anyway, I've always been lucky – depends which way the wind is, my old auntie used to say. So far, it must have been right for me. And if it's not – well, there's always Becky Swan.'

'The *witch*?'

'So they calls her. She's helped many a girl.'

Rebecca lay down. The candle stump was almost burned down and would be needed for the morning. She pinched it out between her finger and thumb, then lay staring into the darkness.

How long would Francis be away? And when he came back – would he have forgotten her, as Polly evidently expected to be forgotten by Vivian? Was this love that seemed so strong, so sure, to prove no more than just a flirtation, a passing fancy?

She did not believe it. Francis had said he loved her.

But – wouldn't Polly say that they *all* said that?

Isabel was feeling strangely calm. The desire for food had left her completely now; she no longer felt hungry. The sight or smell of it repelled her. Mealtimes were an ordeal yet, at the same time, a challenge she almost enjoyed. Each time she left the table having frustrated all efforts to make her eat, she felt a flutter of triumph.

She seemed to have reached another level of living, a high plateau where the air was clear and cold and everything could be seen with an extra sharpness. Her mind seemed to float loose from her body, and she felt almost as if she were transparent. It became a goal: to become totally transparent, clear as glass, so light that her feet would float above the ground.

She felt a quiet, pitying scorn for the grossness of those who had not attained this almost spiritual state, who still believed that the consumption of huge quantities of food was necessary to keep the human body alive, who fell on three meals a day as if they were starving. Starving! They didn't know the meaning of the word. How could they know the exquisite pleasure of very slowly eating the few morsels that were all she allowed herself each day? How could they understand that such pleasure was only possible when the experience itself was rare?

You didn't enjoy that, she would think, watching her brother Vivian dispose of a plate piled high with meat and vegetables followed by a large helping of pudding. You might have enjoyed the first mouthful or two – but that's all. The rest was hardly noticed.

Isabel had discovered the secret of enjoying food – only to eat the first mouthful. And so this was all she ever did.

'What's the *matter* with it?' her mother would ask in despair, looking at the untouched food. 'It's delicious. You used to love veal. And it's so delicate – so good for you. Try a little more, Isabel, please.'

But Isabel, having eaten one tiny mouthful, shook her head and pushed the plate away.

Isabella looked at her in exasperation.

'You're doing this deliberately. You're simply trying to worry us. You think that by starving yourself, you'll get your own way. Well, miss, let me tell you this – you *won't*. Childish tantrums won't help you get your own way now, any more that they did in the nursery. Your father and I are agreed on this. You'll never be permitted to marry Francis, and you might as well make up your mind to it. In any case, he's gone to London now. No doubt he's forgotten all about you.'

Francis. There was a twinge of pain in Isabel's mind as she heard the name, but it was more like the remembered pain of a toothache that had been cured. Vaguely, she remembered the ache of her love for Francis, but it was long ago now. Did she still love him?

She shook her head. Love was a concept she had almost forgotten. It had been relegated to her past, like the enjoyment of a spring day, a walk in the woods, a meal. She had gone beyond those pleasures now, passed through some strange barrier into her world of bright light and icy air. She had detached herself from the world she had always known. Wherever she was now, it had become her world, and she had no wish to return.

Jeremiah came to visit her. He talked with her mother and Maria, seeing that Isabella was fast losing patience and that Maria was half sympathetic towards Isabel, half irritated. He looked at his daughter, the one who had always been his secret favourite, and his heart sank. She was so thin, so pale, and had such a strange look in her eyes. It was as if she had travelled far away, too far for him to reach.

'Isabel, my dear,' he said as they sat alone in her room, for she seldom came downstairs now. 'Isabel, you must try to pull yourself out of this terrible decline. What good is it doing you?' He looked at her sadly. 'You can never have him, you know. You can never marry Francis.'

Isabel said nothing. The pain touched her mind again, pricked at her heart. She tried to turn away from it, but it was still there, like an itch she could not scratch. She looked at her father, her eyes like bruises in her face, and he took her hands in his and looked at the fingers, thin and white as bones. A fine downy hair had begun to grow on her hands and arms.

'If it were possible to give you what you want, believe me, I would. The fact that you and Francis were cousins wouldn't—'

'But we're not. Francis was adopted.'

Jeremiah sighed. He could not meet her eyes.

'Isabel, believe me, you *cannot* marry Francis. And I can't tell you why. You must forget him, and begin to live your life again. You're beautiful, intelligent – you can't waste your youth like this. You must begin to eat again, take an interest in yourself. The weather's improving now – you could go away, take a holiday. Your mother would go with you. Or Sarah, perhaps. You could go abroad – to Italy, perhaps. It's warm and sunny there, it would do you good. But you must regain your strength first.'

Isabel looked at him. Her expression was strange – faraway, as if she had barely heard his words. And – almost pitying.

Jeremiah saw the look. And felt a terrible premonition that nothing could save his daughter now. She was doomed.

Doomed by his own past.

In spite of his words on that first evening, Francis could not help enjoying the excitement and stimulation of London. It was so busy, so bustling, so different from Kidderminster. He accompanied Vivian to the large furnishing shops who would order carpets from Pagnel's, to the homes of gentlefolk too grand to visit shops, who would order carpets for their own homes, often specially woven to match the pattern of the ceiling above. He walked along the wide streets, gazing up at the huge buildings that towered on every side.

'Wonderful, isn't it,' Vivian said in his ear. 'Who'd ever want to live in a backwater like Kidderminster after this?'

'Kidderminster isn't a backwater,' Francis said slowly. 'It's real – more real than this. Kidderminster, and places like it, are where the real things happen – the industries that London depends on. If we weren't making carpets, mining coal and iron, manufacturing all the goods that London needs to sell, there'd be no reason for a capital city to exist. All these people – they're selling and buying, but they're not *making* anything. And some of them aren't even doing that.' He looked at the men and women passing them. 'They're either parading their own wealth for others to admire or envy, or they're reduced to thievery – they've no way of earning money so they must steal it from others.'

'Trust you to take a prudish attitude,' Vivian said carelessly. 'You always take a gloomy view, Frank – why, these people are the salt of the earth. Cockneys – sharp as needles and as full of life as a barrel load of monkeys. Look at those boys over there – lively as crickets. I daresay they're not above dipping their hands in a gentleman's pockets, but that's something you must always watch for. And a few days in gaol will soon teach 'em a lesson. As for being unable to earn money – why, anyone can pick up a living by holding horses, running messages and suchlike. There's less need for poverty here than in your precious Kidderminster. If any man goes hungry in London, it's his own fault.'

Francis said nothing. He had become even more aware, since they had arrived in London, of Vivian's attitude to the poor. He was like a carthorse, wearing blinkers that allowed him to see only what he wanted to see. As far as Vivian was concerned, the problems of poverty either did not exist or were self-inflicted. Or – worse still – he saw poverty as a necessary part of the general economy.

'They wouldn't work if they weren't half-starved,' he said. 'Look at them – lazy as cats, sprawled in the sun drinking gin. Pay 'em more and they'd work less. Well, isn't it natural? Wouldn't you, if you had to slave in a factory from morning till night?'

'So perhaps we should improve their working conditions,' Francis suggested. He thought of Rebecca and her anger over the way in which the working classes were forced to live, and felt a pang. Was she missing him as he missed her?

Vivian stared at him and laughed his loud laugh.

'And take even less profit? Just so that they can live in the lap of luxury?' He shook his head. 'You're not thinking straight, Frank. It's being brought up by a schoolmaster – Uncle Geoff's never lived in the real world. He doesn't know what it's all about. But you're going to have to learn, if you want to make a success of business.'

They walked on along the Haymarket. As Vivian had promised, at this time in the evening it was filled with people out for an evening's pleasure. Carriages drew up at the pavement and richly dressed women were handed down by gentlemen in clothes finer than were ever seen in Kidderminster. Others strolled along the street, looking into shop windows and going into the restaurants where they could eat foods Francis had never heard of, and drink wine or coffee in lavishly decorated surroundings. He looked into one as they passed and saw that the walls were covered with mirrors edged in gilt; the customers were reflected on all sides, so that it seemed that a crowd of glittering people stretched away, talking and laughing, into a shimmering distance.

There were other strollers, too. Women and girls dressed from the high styles of the latest fashions, their cloaks and bonnets richly trimmed, to the plainest of gowns, as demure as Quakers. One of them glanced at Francis as she walked by and he was startled by the flash of her eyes. It was far from demure; and he realised that these were the women Vivian had spoken of, the women who offered their favours for money, the women who were lost to love.

'Take your choice,' Vivian murmured. 'A stylish

367

lady or a pretty little milliner. Oh, yes – you'll find 'em all here. Mostly they claim to be governesses, clergymen's daughters as often as not, seduced and led astray, then abandoned. Some of 'em may be, for all I know. But there's a good many girls – milliners, shopgirls, housemaids and so on – in regular work, eking out their pay with a little dalliance during the night. As I told you – there's never any need to be poor in London. Not for a woman, anyway, so long as she's passably good-looking.'

Francis looked at the women who paraded constantly along the street, approaching any man on his own or with a group of others. He and Vivian had already received several offers themselves, from girls who looked at them with saucy eyes that seemed to promise fun, and women who gave them a hard stare and offered what was little more than a business arrangement. Vivian shook his head at them all.

'We can do better than this,' he remarked. 'I know a little restaurant in James Street, not far from here. The bawd there keeps a good house – pretty girls, all fresh from the country, she never keeps one more than two or three months. Passes them on to another house then. What about a nice rosy-cheeked milk-maid to remind you of home, eh? Or a sweet little virgin, if she's got any in stock?'

Francis opened his mouth to tell Vivian that he wasn't interested, that he wanted none of this 'entertainment'. The whole business sickened him. He thought of Rebecca's fears that she might in the end be forced to this, degraded as these girls were degraded, risking violence, perversion, pregnancy and disease. Risking death.

But before he could speak, another woman had come up to them. She was fair, with yellow curls that fell to her shoulders, and bold blue eyes. She was dressed in a manner that suggested she had either suffered hard times or was about to; her clothes were not quite stylish, not quite well looked after, not quite clean. She began her little speech, as they all did, with scarcely a glance at their faces. And then she looked up. Francis saw her eyes widen as they saw his face; he saw the colour leave her cheeks as she turned her glance upon Vivian.

He stared at her. Had he ever seen her before? There was something familiar in the way she turned her head, in the way she put up her hand to brush back her tangled curls.

At his side, he felt Vivian stir and turned to look at him. There was an expression of disbelief on his cousin's face.

'Bessie Himley . . .' Vivian said slowly. 'So, I've found you at last . . .'

Rebecca finished cleaning the library fireplace and leaned her head against the arm of the chair she and Francis had so often shared. She remembered the way he had held her in his arms, the feel of his arms about her, his lips on hers in the kisses that had lit such a fire of longing in her heart.

Was he never going to come home?

He had left London, they'd heard, and gone north to Yorkshire, and even further than that, to Scotland. He would be looking at yarns, seeing the sheep which provided the wool for the carpets woven in Kidderminster. He would be looking for new methods of making carpets, trying to find ideas for new designs.

He had been away for six weeks, and Rebecca was beginning to think she would never see him again.

Wearily, she rose to her feet and picked up her box and pail. She always seemed to be tired these days. And her breasts ached and felt tight and sore in her bodice. As she came to her feet, a wave of faintness shook her; she felt suddenly sick and sank to her knees, trying to hold back the retching.

The door opened and Polly came in. She took one look at Rebecca and hurried over, putting her arm around Rebecca's shoulders.

'Becky! Whatever's the matter? Are you poorly?'

'I don't know,' Rebecca gasped, leaning against Polly's bosom. 'I just felt queer all of a sudden. I've been like it the past two or three days – it comes over me all of a sudden and then goes off again. I haven't been properly sick, but I feel real bad at times.'

Polly stared at her.

'Is it mostly in the mornings?'

'No – it's any time. I suppose it's worst in the mornings, but it seems to go on all day. Why?' Rebecca looked up and drew in a quick breath. 'Poll – you don't mean—'

'Could you be?' Polly asked. 'I mean – have you . . . is there someone . . . ? Becky, you've been looking peaky for days now. You must know what it is.'

'A baby,' Rebecca said, and sank back on her heels, staring at Polly with a white, frightened face. 'Polly, I'm going to have a baby. That's it, isn't it? That's why I've been feeling like this?'

'I should think so,' Polly said grimly. 'My God, Becky, for you to get caught – you of all people.'

'It was only once,' Rebecca whispered. 'I never thought – it was only once.'

Polly tightened her arm about Rebecca's shoulders. 'Once is all you need, Becky. Anyone can get caught – you've just been unlucky. You should have looked to see which way the wind was blowing.'

Rebecca folded her arms across her stomach. A baby. Francis's baby. But Francis was away and might not come back for weeks – months. In the meantime – what was she to do?

The sickness washed over her again, and she turned her head into Polly's shoulder and wept.

Chapter Sixteen

After nearly six years in London, Tom Himley considered that he knew the city pretty well. The teeming streets, the narrow alleyways, the hidden corners that had been so daunting when he and Bess had first arrived, were all familiar territory to him now. It was difficult to remember that he had ever been lost amongst the tall buildings.

He had learned his way about by a variety of methods, while struggling to earn the money to stay alive. He had held horses while their owners ate dinner in restaurants, he had run errands and taken messages, he had swept yards, served in taverns and done a multitude of other jobs – anything that would bring in a few coppers without drawing too much attention. Sometimes he had been offered a permanent job by some gentleman impressed by his willingness and honesty. But Tom had never accepted; he had been afraid to step into the world where he might one day be recognised, by Vivian Pagnel perhaps. Or otherwise discovered and exposed as a murderer.

For the same reason, he never tried to go back into weaving. There were silk-weavers at Bethnal and Tom knew that he could quickly have adapted – hadn't Kidderminster also been a centre of silk-weaving, and hadn't his own father and grandfather been silk-weavers? But who was to know whether the long, creeping tendrils of the grapevine might stretch as far as a silk-weaving shop in Bethnal Green? It was better to be hidden in the streets, known to nobody. Even then, he was in constant dread that someone would one day lay a heavy hand on his shoulder, take him before the magistrates and condemn him to hang for Jabez's death.

Most of the time, Tom was too busy and too anxious to think much about the early days when he and Bessie had first come to London. But occasionally something would remind him. An old crone, sitting alone in a tavern, who looked like Sal Preston. A glimpse of a girl fresh from the country, looking bewildered and lost. The sight of a young face peering hopefully at passing men, looking for trade.

It still angered him, to think what he and Bess had been reduced to – Bess in particular. And he never stopped reproaching himself for not having taken better care of her.

'Don't be daft,' Bess said when he expressed this regret. 'What else could you do? You only went to look for that place that Mr Vivian give us the address for. And I was more dead than alive, you had to leave me behind. We didn't know what old Sal was.'

'I ought to have realised,' Tom said, but he knew that she was right. It was no use going over old ground. And although six years in London had made him as sharp-witted as any native Cockney, he knew that he could not be blamed for having once been a green boy, as ignorant and innocent as a newborn babe.

Standing at the head of a horse, outside one of London's most popular restaurants, he would think again and again of those early days in the city. The panic of having lost his way, of falling prey to the girl who had first befriended and then robbed him, the despair of losing Bess, of sleeping rough, huddled in doorways, of begging for food. The bewilderment of that cold, foggy evening when he had at last, days later, found Sal Preston's house again and asked for Bess, stayed with him. The look on the pale, tired face of the girl who answered the door; her shaking head, her denial that Bess had ever been there.

'I dunno who you mean. Sal never brought nobody back. And we wouldn't know anyway – we're respectable working girls here, we minds our own business.' She brushed back tangled yellow hair and stared at him curiously. 'Here, haven't I seen you before?'

'Yes,' Tom said, snatching at her admission, 'the other day when Sal brought me and my sister here. If you remember me, you must remember her.' He found himself pushed aside by another girl who had just come in from the street, followed by a man who gave Tom a brief glance before going up the narrow stairs. 'What sort of place is this, anyway?' he demanded, remembering the girl he had met, the one who had taken him to her room. Suddenly he knew what must have happened to Bess. He stared at the face that ought to have been pretty but was wan and dissipated, with skin that was once creamy now coarse and grimy, eyes bleary. 'You've seen her,' he said with angry certainty, and reached out to grasp her arm. 'Tell me where she is – you got to tell me.'

The girl laughed shrilly, but there was an edge of fear in the sound. 'Here, you let go of me – it costs money to touch one of Sal Preston's bawds, didn't you know that? Yes, that's what I am – what we all are here – bawds. And so's your sister by now, if Sal's got her claws into her. And it ain't no use you looking like that – you shouldn't've left her here in the first place if you didn't want nothing to happen to her.'

Tom let go of her arm. He stared at her. A great

wash of despair and regret overcame him and he leaned against the wall, trembling.

'Bess a bawd? Our Bess? But she'd never—'

'Sal Preston don't give a girl much choice,' the girl said bluntly. 'She's got clients that'll pay well for a fresh wench. And know how to tame one that's not too willing. They like it that way.' Her eyes were flat, uncaring. 'Look, mister, it happens to us all. And it ain't a bad living, while you got your looks. At least your sister got a room, she don't have to go begging in the gutter or walking the parks. That ain't no fun on a cold winter's night, I can tell you, and the money's not so good either. What man's going to pay well to lay on the cold grass? Maybe it's better not to ask.'

Tom felt sick. His sister, bright, light-hearted Bess who had never wanted anything but a good time, and had never had it – a bawd, forced out of what little innocence Jabez Gast might have left her. Doomed to become what this girl before him had become – a slattern, a slut, with hard eyes and a coarse tongue.

'Where is she?' he asked dully. 'You might as well tell me. I can find her, you know.'

The girl hesitated. Then she shrugged.

'Look, I dunno if it was your sister. But there was a girl – it might have been the day you come here, or the day after, I dunno. Sal took her away. She ain't been here since. It might not have been your sister at all, mind. I'm not saying it was. I'm not saying nothing.'

'Took her away?' Tom stared at her. 'But where? Where would she take her – and why?'

'Why? Maybe because she didn't want her found. I dunno, do I? I told you, I'm not saying nothing. I *dunno*.'

'But you know where she'd have taken her,' Tom said. 'You know where that girl's gone. You can tell me that – even if the girl's not Bessie.'

'I can't. I dunno where she's gone. I dunno nothing.'

The girl was looking frightened now, her eyes flickering uneasily up and down the street as if she were afraid of being seen. As they stood there, the man came back down the stairs, followed by the other girl. He glanced again at Tom and pushed past. He was breathing heavily.

'You still here?' the other girl asked, as she adjusted her shawl. 'Coo-er, Meg, you're taking a chance, ain't yer? If old Sal catches you gossiping here when you oughter be bringing in the cash—'

'I know.' Meg turned quickly to Tom. 'Look, you'll have to go now, I can't hang about here. I got to work—'

'Not until you tell me where my sister's gone,' Tom said, feeling suddenly sure of himself. 'You know where that hag took her, and I'm going to stay here till you tell me. I don't care what trouble I make, see? I'll stop right here – on this doorstep – till you tell me where my sister's gone, and you can do what you like.'

The two girls stared at him. Then the second girl said, 'Is he after that kid what Sal took over Russell Street?'

'Russell Street?' Tom said quickly, and Meg rolled her eyes, then nodded with resignation.

'All right. Yes, that's where she went. Sal's got another house there. Near Covent Garden. I dunno the number – but you only got to ask. And I'm not telling you no more than that. And if Sal ever asks, I'll say I never seen you in my life, understand?'

'Of course I understand.' Tom looked at her helplessly. 'Look – I wish I could give you something, but I've been robbed—'

'Oh, yes, that's what they all say.' Meg turned away

with a gesture of contempt. 'You go and look for your sister, if sister she really is, and keep away from me, that's all I ask. I don't want no trouble with Sal. She looks after her girls all right, does Sal, so long as we behaves ourselves, and I don't want to end up walking the parks.' She began to close the door. 'Go on – get off out of here now. You're no good to me, and that's the truth of it.'

The door closed. Tom looked at it and then at the other girl. She was watching him with a curious expression on her face.

'Well, that's the first time I seen Meg turn away a likely young man,' she observed. 'You'd better do as she says – get away from here. If what she says is true, Sal ain't going to be too pleased to see you round Russell Street either. Nor your sister, I shouldn't think.'

'What do you mean? Why shouldn't she want to see me? She never wanted to end up like this—'

'Well, you didn't do much to stop it, did you? By all accounts, she's set on the primrose path now, while you've been off losing all your money – what good d'you think you're going to do her now? It's too late to save her from a fate worse than death – Sal will have seen to that.' The girl's laugh was raucous. 'She'll have got used to it now – ah, and used to three meals a day, too. Sal feeds us right, you got to give her that. She looks after us, too – better'n you can. Your sister won't even want to give you time of day now – you see if she don't.'

She went off down the street, while Tom stood on the doorstep staring after her. He turned and looked at the house. The door remained firmly closed. A scrap of curtain moved in one of the windows, then hung still.

Slowly, Tom moved away and stumbled down the dark, rough-cobbled street. There were few people about. A crone sat in a doorway, mumbling to herself. A drunkard weaved his way down the middle of the road. A thin, bony dog chased a scraggy cat into a corner, where they disturbed a man and woman standing pressed against the wall. The man cursed and kicked, the cat yowled and the dog yelped and scampered away. The woman laughed, and a chill ran through Tom's body. It could have been Bess's laughter.

Had she really been brought to this? Was she, even now, lying with some man, a stranger she might never see again, forced to give herself for money, for food? How had it all come about – and how could he have managed any differently, any better?

Miserably, Tom roamed through the streets. He was barely conscious of the gnawing hunger in his belly and had forgotten how long it had been since he had last eaten. He had no money for food, nor any idea of how to acquire any. He looked up from time to time at the street names, wondering whether he was anywhere near the place Bess had been taken to. But after the girl's words to him, he no longer knew whether he should continue to search for his sister. He hadn't been much use to her so far – would she be pleased to see him now? Or would she turn away from him in disgust, saying he'd let her down? He wouldn't blame her if she did.

'Here – you, lad! Hold this horse for me, will you?' The voice rang out commandingly and Tom turned his head. He was in a wider street now, better lit, with shops that were still open and several coffee-houses with windows steamed up and noise and laughter coming from within. The man who had called to him had just dismounted from a tall black horse which was drinking from a trough.

'I'm going in here to do some business,' he said as Tom drew near. 'I need someone to look after Brandy for me. You look an honest fellow – are you?' His sharp eyes assessed Tom. 'There'll be a few pence in it for you, if you keep a good eye on him. Mind, I can see you from inside, so don't try any tricks.' He handed over the bridle. 'Let him have a good drink and then keep him quiet. He's a good enough brute.'

He disappeared into the coffee-house and Tom stood uncertainly, the bridle in his hand. He had never had much to do with horses; there had been plenty in Kidderminster, but they had not come much to the weavers' cottages. Sam Hooman had had one, and Tom had sometimes helped groom and feed it. He had been fond of the animal, and sorry when it had slipped on ice and broken a leg and had to be destroyed.

The fog swirled around as he stood in the road. Other horses clattered past, dragging carts full of goods, or curricles and phaetons with grandly dressed people sitting high above the road. Warm, yellow light spilled from doors and windows; he could smell coffee and pies and was suddenly aware of his hunger. The horse snorted and tossed his head and Tom automatically put up his hand and stroked the long, soft nose.

'I see you've got a hand with animals,' a voice said, and Tom turned to see that the man was back, already checking the girths. He felt in his pocket and drew out a few coins, handing a couple to Tom. 'Care to earn a little more tomorrow? I need someone to see to him while I do business – don't care to trust most of the cadgers round these parts. Well?'

'Yes, sir – thank you, sir,' Tom stammered. 'Where do you want me to be?'

'Oh, here'll do. Nine o'clock sharp – if you're not here I'll look for someone else.' He swung into the saddle. 'Name?'

'Er – Tom.' Just in time, Tom realised that it might be better not to tell his real name. He knew little of the processes of the law, but thought it quite possible that every magistrate and watchman in the country had been warned to look out for Tom Himley. 'Tom – Tom Broome.'

'I'm Jacob Bright. They all know me hereabouts. Well, Tom Broome, if you serve me well you may do yourself a good turn – my last ostler fell under a brewer's dray last week and got trampled by the shires. They've got big feet, those animals. Careless of him – lost himself a good position.' He laughed. 'Still, it was over quick enough. You'll be here at nine then.' He touched the horse's sides with his heels. 'Get up, Brandy. It's too cold to stand about.' And the horse clattered away into the fog, merging with the darkness, the sound of its hooves blending with the other sounds of the street.

Tom stood looking after him. He looked down at the money in his hand. Enough to buy food for tonight. Enough even for something to eat in the morning. And the promise of more to come tomorrow.

It was possible, after all, to live in London. It was possible not to starve, without resorting to thievery.

He went into the nearest pieshop, feeling more light-hearted than he had done for days. Tonight, he would eat. Tomorrow, he would earn some more money. And then he would find Bessie and take her away from the life she had been forced into.

381

Now here he was again, standing outside a restaurant, holding a horse. It was as if he had come round full circle. And nothing had worked out as he had imagined it.

Jacob Bright had employed him for three days, paying him well and giving him a hot pie and a pint of ale to drink when he went to eat his own lunch. They had travelled over the city, with Tom walking at a fast pace beside the horse as Jacob went from place to place to conduct his business. Each evening, he had named the place and time for Tom to meet him next day. And because he had made it clear that he expected his ostler to look presentable, Tom had found cheap lodgings for the night and washed before going out in the morning.

'You'll do for me,' Bright declared on the last day. 'You're honest, or seem to be, and you're the quiet sort, not loud-mouthed. I like that. Now, I've got to go home tomorrow, back to Berkshire. You can come with me if you like, and work as a handyman while I'm there, or you can stop here in London and find your own employment meantimes. But I want you available whenever I'm in Town, d'you understand? Now which is it to be?'

Tom stared at him. 'I can't go to Berkshire, sir—'

'Why not?' The question was barked at him.

'Why, because I've a sister here—'

'Bring her along as well,' Bright said casually. 'We're always looking for maidservants. The silly wenches get themselves into the pudding club or go off and marry the gardener's boy or such. We can find a place for your sister, I've no doubt.'

'But I don't know where she is. I've been looking for her – we lost each other, first day in London.'

Tom felt despair wash over him again. Where could Bessie be now? After so many days, what was happening to her? He ought to have searched for her before – but he'd needed money so desperately. He'd needed to fill his own belly.

Bright stared at him, then laughed abruptly.

'Lost each other! And you hope to find her again? You're crazy, Tom. You'll never see her again in all this hugger-mugger. Anyway, she'll have picked up with some fancy-man by now – won't want big brother coming along and telling her what's what.' He laughed again. 'So – are you coming with me or not?'

Tom shook his head. 'I've got to find her, sir.'

Jacob Bright shrugged. 'Well, it's your choice. Though I think you're a fool. Still, if I see you next time I come to London I'll take you on again, and maybe you'll have realised then which side your bread's buttered. Now I must go. Up, Brandy.'

He gave Tom a nod and turned the big black horse round. They disappeared down the street and Tom stood looking after them.

Had he been a fool? Was Jacob right – had he lost Bess for ever? Would he have been more sensible to take up the offer, go to the country and start a new life as Tom Broome, far from anyone who might have known him in Kidderminster?

But he couldn't abandon Bessie as easily as that. He had to go on searching. And meanwhile, he could earn enough money to keep himself alive. Enough to take care of her, too – when he found her. Unless she had, as Jacob Bright asserted, found herself a 'fancy-man' to keep her.

And even that would be better than the fate he'd feared for her.

After only a few days, Bessie had given up all hope of ever seeing her brother again.

She was now acknowledged as one of Sal Preston's wenches. As yet, she had not been permitted to go out of the house; her clients had been brought to her room, where she had waited trembling and afraid, aware that her fear was an added attraction yet unable to hide it. And as the men to whom Sal sold her body took their pleasure with rough brutality, so she grew more afraid.

'You oughter fight back a bit,' Maud said one evening. Maud was the girl Sal had deputed to instruct Bess in the art of pleasing clients. 'At least they'd go away with a scratch or two to remember you by. Some men likes a bit of a fighter.'

'But I don't want them to like me,' Bess said, sitting up on the bed to sip the broth Maud had brought. 'If they like me, they'll come again. I'd rather they left me alone.'

'Well, they won't do that.' Maud was small and dark, with eyes that were still bright. 'Sal won't let 'em. Long as you're here, you'll have to work. And it ain't so bad. You can eat, you got somewhere dry to sleep. What more do you want?'

Bess looked at her. 'How did you come to be here, Maud? Did Sal pick you up, same as she did me?'

'More or less. That's how she gets most of her girls. Mind, it weren't quite the same with me. I used to live in Dover and I got friendly with a soldier there. There wasn't much for me at home, only drudgery – I worked for my mum and dad in the shop they had, and they wouldn't let me out more'n once a week, I had to work all the time. So when this soldier asked me to go with him, I did. I liked it. He was good to me – give me money and presents. I got a room near the barracks so we could see each other often. I thought he'd marry me one day.'

'What happened to him?' Bess asked when Maud fell silent.

'Oh, nothing happened. He just got tired of me, see. So then I took up with one of his mates, but that didn't last either. I was with a sergeant when the regiment moved to London, so I moved with them. Then they went off again and I decided to stop in London. I could see there was plenty of custom to be found here, and I was a bit tired of soldiers. Only it's not so easy when you're on your own. I got a room, but it wasn't much and I had to find my own food and all. So when Sal spoke to me, I was glad enough to fall in with her.'

'So you never started like – like I have? You didn't have men forcing you, thinking you were a virgin?'

Maud grinned. 'No, I never had that. I don't hardly remember *being* a virgin. I don't reckon I ever was, not really. My dad saw to that when I was still little.' She looked at Bess. 'You want to stop worrying about it, you know. Lay back and let go. It hurts all the more if you're scared. If you don't want to fight a bit, just let 'em get on with it. It's over all the quicker then.'

'Is that what you do?'

Maud laughed shortly. 'Me? I been doing it so long I don't even think about it any more. See, when I started it was something I enjoyed doing. And men like that too. It makes 'em feel good. So now I just go on as if I do, even if I'm really thinking about a new ribbon or what's for dinner that day. They can't tell the difference and they'll pay well. And come back again.'

'But I don't *want*—' Bessie began, but Maud interrupted her.

'I knows you don't want 'em to come back, kid. But see here – you're going to get men anyway, and they might as well be ones you know. You can get to know their ways then, see, and you knows what to expect. Better'n a string of strangers, ain't it?'

'I suppose so,' Bessie said after a moment.

'Course it is. Look, it's in your own interests to give 'em value for money. Some of 'em can get real nasty if they think they've bin rooked. Look at Suzy the other day – feller give her a black eye and nigh on bust her nose. You don't want that happening to you. And you've just about had your run as a virgin. Sal won't be able to pull that much longer.'

'So I've got to start pretending I like it,' Bessie said, and thought of how she and Nell had giggled together back in Kidderminster as they'd wondered what it would be like to get behind a wool bale with Mr Vivian. Mr Vivian . . . what would he do when he found she and Tom had disappeared? Would he come to search for them? Or set the constables on them? 'But I don't know how to pretend that,' she wailed. 'I don't know what to do.'

Maud grinned. 'Don't worry about that, duck,' she advised. 'Just you listen to your Auntie Maud. I'll tell you all you need to know . . .'

After a while, Bessie was allowed to go out alone. She had been several times with Maud or one of the other girls and had seen how they went about soliciting for new clients; on the last two occasions she had found her own men, practising what Maud had taught her and discovering that it worked – the upward glance, the suggestive voice, the sensuous movements of her body. She had taken them back to Sal's house with a sense of triumph, mixed with contempt for the men

386

who were so easily drawn. What did they get out of a half-hour tumble on a greasy bed that was worth paying for? She wouldn't have given a farthing for it herself and she despised those who were so ready to pay.

Still, she seemed able to please them well enough now. She'd listened to Maud's instructions and tried lying back and letting it happen, though it hadn't been easy; her whole inside had tightened up and cringed whenever a man had entered her, so that his thrusting organ became a weapon as brutal as any cudgel or bayonet. But once she'd achieved it ('think about summat else,' Maud had advised) she'd found that it really did work. And from there, it wasn't so difficult to pretend to the pleasure she had never experienced. 'Just a bit of whimpering and moaning, that's all you need. And breathe quicker, towards the end.' Bess, whimpering, moaning and breathing quickly, had found it all to be good advice. The men liked it and came back for more. Sal was pleased. Bess found herself being given better food and even a little money. She bought herself some ribbons and threaded them through her hair. She began to reckon up just how much could be earned this way.

Sometimes she thought of Tom, and wondered what had happened to him. But she never really expected to see him again.

It was on the third time when she went out alone that she caught sight of his familiar figure, standing outside a coffee-house. He was holding the bridle of a large grey horse, stroking its nose as it drank from a trough. He looked thin and weary and disheartened.

Bessie stopped. She drew into a corner. Her heart thumped and she stared at him hungrily. She wanted to rush out, to run to him. She could not understand why she did not do so.

In those first few days, after she had woken from her drugged sleep in Sal's room and realised, slowly, what was happening to her, Bess had waited for Tom to come and rescue her. She had been unable to believe that he would not find her, that he would not come storming into Sal's house and take her away with him, away to some place of safety where all would once again, miraculously, be well. She had strained her ears for his voice, started up at every knock on the door, gazed from the window in the hope that she would see him come walking down the street.

But none of these things had happened. Tom had never come. And Bessie had come to believe that he wouldn't. That she would never see him again. That he had – perhaps – given up the search. Even forgotten her.

And here he was. Standing apparently unconcerned, holding a horse. Not even glancing up and down the street in the hope of seeing her, but looking instead at the horse, talking to it, stroking its nose.

Bessie left her corner and stalked across the road, kicking aside the rubbish that littered the cobbles, ignoring the men who crossed her path, forgetting that she ought to be practising her new skills on them, forgetting that Sal would be expecting her back with a new client. Her eyes were stormy, her bosom heaving with a breathing quick enough to please any man. She was unaware of the admiring glances she attracted, or the suggestive remarks passed by the errand boys and street sweepers. She swept across the street like a queen and came to a halt in front of Tom, her chin tilted.

Tom turned his eyes away from the horse and looked down at her.

For a moment, there was complete stillness. She saw disbelief in his eyes, followed by relief, delight, joy. And her own temper vanished as quickly as it had come.

'Bessie,' he whispered incredulously.

'Oh, Tom – *Tom* . . .'

She held up her arms and he caught her against him. They held each other as they had not done since they were children – as they never remembered having done in their lives. She felt his heart thumping against hers, and buried her face against his shoulder. 'Tom – Tom – Tom . . . I thought I'd never see you again . . .'

He held her away from him, his eyes searching her face.

'Where've you been, Bess? What's been happening to you? I looked for you – I went back to the house and you were gone—'

'I know. Sal took me away—'

'A girl told me she had another house, somewhere near Russell Street. I've been there asking, but nobody would tell me anything. They said they'd never heard of Sal Preston—'

'It isn't Russell Street. It's Maiden Lane – and that's a joke. And nobody'd tell a stranger anyway, case he come from the constables. Tom, what have you been doing all this time? How have you been living?'

'Like this.' He nodded at the horse, who had finished his drink and was staring at them incuriously. 'I pick up a few bob one way and another. But what—'

A man came out of the coffee-house and approached them. He glanced at Bessie, then took the bridle from Tom's hand. His face was hard and angry.

389

'Is this what I pay you for, Ostler? Talking to drabs in the street while you're meant to be taking care of my animal? Damned if I pay you for that – old Jorrocks here could have been cut away and stolen while you've been spooning here, and you left with just the bridle to hold on to.' His glance sharpened, and Bessie realised that she knew this man, as he did her. She had lain with him, in her first days at Sal's house, when she was still terrified, still being sold as a virgin. 'And I'll wish you well of this one,' he added contemptuously. 'It's like bedding a rabbit. I prefer a woman with a bit more juice about her.'

He swung up into the saddle and jerked the horse's head up. Tom stared up at him, then turned to his sister.

'Bess?'

Bess looked back at him, her eyes stony again.

'Well, what did you expect? Left with Sal Preston – no money, nowhere to go. What did you expect me to be doing, Tom Himley? Running a milliner's shop? Waiting on some fine lady? Haven't you *seen* what this place is like? Haven't you seen what happens to girls like me in London?'

Tom shook his head. Misery hollowed his eyes. 'I know, Bess. I saw the girls at that other house – I knew then what you must have come to, but I suppose I still hoped, somehow . . .' He shrugged helplessly. 'I didn't know what to do – where to look—'

Bessie touched his arm. 'It wasn't your fault, Tom. She told you the wrong place, on purpose.' She looked at him, struck by a sudden thought. 'Did you ever find James Street?'

Tom looked down at his feet. 'I did, in the end. But—'

'And Mr Vivian?' she interrupted, suddenly eager.

'Was there a message from him? Did the woman give you a room – a job? Can we go there now?' The idea of escape from Sal and the life to which she had resigned herself suddenly rose again, bright and shining as if it had never dimmed. Of course, she knew now what Mr Vivian would expect – but wouldn't it be better, being his mistress, his kept woman, than this life of cadging and soliciting and giving herself over and over again to a succession of strangers . . . ?

Tom raised his eyes and the look in them shocked her into silence.

'Bess, it's not like that,' he said miserably. 'That first – day looking for James Street – I dunno where I went, I got lost, I had to ask my way. And there was a girl – she seemed all right, same as Sal seemed all right. She told me she had a friend would know. She said if I went back with her . . .' His voice trailed away and Bess stared at him, knowing already what he was going to tell her. 'She robbed me, Bess. They took it all – the money, the letter, everything. I had to fight to get out – I still don't know whether I did for the man she was with. And when I went to the place Mr Vivian sent us to – the woman there just laughed in my face. I couldn't blame her. I looked a real crow by then.'

'So we can't go there,' Bessie said flatly, and he shook his head.

'All the same, Bess, now we've found each other it's got to be better. We can find somewhere to live – a room somewhere, there's some cheap houses round about – I'll get permanent work. There's this man I worked for first off, Mr Bright, he offered me a job in the country, said I could bring you too—'

'Where is he now?' Bessie asked quickly, but again Tom shook his head.

'He went back, Bess. He said he'd look out for me

when he come again but I haven't seen him since. But there's others, I could—'

Bess shook her head. Her eyes had hardened again, their expression flat and disillusioned.

'It's no good, Tom. It won't work. You're dreaming. How can you keep us both, just by holding horses while they has a drink at a trough? This is London – not some sort of heaven. Look – I've been through the mill now. I know what it's all about. I've learned a lot since you left me at Sal Preston's. I can make enough money to live on. I can keep a roof over my head and food in my belly. I'm not going to throw all that up just because we've found each other again. It'd be daft.'

'But you're—' Tom stumbled over the words. '—Bess, the way you're living, you're a – a—'

'A strumpet. A doxy. A drab. There's a hundred words for what I am, Tom.' She looked at him, her blue eyes defiant. 'I don't like it much, but it's no worse than standing all day at a loom. It's no worse than being raped by Jabez Gast, for nothing. At least I gets paid for it now. And there's always a chance of taking some feller's eye and getting married from it. You don't have to laugh. A lot of Sal's girls have got their own fancy-men – soldiers, some of 'em, or footmen at big houses, even constables. They're saving up to get wed. And I heard of a girl who got took up by a duke. S'pose that happened to me, eh?'

'Oh, Bess,' Tom said sadly. 'Bess, Bess. If our Mam could see you now – hear you talking like that—'

'Well, she can't. No more's she going to.' Bess looked at him. 'Tom – what say we find somewhere together one day, set up in business? I can bring in the clients – I know what's what. Just a few regulars, that's what I'd like. And you could look after things, like—'

'I'll not act as bully for you,' Tom said quickly. 'There'd be no robbing. It'd have to be honest.'

'It would be.' She smiled at him. 'Look, I'll have to go now – Sal will be sending out to look for me. But let's meet again, tomorrow, and talk some more. We could do it, Tom – we could set up together, us and maybe one or two of the others. We'd only need a room to start off with. Think about it, eh? And then you could write and tell Mam and Dad we're all right – they must be worried half out of their minds. They needn't know what's really happened. You can say we've got good jobs. It'd make 'em feel easier.'

She gave him a nod and turned, slipping away into the crowd. When she looked back at the corner, Tom was still in the same place, gazing after her.

Bessie began to ply her new trade again, pacing slowly along the pavement, looking up into the faces of unaccompanied men, wheedling them with soft promises. Within a few minutes, she was taking a young clerk back to her room at Sal's house. And as she lay back on the grubby bed, letting him fumble with her body, she thought again of her meeting with Tom.

They could make a good life together, she and her brother. Gentle though he was, he had killed one man, and possibly two. He would be a good protector. And a girl setting up on her own needed protection, from someone she could trust.

They could rent a room. Tom could be out earning money however he liked, while she practised the skills Maud had taught her. After a while, they could find somewhere better – bigger. They could end up with a house of their own. They could become known. They could aim for a better class of man – nobs like Mr Vivian. She could stop doing it herself and employ girls, like Sal did. Except that she'd never be like old Sal.

The clerk gave a grunt and Bessie remembered her duty and squealed, twisting her legs about him. You never knew. He might end up as Lord Mayor of London. It would be worth a bit of effort now to have a Lord Mayor amongst her clients.

It hadn't worked out exactly as Bessie had planned. She and Tom had met, talked and come to an agreement. They would do as Bessie suggested and find a room of their own. Tom would not act as 'bully' – he was still unhappy about Bessie's profession – but he would bring in whatever money he could earn and keep the roughest of her customers away. Stealing from them was forbidden. However Bess earned her money, it had to be honest.

Bessie agreed with this and, after a few more months with Sal, managed to save enough to leave and move into a shabby, damp basement with Tom. There was a bed, a table and a couple of chairs, some old curtains and linen, some dishes and utensils. Bess swept the floor, lit a fire in the fireplace and then set out on her first day of independence.

Bringing in the men was easy enough. But somehow Bess had never managed to struggle out of the level in which she had found herself with Sal. Her clients remained the workmen, ostlers, tavern waiters and young clerks they had always been. If she ever attracted anyone of better class, the sight of her basement room was enough to send them backing away up the steps. And it seemed that she would never be able to afford anything better.

There were other problems, too. Pregnancies – after the first few weeks, Bessie had realised that she'd been 'caught'. It might even have been Jabez Gast's. Fortunately, she had still been with Sal then and went at once to Maud for advice. Maud was unsurprised.

'It happens to us all,' she remarked before taking Bessie to see an old crone who lived at the top of a house near by and provided Bessie with medicine which brought her to bed for several days but rid her of the encumbrance. After that, Bessie had done as Maud advised and acquired a length of pig's intestine, sewn securely at one end. Any client who refused to use it must pay double and remember to withdraw in time. But there were still those who didn't or wouldn't remember, and Bessie paid more than one visit to old Moll in her attic.

And there was disease. The clap was common enough and could be cured. But there were others that were much feared – though the pig's intestine was supposed to protect against them, provided you washed it pretty often – and Bessie was always anxious about a new client. That was why girls liked to keep to one man. Apart from anything else, it was safer.

And, lastly, there was Tom.

'Can't we get out of this game, Bess?' he would say as yet another client departed and he was at last allowed into the basement for a few hours' sleep. 'I never thought you'd be dragged down to this. Look, I'll go back into weaving—'

'And have someone remember your name? Talk gets about, Tom, you know that. Weavers move around. Someone'd know you, someone'd remember. It's not worth the risk.' She looked at him. 'It's me'll hang as well as you, Tom, if we're found.'

He sighed, knowing there was truth in her words.

Yet how could he stand by and watch his sister prostitute herself, giving herself to any man who would pay a few shillings? He would try again, begging, pleading, but Bess shook her head. She felt secure doing this. She knew where she was. She could support herself, and Tom too if need be. It was better than standing at a loom. And one day she'd get married – there was that pot-boy at the King's Head, he was going to do well for himself, they could buy a tavern and live rich. Or the footman down in the Square, he was going to make butler one day, anyone could see that. He fancied her for a wife, he'd said so many a time.

By the time her sister Rebecca had grown up enough to fall in love, Bessie and Tom were an accepted pair around Covent Garden. They had two rooms now, one for Tom so that he could be at home when Bessie was working. And Bessie could afford new ribbons for her hair and paint for her face.

She was wearing a new ribbon when she went out that day and decided to try for some new clients. And the two young men approaching her seemed a likely enough pair. She went up to them with the half-bold, half-demure manner that had been so successful.

'Wouldn't you like a good time for half-hour or so, misters?' she said softly, not looking up at their faces. 'I can promise you some pleasure. I got a room near here – only a step to walk. What do you say, lads, eh?' She peeped upwards. 'One at a time or both together, I don't mi—'

She stopped abruptly. She looked from one to the other. She felt the colour leave her face as slowly, without thinking, she put up her hand and brushed back her tangled yellow hair.

'Bess Himley,' Vivian Pagnel said slowly. 'So, I've found you at last . . .'

Chapter Seventeen

Bessie Himley? Could this really be Rebecca's sister? This . . . this slattern, with the brassy yellow hair and the dress so low-cut he could almost see the nipples on her full breasts, this woman of the streets whose calling was so apparent? Was this what she had come to?

Without Vivian, Francis would not have recognised her; it was years since he had seen her and he did not even remember those brief glimpses in the carpet shop. He would have walked past, brushing her aside as he had brushed aside all the other drabs who had come wheedling up to them. But at Vivian's exclamation, he stopped dead.

Rebecca had said she was working in a house, as a lady's maid. And Tom had a job, too, looking after horses, well paid and respected. What had happened to them? Or had none of it been true in the first place?

The girl stared up at them, her eyes wide with disbelief. Then her face paled, her eyes darkened with fear and she turned as if to run. But Vivian shot out a hand and caught at her arm.

'Not so fast, my doxy! Come here and look at me – you *are* Bess Himley, aren't you? Don't try to deny it.'

She shook her head, plainly terrified.

'No – no, sir, that ain't my name, I don't know no one of that name, you got me mixed up with someone else, sir, there is a girl called Bess around here somewhere, I've heard tell of her though I've never seen her, but I ain't Bess, sir, my name's – my name's—'

'Sarah, perhaps? Or Jane? Or maybe it's Martha?'
Vivian smiled. 'Take your choice, my pretty. Which is
it to be? Or perhaps you'd rather be Hannah, how
does that suit you?' He watched Bess's shaking head
for a moment, then laughed. 'Difficult to choose,
isn't it? Let's settle for Bess after all, shall we? I'm
sure you'd answer to it if someone called out to
you – your brother Tom, for instance. That *is* him
over there, isn't it?'

Involuntarily, Bessie turned her head and Vivian
laughed again. 'You see, Francis? It's her, all
right – the drab that sliced old Jabez Gast's throat
open for him and then ran away, leaving his blood all
over my new drawing room carpet. My wife was very
disappointed over that carpet,' he said to Bessie. 'But
that's not all you owe me for – is it? What happened
to the money I gave you – eh? And why didn't you go
where I said?'

Francis looked at the frightened girl and felt sorry
for her. Rebecca had always insisted that she and Tom
could not have killed Jabez intentionally, and he
believed her. And who knew what that experience had
done to the pair of them, or what hardship they had
suffered in the years between?

'Well?' Vivian was demanding as he shook Bessie's
arm. 'Out with it – the truth. What did you do with
that money? And why didn't you wait?'

The tears made tracks down Bessie's dusty face.
She tried to pull her arm away, but Vivian gripped
more tightly. Francis could see the soft flesh
reddening as his fingers pinched it, and he stepped
forward protestingly.

'Vivian, stop it – you're hurting her. Let her go.'

'And have her escape me again? Frank, this is the
girl who killed one of my best weavers and then ran

398

off with a bag full of money. I've been looking out for her for five or six years past – you can't expect me to let her go now. I want to know what she's been doing, she and that precious brother of hers.'

'All right, but you don't have to twist her arm off.' Francis laid a hand on Bessie's shoulder and she turned her white face up to him. 'Why don't you come and have a cup of coffee with us?' he suggested. 'Then we can talk. I'm sure you want to know about your family back in Kidderminster, don't you? Your sister—' Belatedly, he remembered that the girl did not even know her parents were dead. 'Come and talk for a few minutes,' he added gently. 'Mr Vivian won't do anything to hurt you.'

'I didn't ask you to speak for me,' Vivian said sharply, not letting go of Bessie's arm. 'But I agree – this would be better discussed somewhere more comfortable. We'll go in here.' He jerked his head at the nearest coffee-house and they made their way in and found an empty table. A serving girl came over to them, her eyes curious as she stared at Bessie, and a few minutes later brought the coffee Vivian had ordered.

'Well?' Vivian said as Bessie picked up her cup with trembling fingers. 'Now you can tell us the truth. And quickly, too – we didn't come here to waste time talking. There are better ways to spend an evening, as no doubt you know.'

'I didn't ask to come in here,' Bessie muttered. 'I got a living to earn.'

'I've already paid for your time,' Vivian said abruptly. 'Remember – six years ago? And more than paid for it. You owe me this, at the least. What happened?'

Bessie stared at her cup. Francis felt again the pity

399

he had felt for her a few minutes ago. Beneath the veneer of hardness that had grown around her, he sensed the vulnerability of a young girl brought to London, going in fear of her life, knowing nobody, an easy victim for the bawds who preyed upon innocent country girls. Even after all this time, he thought, there was still a trace of innocence there. And he remembered again that this was Rebecca's sister, the girl who had helped to bring Rebecca into the world, had played with her as a baby, treated her with careless good nature as she grew up, giggled and laughed her way through a life that had brought her little real fun or pleasure. He remembered Rebecca's face softening as she talked about her childhood during those early morning meetings in the library.

'Tell us what happened,' he said quietly.

Bess lifted her head and looked at him. He met her eyes steadily, trying to convey to her his friendship. Whether or not she recognised it, he could not tell, but after a few moments she began to speak.

'We got to London all right. We come on the coach, like Mr Vivian said. Then we didn't know where to go, see? We met this woman, Sal Preston, and she said she could help us. She said James Street was a long way away and we wouldn't have time to get there that night, and we could stop over in her house.' Bess looked down at her cup again. 'She seemed all right. We didn't know. We didn't know what else to do.'

Vivian stared at her. 'So you fell in with some old crone? And what then? Are you going to tell me she kept you prisoner – she and that brawny brother of yours?'

'Not him, no.' Bess looked at Francis as if pleading with him to understand. 'She sent him off early next morning, telling him James Street was right over the other side of London. Then she took me to another house she had – told me Tom was coming back there to collect me. Only it weren't true – he never even knew she had another house. And while I was there—' Her eyes lost their vulnerability, became hard and flat '—well, it can't be hard for you to guess what happened to me, sir. I was near enough a maid, and scared enough to stay that way for a while. Sal had a lot of gentlemen who liked that sort of thing. She made a lot of money out of me, those first weeks.'

Francis stared at her. 'You mean she brought men in to – to defile you?'

'You can call it that, yes, sir. Only I was *defiled* already, wasn't I.' She turned her eyes on Vivian. 'Tom and me never killed Jabez deliberately. If he hadn't gone for me already, it would never have happened. And it was an accident anyway.'

'All you have to do is prove it,' Vivian said silkily. 'I'm sure the magistrate would be interested, even after all this time.'

'You're not going to give her up now,' Francis protested. 'Especially since you helped them to escape.'

'Yes, there is that,' Vivian agreed. 'Although it's only her word against mine that I did, after all.' He turned back to Bessie. 'And what about your brother, the gallant Tom? Did you ever see him again?'

'Yes, sir. He hung around asking and searching and picking up a few jobs, and one day we ran into each other in the street. It was too late for me to change by then – Sal had got me working for her and there didn't seem to be anything else I could do. We saved up a bit and I left Sal and we set up in a couple of rooms of our own. Tom works same as he was already doing, and I – do what I'm doing.'

'And my money? You spent that, I suppose, on fancy clothes and gin.'

'No, sir, we didn't. Tom was robbed of it the first night he was lost, looking for me. He hadn't got a penny. He was near starving when we found each other again.'

Francis gazed at her. What a pitiful tale. He visualised them, brother and sister, already shocked by the disaster that had overtaken them, arriving in London, bewildered by the teeming streets, the hurrying crowds, the babel of voices all about them. Separated, distraught, at the mercy of all the scum of London's underworld.

Bess met his eyes.

'Please, Mr Francis, tell me. Where's our Becky now? And me mam and dad, how are they? Tom and me – we wrote and told them we were all right, working in fine houses, earning good money, but it weren't true. And after that – well, we couldn't write again. But it didn't mean we'd forgot.'

Francis touched her dirty hand.

'Bessie, your sister works at Pagnel House. She's a housemaid now.' He wanted to add that he loved her, wanted to marry her, but the idea seemed ludicrous in these surroundings. It was almost unbelievable that this girl, tattered and painted and blowsy, was the sister of his sweet, modest Rebecca. 'Your parents—' he paused and saw by the flicker in her eyes that she knew the reason for his hesitation. 'They're dead, I'm afraid,' he said gently. 'They died within a few days of each other, back in the winter.'

Bessie was silent. Then she sniffed and wiped her nose on her sleeve.

'Well, it's probably just as well. They never had much of a life – they're well out of it. Wish I could go

402

the same way.' She looked at Vivian and there was a curious pride in the tilt of her head, as if she had discovered deep within her the shreds of a forgotten dignity. 'And I suppose I will, if you has your way, Mr Vivian. Thieving, murder – you can pin the lot on me, can't you? And watch me swing – you'd enjoy that.'

'I can think of something I'd have enjoyed far more, if you'd had the sense not to get caught up in this game,' Vivian said. His eyes moved over her. 'You're still a pretty enough wench, Bess, if you'd only clean up and dress better. You're working in the wrong market. You'd be better off as one man's paramour than a shilling lay for all comers.'

'Well, it ain't so easy to get on, not in this world,' Bessie said sulkily. Her nasal Kidderminster accent was overlaid now by tinges of Cockney. 'By the time I've got food and ale, and paid for me room, there ain't much money left for ribbons and such. And there's medicines too, stuff like that. I did have a friend, but he couldn't give me enough to keep me – I had to go on working. What else could I do? *I* don't want to starve. And it ain't easy, getting work without a character.' She looked at Vivian and her eyes sharpened. 'Still, here I am now, Mr Vivian,' she said and Francis recognised with a shock the wheedling tone in her voice. 'And willing enough to pay back that money I owe you, just the way you meant. S'long as I gets enough to eat and drink in the meantime.'

Vivian stared at her, then laughed. 'Well, you've a nerve, I'll say that for you. As if I'd want you the way you are now. No, I'm well suited, thanks very much, tasty little French piece I keep tucked away in London. Not that I object to an occasional taste of the exotic, just by way of variety – but that hardly

403

describes you, does it? Maybe Francis here would like a roll with you; he needs teaching a few tricks, unless that little sister of yours has beaten you to it.'

Francis jerked round in his chair and stared at Vivian. 'What the hell do you mean by that? Rebecca's got nothing to do with this. You'll keep her name out of it, do you understand?'

Vivian looked at him in surprise and Francis felt his face colour. Too late, he realised that the words had been one of those taunting remarks that Vivian liked to make, with no regard as to whether or not they might be true. His biting tongue was likely to snap at any target and would occasionally find one that he hadn't been aware existed.

Now he was looking at Francis with glinting eyes, his brows raised in amused speculation.

'Well, and what little hornet's nest have we stirred up here, then? You and the little Rebecca, hmm? No wonder she was so reluctant with me. But a little firebrand once she overcomes her reluctance – don't you agree, cousin?'

Francis felt the colour deepen to scarlet in his face. He curled his hands into fists, repressing the sudden violent urge to smash them into Vivian's cockily smiling face.

'Or didn't you get that far?' Vivian asked. 'A pity. That modest exterior conceals quite a—'

Francis stood up. He was trembling.

'I'll ask you to come outside and repeat that, Vivian.'

Vivian let out a hoot of laughter.

'Come outside! Frank, what melodramatic romances have you been reading? The age of the duel is past, didn't you know? In any case, I'd never dream of scrapping over a housemaid – they're two a penny,

404

here today and gone tomorrow. No doubt the little hussy has slipped out for half an hour with the butcher's boy and forgotten us both by now. They're all the same, these wenches. Well, it's in the blood, isn't it – look at her sister here.'

Francis glanced unwillingly at Bessie. He did not want to believe what Vivian was insinuating – that he, too, had possessed Rebecca's sweet body, that he had lain with her in his arms and kissed those soft lips. He did not want to believe that it was 'in the blood' – that Rebecca was like so many girls of her class, ready to give herself to any man for a shilling or two. He *would* not believe it. He had talked with her, fallen in love with her – and he was ready to swear that she had fallen in love with him.

Yet she had offered herself, on that warm spring afternoon. She had given him her lips, she had guided his hands to her body . . .

And Bess, her sister, was looking at him now with a hard cynicism that struck cold at his heart. She had been selling herself for six years past, walking the streets of London ready to take any man to her bed, provided he could pay her price. She did not find it at all hard to believe that Rebecca might have succumbed to both Vivian and himself.

'It's not true,' he said passionately. 'Not Rebecca. I won't believe it.' He looked back at Vivian. 'You simply said it for fun – for something to say.' But for all his determination, there was an edge of appeal in his voice – as if he were asking, begging, that Vivian should reassure him.

Vivian's smile grew. 'Well, that's something you'll never know, isn't it, unless the little lady herself chooses to tell you. And then you can only be sure if she confirms it – you'll never be *quite* sure of a

denial, will you?' He laughed again, and Francis felt a
renewed surge of fury. But it was useless to give way
to it. He would only make himself look ridiculous.
And give Vivian even more cause for mirth.

Vivian looked up at him.

'Sit down, Frank, do. You make my neck ache,
towering up there like the wrath of God. Let's forget
about the wenches back in Kidder and think of the
ones in London. This one especially.' His eyes glinted
at Bessie. 'What shall we do with her, eh?'

'We'll do nothing.' Francis sat down, but his anger
was still there and it emerged in his voice, hardening it
so that it sounded suddenly less the voice of a boy,
more that of a man who meant what he said. 'Bessie's
had a hard enough time, without you making it worse.
What has she ever done to you, after all? She came to
London at your instigation—'

'I helped her escape a topping she fully deserved.
Let's get it right,' Vivian broke in.

'—and was unfortunate enough to fall into the
clutches of a bawd. But would she have been any
better if you had had your pleasure of her first? You'd
have tired of her in a month or two and she'd have
been exactly where she is now – on the streets. What
does she owe you? Tell me that.'

'The money I gave her and her brother. My best
weaver. The risk I took—'

'Which you thoroughly enjoyed. I can imagine just
what kind of thrill it gave you to smuggle the two of
them away from Kidderminster. As for your weaver,
if he hadn't raped her he'd be alive today. And I
believe it was an accident anyway – though if it
wasn't, he deserved to die. Men like him are abusing
young girls every day, taking their pleasure with never
a thought of what the consequences might be. Yes,

and you're as bad,' he went on, hardly caring what he said to Vivian now as he thought of Rebecca, so fragile, so true, being forced to accept this man's advances. 'You'll tumble a housemaid and forget about it in half an hour, and never mind whether she wants it or not. As for the money you gave them – that was no more than fair recompense for the danger you allowed her to be in, you and your twelve and twelve working, knowing that young girls were likely to be alone with men, knowing that this kind of thing went on. But you didn't care, did you? You didn't care how they lived or died, so long as you got your fine new carpet for your drawing room.' He flung Vivian a look of withering scorn. 'And I take part of the guilt upon myself – because I designed that carpet. It was on a design I made that Jabez Gast ravished this girl and bled his life away.'

There was a long silence. Then Vivian laughed again, but the cocksureness had gone. He sounded uneasy, as if he were attempting to regain a shaken confidence.

'Well, you do get heated when you've a mind, Frank. I never thought you had it in you. And – since you seem to feel some measure of responsibility for this girl's *sad* plight – perhaps you'll tell us what you mean to do about it. I think you'll agree I did all *I* could to help the poor mistreated soul.'

Francis gave him another scornful look. Then he turned to Bessie.

'Let's leave here now, Bess. Take me to your brother. I want to meet him and talk to him. I've an idea we could improve your position.' He glanced back at Vivian. 'I take it you won't try to interfere. After all, I've heard you admit that you helped the two – miscreants – to escape justice. It isn't merely their word against yours.'

Vivian stared at him, then shrugged and took out his snuffbox.

'Do as you like, Frank. I must say, it seems a dreary enough way to spend an evening in London. You won't mind if I don't accompany you? I feel a need to pay a visit to my little French lady's love-nest. The charms of Covent Garden and its surroundings have palled rather.'

'I don't mind at all,' Francis said, 'if you don't accompany us.' He stood up and held out his arm for Bessie to take. Slowly, unbelievingly, she rose and laid her hand in the crook of his elbow. 'I daresay I'll see you tomorrow, Vivian.'

Vivian did not answer. He watched them go. Then he put away his snuffbox and got up, swaggering to the door.

Francis and Bessie had disappeared from sight.

Tom was dubious.

'Look, you don't need to worry about me,' Francis said, seeing the other man's wary glance. 'I'm not going to tell anyone where you are. I'm not going to set the magistrates on you. What happened six years ago is over, as far as I'm concerned, and I believe you when you tell me it was an accident. I just want to help you.'

'Why?' Tom asked directly.

Francis hesitated.

'Because I think you've had a bad time. Because I think the Pagnels owe you better. And—'

'Because of our Becky?' Bess said quietly, watching him. 'It's true, is it, about you and her? And Mr Vivian, too—'

'No!' Francis broke in sharply before she could finish. 'No, I don't believe that's true. But Rebecca

408

and I – yes.' He looked at them both, wondering if they could believe him. 'But it's not the usual story. I love her. I want to marry her.'

'Marry her!' Bessie gave a short laugh. 'A Pagnel, marrying a Himley. That'll be the day. I'd like to see that, I would.'

'Well, I hope you will. But it's you we have to think about now.' Francis looked at Tom. 'You were apprenticed as a weaver, weren't you?'

'Aye, I was.'

'And you were a good weaver? You liked the work?'

'As much as anything else, I suppose. Yes, I reckon I was good enough.'

'Would you like to go back to it?' Francis asked quietly.

Tom shook his head at once.

'No, that'd never do. See, I thought of going up Bethnal and getting work in the silk-weaving. But I was always scared of someone hearing about me – putting two and two together, like. Folk move around in weaving, they go from Kidder to Wilton, or they move from silk and bombazine into carpets. I'd always be scared—'

'But there's no need to be,' Francis said. 'Look, it's six years ago now. And if you change your name, who's to know there's any connection? You've let this fear get too much for you – you're not thinking straight. You can get out of this life you're leading now, make something better for yourselves, you and Bessie.'

Tom gave him a wry look. 'You think so. What d'you imagine a weaver earns? You told us you went to our dad's cottage. Were they living rich?'

'No. But this would be different.' Francis leaned

409

forward. 'Tom, I want to help you. I want to set you up in your own weaving business. *Our* business. Making carpets, to my designs – on a small scale at first, but who knows what it could lead to? I've got ideas – about designs, about production methods – ideas my uncle wouldn't countenance. He's of the old school, he doesn't take easily to new ideas. He doesn't believe that the weavers should have their own say in matters, he's against the unions – he believes that with a fair employer there's no need. But you and I together—'

Tom stared at him. Then he looked at Bessie.

'What d'you think, Bess?'

She turned her eyes from one to the other. The doubt was there in her face, too. Trust was something she and Tom had discarded long ago. It wouldn't return easily.

'We'll think about it,' she said.

Starting his own weaving business in partnership with Tom was less easy than Francis had hoped.

For one thing, Bessie had been hard to persuade. She regarded Francis with only a little less suspicion than that with which she looked on Vivian; he was a Pagnel, and Bessie had made up her mind to have no more to do with Pagnels. Her wariness would fade, he was sure. But before it could even begin to do so, he found himself leaving London and travelling north.

'My father wants you to go to Yorkshire,' Vivian observed one morning as they sat at breakfast. He looked at the letter in his hand. 'You're to visit our yarn suppliers in Halifax – perhaps go on to Scotland.'

Francis looked at him in dismay. 'But I thought we were to return to Kidderminster soon.'

'I'm going back at the end of this week.' Vivian passed the letter across. 'See for yourself.' He smiled. 'It seems that your room is preferable to your company. Or perhaps you'd rather look on it as a compliment to your abilities.'

To Francis, it was neither. He thought only of the enforced separation from Rebecca. And as he lay on a succession of hard inn beds, on the way to Halifax and then in a succession of northern towns and cities, his longing increased.

It seemed so long since he had seen her. His departure had been so abrupt – there had been no time for more than a hurried goodbye, a brief, snatched kiss, a promise to come back soon. But the promise had been broken already. Weeks had gone by, begun to stretch to months, and still there seemed to be no prospect of a return to Kidderminster.

He stared into the darkness. How was Rebecca now? Had she given up hope? Was she thinking that he no longer loved her, that it had been no more than a passing game? Had she – worst thought of all – forgotten him?

If only he could communicate with her. But a letter was out of the question. It would be seen, remarked upon, enquired about. It might even lead to Rebecca's dismissal.

He must go home soon. He must see her. He must put things on a proper footing between them. Whatever might be said, he was determined that Rebecca and he should be married, and soon. The fact that she was a housemaid was immaterial. At least it was more suitable than a marriage with Isabel.

At the thought of his half-sister, Francis sighed. He felt deeply sorry for Isabel. She had, in all innocence, chosen the one man in the world who was out of her reach, and nothing could be done about it. If only she could forget her hopeless passion; if only she could recognise it as an infatuation and go on with her life as a young girl should, enjoying the parties, the attention, the light flirtations that every girl should enjoy. If only she could love someone else as a woman should love.

But Isabel had never wanted to be a woman. The whole idea of the state had appalled her. She had fallen in love with Francis as a refuge from growing up. She had seen him as her childhood playmate and believed that they could extend that childhood together.

And now, with her escape into a lifelong childhood forbidden her, she had taken a different refuge. She had gone into a decline.

There was little, Francis had been told, that the doctors could do about a decline. It began with a disappointment, usually over love, or perhaps a family quarrel. From a simple reluctance to eat, it became a real inability. The girl grew thinner, though she often refused to believe it. She saw herself as fat and ungainly, wrapped herself in layers of clothing to hide her thinness, and to keep warm, and became almost frightened at the thought of eating. She stopped growing as a woman; her body reverted to its own childhood. And no amount of pleading, coaxing, cajoling or scolding could change her.

Isabel had been taken back to Pagnel House and lay in her bed, weak and pale, refusing all but the smallest morsels of food. And begging, constantly begging, to see Francis.

'It would, however, do no good for you to come home,' Jeremiah wrote to Francis. 'The doctors are agreed on that. Seeing you again would only start the symptoms afresh, resulting in a greater disappointment. For as you know, my son, there can be no possibility of any affection between yourself and Isabel. She must forget you – and you must stay away until she does.'

Francis knew that his father laid no blame on him for this situation. But that was of no help. He wanted to go back to Kidderminster. He needed to go back. Because he wanted – he *needed* – to see Rebecca.

And it seemed that it was to remain impossible to do so.

Francis sighed and sat up, feeling for the tinder to light his candle. Perhaps if he read for a while . . . But even as he picked up a book, he knew that it would be of no use. Rebecca's face danced between him and the words, her voice sounded softly in his ears. He remembered her eyes as she looked up at him, that afternoon in the woods. He remembered the feel of her body, so soft and yielding beneath him. He remembered her kisses, so sweet and shy at first, then so passionate. He remembered the love that had enveloped them, the warmth of its aura around them as they lay closely entwined on the deep bed of moss.

Rebecca, Rebecca, he thought longingly, and knew that he must go back soon.

Chapter Eighteen

'Expecting!'

Mrs Hudd stared at the two girls. She shook her head slowly, then sat down. Her face wore a curious expression, a mixture of pity and exasperation. She looked from Polly to Rebecca. Her glance lingered on Rebecca's white apron.

'You silly girl,' she said. 'You silly, silly girl. What did you want to let that happen for?'

Rebecca felt the tears come to her eyes. She thought of that magical afternoon with Francis. How had it come to this? If only he would come back – but he was in Yorkshire now, and there was no word of his return. She had known for some weeks now that she was pregnant and had been hiding the knowledge in the hope that he would soon come back. But now she had been forced to confide in Mrs Hudd.

'I didn't think . . . It was only once, and Polly said—'

'Here,' Polly said, 'don't you go blaming me. I didn't even know you had a young man.'

'I should think not indeed,' Mrs Hudd said hotly. 'You both know that followers aren't allowed. What the mistress is going to say, I just can't imagine.'

'Oh, Mrs Hudd, does she have to know?' Rebecca asked in terror. Surely it couldn't be long now before Francis returned, and then all must be well. But the housekeeper gave her withering glance.

'Of course she'll have to know, you silly girl. You can't hide a bellyful of arms and legs. And what were you planning to do – hide it away in the attic and pretend we've got mice? How far gone are you?'

Rebecca thought again of that first day of spring. The buds on the trees and hedges, just beginning to open to a light, filmy green. The primroses starring the banks with yellow. She looked at Polly, who answered for her. 'We reckon it must be nigh on three months, Mrs Hudd.'

'Three months! That's getting too late to have anything done. Why ever did you leave it so late? And what does the man say about it? Is he going to stand by you?'

Rebecca flinched. She opened her mouth, then closed it again. What could she say? She couldn't tell anyone it had been Francis who had held and loved her. The magic would be gone, the beauty soiled by other people's knowledge. She stared at the floor, and again Polly answered for her.

'Please, ma'am, Becky says he doesn't know.'

'Doesn't know? That's ridiculous. Of course you must tell him.' She gave Rebecca a sharp glance. 'I suppose – you do know who he is, Rebecca?'

'Of course I do.' Rebecca raised her eyes indignantly. 'It was only once, I tell you – I've never been with anyone else but—'

'Anyone else but who?' Mrs Hudd waited a moment, then said impatiently, 'Come on, girl, you're not helping yourself by behaving like this. You'll have to say in the end.'

'I can't. Not now. Not yet.' Not until she had seen him again; not until she knew their love was real for him, too, and not merely a way of passing an empty Sunday afternoon.

'Not *yet*? Now whatever does that mean? Do you think this baby's going to wait? It's not. It's going to

grow – get bigger – and so are you. Everyone's going
to be able to see—'

'I know that!' Rebecca's heard the anguish in
her voice. 'Do you think I don't know about babies?
I saw my mam carry enough, though none of them
lived after me. But it's no good asking me to tell
you who it was – I *won't* and that's all there is
to it.'

'So what are you going to do?'

'I don't know,' Rebecca said miserably, and the
tears began to fall.

Mrs Hudd sighed.

'Well, I don't know what you expect *me* to do about
it. You know perfectly well what the rules are. No followers. And goodness knows we take enough care of
you girls – when you ever get the chance for such
goings-on I don't know. You're only allowed out to go
to church or see your family. That's it, I suppose –
you've been slipping off to meet soldiers and such on
the sly, when you ought to have been saying your
prayers. Well, this is the wages of sin and I must say
you deserve them, you sly minx.' Her exasperation
began to turn to anger. 'When I think of all I did for
you – taking you in when no one else would have
done, coaxing the mistress to give you a chance. And
your poor mother, what would she have said? Poor
Fanny – it's a mercy she's not here to see this. She had
trouble enough, without another daughter bringing
shame on the family—'

Through her tears, Rebecca was aware of Polly
stepping forward. She put out a hand, but Polly
ignored her protest and answered the housekeeper in a
way she would normally never have dared do.

'Please, Mrs Hudd, don't go on at Becky like that.
She's upset enough. It's her's got to have this babby,

not us. And she hasn't been off the sly – not really. Only that once—'

'—which it seems was quite enough,' Mrs Hudd said grimly. 'Well, all right, I'll say no more. I'll grant she's got troubles and to spare, with this lot.' She addressed Rebecca again. 'You realise you'll have to leave, don't you? The mistress will never keep you on now, not in that condition.'

Rebecca raised a tear-streaked face. 'But what shall I do? If I can just stay on for a few months longer—'

'A few months! The baby will be born in a few months – haven't you realised that yet? I'll keep you as long as I can, of course, but once it starts to show I'll have to go to the mistress. As for what you'll do – I don't know, do I? You should have thought of that before. I suppose you'll go to the workhouse, like many a girl before you. I'll be sorry to see it, but what more can I do?'

Rebecca looked at her. The housekeeper was a strict, almost autocratic figure, but she had shown a kind heart on several occasions. This time, however, there really was nothing she could do to help. Followers were strictly against the rules and any girl finding herself in Rebecca's situation could except instant dismissal. By allowing her to stay on until her condition showed, Mrs Hudd was risking her own position. Rebecca could not expect any more than that.

If only Francis were here. Ever since she had first suspected the truth, Rebecca had been hoping for his return. Francis would know what to do: Francis would look after her. She never seriously considered the thought that he might actually marry her – as he had said he wanted to do – but he would have done *something*.

Polly had wanted her to go to Becky Swan, who was

said to be a witch and who had helped many a girl in trouble. But Rebecca had refused point blank. Get rid of Francis's baby? She would sooner die.

'And that's just what you'll do, too,' Polly said at last, exasperated. 'Becky, you *know* what happens to girls like us when they gets caught. Unless they can get wed, it's the workhouse. And more comes out of there dead than alive, you know that.'

'I can't help it. I can't kill my baby.' And Rebecca folded her arms across her stomach in the age-old protective manner of all women, and thought of the life that lay beneath them. Her child and Francis's. A heart, created by their love, already beating somewhere deep inside.

She folded her arms across her stomach again now, and looked up into Mrs Hudd's face.

'I'm sorry, ma'am. I know you've been kind to me, you and Mrs Atkins. Taking me in when our Bess and Tom ran away. And helping when Mam died. I never meant anything like this to happen. But—'

'It's all right, Rebecca,' the housekeeper said when Rebecca's voice trailed away into silence. 'You don't need to say any more. You're not the first girl this has happened to, and you won't be the last. I'll say nothing to anyone until I have to. But after that – well, I'm afraid you're on your own, my girl. Unless you can get the father to stand by you!'

The father. It sounded strange, hearing Francis referred to in that way. Rebecca wondered what Mrs Hudd would say if she knew the truth. Probably very little more than she had already said. It was common enough, after all, for a housemaid to be seduced by the young gentleman of the house. Polly had hinted enough about herself and Vivian. But she had been luckier – or more careful. She knew too much to end like this, with a swelling stomach and no one to turn to.

'Well,' Polly said as they went up to their attic bed-room, 'at least she didn't turn you away out of hand.'

'It's only a matter of time though, isn't it.' Rebecca sat down wearily on the edge of her bed. 'Another month and I'll start to show. The mistress is going to know then – that's if she don't notice sooner. If only I didn't feel so sick all the time . . .'

'That'll wear off now you're three months gone. You'll feel better any day now.' Polly looked at her. 'Becky – Mrs Hudd was right, you know. The feller – he ought to help you, somehow. Why don't you tell him – even if it's over now? Why should he get away with it?'

'It's not like that, Poll, I told you.' Rebecca sighed and lay back. 'He's not getting away with it. And I can't tell him – not now. I just can't.'

'He's married, isn't he,' Polly said, and shook her head sadly. 'Oh, Becky . . . you of all people. I'd never have thought you'd end up this way.

Nor did I, Rebecca thought as she rolled at last into bed and snuffed out her candle. That day in spring, when everything was so magical, and loving seemed right and sweet and true . . . I never thought it would end like this. Oh Francis, Francis, where are you? Why, why, *why* can't you come back to me?

In the factories that summer, women and girls fainted from the heat, children stumbled in their work and were often injured by machinery, and men drank more ale than usual and gave vent to shorter tempers. In the carpet shops, the smell of size and urine hung like a miasma in the air, and over everything lay a pall of smoke from the increasing number of factory chimneys.

The heat was almost too much for Rebecca. Aware that each day her figure was thickening, she dragged herself through her chores, keeping as much as possible away from Isabella's gaze. But she knew that it could not be long now before her condition was noticed, and what would happen then, she dared not think.

'You'll have to make some sort of plan,' Mrs Hudd said to her in despair. 'Susan can't keep on sending Polly to answer the mistress's bell – she's going to ask for you some time. And she knows a belly-bump as well as the next woman. She'll see right away.' She paused and then added, 'I'm sorry to have to say it, Rebecca, but if she doesn't notice it herself I'm bound to tell her soon. I can't let it go much longer.'

'No, I know.' Rebecca looked miserably out of the housekeeper's window at the dusty garden. If only Francis would come back. But although Vivian had come home from London weeks ago, there was no sign of Francis's return. He had gone to Halifax, then to Scotland to look at wool and try to discover more about a certain dye that was being used. And then he had gone back to London.

The talk was that he could not come back until Miss Isabel was better. It was well known by now that her decline was due to her passion for him and her parents' refusal to allow them to marry – although why the match should be frowned upon, nobody seemed to know. Only Rebecca knew that Francis himself had never wished it. As far as the other servants were concerned, it was romantic and sad – but for Isabel, fasting away to nothing in her room upstairs, it was death.

Her first nervous jealousy past, Rebecca felt deeply sorry for Isabel. She had waited on the girl when Isabel had first been brought home from Vivian's house, and had grown to like her. She had watched anxiously as Isabel picked at the food on her tray, and tried to persuade her to eat. But Isabel merely shrugged and turned her face away. It was as if she feared the food Mrs Atkins prepared so carefully to tempt her; as if it she saw it as an enemy.

Isabel was fading away, and there seemed to be nothing anyone could do about it. But at the moment, Rebecca was more concerned with her own fate. If Francis did not return soon, she would be dismissed. And she did not know what she would do.

'What about your brother and sister in London?' Mrs Hudd asked. 'Couldn't you go to them?'

Rebecca looked at her. She could see that, kindly though the housekeeper was, there was not much more help to be had from her. Mrs Hudd had her own position to think of. If she were seen to be helping Rebecca – and thus condoning her sin – she might well find herself dismissed along with the housemaid. It was not to be expected that she should risk that.

Go to Bessie and Tom?

But perhaps it wouldn't come to that. Francis *must* come back soon. And then, surely, everything would be all right.

But as she lay in her narrow bed at night, her hands on her swelling stomach. Rebecca was chilled by a fear that everything would not be all right. She saw herself turned away, stumbling down the path with her few possessions, standing at the gate not knowing which way to go. She saw the dreadful alternatives: the workhouse with all its horrors, or the long walk to London. She would never be able to do it. She still felt ill for much of the time. And her small savings would not pay her fare.

She saw herself dragging slowly along the roads, an easy target for footpads; falling, exhausted at last, into a ditch to lie there until she died.

Other girls in her position had taken their own lives. There was one only last year, a parlourmaid working for one of Mr Pagnel's friends. She'd been found floating in a pond. But that was a sin, too, a sin even greater than the one she had committed – which didn't feel like a sin at all. And besides, there was still Francis. One day, he must return. And then . . . Then?

Her thoughts chased around in her head like dogs on a treadmill, too weary to go on yet unable to stop. Rebecca lay through the long, hot nights of the summer, and felt the cold, damp hand of despair.

The day came very soon after that.

Polly, who had quietly appeared upstairs whenever a housemaid was summoned, fell on the stairs while carrying down a heavy pail of water, and sprained her ankle. Sitting in the kitchen, she stuck it out in front of her on a footstool and they all watched as it swelled.

'Cold compresses,' Mrs Atkins said, 'that's what's wanted. Tilly, run down to the fishmonger's and get some ice. Well, you're a fine one,' she went on to Polly. 'That's put paid to your going to the Midsummer Fair. You'll not be able to put that foot to the ground for a week or more. You'll have to do jobs you can do sitting down – vegetables and such. Becky'll have to do your jobs in the house.'

The same thought struck them all at once. They turned and gazed at Rebecca.

'She'll see it straight off,' Susan said, looking at Rebecca's apron. 'You don't hev much of a bump yet, but you're a sight thicker.'

'Maybe she'll just think I'm getting fat,' Rebecca said, but without much hope. She knew that even if Mrs Pagnel did not notice her condition at once, it would become apparent soon enough. And then she would expect Mrs Hudd, Mrs Atkins and Susan to have realised it, too – and report it to her.

'Well, it can't be helped,' Mrs Atkins said. 'You'd better answer her bell next time she rings, Becky, and see what happens. And you'd better be ready to pack.'

Rebecca looked around at their faces. They were all so familiar, the only 'family' she had left. They were sympathetic; not one of them blamed her for the situation she was in. Each one knew that it could easily have happened to them.

Yet there was nothing they could do to help her. They knew it, and their helplessness showed in their pitying faces. Rebecca knew it, and the knowledge lay heavy in her heart.

Suddenly a bell tinkled on the wall above their heads.

'The mistress,' Susan said, and her eyes fell on Rebecca.

For a moment, Rebecca wanted to refuse, to cry out and beg Susan to go in her place. But she curbed her tongue. It would do no good. She could not be shielded for ever. And even if Polly hadn't fallen, the truth must have come out soon. She was almost four months gone; her condition could not have been ignored for much longer.

She turned and went up the stairs that led out of the kitchen and along the corridor to the green baize door.

Isabella was waiting in her boudoir.

'Oh, there you are. You took your time.' Her eyes sharpened. 'Where's Polly? She usually attends me.'

'Please, ma'am, Polly's fallen and hurt her ankle.'

Rebecca stood respectfully just inside the door, hoping that Mrs Pagnel would not look carefully at her. Often, she did not, treating her maids as if they were mere objects, machines to carry out her orders. But Isabella beckoned her further in, irritation creasing her face.

'Don't stand hovering there, girl. Come in properly. It's Rebecca, isn't it. Goodness me, it's so long since I saw you, I'd almost forgotten you worked here at all. You always sit at the back at prayers, you're like a mouse.'

Rebecca moved forward reluctantly, afraid that now that Isabella had noticed her, she would see the truth. But Isabella had already lost interest. She was picking over a mess of embroidery silks, complaining that Isabel's kitten had tangled them up and demanding that Rebecca should unravel them. 'We only brought the animal in to try to amuse the girl,' she said pettishly. 'And she takes almost no notice of it. She seems to have lost interest in everything these days. Well, if she thinks her behaviour is going to get her what she wants, she will just have to think again. All this silly starving – what good does she think it will do her?'

'I don't think she expects it to do any good, ma'am,' Rebecca said, taking the silks over to the window for a better light. 'I don't think she *can* eat, now. It's as if she was really ill.'

'Really ill! And what might you know about it, miss? The idea – a housemaid telling me she thinks she knows better than I do, over my own daughter.' Isabella's face flushed unbecomingly. She had grown fat lately, as Isabel had grown thin, and her puffy cheeks were blotched with ugly colour. '*What* did you say Polly's done to herself?'

'She's hurt her ankle, ma'am, falling down the stairs. Mrs Hudd say it'll be a week before she can walk again.'

'Stupid girl,' Isabella said dismissively. 'And I suppose that means the whole house will be disrupted, just because of one careless housemaid. Haven't you finished sorting those silks yet? It's a simple enough job, surely.'

Rebecca parted a length of blue from a strand of red and looked down at them. They were the colours her father had woven into his carpets. Sitting at his loom in the cold, bare hovel he had called home, while first Bessie and then Rebecca stood beside him, working the sword and the wire. Working long hours, all through the day and sometimes into the night, the loom clattering ceaselessly, just so that he could earn enough money to keep himself and his family alive. So that people like Isabella Pagnel could sit in expensively furnished rooms, with their feet on that same carpet, complaining over a few tangled strands of silk.

She thought of the discontented, spiteful face of the woman who employed her. She thought of the rest of the servants, her 'family', who had stood by her in trouble and were risking their own jobs by pretending that they knew nothing of her condition. She thought of Mrs Hudd and Mrs Atkins, neither of them young, being turned out to live on what savings they had, and then to tramp the streets or go into the workhouse.

No. She couldn't let that happen. These people had been kind to her. They'd helped her through difficult times. Certainly, they had also been sharp and snappy with her, certainly Mrs Hudd had been strict and exacting in her demands, certainly Mrs Atkins had more than once lost her temper in the flurry of preparing an elaborate meal – she had once boxed

Rebecca's ears so hard that her head had sung for the rest of the day – and certainly Susan had been bad-tempered and sometimes unfair, especially early in the mornings.

But there had been good times, too, times when they'd been merry together. Christmases when they'd been permitted to have their own parties, with home-made wine that Mrs Atkins had kept for several years in the pantry, and dancing and games. And evenings when everything had gone well and they'd finished their work and sat together by the kitchen range, with Oddjob telling stories and Mrs Atkins passing round some sweetmeats made that afternoon.

She could not repay them by dragging them all into her own trouble. Neither could she wait any longer for Francis to return. And – she faced it at last with a sinking recognition that it might well be the truth – even if he were to walk in through the door at this very moment, she had no guarantee that he would help her. He might by now have forgotten all about her. He might even have found some other girl, someone from his own class, better suited to be his wife.

That might even be why he was staying away so long.

I'm on my own, Rebecca thought. And out of the cold loneliness of her despair, came the beginnings of a new strength. On her own . . . but although the words had a bleakness, there was also a kind of strength about them. On your own, you could make your own way. On your own, you stood or fell by your own decisions.

She still had herself. She still had strength of will, determination. She was alive; she would stay alive. She would survive.

And the child would survive with her. It was hers; it was all she had.

The silks were now laid out neatly side by side, their

colours glowing like jewels. Rebecca carried them back to the small table where the cloth that Isabella was embroidering lay in a tumbled heap.

'Is there anything else I can do for you, ma'am?'

Isabella looked at her fretfully. 'Do? I can't think what *you* could do for me, no. I'm used to Polly now . . . No, you may go, no doubt there's plenty of work for you in the kitchen. Tell Polly she must get well soon – I can't manage without someone who knows me.' She sounded like an invalid, Rebecca thought as she bobbed her curtsy and turned to go from the room. Well, Polly was welcome to her. Rebecca would rather clean out fireplaces any day.

Nevertheless, while Polly was unable to walk it was clear that many of her tasks would fall to Rebecca. And on that first afternoon, when she went back to the kitchen, the others were all waiting anxiously to hear what she had to say.

'No, she didn't notice,' she told them. 'At least, I don't think she did, and she never said anything.' She looked at Mrs Atkins. 'But she's going to see it soon. And I don't want to get anyone into trouble on my account. I think someone'd better tell her. And if you want the truth, I'd like to get it over with.'

Mrs Atkins looked at Susan. 'Well, it's not my place—'

'Nor mine,' Susan said in alarm. 'We'd better tell Mrs Hudd.'

Nobody suggested that Rebecca should tell her mistress herself. That would raise the immediate question as to why the senior servants had not known. Even now, there would be demands regarding the discipline below stairs, the possibilities that existed for housemaids to lose their virtue. Nobody would escape the ensuing retribution.

'Well, I suppose it must be done,' Mrs Hudd agreed when they talked it over later. 'With Rebecca going in to the mistress every day, she's bound to notice. Better I tell her before she does. And you never know, she might take a charitable view.' But she spoke without hope, and everyone knew it. There was little charity – apart from the 'good works' she did in public – about Isabella Pagnel.

'Expecting a *child*?'

The way Isabella repeated the phrase, it might have been less shocking if Rebecca had been expecting an elephant. She dropped her embroidery and stared at the two figures standing before her; Mrs Hudd, stiff and upright in her black dress, Rebecca subdued in cap and apron. Rebecca kept her eyes down. To meet her mistress's eyes now would almost certainly be deemed brazen insolence, and be of no help at all.

'Did I hear you aright?' Isabella asked after a moment. 'Do you really mean to say that this – this young woman – is expecting a *child*? In *my house*?'

'I'm afraid so, madam,' Mrs Hudd spoke sorrowfully. 'And very surprised I was to find out – Rebecca always having been such a modest and well-behaved girl. I can't believe it's her fault, madam – and if you could find it in you to give her another chance—'

'Another *chance*? Another chance to do what? Bring further shame on the house? This reflects on me, you know, as well as you, Mrs Hudd.' Isabella's eyes narrowed. 'And you might tell me just how such a thing could have happened. Do you not supervise the maids?'

Mrs Hudd drew herself up and Rebecca quickly intervened. After all, she could lose nothing by defending the housekeeper, whereas Mrs Hudd might well lose her situation if Isabella took it into her head to be spiteful.

'Please, ma'am, Mrs Hudd does see that we don't misbehave. It wasn't her fault. I – I deceived her about where I was going one Sunday. I should have been at church . . . I'm sorry, ma'am. It was only once – I never thought—'

'Be quiet!' Isabella turned a look of disgust on her. 'I'd rather not hear the squalid details, if you don't mind. It's bad enough having a maid in my house carrying on in this way, without having to hear her *talk* about it. Well,' she turned her attention back to the housekeeper, 'you'd better look out for another maid at once. This *would* happen, just when Polly's unable to work properly. And it's a pity you couldn't follow her example, miss,' she added to Rebecca. 'Now, Polly's a sensible girl, who takes a proper pride in her self and allows no liberties. You won't find *her* coming before me to confess to being in this condition.'

Not as long as the wind blows the right way, Rebecca thought. But before any more could be said, the door was open and Jeremiah burst into the room like a tidal wave. He saw the three women and stopped in surprise.

'Hullo! What's going on here? You all look very solemn.'

Isabella sighed.

'Well, I suppose you may as well know now, Jeremiah. You'd have to know anyway. It's this – this young woman here.' Isabella indicated Rebecca with a gesture of distaste. 'Mrs Hudd's just brought her to me. It seems that she's in a – a certain condition.' She drew in her lips, folding them around her teeth, and looked down her nose.

'A certain—' Jeremiah looked from his wife to

430

Rebecca, then at Mrs Hudd who met his eyes without expression. 'You mean she's—'

'Yes, she is,' Isabella said before he could finish. 'The foolish, irresponsible girl. Well, she's brought it all on herself and I've told her so. She'll have to go, of course, and at once.'

'My dear, are you sure?' Jeremiah looked at Rebecca and she lifted her head and returned his look, reminded suddenly of Francis; he had just that direct, compassionate way of looking straight into a person's eyes . . . She was stabbed by a sudden fierce longing for Francis. Why wasn't he here? He'd told her he wanted to marry her – had he meant it? At that moment, looking into the concerned eyes of Jeremiah, she felt certain that he had. But if she left this house now, would he look for her?

'Of course she must go,' Isabella said sharply. 'I can't condone immorality amongst my maids. I'm surprised that you should even suggest it.'

'But where will she go? *Have* you anywhere to go, Rebecca?' he asked. 'Parents – a home—?'

'Her parents are dead,' Isabella said before Rebecca could answer. 'Don't you recall the fuss when her father died and she brought the mother here to die in my kitchen? I was most forbearing then, I listened to Francis's pleas and allowed him to arrange the funeral, I gave the girl time off from work, said nothing when the whole household was disrupted over the unfortunate affair – and not only that,' she went on, her face reddening as her indignation grew, 'let's not forget the circumstances in which she first came here. Yes, Jeremiah, you may have forgotten, but I haven't. It was her brother and sister who murdered that weaver – the best in Kidderminster, Vivian said – and took flight and were never seen again. I had doubts at

431

the time, but Mrs Hudd persuaded me – said the mother had worked here as a girl and was a good, honest soul.' Her cold, protuberant blue eyes glared at the housekeeper. 'I should have followed my instincts then and refused to take the girl in. I should have known she'd be nothing but trouble.'

'My dear, is that fair?' Jeremiah protested. 'Rebecca's been with us for – what, five years, six—'

'Six. But that's—'

'And she's never given any trouble before, has she? If she has, I've heard nothing of it.' His tone implied that if she had, he would certainly have heard about it. 'Even this may not be her fault. Young girls are forced, sometimes, you know – or even if not forced, taken advantage of—'

'I've already said I don't want to hear about it!' Isabella was almost beside herself now. 'And I'll be grateful, Jeremiah, if you'd kindly stay out of this matter. *I* deal with the servants, the way I think fit. And this is a matter I simply will not condone. The girls know the rules – no followers. No, Rebecca must go. I want her out of this house by tomorrow morning at the latest.' She looked at Mrs Hudd again. 'And I'll wish to have more words with you on this subject, Mrs Hudd. I'm not at all satisfied with your surveillance of the staff. This would never have happened if you had been properly vigilant.'

Mrs Hudd opened her mouth to reply, but before she could speak the door opened yet again and Susan came in, looking flustered. She glanced at Rebecca and the housekeeper and pushed past them to address her master and mistress.

'Please, madam, sir – it's Miss Isabel. I think you ought to come – she seems real poorly. Sort of fainting and raving both at once, and me and Tilly don't know what to do for the best. And she keeps being sick, and there's nothing in her poor stomach to bring up – it's awful to watch . . .' She began to cry and pulled her apron up over her face.

Isabella stood up at once, her face pale. Jeremiah came forward quickly and took her arm.

'We'll go to her at once. Mrs Hudd, if you'd come with us . . . ? And Susan, we may need your help, too. And Rebecca?' He glanced at his wife, who hesitated.

'Rebecca has been dismissed. But there's no reason why she shouldn't still make herself useful. Goodness knows it's going to be difficult enough, without Polly.'

She turned and hurried out of the room, followed by Jeremiah and the servants. Rebecca, somewhat hesitantly, brought up the rear. Going up the stairs to Isabel's room, Jeremiah paused and looked down at her. Rebecca returned his look doubtfully.

'Don't worry too much, my dear,' he said quietly. 'I'll do my best to help. You've been a good servant and I don't want to see you turned away with nothing.'

He went on ahead of her, leaving Rebecca to wonder just how much he knew or suspected. He must have some idea about herself and Francis, surely – or why would he care what happened to her?

For the first time, she began to feel a tremor of hope.

Isabel was lying in bed when they came into her room. Her body was so thin it made barely a ripple in the bedclothes, her face so pale it was almost lost in the white sheets. Her eyelids flickered when her mother bent over the bed, but there was no other sign of recognition. If she had been raving, as Susan had said, she was now exhausted and lay completely still.

433

'I'll send for Dr Cully,' Jeremiah said at once. 'Susan – send the bootboy, he's a good runner. Tell the doctor he must come *at once*. And then make some tea and bring it up, your mistress will need it.'

'Tea?' Isabella said in a high voice as Susan hurried from the room. 'Tea? How can you talk of tea at a time like this? Can't you see – can't you see she's dying? My baby – *dying*. And all you can talk of is *tea* – oh, how can you be so inhuman?' She turned on her husband, her eyes wild, her mouth distorted, and raised her fists to pummel his chest. 'You don't care – you don't care – nobody cares but me. It's *our daughter* lying there, and you don't care . . .'

'Isabella!' Jeremiah spoke sharply. He caught his wife's wrists and held them so that she could not beat him. 'My dear, control yourself. Of course I care. But hysterics aren't going to help Isabel, or anyone else. We must keep calm. The doctor will be here soon—'

'And what will he do? What has he managed to do so far? We called him in right at the start and he's done nothing. He's a fool.'

'Not a fool, no.' Jeremiah looked gravely at the bed. 'Isabel has declined steadily ever since her disappointment over Francis. It may be that he is the only person who could have prevented this.'

'Are you saying we should have allowed her to marry him?' Isabella had quietened a little now, but her voice was hard, as if even Isabel's pitiful condition would not change her mind.

'No,' Jeremiah said sadly, his eyes on the still, white figure in the bed. 'No, we could never have allowed that.'

He released Isabella's hands and went to the bed. Rebecca, bending over to smooth the pale brow, moved aside a little, but he motioned her to stay were she was.

'You've waited on my daughter, haven't you?' he murmured, and Rebecca nodded. 'Stay with her now, then. It may comfort her to know you're here.' He drew a chair forward and pressed Rebecca's shoulders gently so that she sat down in it. 'Just stay with her. It may be all we can do.'

Rebecca's eyes filled with tears. She sat close to the bed, holding Isabel's thin hand softly in hers, feeling the bones, thin and brittle as a bird's, and sadness pierced her heart. It was so like that winter's day when she had sat beside her father's deathbed; the same encroaching greyness, the same aching sense of inevitable loss. And again, as she had sat in the kitchen downstairs, trying to spoon a few morsels of soup between her mother's blue lips and knowing it was useless. The same fate, the same road for them all.

There were óther things to remind her of those sad moments. Her father had died in abject poverty, his body wasted as much by starvation as by the disease that had claimed him. And Fanny, too, had been worn to a shadow, having given up what food they had to try to keep life in her husband, taking only enough to keep her by his side until she was no longer needed.

Like Isabel, their bodies had been little more than skin and bone. But there the similarities ended. For Isabel had never been forced to go hungry. For her, there had been food in plenty, every delicacy she could desire. Her starvation had stemmed, not from necessity but from some other, more mysterious reason.

From love?

Jeremiah had placed another chair on the other side of the bed and he pressed Isabella into it. Rebecca watched as Isabel's mother took the other thin hand and held it in her own, caressing and weeping over it. She remembered Isabella's attitude towards her

435

daughter's illness when it first began, and as it had progressed. She had been impatient, angry, indifferent by turns. Never, until now, had she appeared to take the situation seriously or realise what could actually happen.

'Oh, my baby, my baby . . .'

Isabel made no sign that she heard or felt their presence. She lay quite still, already little more than a wraith. Her eyelids were a pale, icy blue, almost transparent, and the rounded shape of her eyeballs showed clearly through their thinness. Her eyes, Rebecca remembered, had been of little use to her lately; she had seemed to be retreating into a world of darkness, holding out her skeletal hands and saying over and over again that everything had gone into a fog, that she couldn't see properly. There had been pain, too, pain in her back and a breathlessness as if her lungs would not properly function. It was as if her body were breaking down.

The door opened and Susan came in and whispered that the doctor was here.

'Show him in at once,' Jeremiah said from the foot of the bed, and Isabella leapt up and ran to the door.

'Doctor Cully – oh, doctor, thank goodness, you've come. She's dying, my baby's dying – you've got to do something. You've got to stop it. You can't let this happen, you can't, I won't let you . . .' Her hands were fists again, raised as if to pummel him as she had pummelled her husband, but Jeremiah stepped forward quickly and caught her arms in his big hands.

'Isabella, calm yourself. This behaviour does no good. It can't help Isabel, and it won't help you. Now, be quiet.'

But Isabella was past reason. The sight of the doctor

seemed to have released a dam of pent-up hysteria; it flooded out of her in a stream of tears, incoherent pleas and accusations, wild cries and screams that filled the air until at last Jeremiah dragged her struggling from the room, indicating to Susan to follow. Mrs Hudd took the chair by Isabel's bedside and folded the thin hand in hers. She did not look at Rebecca.

The doctor closed the door so that Isabella's voice could be heard only faintly as Jeremiah half carried her to her room. He came across to the bed and looked gravely down at the still figure.

'I was afraid it was coming to this. The last stages of the decline are very rapid, I fear.'

'There really is nothing to be done, then?' Mrs Hudd asked quietly.

The doctor shook his head. 'We can only wait now. Is there dropsy?' He lifted the covers and Rebecca saw with a shock that Isabel's skeletal legs had swollen to a grotesque caricature of plumpness. 'I thought so. It will not be long now.' He paused. 'It's hot. Draw back the covers and let her body cool a little. She may as well be as comfortable as possible for the last few hours.'

Rebecca's eyes filled with tears and she looked across the bed to see that the housekeeper was weeping softly. Between them, Isabel lay as if already dead; but when they drew the bedclothes from her body, there was a very slight rise and fall of her withered breast and a visible beating of her heart under the thin covering of her nightgown, to betray the fact that there was still a kind of life there.

But not real life, Rebecca thought sadly. And if the doctor were right – and who could doubt that he was, that Isabel was doomed – it would be better if death came quickly. A soft brush of its dark hand across that still, white face; a kiss from its cold lips; and all would be over.

But death, she already knew, took its own time. And it was many hours before Isabel died; hours during which Rebecca sat quite still by the bed, refusing to let go of the hand she held. Hours when other people came and went – Jeremiah, Susan, Mrs Hudd and, for a few tearful moments, Isabella who was able only to whisper a stricken goodbye before being led again from the room.

It was towards midnight, with the nightingale singing outside the window, when Rebecca saw the flutter of Isabel's heart still at last. The flattened chest rose and fell no more. And through her own weary sadness, she almost believed for a moment that something was leaving the room; a soft brushing sensation, as if Isabel's spirit had flown from the window to join the singing nightingale.

There was much to do before the funeral. Relatives must be notified, arrangements made, rooms prepared and food cooked. Mrs Atkins ordered several large hams and these took their turn in the big oven. Polly, in her chair at the table, was kept busy preparing vegetables and salads, mixing and beating mixtures for cakes and puddings.

'It in't just the funeral itself,' the cook said, pausing in her labours. 'It's all those people coming up from Dorset to stop. Hand me that pan, Becky, and fetch a dozen eggs.' She looked at the array of dishes. 'Seems queer, don't it, us making all this food for poor Miss Isabel, when she starved herself to death.'

Mrs Hudd, who had come into the kitchen to relay Isabella's latest orders (which changed, it seemed, more often than the weather as she slowly recovered from her prostration of grief), sighed and nodded. Her eye fell on Rebecca, returning from the larder.

'Have you made any arrangements, Rebecca? The mistress is bound to remember she dismissed you.'

Rebecca set down the pan Mrs Atkins had asked for, and put the eggs in a bowl.

'I suppose I'll try to get to London and find Bessie and Tom. He gave me an address in the letter he wrote, but I don't know if they'd still be there . . .' She felt a flicker of anxiety. Tom had been curiously evasive in his letter, as if reluctant to say much about the life he and Bessie were leading in London. She could imagine herself arriving there, at the address he had given, to find that they had moved on, no one knew where. The thought of being alone in London, with her baby's birth drawing nearer, was frightening.

If only she could contact Francis. But only his uncle and aunt would know where he was likely to be found. And it was impossible to ask them.

'Well, you'd better be thinking about it.' The housekeeper's voice was kind but brisk. 'As soon as the mistress remembers, she'll have you out, make no mistake. And she's got a spiteful turn of mind, you know that. Hurt her, and she's like to kick out at whoever's nearest. And she's carrying on now as if poor Miss Isabel's death is everyone's fault but hers.'

It was rare for Mrs Hudd to be so open about her employers, and Rebecca knew that what she said was true. Isabella Pagnel might make more of her sufferings than anyone else, but she never liked to suffer alone. If by hurting someone else she could lessen her own pain, she would have no scruples in doing so.

'Now, then.' Mrs Hudd was frowning at a list she held in her hand. 'Have you got the rooms ready,

Susan? The blue room for the mistress's uncle from Dorset, the pink one for the master's cousins . . . Oh, and Mr Francis's room, of course—'

'Franc – Mr Francis?' Rebecca broke in before she could stop herself. 'Is – is he coming home?'

Mrs Hudd and Susan both turned to stare at her.

'Well, of course he is. He was poor Miss Isabel's cousin, after all.' And the cause of all this trouble, Mrs Hudd could have added, but it was implicit only in her expression. 'Did you think he'd stay away, and cause tongues to wag even more?'

'No – no, of course not,' Rebecca murmured, and escaped from their curious glances to fetch Mrs Atkins some more pans. In the larder, out of sight of the others, she stopped and leaned her hot forehead against the wall.

Francis coming home! Why had it never occurred to her? In the upset and turmoil of Isabel's death, the possibility had never entered her head – yet now, she could not understand how it had ever escaped her.

He might be on his way, even now. He might come through the door at any moment. He would see her – and in the first moment, she would know whether or not the love that had flowered between them still lived. She would know the truth.

Her heart thumped. Francis coming home . . . coming home . . .

'Hev you gone to sleep in there, Becky?' Mrs Atkins called. 'I want those pans today, not halfway through next week. There's work to do out here, in case you hadn't noticed.'

Rebecca picked up several pans at random and scuttled back to the kitchen.

'I'm sorry, Mrs Atkins. I wasn't sure which ones you wanted.'

The cook stared at her in exasperation.

'Well, not those for a start. I'm making cakes, not jellies. And I don't want a fish-kettle, either. Really, Becky, if you don't perk up your ideas a bit, you'll be looking for another place—' she remembered suddenly that Rebecca would indeed soon be looking for 'another place' and stopped, her face growing redder than ever. 'Well, all right, girl,' she said in a grumbling but kindlier tone, 'you go back and get the cake tins for me, and don't worry. We all know you've got more on your mind than a funeral. But do try to help while you're here, there's a good girl.'

'Yes, Mrs Atkins,' Rebecca said, going back to the larder. But although this time she brought out the right pans, and although she made no further mistakes that afternoon, her mind was never on her work. She could think of only one thing. That Francis was coming home.

Isabella Pagnel caught sight of Rebecca just as the family was setting off for the funeral.

The servants had been in the kitchen ready to go upstairs and pay their respects before leaving for the church. Rebecca had lingered, meaning to stay out of sight although she would have liked to go to church with the others; she had been fond of Miss Isabel, after all, and had been with her when she died. But at the last moment Isabella had taken it into her head to come down to the kitchen to issue a few last-minute orders, and there had been no time for Rebecca to conceal herself.

Isabella stopped dead.

'What's that girl doing here?'

Her voice was trembling. Rebecca glanced from side to side, but escape was out of the question now.

441

She saw Jeremiah step forward quickly and take his wife's arm.

'What girl, my dear?'

'That one.' She pointed a shaking hand. 'That one, ready to bring disgrace on the house. I dismissed her. What is she doing, still here?'

Jeremiah shook his head.

'Don't worry about it now, my dear. Probably Mrs Hudd wasn't sure of your instructions. It was on the day poor Isabel was taken so ill, if you remember, and—'

'I know perfectly well when it was,' Isabella snapped. 'And I know that my instructions were quite clear.' She turned on the housekeeper. 'Mrs Hudd, I hope you have some explanation for flouting my orders in this way. I shall speak to you later. Meanwhile, that girl must go.'

'My dear, not now—'

'Yes, *now*. I won't have her in the house a moment longer,' Isabella was shaking with passion. 'I want to see her out of the house before we leave. I don't want to go to my daughter's funeral knowing that this – this *harlot* is still here.'

'Isabella, calm yourself—'

'*No!*' she screamed, turning on him. 'No, I will *not* calm myself – not until *that girl has gone.*'

There was a moment's silence. Rebecca looked at Jeremiah Pagnel. He looked back at her – sorrowfully, she could have sworn – and then sighed.

'Very well, my dear. The girl will go at once. Go upstairs and rest for a few minutes, and I'll see that she's gone before we have to leave for the church.' He glanced at Susan. 'Take your mistress up to her boudoir and give her something to steady her nerves. She's very upset today, and who can blame her?'

Susan led Isabella out of the kitchen. The other servants stood silently by as Jeremiah turned to Rebecca.

'You heard what my wife said, Rebecca. I'm afraid you will have to leave.'

'Yes, sir. My bags are packed. I only stayed on because there was so much work to do.'

He nodded. 'What are your plans?'

'I was going to go to London, sir, to my brother and sister.' I was hoping not to have to go anywhere, she thought. I was hoping Francis would be here by now. But he had been delayed on the road and no one knew when he might arrive.

Jeremiah nodded again, then beckoned to the bootboy. 'Go and get the carter to come here at once. Tell him he'll be paid well. I want him to take Rebecca to catch the London coach – I'll pay your fare,' he added to Rebecca. 'You'll need all the money you have when you get there.' He felt in his pocket and produced a handful of coins. 'Take this. It should be enough to cover your fare and board and lodgings when you arrive, if you should need them. And take care.'

'Yes, sir,' Rebecca murmured, staring at the money in her hand. Sovereigns . . . Together with her own meagre savings and a few coins the other servants had collected to give her, they would certainly help her through the first, most difficult days. And then? She dared not look ahead.

'Thank you, sir,' she said, and looked up at him. And saw again that strange resemblance to Francis. That look in his eyes; that curve to his mouth.

She turned quickly and went up the back stairs to her attic room. Her bags were there, packed; she picked them up, light as they were, and carried them down the stairs. The other servants were grouped there together, talking in low voices. Jeremiah had gone.

Rebecca looked at them, her eyes filled with tears. She went round and kissed each one. They murmured to her, words that meant little but had to be said. They hoped she would find Bessie and Tom; they hoped she would find a comfortable place; they hoped everything would be all right about the baby. They hoped that one day they'd see her again.

Rebecca went to the door and climbed up into the cart. Her throat ached. She sat on her bags and looked down at their faces, and then the carter whipped up his horse and the cart lurched forwards.

They turned the corner. And Rebecca set out on her new life, with no knowledge of what awaited her, and little hope. She would never see Francis again now.

She did not even see the small hired carriage that came bowling down the street, its horse trotting as fast as its driver could make it. She did not see the pale, fair face that stared out of the window. She caught the London coach with only minutes to spare, unaware that she had actually passed Francis on the road; unaware that he was at that moment standing at his cousin's graveside, grieving over the waste of a young, vibrant life, while part of him waited impatiently for all to be over so that he could find Rebecca again.

Chapter Nineteen

'Dismissed? Rebecca has been *dismissed*?'

Francis half rose from his chair, a small cake about to touch his lips. He set it back on his plate and stared at his aunt, who looked back at him in some astonishment.

'Yes, dismissed,' Isabella said sharply. 'Why should that be of such surprise to you, Francis? Indeed, why should it concern you at all? I presume I am allowed to arrange affairs in my own house, without consulting you.'

'Of course, Aunt.' He felt his heart kick, his mouth grow dry as he sought for words. 'But – I thought Rebecca suited you. She'd been here for several years, after all. Why—'

'Really, Francis. Don't you think you're being somewhat ill-mannered, interrogating me in this way in my own drawing room? I've told you, Rebecca has gone and the new maid, Elsie, seems to be shaping quite well. That's really all you need to know – more, in fact. The servants are no concern of yours.'

Francis stared back at her. His skin chilled as if the blood had left it to drive his thumping heart. He had been waiting ever since the funeral to find out where Rebecca was. Not seeing her at the service, he had assumed she had remained behind to see that all was ready for the family's return. There had been too many people around then for him to look for her, and for the next two days he had been swept up in a turmoil of family meetings, greetings and partings. His eyes had searched for Rebecca constantly, but she had made no appearance; other maids and footmen had waited on the family and guests. Only when he crept down to the library early in the morning and found a strange maid doing the polishing and dusting that had been Rebecca's tasks, had he begun seriously to worry.

And now, making what he had hoped his aunt would accept as no more than a casual enquiry, he had been given – with equal casualness – this news. That Rebecca had been dismissed. That she had left Pagnel House.

Bewilderment warred with guilt that he had not sought her earlier. But he had assumed she must be there. She had always been there . . .

And he knew an icy fear that he had lost her. Lost Rebecca . . .

'But where did she go? She has no family in Kidderminster. Has she found a new position somewhere? I still can't understand why—'

'And *I* cannot understand your interest in the matter,' Isabella said curtly. 'I told you, Francis, it's nothing to do with you. Rebecca's dismissal was over a matter I prefer not to discuss – it's not the subject for a drawing room. As for whether she has found a new situation, I should very much doubt that. She went from here without a character, and as soon as any employer recognised her condition—' She stopped abruptly and a red stain spread over her face and neck. 'Please let us speak no more of it,' she said and reached for her tea.

Francis stared at her. What did his aunt mean? Rebecca's *condition*? Surely . . . The suspicion crept into his mind and settled there like a dark, crawling insect. Surely she didn't mean—

The door opened and Jeremiah came in, his sombre face lightening a little at the sight of the tea. He glanced quickly from his wife to Francis and his eyes narrowed a little.

'Is something wrong?'

Isabella spoke at once.

'Nothing at all, Jeremiah, except that Francis seems to think fit to question my arrangements regarding the servants. His journeys away from Kidderminster seem to have set some strange ideas in his head. Perhaps you'd like to remind him how we do things here. Or perhaps he would prefer to return to London, or the North, if they suit him so much better.'

She had never liked him, Francis thought, flinching a little under her bitter sarcasm. But now she seemed positively to hate him. He knew that she blamed him entirely for Isabel's death. Perhaps she was right – it would be better to return to London. But not without Rebecca.

'I was simply asking what had become of the maid, Rebecca, who used to wait on us,' he said. 'I didn't mean to cause offence. But my aunt tells me she's been dismissed.'

He saw Jeremiah give his wife a quick glance, and his fear grew.

'That's right,' Jeremiah said after a moment. 'She was dismissed. Only a few days ago, wasn't it, my dear? I think she actually left on the day of poor Isabel's funeral.'

At the mention of her daughter's funeral, Isabella gave a cry and covered her face with her handkerchief. Jeremiah immediately moved to lay his arm across her shoulders.

The words hummed through Francis's brain,

repeating themselves over and over again. On the day of the funeral? On the day of Isabel's funeral? It could have been only just before he arrived. He might even have passed her on the road.

'But *why*?' he asked, a note of desperation in his voice. 'And where did she go? Fa – Uncle, I must know.'

Jeremiah's eyebrows rose. Isabella looked up from her handkerchief and stared at him.

'Must know? *Must?*'

'Please,' Francis said, controlling his voice with some difficulty, 'tell me why Rebecca was dismissed and where she has gone.'

'Very well,' Isabella said in a hard, high voice. 'Since you insist on knowing, I'll tell you. The girl was dismissed for immoral conduct. She had evidently been . . . consorting . . . with some man.' She spoke disdainfully, as if a man were some lower species of life. 'Her condition became apparent and I had no choice but to dismiss her. As for where she went, I do not know, neither do I wish to. And now, may we please leave this distasteful subject and—'

Her condition . . . her *condition*. That could, surely, mean only one thing.

He searched for the right words. 'Rebecca was . . . expecting a child? Is that what you're trying to say?'

'Francis, *please*—'

'Francis—'

'No!' he said, his voice suddenly stronger, overriding his aunt's shrill protest and his father's deeper rumbling attempt to stop him. 'No, let's stop beating about the bush and find the truth. Is that it? Is that what happened?' Isabella had buried her face in her handkerchief again, and he looked at Jeremiah.

Slowly, the older man nodded; 'I'm afraid so,

Francis. And you know the rules your aunt applies to the servants. I was sorry to see her go, she was a good, well-mannered maid and pleasant in her behaviour, but—'

'She was more than that,' Francis said in a low tone. 'She was the girl I meant to marry. And if she was expecting a child – that child was mine.'

There was a sudden silence. Isabella lifted her face again. Jeremiah took his hand from her shoulder and straightened himself. Francis faced them both, his body quivering, his mind still trying to take in the truth. Rebecca pregnant. Rebecca expecting his child. And gone – gone – no one knew where.

But somebody must know where.

'Where did she go?' he asked again. 'I mean to know. I must know.'

Jeremiah began to speak, but Isabella lifted a hand and interrupted him.

'Francis, can I believe my ears? Are you telling me that you – *you* – seduced one of my housemaids? That you took advantage of your position here and—'

'It wasn't like that—'

'Then how was it? No – don't tell us. I'd rather not hear the details. I've never had to listen to such talk before in my own drawing room and I do not intend to begin now. It's too disgusting. To think that this has been going on under my own roof!' She lifted her handkerchief to her face again and turned to her husband, but he had stepped away from her. His eyes were on Francis and there was a curious expression in them.

'Rebecca is carrying your child?' he said quietly, and Francis nodded.

'It wasn't a seduction. I love her. I want to marry her. You must tell me where she's gone.'

'Must? *Must?*' Isabella cried again. 'Francis, please remember to whom you are speaking. And remember your own position, too. You live here, yes, but as an employee, not as a member of the family. You are *not* a member of this family – you never have been.' She turned to Jeremiah. 'I always knew it was a mistake, letting Geoffrey and Enid take in this – this foundling and treat him as their own. And you've condoned it – you, with your so-called kindness and benevolence. Well, now you can see what it's brought us all – shame and disgrace. One of my best maids seduced and ruined, and all because you would bring bad blood into the family.'

As she spoke, her face scarlet with anger and her eyes wild, the door opened and Vivian came in. He stopped in surprise at the sound of his mother's raised voice, then closed the door behind him and came forward.

'What's all this?' he asked, straddling the hearthrug and looking round at them with an air of amused interest. 'Shame and disgrace? Seductions? Bad blood? It all sounds fascinating.'

Isabella turned to him at once.

'Vivian! Oh, Vivian, thank goodness you're here. I've just been hearing the most dreadful things, things such as I never expected to hear in my own drawing room – I hardly know how to tell you—'

'Isabella, my dear, please—' Jeremiah began, but Vivian interrupted him.

'Dreadful things, Mother? What dreadful things? Do tell me.' His eyes were gleaming and he glanced at Francis with speculation. 'Surely Frank hasn't been besmirching the family honour? He wouldn't know how.'

Isabella gave a little cry, and Jeremiah stepped

forward, his face dark and angry. 'Vivian, this is not a joke. Your mother is genuinely upset. And I think we should leave the subject now and discuss it later. My dear, have some more tea, it will calm your nerves. Francis, ring the bell for more hot water.'

'I'll do it.' Vivian reached behind him for the bell-pull. 'But you can't leave it there, Father. Obviously some family crisis is taking place, and I want to know what it is. I heard the words "shame" and "disgrace" being bandied about as I came in. You can't expect me to leave it at that.'

Francis looked at him with pure dislike. After his father's rebuke, Vivian was making a poor attempt at repressing his curiosity; a prurient interest showed in his voice and his eyes glittered as he glanced from one to the other.

Isabella reached out her hand, and Vivian leaned down and took it in his.

'Tell me what's happened, Mother,' he said softly, and Francis saw her eyes fill with tears.

'It's that girl – the housemaid, Rebecca. I was forced to dismiss her, on the very day that poor dear Isabel was – was buried.' The tears were flowing down her cheeks and she spoke through sobs. 'She was – well, in a certain condition. It would have been apparent to everyone within a fortnight. I couldn't keep her here, could I?' She held his hand in both hers, gazing up at him in appeal. Vivian looked down at her and a small frown appeared on his forehead.

'Well, of course not, Mother. But why so upset? These things happen. And why is Frank so—' He broke off suddenly, glanced at Francis and whistled. A grin appeared on his face. 'You don't mean – *Frank* – well, I'll go to sea!' He began to laugh.

'Vivian!' his mother cried. 'It really is *not* amusing. You haven't heard the whole story yet. You cannot imagine—'

'Oh, I think I can,' Vivian said, his eyes gleaming. 'It's not so uncommon, after all. Plenty of young men do what Frank's done – tumbled a housemaid and left her with a souvenir—'

Jeremiah reacted quickly, his voice loud in the normally quiet room. 'Vivian, that's enough! I'll thank you to remember where you are—'

But he was interrupted by Isabella herself, her voice like ice as she looked first at Francis, then back at Vivian.

'Perhaps plenty of young men do behave in this fashion.' Her words sliced the air, cutting across Jeremiah's so that he fell silent. 'But not young men of my family – in my house.'

There was a short pause. Then Vivian said, his silky voice almost casual, 'But Francis isn't of our family, is he, Mamma? Not truly.'

'No,' Isabella said, and Francis could hear in her tone all the rejection, all the antipathy she had only ever dared to hint at before this day. 'No, he is not at all of our family.'

Francis was aware of Jeremiah's sudden movement. He broke in quickly, unable to remain silent any longer. The matter of his own birth was immaterial – it was Rebecca who mattered, Rebecca who was lost to him through his own carelessness, his own assumption that she would be always there, waiting for him.

'Please – none of that matters. The important thing is that I want to marry Rebecca – I *must* marry her. And nobody seems to know where she is. Nobody even cares.'

'*Marry* her?' Vivian stared at him. 'Oh, come, Frank, that's going too far. Give her a few sovereigns to take away with her, by all means, if you feel kindly towards the wench. But marriage – that's totally unnecessary.'

'It's totally necessary,' Francis retorted. 'Because this wasn't just a "tumble" as you so coarsely put it, Vivian. I love her – something you might not understand. And I want to protect her, and our child. I want to marry her. I *will* marry her.'

'Then if you do,' Isabella said, her voice now icily cold, 'you will leave this house.'

Francis bowed his head. Vivian lifted his eyebrows, looking at him as if he were some strange species of animal, then laughed again. He looked at Jeremiah.

'He's gone mad, Father. You'd better have him committed to an asylum. And Mother's quite right. He couldn't possibly bring the slut here.'

'He could,' Jeremiah said quietly, and stood up straight. They all stared at him. Isabella opened her mouth, but he lifted one hand, motioning to her to be quiet. He moved around the low tea table, facing them all.

'I shall do all I can to help Francis find this girl,' he said slowly. 'And if he wishes to bring her here, then he shall do so. Because the child she carries is my grandchild. Perhaps my grandson.' He looked at Vivian, and his eyes were hard. 'Perhaps the only grandson I shall ever have.'

Rebecca's journey was as harrowing as that endured by Bessie and Tom six years earlier. She had never before been on a coach and found the jolting almost unbearable. Cooped up inside with other passengers, she was stifled by the heat and felt sick and faint. She was thankful for the stops and reluctant to reboard the coach; only the thought of being with her brother and sister again persuaded her to continue.

But at last they found themselves clattering through the streets of London's outskirts and she roused herself to take an interest. This was the city everyone talked about, the centre of the country where everything important happened. The King lived here, the one who had stood Regent for so long for his father – Rebecca remembered her mother and other women in the bobbin-winding shop talking about the mad king. It seemed so long ago, that brief childhood. She wondered if she would see his palace, and craned her neck out of the window, but saw only mean, narrow streets littered with rubbish.

The laws of the country were made here, too. And all the fashions that Mrs Pagnel and her daughters pored over and tried to copy came from here. She looked out again, expecting to see important men in tall hats and stiff collars, with women dressed in glittering finery. But there were only slouching men in scruffy clothes, and women with wan, pale faces who clustered together in corners and hid bottles in their tattered shawls.

The streets grew more crowded. They were filled with vehicles of all kinds – phaetons, curricles, carts, coaches of all sizes – as well as men on horseback and a thrusting crowd of people on foot. Rebecca stared out, half afraid, seeing something hostile in the eyes that stared back at her. A man leered and whistled, a boy sniggered and made a rude gesture, a woman grimaced, as if Rebecca and her fellow-passengers were enemies. She drew back, her heart thumping a little, aware that she was shaking.

'Don't worry, love.' The fat woman beside her had

taken Rebecca under her wing and offered comfort through most of the journey, as well as her own life history and that of her married daughter, whom she was visiting in London. 'They're just envious, 'cause they think we're rich to be travelling by coach. It don't mean nothing.' She gave Rebecca a friendly glance. 'You say you're going to your sister? She'll be expecting you?'

'No – not really.' Rebecca felt her face colour. 'I didn't have time to let her know I was coming – it was all rather hurried—' She saw the curiosity in the bright eyes; she had managed to evade most of the woman's questions until now, with a sickness that needed no feigning. 'Bess doesn't read anyway,' she added truthfully enough, 'so it wasn't really much use writing.'

'Ah, well, I hope you find her all right. You've got an address?'

'Yes.' Rebecca looked out of the window again. 'Oh – look. What's that? Is it the King's palace?'

The woman leaned past her, and shook her head, laughing. 'That? Nothing like it, my dear. That's just some big house, nothing special hereabouts. You'll see plenty more like that.' She went on to describe to Rebecca the grandeur of some of the houses in London, the exclusiveness of the squares with their gardens, the spaciousness of some of the great streets in the heart of the city itself. And by the time the coach came to a stop and the passengers disembarked for the last time, she had forgotten Rebecca's business in her eagerness to meet her own family. She paused only long enough to give Rebecca a quick hug before going off to the embrace of a plump young woman who could have been herself, twenty years earlier. Rebecca was left standing beside the road, quite alone.

The other passengers dispersed. The coach disappeared into an inn yard. Rebecca picked up her bags and stood undecided, not sure which way to go. She looked about her at the hurrying people, but none of them gave her more than a passing glance. She felt suddenly cold, lonely and more than a little frightened.

Until now, she had not realised just how big London was. How could she possibly find the address Tom had given? Who would know? Who, out of all this uncaring throng, would spare the time for a stranger?

Slowly, she began to walk along the street.

Jeremiah and Francis faced each other in the library. Isabella had been taken upstairs by Susan, sobbing and still half hysterical. She had clung to Vivian, declaring that he was the only one left she could trust, and he had promised to go to her as soon as she was settled in bed. But although his voice had been solicitous and tender, there was still an imp of devilment in his eyes, and Francis knew that he was the only one of them to be enjoying the situation. And trust him, Francis thought bitterly: scandal had always been one of Vivian's pleasures, even when it threatened to touch his own family.

'Well,' Jeremiah said at last, 'this is a pretty state of affairs.'

'Yes. I'm sorry.'

'Sorry?' Jeremiah looked at him as if startled. 'I'm not asking for apologies. What have you done that I haven't done ahead of you – other than have the courage to face up to it. All the troubles in this house have stemmed from my misbehaviour, not yours. Or from my cowardice.' He shot Francis a brooding look. 'If I'd been honest to begin with, you'd have been acknowledged as my son from birth. Little as

Isabella would have liked that, it wouldn't have resulted in what happened to poor Isabel. Or perhaps to the unfortunate girl Rebecca. Nothing would have come about as it has.'

'But it's useless to look back,' Francis said gently. 'So many other things would have been different too. My aunt – she would have refused ever to allow me into the house. Isabel might not even have been born. Who knows what might have happened?'

Jeremiah sighed. 'You're right, of course. And none of it helps now. We have to decide how best to deal with what *has* happened, and I'm damned if I can see my way through the wood.'

'It seems simple enough to me,' Francis said. 'I want to marry Rebecca. I need to find out where she went. If I am never to return to this house, as my aunt has demanded, then I must stay away and make my own way—'

'No! I'll not have it.' Jeremiah took two steps to reach Francis and laid his big hands firmly on his son's shoulders. 'Francis, you know that even before I told you the truth, you were always my son. In my heart, I never really gave you up. I was compelled to acknowledge Vivian as my heir – but I always intended that you should have a special position in my business. Thanks to your talent as a designer, you've made your own place. And I won't see you lose it now.'

'And how will you live with my aunt if you insist that I stay here? She'll never forgive you as it is; if I am here, under her eye, she'll never let you forget the hurt you've done her. I have to go. You know it. And besides – I must find Rebecca.'

Jeremiah gazed into his face, then sighed and nodded. 'Very well, Francis. Go. If you feel you must.

But there will always be a place for you here. You must believe that.'

Francis shook his head slowly.

'Not while my aunt is alive, Father. I can never come back while she is here.'

'To think how he betrayed me,' Isabella wept. 'All these years, he's been deceiving me. First that slut of a governess – oh, I remember her well, a sly minx if ever I saw one – and since then, who knows how many women. And all of such low class, too. Governesses! Housemaids! I suppose they share his disgusting tastes.' She turned her face aside on the pillow and closed her eyes, tears trickling from beneath her lids.

Vivian took his mother's hand.

'Don't distress yourself so, Mamma.' His voice was soft and caressing, but there was a gleam in his eye. 'Many men have these aberrations. It means nothing.'

'Oh, I know that's what they all say!' Isabella tossed in her bed. 'But that does not make it any easier for a wronged wife to bear – especially when she's been deceived into entertaining her husband's by-blow in her own house. Can you imagine how that makes me feel, Vivian? Can you even begin to conceive of my feelings, knowing how Jeremiah must have been laughing at me behind my back, all these years?'

'Of course I understand, Mamma,' Vivian said soothingly. 'And I can see how very distressed you are by it all – as, indeed, you have every right to be.'

'He must go.' She caught at his hands, staring up at him with wild, feverish eyes. 'You do agree, don't you? That – that boy, that deceiver – he must go at once. Why, it was obvious that he knew all about it.

458

The two of them have been plotting behind our backs, Vivian – plotting against *you*. No doubt he intended to take your inheritance away from you – as if it were a *birthright*. And he no more than a – a—' She choked over the word, but Vivian supplied it, almost under his breath, almost savouring it as it lay on his tongue.

'A bastard. Forgive me, Mamma, but it *is* the only word . . . Well, we always knew he must be. And Uncle Geoffrey and Aunt Enid – they must have known of this, too—'

Isabella flung herself about in the bed. 'They must! And how many others, do you suppose? How many people have been conspiring behind our backs? Laughing, gossiping – oh, it's intolerable. I cannot bear it, I simply cannot bear it.'

Vivian laid his hand on her shoulder. 'Now, Mamma, don't upset yourself so. Nobody else knows of it, I'm sure. Don't you think I would have heard if there had been gossip? And nobody else need know, either. Father won't want it spread abroad any more than you do. And if Frank leaves Kidderminster – well, who will be surprised at that? He's been away for months, it can soon be put about that he preferred to set up on his own.'

'And how will he do that,' Isabella asked, 'with no money of his own? For I won't have Jeremiah giving him money.' She pulled herself up into a sitting position and looked directly into Vivian's eyes. 'The money for the business came from my own fortune – and though it may be my husband's in law, he knows who truly holds the purse strings in this house. And I will not have one penny going to that by-blow – not one penny.'

There was a short silence. Vivian looked at his

mother and saw the implacable determination in her eyes. He smiled slowly, picked up her hand and kissed it.

'Have no fear, Mamma,' he said softly. 'Father will understand you, I know. He won't go against your wishes.'

Rebecca stood at the corner of Drury Lane and gazed about her.

The bustle here was worse than any she had yet experienced. People scurried about as if their lives depended on the keeping of a thousand appointments. They hurried up and down the maze of narrow alleyways and courts, brushing past Rebecca as if they did not see her. The air was filled with their shouts and chatter, and from the fruit and vegetable stalls that filled whatever space was available came the calls of the stallholders.

Rebecca found herself shoved aside as a burly man thrust his way out of the doorway behind her. She half stumbled, regained her balance and looked around in some despair. Would anyone in this impatient throng ever stand still long enough for her to ask directions?

She saw a girl coming towards her – walking slowly, pausing every now and then to look up into the face of some passer-by and ask some question. Was she lost too? But she did not appear to be asking the way. Her question, whatever it was, seemed to bring the same brief answer from each person she asked – a shake of the head, little more. And she did not seem disconcerted by this, simply wandered on, her smile never fading, her manner still as friendly.

I'll ask her, Rebecca decided, and stepped in front of the girl as she came near.

Immediately, the girl stopped and stared at her.

Her smile disappeared; her eyes were hard and cold.

'Here, what d'yer think yer up to? This is my patch.'

Rebecca blinked. 'I'm sorry – I don't understand—'

'In a pig's ear,' the girl said coarsely. 'Look, you don't clear off I'll get my bully to come and see you off. And will he be gentle with you? Oh yes, I'm sure he will. Wouldn't hurt a fly, my bully wouldn't, I don't think. You'd better get out fast if you know what's good for you, see?'

'I don't know what you're talking about,' Rebecca said desperately. 'I've only just arrived here. I don't know London at all. I'm looking for my sister—'

'Then you'd better find her, quick,' the girl advised her. 'This ain't no place for gabies.' She looked at Rebecca curiously. 'Here, you talk funny. Where are you from?'

'From Kidderminster,' Rebecca said, but the girl's face was blank. 'I told you, I've come to find my sister. She lives around here somewhere. Near Covent Garden, I was told – that's right, isn't it? Is Covent Garden near here?' As yet, she had seen nothing that resembled a garden, nothing but streets and buildings. Covent Garden sounded pleasant, a haven of peace in all this bustle. Once she reached it and found Bess, everything would be all right.

'Covent Garden's near here, yes. But I don't know anyone there from – where did you say you come from?' The girl shook her head and began to look impatient again. 'Look, I dunno what this is all about, but if you got a sister, I can tell you, she don't live near here. I told you, this is my patch.'

'Then could you tell me where this place is?' Rebecca fumbled for the creased piece of paper that was Tom's last letter to her. 'Martlett Court. That's where she lives – do you know it?'

The girl looked at her curiously. 'Yes, that ain't far away. Is that where your sis lives? What's her patch, d'you know?'

Rebecca shook her head uncomprehendingly. 'What's a patch? I don't think Bess has got one. This letter doesn't say anything about it.'

The girl cackled. 'Nor would it, if that's a letter home. We don't boast about our trade round here. I take it she's same as the rest of us.'

'I don't know. She works in a big house. My brother's a handyman.'

'Oh yes, and the King comes down here for his breakfast every morning. Well, you want to find her, you go that way, see? Down the road to the corner, then turn right. That's Martlett Court. But don't expect no grand houses.' She cackled again, then gave Rebecca a push. 'Go on, then. I ain't got time to stand here a-jawing with you. I got work to do.'

Rebecca started to thank her, but the girl pushed her again and she picked up her bags and set off in the direction indicated. Her heart was beating quickly. Was she really about to see her brother and sister again, after all these years? Would she even recognise them?

The summer evening was fading as she trudged along the littered street, but there were still as many people about. She passed other girls like the one she had spoken to, girls who sauntered along as if they had all the time in the world, looking up into the faces of passers-by and speaking in wheedling voices. They looked at Rebecca with the same hostility and she averted her eyes and hurried past, wondering what threat she posed to them. From coffee-houses and taverns came the sounds of voices and laughter.

Straight down the road to the corner, then turn right . . . And here it was. Martlett Court.

Rebecca stood for a moment, looking up at the nameplate. A flutter of nervousness caught at her throat. Suppose Tom and Bess didn't want her? Suppose they couldn't help her?

Slowly, she walked down the narrow street, looking up at the buildings, fighting a feeling of disappointment. This wasn't the grand London square, with the big houses surrounding a tree-shaded garden, that she'd imagined. Martlett Court was little more than a mean, narrow alleyway, the buildings on either side so tall that it seemed impossible that the sun would ever shine here. And the dankness of the air seemed to confirm that it rarely did. Was she in the right place after all? Could Tom have given the wrong address? Or was there more than one street with this name?

She looked again at the letter. Number 23, Tom had written. Some of the houses had numbers on, some hadn't. She found 17, 19, then a door that had no number on it. That must be 21. And the next one – 23. She stopped and looked up at it.

The house looked back at her. Tall and narrow, its windows like blank eyes, it exuded the same hostile air as the girls who paraded up and down Drury Lane. Its walls were grimy, its windows dull. She saw a face staring from one of them and moved eagerly, ready to wave, but the face vanished. Nobody came to the door.

Rebecca hesitated. There was something unfriendly about that door. She felt reluctant to knock on it. Almost, she turned away.

But she had to find somewhere to spend the night. She had slept in the open last night, hidden in a doorway, terrified of being discovered and attacked. She could not face another night like that. She must find Bess and Tom. And this was the address on Tom's letter. They must be here. All she had to do was knock.

She raised her hand. But before she could grasp the knocker, the door swung open and she found herself looking into the creased face of an elderly woman.

'Oh,' Rebecca said, taken aback. 'I – I'm looking for Bess Himley. And Tom. They – they work here.'

'Himley? No one of that name here.' The old woman started to close the door, then stopped and peered closer at Rebecca. 'Bess and Tom, d'yer say?'

'That's right.' Her heart had sunk, now it began to lift again. 'Do you know them?'

'I knows a Bess and Tom Broome. Not Himley. You sure you ain't made a mistake?'

'No, it's Himley.' She stopped, thinking. They could have changed their names. Tom had never mentioned it, but then he'd never expected a reply to his letters. And Broome was a Kidderminster name.

'It could be Broome,' she said slowly, staring at the grime-ingrained wrinkles of the old face. 'Bess has got yellow hair and big blue eyes. And Tom's tall, with brown hair.'

The woman nodded. 'Could be them. Mind, I never had much to do with 'em meself. I keeps meself private, better that way. But Tom Broome's a decent enough lad. Too good for round here, I allus thought.'

'That sounds like my brother,' Rebecca said eagerly. 'Are they here now? Can I see them? Can you tell them I'm here – Rebecca, Becky, their sister?'

The old woman stared at her. Her pale eyes were watery, her lips loose. She shook her head, lifted a clawlike hand to her mouth, started to back away and close the door again.

'Please,' Rebecca begged, suddenly afraid that the crone was going to close the door in her face. 'Please, don't go. Just tell me if I can see Bessie and Tom. I'm their sister. And I've come such a long way.'

'You can't see 'em.' The voice was little more than a cracked whisper. 'You can't see Tom and Bessie Broome – not here, any road. They ain't here any more. They went – oh, three weeks, a month gone. After the gentleman come here arskin' for 'em. And that's all I got to say. I ain't looking for trouble.'

The door closed with startling suddenness. And Rebecca stared at it; her heart sinking heavily in her breast. The summer evening was suddenly cold.

'But I'm their sister,' she found herself whispering again. 'And I've come such a long, long way . . .'

Chapter Twenty

Francis was only a few days behind Rebecca when he set out for London. He had left Kidderminster as quickly as he could, though frustrated by the things that must be done before he could go. But with the knowledge that she had gone to London, together with the address he had in his pocket for Tom and Bessie, he was confident of finding her easily.

'You're set on marriage, then,' Enid had said to him when he had gone with Jeremiah to his old home, to tell his adoptive parents what had happened. He saw her face soften. 'You really love the girl?'

'I love her,' Francis said steadily. He coloured. 'It wasn't just a - a tumble. I didn't intend it to happen until after we were married. But—'

He saw understanding on the faces around him. His father, Jeremiah, whose own illicit love had brought him into existence, twenty-two years ago. The couple who had brought him up - his uncle and aunt, whom he still thought of as the parents they had always been to him - who knew all the truths of his life. He looked at Geoffrey's worn face and thanked God for his unworldliness, and he looked at Enid and felt a wave of gratitude for her compassion.

'I must go and find her,' he said simply. 'And we'll marry - there's nothing to stop us. And if I can never come back to Kidderminster—'

'You *will* come back,' Jeremiah broke in. 'I'll not see you go from here for ever, Francis.'

'You know what my aunt has said,' Francis

answered. 'She won't have me in the house, or in the business—'

Jeremiah came to his feet. He looked like an angry bull. 'She doesn't rule the roost. Am I not master in my own home? Can I not do as I wish?'

'And can she not make life intolerable for you if you do?' Francis retorted. 'Uncle – Father—' he looked helplessly from one man to the other—'how can I stay here and be a thorn in my aunt's side? None of this is her fault. She's just lost her daughter,' his eyes filled with tears at the thought of Isabel, 'and now had this thrust upon her. I can't make matters even worse – and neither can you. We owe her better than that.'

Jeremiah stared at him, then turned away and sank back into his chair. He looked suddenly weary, defeated. He sat silent for a moment, then spoke.

'You're right, of course. I can't subject Isabella to any more misery. God knows, she's selfish and shallow enough, but it's true that none of this is her doing. And she's kept her side of the bargain I made with her when we married. She's borne me two more children – it's no blame to her that they were both girls – and I've had the use of her fortune to build up my business.' He raised his eyes and there was pain in them as he looked at Francis. 'You'll have to go, my son. Go and find your housemaid and wed her, if you must. You're fortunate at least in that you *can* marry her. Your life, at least, need not be a desert.'

It was the most he had ever said about his marriage, and the other three were silent for a moment. Then Geoffrey turned to Francis and asked, 'Have you enough money for this journey? How will you live?'

Before Francis could answer, Enid got up and went to a bureau that stood against the wall. She opened it and took out an old leather purse.

468

'Here,' she said, holding it out to Francis. 'I've been saving it for you, ever since you first came here. I always thought you might need it some day. There should be enough to keep you for a few months, perhaps longer.'

Francis stared at it. He took it slowly, opened it and looked inside. Then he raised his head.

'I can't take this. You need it—'

'We've managed without it so far,' Enid said imperturbably, sitting down again. 'I told you, I saved it for you.'

'And I can give you an allowance, too,' Jeremiah said. He raised his hand to quieten Francis's protest. 'I know what Isabella said – but I mean to have my own way in this. The business is mine – it's for me to say what is done with the money it makes.' He clenched one big hand into a fist. 'In God's name, Francis, you cannot expect me to let my only son disappear without giving him any assistance at all? Why, if I had my way I'd be setting you up in a business of your own, yes, even if it meant you were to be in competition with me. If I had my way, things would be very, very different.'

'But that's just what I mean to do,' Francis said. 'I mean to start my own business. I have a weaver ready to begin whenever we can find premises and buy the loom and materials. I have designs ready, and a supplier of yarn.' He looked at his father with a trace of apology. 'I didn't mean this to be in competition with you – I had hoped to discuss it with you, to suggest that we might start it together. But now . . . it seems the right moment to start up on my own.'

'It is indeed,' Jeremiah said, staring at him. 'But where do you intend to start your business, Francis? And who is the weaver you hope to employ?'

'Why, Tom Himley, of course,' Francis said, as if there had never been any doubt in the matter. 'Tom Himley – Rebecca's brother.'

Rebecca walked back to Drury Lane and stood looking hopelessly up and down. It was dark now and the people had changed; the street was just as crowded but less bustling. People were going to theatres, to restaurants; they were finely dressed and talked in loud, high voices, taking little notice of the ragged boys and girls who slipped amongst them looking for pockets to pick or bags to snatch. Girls dressed in gaudy clothes, their faces painted and necklines low, strolled to and fro, looking into the faces of unaccompanied men. Now and then, a man would accept a girl's invitation and they would disappear down a side street, his hand already straying over the swaying rump.

Rebecca was in no doubt now about these girls. She had genuinely not realised at first what they were, had not understood their hostility towards her – a stranger on their 'patch'. Now she understood and felt sickened. Was this what her sister was doing? Was this why Tom had said so little about the 'jobs' they had? Was this why they had apparently been forced to move from their address?

She would never find them now, she thought miserably. They could be anywhere in this seething mass of people. There was no possibility of discovering their present address, and a chance meeting would be a coincidence she could not believe in.

What was she to do? She touched her stomach. The child was growing fast; she had felt the first fluttering movement only a day or two ago, and been filled with a strange exhilaration. Now the thought brought fear.

How was she to live, in this strange, uncaring city where every woman seemed to be a prostitute, where nobody knew her and she could never find the family she sought? How was she to give birth to a child, look after it, bring it up? Francis's child . . . The tears stood hot in her eyes, made burning tracks down her cheeks. It had all seemed so beautiful, so right, that day in the woods; and now it had come to this.

She felt in her pocket for the money she had left. Enough for a few nights' lodging, perhaps, and food to keep her alive. And then what? Starvation? Or must she go the same way as the girls who passed her, dressed in finery which would look merely tawdry in cold daylight? And what man would pay for her favours, as her body swelled and became more and more misshapen?

She came to a tavern and hesitated at the door. At least she might as well eat while she could. And perhaps they had rooms to let; she could sleep in a bed, even if it must be shared with others, and then try again tomorrow to look for Bessie and Tom. What else was there to do, after all – even if she knew at the start that the search was hopeless?

She went inside and sat down at a table. It was already occupied, by a middle-aged woman with a long nose that almost met her chin, and the drawn-in, purse-string lips that denoted a complete absence of teeth.

' 'Ullo, ducks,' the woman said as Rebecca sat down. 'On yer own, are yer? Bit down on yer luck?'

Rebecca looked at her. The crone's face was ugly, but there was a kindness in her eyes and a softness in her voice. It was the first hint of kindness that Rebecca had found since arriving in London. She felt an overwhelming need to pour out her troubles, to have someone else to help her solve them.

'I don't know what to do,' she said. 'I've only just arrived in London. I'm looking for my brother and sister, but they've moved and I can't find where they are.'

The old woman looked at her. Then a smile spread slowly over her pinched features.

'So you're all by yourself, are yer?' she said. 'And lost yer fam'ly, too. Well, if that ain't the saddest thing I ever did hear. But never mind, me duck.' She reached a skinny hand across the table and patted Rebecca's arm. 'You struck lucky, coming in here. Of all the folk in London, I reckon you've hit on the very one to help you the best. Now, you just get some grub inside yer, that'll make you feel better for a start. And then I'll take you round to my house and you can kip down comf'table for the night afore we starts out to find your sis. Live round here, do she?'

Rebecca lifted her hands. 'I don't know. They did. But now – I'm not sure.'

'Well, we'll find 'em, sure enough. No doubt about that. Old Sal knows everyone round here.' The hag grinned her toothless grin. 'You're lucky you fell in with me. You can trust me, eh, girl? Just trust me . . .'

Bess Himley closed the door after her departing client and leaned on it for a moment, looking around the room.

How many homes had she and Tom had since coming to London? She had lost count now. A series of damp, dreary and uncomfortable rooms, all in houses that threatened to tumble down around their ears for lack of care; some of a squalor she had never seen even in the poorest parts of Kidderminster, others no worse than the weaver's cottage in which she had been born. Try as she and Tom might, they had never been able to raise themselves above the level they had found when Bess first left Sal Preston's house. There had even been times when she had been tempted to return to the bawd.

But now, it seemed that they might at last see an improvement in their fortunes. The money that Francis Pagnel had given them before he left London had secured them these two rooms in a better house, in a street wider than the alleys they had lived in until now. And Bess had bought a new dress, new ribbons for her hair.

'I can get a better sort of gentleman now,' she told Tom as they ate their first meal in their new abode. 'Charge more. We're on the up and up now, Tom boy.'

Tom looked unhappy.

'Don't you think you could give it up now, Bess? You know I've never liked you doing this. And it's not doing you any good. You're looking tired – peaky. And that sore throat of yours don't seem to get any better. If I can just find somewhere to set up a loom, like Mr Francis said—'

'And employ me as your draw-girl?' Bessie said contemptuously. 'No thanks, Tom. I done all the drawing I'm going to do. 'Sides, all that's just a pipe-dream. You don't really think he's going to come back and set you up in business, do you?'

'Why not? He was keen, he gave us the money—'

Bessie laughed. 'Tom, you're as gullible as when you first come to London. Mr Francis is like all the rest. Gets an idea and nothing will do but he's got to do it, and then it's all over and on with the new thing. He'll have forgotten all about us by now. No, we'll make good use of the money he give us, all right – but we won't buy looms with it, or yarn. We'll better ourselves and enjoy it a bit. I ain't had such a full belly since we found that sovereign in the street that time. And I want some curtains for the windows and a bit of a rug for the floor, make it look nice.'

'That's not what the money was for.'

'Well, it's the way it's going to be used.' She stared at him, her blue eyes cold. 'And don't let's hear nothing about stealing, Tom Himley – those Pagnels *owe* us that money, every last penny. If it weren't for them and their twelve and twelve, we'd not be here now.'

'It wasn't Mr Francis's fault—'

'He's a Pagnel, isn't he? Well then. Anyway, you won't see him again – not now we've flitted. He'll never find us here.'

Tom shook his head. 'We said we'd write and tell him, Bess. You said we were moving to get away from Mr Vivian. You said you were scared of him—'

'I am, too.' She shivered. 'He's a real nasty piece of work, Tom. I never really saw it afore – but I've learned about men since we bin here and I can see it in his eyes now. I reckon I had a lucky escape the day Sal Preston picked me up, after all. And so did you. He'd have bled us dry, Tom, the pair of us, and then chucked us on the muck-heap. And he'd do worse now, if he caught up with us again. I could see that, when he got me in that coffee-shop. He had me frighted good and proper that day. I don't want no more risks with that gent.'

'But Mr Francis wouldn't tell him where we were. We could ask him not to—'

'Tom, you're talking through the back of your hat. Of course he'd tell him! And if he didn't, Mr Vivian would find out soon enough. You can't keep a business quiet, not in a family like the Pagnels. No, we keep clear of that lot from now on – just disappear quiet, like we done before. It took 'em six years to find us, and they wouldn't have done then if I hadn't been such a gaby as to go waltzing up to them in the street. I'll keep my eyes open from now on, you can be sure.'

Tom hadn't liked it. But Bess had insisted and, finally, had her own way. They'd used Mr Francis's money to buy a bed from an old woman up the road whose husband had died, and Bess had her rug and curtains. They bought some new cups and plates, too, and a couple of bowls, and some cooking pans. And they had enough left over for a jacket for Tom, all bought from the same old woman, who was going to live with her married daughter. And when Bess had the two rooms to herself, as she did now after her latest 'gentleman' had left, she felt a sense of security and pride that she had never felt before.

It was a pity she was never quite well these days. The sore throat which had begun to plague her in the summer had lingered, and a rash had appeared on her body, making her feverish. She had feared scarlet fever, but after a while the symptoms had disappeared and she had been able to work again. But she had never quite recovered her old energy.

Not that it mattered now. She had acquired enough regular clients not to need to go out on the streets so often. And she smiled to herself as she thought that the money Mr Francis had given them had been enough to help her in her own business. Not at all the kind of business he had intended – but who would want to stand at a loom for hour after hour, when men were so pathetically willing to pay for half an hour on a bed? And now that she had a good bed, in a better room, she could, as she had told Francis, aim higher for her clients. Who knew where she might end up? In the bed of royalty, perhaps. It had happened to plenty of other girls around Covent Garden.

When she thought of her early days in Sal Preston's house, Bessie almost laughed.

Old Sal led Rebecca through a maze of streets. It was dark now, too dark for Rebecca to notice where they went, and she knew she would never remember anyway. But it hardly mattered, when she was so close now to finding her brother and sister at last. She had no doubt that Sal would be able to find them; the old woman did indeed seem to know everyone in the alleyways she hobbled along, and had a word for most of them. If anyone knew Bessie and Tom, she would.

Rebecca was aware, too, that she was almost totally exhausted. The anxieties of the past months, her longings for Francis, her dismissal and long journey to London, capped by hours of wandering and a night spent in a doorway, had left her almost numb with weariness.

They came at last to a tall, narrow house, identical with so many others Rebecca had seen that she wondered at anyone's ability to find their way home. How did they tell the difference between these twisting alleyways, these blank-faced houses? She waited as Sal opened the door, then followed her inside.

'Up them stairs,' the old woman said, lighting two candles. 'There's a room at the top you can sleep in for tonight. It's clean enough – I had a girl stopping in there till only yesterday, nice, clean sort of girl, you won't find nothing wrong. You just go up and make yerself comf'table and I'l bring you up a nice hot drink to help yer sleep.' She gave Rebecca one of the candles and shuffled towards the back of the house.

Rebecca went up the stairs and into the room Sal had indicated. It was furnished only with a narrow bed and a washstand on which stood a bowl and a jug, both cracked. She set her candle on the washstand and sank down on the bed.

After Sal had brought her the hot drink she had promised, she felt her weariness wash over her, and knew she could fight it no longer. Nor was there any need. She took off her dress and lay down on the bed, pulling the thin coverlet over her.

Tomorrow, Sal would take her to Bessie and Tom. They would look after her.

Her last thought was a piercing longing for Francis.

Francis descended from the coach and stood for a moment looking around him. The innyard was full of bustling people: ostlers and grooms leading out fresh horses, rubbing down those that had just come in, serving girls hurrying out for water from the pumps, the innkeeper himself making brief appearances at the door to shout at some loitering potboy. The air was filled with noise – the whinnying of horses, the voices of the scurrying people, the whistling of one of the grooms. And from the street beyond came the rattle of wheels, the clatter of hooves and the cries of street vendors.

A sultry heat lay like a blanket over London. As the coach had driven through the streets, Francis had found himself assailed by the familiar stench of the city, a stench that came from the rotting vegetation and refuse that cluttered the narrow backstreets, the dead cats and dogs that had been left for rats to gnaw, the night soil and household rubbish that was tossed out of doors and windows to wait in gutters and open drains for the rain that might wash it away. Flies, bloated with good living, rose in clouds to buzz around the faces of any who disturbed them, but their buzzing was desultory and they soon returned to their feasting.

Francis went into the inn and arranged for a room. Hastily, impatient to be on his way, he unpacked what was necessary and washed his face and hands. Within a few minutes, he was out, striding along the littered streets, on his way to the address where Tom and Bessie had been living the last time he saw them, when they'd sat together making plans for the new business.

'One loom at first, Tom. Then you can look around for another weaver. It doesn't matter that we shan't be producing much to start with – my designs are going to be demanded by the best people, they'll have a rarity value. We'll soon earn enough to produce more, we can expand.'

He had never had any doubts about his designs. People had already begun to talk about them, to order them specially from Pagnel's in Kidderminster. Jeremiah had been talking of turning over one of his weaving shops entirely to a new line of Francis's designs, making them in the finest quality that only the richest would be able to afford. It would give Pagnel's a name no other carpet manufacturer had. It would give them a lead over their rivals.

Francis had had a long talk with his father before leaving Kidderminster. It had been agreed that he would still continue to design for Pagnel's. But for his own new business, he would use different designs. They would not compete. In any case, he would not for a long time be able to produce in the quantity that Jeremiah's factories could.

'Make a success of this business,' Jeremiah had said, his heavy face sombre as he contemplated his son's departure. 'Maybe one day things will change and we can bring it into the firm here. I haven't given up hope that you'll come back, Francis.'

But on that sultry day, as Francis hurried through the streets, his heart thumping as he thought of being with Rebecca again, it seemed a long way in the future. And although he knew that his livelihood depended now on his success, he could not let that take first place in his mind. The one idea in his head now was the girl he loved, the girl who carried his child. Rebecca . . .

Soon, he would see her again; soon, he would take her in his arms, tell her how much he loved her, assure her that from now on everything would be all right. They would be together – and as long as they were together, nothing could go wrong, nothing could hurt them.

It would take him less than an hour to get to Tom and Bessie's room from here. And Rebecca would be there, ahead of him. In less than an hour they would be together again. They could begin to plan their lives.

Francis scarcely saw the people who thrust and jostled around him. His mind was filled with Rebecca; with his love.

Rebecca woke slowly, her mind muddled and hazy after her heavy sleep. She stared around the dingy room, wondering where she was.

Gradually, her memory returned. She sat up, feeling her head thump as she did so, and stumbled to the window to look out.

The street was wide enough for stalls to have been set up along one side and she gazed down at them, looking at the heaps of fruit and vegetables, the piles of meat and poultry, the neatly laid out slabs of cheese and butter, the churns of milk and the stacks of pies and cakes. A wave of nausea swept over her and she turned aside hastily, and reached the bowl on the washstand just in time.

'So you're awake, are yer?' The door opened and Sal came in just as Rebecca raised a white and sweating face from the bowl. 'Thought I heard yer moving. Not feeling so good this morning?' She set a cracked cup down on the washstand and looked critically at Rebecca. 'What is it – marrow pudden?'

Rebecca nodded weakly. 'They told me I'd get over this once I was past three months, but it hasn't made any difference. Even when I've got nothing inside me, I'm still sick.'

Sal looked into the bowl and nodded. 'Ah, that's just bile. You'll feel better now for a bit, anyway.' She took the bowl over to the window and tipped the contents out into the street. 'Here, have this drink. It'll do you a bit of good even if yer don't hold on to it for long.' She watched while Rebecca sipped cautiously. 'That's it. Just a little bit at a time, that's the secret. So yer stummick don't notice it. Now then – yer said your sister's name was Bessie, right?'

'Yes.' Rebecca looked up eagerly. 'Have you found out—'

'Nah. Not yet awhile. I just wanted to make sure, like.' The old woman looked Rebecca over. 'You look to me as if you could do with a bit more rest. Why don't yer stay here while I goes out and asks around a bit? I'll come back soon's I got any news. How about that? Stay there in bed, be a lady for a few hours.'

Rebecca looked at the bed, then at the window. 'I don't know . . . Suppose Bess is out there somewhere? You wouldn't recognise her—'

'If she's out there somewhere now, she'll be out there again,' Sal said firmly. 'But I don't reckon she's that near here – I knows nearly everyone round here and I don't know no Bess, nor no Tom Himley. But I know lots of coves I can ask. And that'd be wearying work for you. You stop here and rest, like I said. Now – think yer can fancy a bite to eat?'

Rebecca shook her head. 'I can't eat anything before midday.'

'I'll leave yer a bit then, case I'm not back by then. Now—' the crone shuffled out through the door, returning with a plate which she set beside the cup on the washstand '—mind you don't go away afore I gets back. Get out in them streets and you'd be lost quick as a flick of a duck's tail, and likely as not picked up by some bawd and set on the primrose path afore nightfall. And then if I do come back with your sis, we wouldn't know where you'd gone. So you stop here, see?'

'Yes, I'll stay here.' Rebecca sank back on to the bed, thankful for the old woman's kindness. She closed her eyes and listened to the sounds of Sal going down the stairs and out of the door to the street. She listened to the cries of the street vendors outside, and the shouts of their customers. She heard the striking of church clocks. And then the sounds merged into one another and became a background cacophony to her dreams.

Francis was breathless when he arrived at the house where Tom and Bessie had lived. He stood for a moment, looking up at the grimy windows, his heart kicking against his ribs. Was Rebecca in there even now? Was she thinking that he would never come, that she had lost him? Was she afraid of the future, believing that she faced it alone?

He felt a smile pull at his lips as he anticipated that

481

moment of first meeting. The incredulous joy in her face. The delight of throwing his arms about her, feeling that sweet body once more against his. Their first rapturous kiss.

All only a few moments away now. She must be there. She must be inside.

He raised his hand to the knocker, lifted it, let it drop.

Bessie caught sight of Francis as she talked coquettishly with a soldier she had picked up in the tavern. He had followed her outside, but she was playing a game she enjoyed, that of a virtuous maiden only half willing to be seduced. She ducked her head, then looked up through downcast lashes. She let her fingers play idly with the neckline of her gown, shifting it slightly to make it just a fraction more revealing.

'I don't know what you think you're doing, talking to a girl like that,' she protested, giggling. 'What my gentleman friend would say if he could hear you—'

'You've got a friend, then?' The soldier's eyes travelled down appreciatively. 'See a lot of you, does he?'

Bessie gave a little scream of laughter. 'I don't know what you mean! Anyway, he's not *really* that much of a friend. We just has a drink together now and then, *you* know. Bit of a kiss and cuddle, nothing more than that.'

'That so? Well, maybe we could do the same, eh?' He put his hand on her bare arm, moved his fingers against her skin. 'I might be able to show you one or two things your gentleman friend hasn't got around to yet.'

Bessie giggled again and pulled ineffectively at his hand. 'Well, I dunno . . .'

'Come on,' the soldier said persuasively. 'He can't

be much of a man if all he's ever done is kiss and cuddle a bit. Girl like you needs a real man . . . someone like me. Show you what it's all about. How about it, eh?'

'I dunno,' Bess said again, but with a little less doubt in her voice. She allowed him to come a little closer. 'Tell you what – I got a room near here. We could go back there for a bit, if you like. Talk about it – nothing else, mind. I'm a good girl.'

'Course you are. I'm not suggesting anything else.' He grinned into her face. 'Just a talk, and maybe a kiss or two. Nothing else.'

Bessie turned to lead him along the street. And as she did so, she saw Francis, walking slowly along the road towards them. For an instant, she froze; then she grabbed the soldier's wrist and jerked him into the nearest alleyway.

'Here,' he protested, 'what's the hurry, all of a sudden?'

'It's my friend,' Bessie snapped. 'Coming along the street. I don't want him to see us – we'll go this way.'

The soldier laughed. 'Jealous sort, is he? Well, I'm not afraid of him – not a feller that has a girl like you and only gives her a kiss and a cuddle. We'll give him something to be jealous of, shall we?'

He dragged her against him in the alleyway and fastened a hot, wet mouth over hers. Bessie struggled for a moment, terrified that Francis would see them. But as the soldier's lips grew harder and his hands began to move brutally over her body, she caught sight of Francis passing the entrance to the passageway. She turned slightly, more closely into the soldier's arms, hiding her face and half closing her eyes.

She saw Francis pause at the end of the alley. For a moment, his eyes were on her and she prayed that the

shadows hid her face. Then he passed quickly on and
was gone.

'All right,' Bessie snapped, dragging herself out of
the soldier's arms, 'that's enough of that. It's half a
crown if you want it here – five bob to come back to
my room. Take your choice.'

The soldier stared at her. 'But I thought—'

'Thought you'd got a fresh wench? Round here?
You'll be lucky!' Bess laughed shortly. 'Come
on – make up your mind. I can give you a good time,
whichever way you want it, but it's better on a bed.
On'y I don't have time to waste, see? I got a living to
earn.' She looked at him impatiently, then back
towards the street. Francis might come back at any
moment. 'Which is it to be?'

Francis barely noticed the couple clasped together in
the alleyway. He looked down into its shadows as he
passed, as he paused and looked into every alleyway,
in the vain hope that he might see Rebecca, wandering
as aimlessly as he. But the two figures were pressed
too tightly together to be recognisable, and it was
obvious enough what their business was. Francis gave
them a cursory glance and walked on.

Even now, after two weeks of searching for
Rebecca, he found it almost impossible to take in
what had happened. Since that first day, when he had
gone so full of hope to the house where Tom and
Bessie had been living, only to find them gone, the
truth had refused to seem real. He could still barely
believe it – that Rebecca was lost to him as surely as if
she had flown to the moon; that in the teeming streets
of London he had as little hope of finding her, or her
brother and sister, as of finding a feather in a snow-
storm.

Over and over again, his mind returned to that scene, as if searching for some hidden clue he had missed, some vital piece of information which could lead him to Rebecca. It was useless, he knew, to keep going over it. Yet, as he tramped the streets day after day, returning exhausted and hopeless each night to his room, he still relived it, saw again the tall, narrow house, the grimy walls, the battered door. He felt the splintered wood against his knuckles, knew again that kicking of the heart as the door slowly opened – and felt once more the bitter disappointment as the girl who opened it stared at him and shook her head.

'Gone?' He stared at her. 'What do you mean, gone? *Where* have they gone?'

The girl shrugged. She had only opened the door because she was expecting one of the costermongers who often called in at this time and, although she'd liked Bess and Tom well enough, they were of no more interest to her now that they'd left.

'I dunno where they've gone. They didn't tell me nothing – why should they? Just upped sticks and went. Here—' she looked more closely at Francis '—you've bin here before. I seen your face. One of Bess's gentlemen, are yer?'

'No, I'm not!' Francis snapped out the words, then regretted it. 'I'm a friend of theirs. A good friend.' He hesitated. 'There hasn't been anyone else round here asking for them, has there? A young girl? Hair the colour of chestnuts – dark eyes – skin like velvet—'

The girl stared at him, then gave a hoot of laughter. 'I ain't seen no one like that in my life – not round here. You're in the wrong street, mate. Yer wants the Palace for that. No, there's bin nobody asking after Tom and Bessie Broome, not to my knowledge.'

'Broome? But she might not have been asking for

485

that name. She might have asked for Himley.' He looked at her hopefully, but she shook her head. 'Well – look, if anyone does come, will you give her this address?' He scribbled it down hastily on a slip of paper and handed it to her. 'Please – don't lose it. It's important.' He fumbled in his pocket, found a sovereign and pressed it into her hand. 'Please. And I'll come back anyway, to see if anyone's been.'

The girl stared at the money, then back at him. 'Coo . . . it really is important to you, ain't it?'

'Yes,' Francis said, 'it really is.'

But as he walked, day after day, along the burning streets, his feet avoiding the heaps of rubbish, his nostrils twitching at the reek of decay that rose on every side, he wondered if she could possibly realise just how important it was. If she would even bother.

'You mean you saw Francis Pagnel and you never let on?' Tom stared at his sister. 'But he weren't against us, Bess. He wanted to help. What on earth did you do that for?'

Impatiently, Bess slapped a loaf of bread on the table and began to hack chunks off with a blunt knife.

'I told you, we keeps our heads down when that lot's about. They mean trouble, Tom – trouble for us. Oh, Mr Francis might mean well enough – I don't say he doesn't – but get mixed up with him and Mr Vivian will find out. And last time we saw him he had a nasty look in his eye. He'd give us up soon as look at us, Tom, I know he would. And I don't want to swing for old Jabez now, even if you do.'

'I don't, Bess. You know I don't. But Mr Francis gave us money. I don't feel happy about what we did with that.' He looked around the room, poor and shabby enough yet more comfortable than any they had ever known, and all furnished with Francis Pagnel's money. 'We ought to try—'

'To pay it back?' Bessie snorted. 'I told you, it's no more than what they owed us, the lot of them. And he wouldn't even miss it. It's just a night out to him. That sort, they'd lose that at cards and think they'd done well, you know that. No, we don't have no more truck with Pagnels, that's definite.'

Tom looked at her and sighed. He took the chunk of bread she handed him and cut a piece of cheese to go with it. He drank his ale and they talked of other things. And then, a short while later, he went out. He had regular work now, looking after the horses at a nearby inn. And Bessie needed the room again, to ply her own trade.

Francis went back to the inn where he was staying. He went to his room and sat on the bed, his head down, hands hanging loosely between his knees. A great cloud of depression settled over him, and he felt his heart like a weight of lead, dragging him down into an abyss of darkness.

He had lost Rebecca. She was somewhere in London – of that he was certain. But he had no idea where she might be, nor any hope of finding her in this seething throng. The idea of a chance meeting, such as he and Vivian had had with Bess, could be discounted. Even that had taken six years to come about.

Equally, he had little hope of finding either Bess or Tom again. Clearly, they had left their address almost as soon as he had left London – whether to escape himself or Vivian, he did not know, but he was forced to conclude that they wanted no more to do with him than with his cousin. They had expressed interest in his idea of setting up a small business – Tom, in particular, had been keen. But there had been a look in Bessie's eye, as if she had doubts, as if she didn't entirely trust him. And could you blame her for that, he thought, considering the treatment life had meted out to her so far. But he had been confident of gaining her trust.

Now it seemed that he'd been wrong – wrong on every count. And as soon as his back was turned, Tom and Bessie had taken his money and slipped away in the night, leaving no clue as to where they had gone.

They would have made sure that no one could find them. That no one from their old haunts would know where they were. They had known Francis, and perhaps Vivian, would come searching for them. They would have left no careless clues.

Francis held his head in his hands and groaned as he thought of what else this meant. Never mind the loss of his new business – that could be started with another weaver. But if he couldn't find Tom and Bessie, then neither would Rebecca. She would be wandering the streets of London, alone, afraid, with a baby inside her growing larger every day. She would never go back to Kidderminster, so even if Tom wrote again with a new address, she would never receive it. She was as lost as if she had disappeared to the jungles of Africa, and had been for almost three weeks. What might have happened to her in that time?

Francis thought of the scenes he had witnessed since arriving in London, a London he had never fully realised existed during his visit with Vivian. The squalor in which most people passed their lives, the dirt and filth which were strewn around, the poverty that stared out of hollow eyes in shrunken faces old before their time – why, even the children who scurried about his feet looked like old men and women in miniature, their faces wizened with hunger and disease.

People as starving, as hopeless as these had no choice but to turn to crime and depravity, he thought as he searched, a little more hopelessly each day, for Rebecca. What else was left for them but prostitution and theft? Why should they not try to steal a lace handkerchief or a sovereign or two from someone whose fine clothes spoke of wealth, whose plump faces denoted a hearty meal several times a day? When there was no honest way of earning a living, why should they not resort to selling their bodies – and indeed, where was the dishonesty in that? The degradation lay in those who used them so shamefully; the men who relieved themselves in a woman as casually as in a privy and cared nothing for the violation of her body, the men who pleasured themselves with children, boys and girls, and laughed at the corruption they created.

Had Rebecca been reduced to this? Was she even now walking the streets, offering her swelling body, as her sister Bessie had done? His sweet, fresh, wholesome Rebecca, who had given herself to him with such innocent delight?

Rebecca, Rebecca . . . Her name hung in his mind, pierced by the arrows of pain that shot from his heart. Why had he ever left her? Why had he stayed away so long?

Rebecca woke to find sunlight struggling through the grime that dulled the window. Outside she could hear the raucous noise of London going about its daily business. She opened her eyes, still half-drugged with sleep, and found Sal standing by the bed.

'That's it,' the old woman said approvingly.

'You're starting to feel a bit more the ticket now. Hungry?'

Rebecca sat up gingerly, but the expected nausea did not wash over her. Doubtfully, she moved her head, but still the sickness did not come. And her stomach felt empty, healthily empty, for the first time for many days, even though it was swollen now with the child she carried.

'I think I am,' she said in surprise. 'I think I could eat something.'

'There's a girl. Well, I ain't got a lot, but I brought yer up a bit of bread and honey – put heart into you, that will. And then we can have a talk.' Sal took a plate from the washstand and handed it to Rebecca. 'Get that inside yer, and then tell me how yer come to be in London. Lookin' for your sister, yer said. But yer ain't a Londoner born, so neither's she – why did she come here, and why d'you come looking?'

Rebecca hesitated. Could she trust this old woman? Tom and Bessie were still wanted, back in Kidderminster, for the murder of Jabez Gast. And there would be a reward for anyone who could tell the magistrates where they were. Would Sal, obviously poor even if she did appear to own this decrepit house, be able to resist a reward? She owed Rebecca nothing, after all – it was the other way about. She must be expecting some return for her kindness.

Or was it just kindness? Was there some hidden plan lurking in Sal's mind – some plan that involved Rebecca, some purpose that had not yet been revealed? Rebecca looked at the seamed face, the cheeks sunken and mouth drawn in by lack of teeth, and felt a sudden twinge of fear. What was going to happen to her?

'Come on,' Sal urged. 'There's nothing I like more

than hearing folks talk about theirselves. And if yer wants me to find your brother and sister, I needs to know a bit about them. Bessie and Tom, that's them, innit? Nice names. Nice family, the three of yer. And maybe they'd be as pleased to find you as you'd be to find them, eh? So – why not tell old Sal all yer can? Eh?'

Why not, Rebecca thought as she ate the bread and drank the milk Sal gave her. What else, after all, could she do?

Sal hobbled down the street, leaning heavily on her stick. Her knees were giving her gyp again, but they always did nowadays and she didn't reckon they'd be getting any better. Times were they were so swollen she had a job to get them moving in the mornings, but she knew that if she once gave in and took to her bed, she'd be there for life. And who was there to look after her? Nobody.

Not until young Becky had happened along, that is. A bit of luck that had been, spotting her in the pub. Sal had hardly been able to believe her luck, catching a fresh young piece like that before anyone else had set eyes on her. Another five minutes and one of the bawds would have cottoned on, and the wench been whipped into one of the bordellos before she knew what had happened.

But Sal Marryat had got there first. And if she played her cards right, she reckoned young Becky was going to be her salvation. It was no fun, getting old in London, even if you were lucky enough to have a house. Sal could rent out rooms to girls and never ask questions, but none of them stayed long and none of them cared tuppence about her. They'd see her dead on the stairs and kick her out for the nightsoil men to cart away. None of them would look after her in her old age.

But Becky might. Becky was young and innocent, fresh from the country. She was already grateful to Sal. And when Sal found that brother and sister of hers, they'd be grateful, too. And if she didn't find them?

Why, who else would Becky have then but Sal herself? And wouldn't she be glad to do whatever she could to earn money to support them both?

Sal smiled to herself as she crept through the streets. She reckoned she'd struck lucky this time, right enough.

Rebecca hadn't thought it was much use trying the house where Bessie and Tom had lived. She'd been there herself, been told that the two had gone, no one knew where. What was the point in Sal going there, to be told the same thing?

But Sal knew better. The old woman Becky had seen would have known her for a stranger to London, and would have been suspicious. What would such a girl want with Tom and Bessie? She wouldn't have wanted any trouble, so she had sent Becky packing.

But she'd talk to Sal. She'd see Sal for someone of her own kind. If there was anything to be told, she'd be likely to tell it to Sal.

It was a long walk to the address Becky had given her, and Sal was hot and tired by the time she reached it. She stood for a moment looking at the door. The house was much like her own, and in the same state of decay. Rebecca's heart had sunk as she stood looking at that door; to her, it had seemed unfriendly and forbidding. To Sal, it looked comfortingly familiar.

She lifted one scrawny hand and knocked.

The street was busy with people. A cart stopped near her and the driver gave his horse a nose-bag while he went into one of the houses. A few children, playing in the gutter, began to tease the animal until the man came out again and shouted at them. They ran away, then noticed a cripple moving slowly down the street and began to taunt him instead. He lashed out with his stick, catching the smallest on the head, and the child fell down and lay screaming. The rest disappeared round the corner.

At last the door opened. A girl stood there, dark-haired, with suspicious eyes. She looked at Sal and began to close the door again.

'No – wait.' Sal put out a hand. 'I just wants to ask yer something. I'm looking for a party what used ter live here. Name of Broome – or Himley. Brother and sister, Tom and Bessie to their mates.'

The girl looked scared. 'Here, what have those two done? You're the third to come arstin' about them. I dunno nothing. Nothing, hear me? They've gone, and good riddance.'

'Look, it's all right,' Sal said placatingly. 'There ain't no trouble. It's just their sis, see, she's come here from the country, hoping to find 'em, and they've flitted and she don't know where. That's all it is.'

'And what about the gent, then? Folk like Tom and Bess don't have that sort coming after them. Not without it means trouble.' She started to close the door again. 'I told him, I don't want trouble. I can get enough of that without trying.'

'I told yer, there ain't no trouble. Just tell me where Tom and Bessie went, and that's all there is to it.' Sal grinned toothlessly. 'Come on, now, you can see I don't mean no harm. And Becky, she's starving for

493

news of them. Got a baby coming and all – she needs her own kin about her.'

The girl looked at her doubtfully. 'Sister, you say? From the country?' She hesitated, then asked, 'Would she have dark brown hair? And a sort of country-looking skin?'

'That's her. Pretty wench, or will be when she gets her bloom back. She's having a miserable time of it with her bellyful, but I reckon that's as much because of her being worried sick about her fam'ly, and about the feller that landed her in the club. Still hankering after him, see. Here – how did yer know what she looked like, anyway?'

The girl sighed. 'I s'pose I might's well tell yer. One of the gents as come here asking after Tom and Bess – he asked about her, too. "Hair like chestnuts" he said – good as poetry, it was. He give me the name of the place where he was staying, told me if anyone else come . . .' She fished in her dress, found a scrap of paper which she handed to Sal. 'Course, he won't be still there – must be a couple of weeks ago now. He'll have got fed up and gone.'

'Still, it's worth a try,' Sal said, looking at the paper. 'And yer got no idea where those two might be? None at all?'

The girl looked at her cautiously. 'If I tell you, d'you promise there'll be no one else coming round here? I can't be doing with any more questions. The constables got their eyes on this house as it is.'

'There won't be no one else,' Sal assured her.

'Well – all right, then. I saw Tom the other day – he was working with the horses in one of the new hotels up Brook Street. Hang around there for a bit and you'll spot him – if he's still there. He moves about a bit, does Tom.'

'I'll find him.' Sal said, her heart sinking at the thought of yet another long walk. 'You're a pal. I wouldn't be surprised if Tom and Bessie ain't very grateful to yer for this.'

The girl did not seem impressed. Gratitude wasn't something that came her way often. She started to close the door again, and this time Sal did not prevent her. She turned and began to limp away along the street.

The catcalls of the children, meeting her as she turned the corner, did not disturb her. She merely shook her stick at them and muttered a few curses which had them fleeing, convinced she was a witch.

Sunk in his misery, Francis scarcely heard the knock on the door. When at last it drove into his consciousness, he merely lifted his head and stared with blank eyes at the wall. The knock came again, and he said in a lifeless tone: 'Yes? Who is it?'

The door opened and a chambermaid stood there, looking at him with curiosity.

'There's someone to see yer, sir. She's downstairs. Shall I bring her up?'

'Someone to see me?' Francis started up, wild hope leaping to his heart. But it sagged again just as quickly. It couldn't be Rebecca – she did not even know he was in London. Nor could it be Bess, who had taken such positive steps to avoid him. And there was nobody else he could think of, nobody at all.

'Who is it?' he asked, unable to quench finally that fluttering hope. 'Did she give a name? Is she young, dark-haired—?'

The chambermaid shook her head.

'No, sir. She's old. Calls herself Marryat, or some such name. And not a very good sort of person either, if yer asks me. She probably wants to sell yer something. We get a lot like that here.'

Francis sank back on to the bed again, shaking his head.

'Send her away,' he said flatly. 'Tell her there's nothing I want from her. And then let me alone. I'll be leaving soon.'

It was late when Sal finally arrived home. Rebecca heard her stumbling footsteps and hurried out of her room, peering into the darkness of the narrow staircase. The house had been noisy enough all day, with the family who shared the room next to hers quarrelling loudly, and a fight going on in the room below. She had stayed indoors, afraid to go out in case Sal came back, though she was feeling so much better now that she longed for a breath of fresh air.

'There you are!' she exclaimed in relief. 'I was beginning to get worried . . . Sal, you look worn out. Come and sit down, do, and let me get you a drink.'

'I'm all right.' The old woman came slowly into the room and sank into the rickety chair. 'My, it's bin hot today. It's got to break soon – then we'll get a storm, mark my words.' She drank greedily of the water that Rebecca handed her. 'That's good.'

'You need a rest. Wherever have you been?'

'Where haven't I bin? I bin all over London, I reckon.' Sal looked at the girl before her. 'You're lookin' better today, Becky. Bin sick today?'

Rebecca shook her head. 'No, nor even felt bad. I reckon it's gone now. I feel fine. And I'm coming with you tomorrow.' She spoke half-defiantly, as if expecting a refusal, but Sal grinned and nodded.

'That's good, 'cause I was going to ask yer to come with me. I got someone I wants yer to meet.'

Rebecca stared at her. Her face whitened. She sank down on the bed, her eyes fixed on the old face.

'You've found them?' she breathed. 'Tom? And Bessie? You've found Tom and Bessie? *Oh* . . . But why can't we go to them now? Why must we wait until tomorrow?' She jumped up and snatched up her shawl.

'Because my old feet won't walk a step further, that's why,' Sal retorted, but there was still a grin on her face. 'You set yourself down again, Becky, and let's get a bit of rest. You've waited all this time – yer can wait a few more hours. And get me another drink of water, there's a good girl.'

'Of course.' Rebecca did as she was told and then sat down again, hardly able to wait until Sal had finished drinking to ply her with questions. Where were Tom and Bessie now? How had she found them? Why hadn't they come back with her at once, to see their sister?

But Sal had barely finished her drink before her chin dropped on her chest and her snores filled the room. Rebecca looked at her and felt a wave of shame. The old woman was exhausted and must be allowed to rest. She was right. The morning would be soon enough.

All the same, Rebecca slept little that night. And through all her joy that she was at least to meet her brother and sister again, there was the sharp pain of sorrow and regret.

Francis was still lost to her. She had no hope of ever seeing him again.

Francis had almost finished his packing. He fastened his last box, strapped up his trunk and then sat down on the bed in the attitude of dejection that still overcame him whenever he thought of the failure of his search. He had been in London now for almost a month, and knew that he could stay here a lifetime and never find the one person he sought. Where could she have gone? Why had everything gone so dreadfully wrong?

His memory took him back to Pagnel House in the winter, when he had got up early to read in the library in the early mornings. He remembered Rebecca, coming in with her housemaid's box, her cinder pail, her brushes.

He remembered the love they had shared that spring afternoon on the deep, soft bed of moss. The pain of parting from her so soon afterwards, with no time for more than the briefest of kisses. The agony of the weeks apart.

He thought of his momentary doubts when Vivian had insinuated that he, too, had possessed that lovely body, that Rebecca was no more than a slut, and his conviction that Vivian had been lying; of his feverish anxiety to get back to her, his longing all through Isabel's funeral for a sight of her face; of his horror when he learned what had happened, his determination to find and marry her.

He had cut himself off from everything for Rebecca. For her, he had left Kidderminster; for her he had come to London, ready and eager to start a new life, a new business.

And now it had all crumbled away, like a castle of clay in hot sunshine.

Nevertheless, he did not intend to give up his search. He would spend the rest of his life, if need be, looking for Rebecca – for, after all, she was his life. Nothing had any meaning without her. But he could not go on living in this inn with all the noise and commotion of such places – there was a noise going on at this moment, an argument of some sort in the entrance down below. He needed somewhere quieter than this, somewhere of his own where he could retreat at the end of the day and be alone with his thoughts, painful though they might be. Somewhere where he could, one day, bring Rebecca and tell her it was her home . . .

He got up and stared out of the window. He had found a small house in one of the squares, within his means to rent, and had taken a lease on it. By tonight he would be there, setting up home for the first time in his life. Tomorrow, he must begin again to think about his own business, the small carpet shop he had planned with Tom Himley. He would need a weaver, someone honest and trustworthy. He regretted Tom Himley; they could have worked well together. But Tom clearly did not want to work with a Pagnel again, and Francis could not, in all honesty, blame him.

The noise down below had increased and seemed to be coming up the stairs. Francis sighed. He would be glad to get away from here. Despair overwhelmed him again and he stared out of the window, unseeing.

When the door opened, he did not move. Expecting the chambermaid to come in, to bring fresh water or clean linen, he could not rouse himself. At the touch on his shoulder, he barely flinched. And then, slowly, he turned his head.

And looked into a face with skin like velvet, framed with hair the colour of chestnuts. Into dark eyes that looked up at him with a love deep enough to soothe all the agony in his heart, yet still asked a question, as if they were not yet sure of his response. Into the face that had haunted his dreams.

'Rebecca . . .' he said slowly, unbelievingly. He

took her in his arms and drew her against him, marvelling at the soft, warm reality of her. He touched her lips with his, afraid that she was a dream, a wraith, afraid that he had lost his senses and begun to suffer from hallucinations.

'Francis?' she whispered, and he felt her melt against his body and knew that she was real.

After a long time, he looked up and saw Tom Himley standing in the doorway, with an old crone he had never seen before but knew must be the one who had come before and been turned away.

How she had brought Rebecca to him, he did not know. But somehow, she had worked this miracle, and he knew that he would be for ever in her debt.

'Rebecca,' he said again, unbelievingly, and laid his lips on the soft mouth turned up so trustingly to his.

Epilogue

'A letter for you, Francis.' Rebecca came towards him as he entered the house, the baby astride her hip. She handed him the packet. 'And even better news – Daniel took his first steps this morning!' She set the baby down on the floor, holding him steady with her hands. 'Show Papa, sweetheart – show him what a big, strong boy you are.'

The baby laughed and thrust his fist into his mouth. His knees gave way under him as his mother urged him to walk across the floor, and he dropped to his hands and knees and crawled instead, reaching fat little hands up his father's trouser-leg. Francis swung him up into his arms.

'Crawling is still easier, isn't it, my son? Never mind, you'll show me soon enough. And now, what's this letter?' He glanced at it. 'From Kidderminster – from my father. Well, I'll read it later. Tell me how your day has been, my love.' He bent and kissed Rebecca and she stood in his arms for a moment, warmed by the love that flowed between them.

'Well enough. Bessie seems a little better. The fever's passed off again. Sal looks after her like a mother.' She looked at the packet still in Francis's hand. 'Don't you want to read your letter?'

'I suppose so. Yes, I do.' He looked at it and a wry smile touched his lips. 'To tell the truth, I'm always a little reluctant to open these letters. I'm afraid of bad news of some kind. But that's silly – how could news from Kidderminster affect us now? We have our own life here, our own business, and it looks like being a success.' His eyes lit up as he laid his arm across Rebecca's shoulders and steered her into the drawing room. 'I've been hearing about the new Jacquard process that they've been using in France. It makes weaving a complex pattern so much easier. It uses rolls of paper, with holes already punched in them to show the pattern, and the loom weaves the colours in automatically – it's difficult to explain, you need to see it in operation to appreciate it. But I think we could well use it ourselves, and Tom agrees. It must come – and the manufacturer to use it first will be ahead of all competitors.' He stood for a moment, looking at the carpet at their feet. 'This was my first independent design, Rebecca, remember? And now it's being bought for drawing rooms all over London.'

'You'll be a success,' Rebecca said quietly. 'I've never had any doubt about that. But open your letter, Francis.'

He drew her against him and she took the baby while he slit open the package. The letter was short enough, and Rebecca listened as Francis read it out to her. The family were all well enough, Jeremiah wrote. Maria had had another child – yet another girl. Vivian was about to leave for America, to study methods there and consider starting up a factory since Americans were reluctant to buy any goods that had not been made on their own soil. Isabella was as usual – from which Rebecca deduced that she still would not allow Francis's name to be mentioned.

She felt sad at the thought that Jeremiah could not openly acknowledge his own son, illegitimate though Francis was, nor his baby grandson. Yet it was not surprising – few wives would condone their husband's infidelity, even though it had taken place almost a quarter of a century ago. And it must be especially galling that Francis had so easily fathered a son, while Vivian seemed able only to sire daughters.

But Jeremiah took care to keep the little family in touch with events in Kidderminster. He had even visited them in London, soon after little Daniel had been born, and Rebecca had been touched by the softening of his big, heavy face as he laid his thick finger against the baby's cheek. She had been warmed further by Jeremiah's acceptance of her, and his kiss as he said goodbye.

'I'm sorry you can't go back to Kidderminster, Francis,' she said quietly as Francis folded the letter again. 'It's your home, after all, and the centre of the carpet industry. You ought to be there.'

He shook his head. 'Home is where we can be together, Rebecca. And one day we shall go back there together, I'm sure of that. Some day, somehow, the way will be clear for us.' His arm tightened around her shoulders and she turned in his arms. 'I have a dream that we shall go to Kidderminster together and make the finest carpets the world has ever seen,' he told her softly. 'We shall found a new dynasty, you and I – a family of carpetmakers whose name will sound through the ages, Pagnel and Son – and Daniel shall be the first of the line.'

'And there'll be a second soon,' she said, looking up at him with a sparkle of mischief in her eyes. 'Some time about the middle of August, I believe. A brother, perhaps, for Daniel – and a second son for the line.'

Francis gazed down at her. Then he drew her close and laid his lips on hers in a kiss that began softly, gently, and deepened to a passionate demand that was thwarted only by the protests of the baby who was half crushed between them. They laughed and broke apart, but the light did not die from Francis's face.

'And if it is not a son?' he asked. 'Will you welcome a daughter, Rebecca?'

'If you will, too.'

'I will welcome any child that is made from our love for each other,' he said gravely, and set Daniel on the floor so that he might kiss her more thoroughly.

But even then, the kiss was interrupted, as the baby pulled himself to his feet and, with a glance of triumph at them both, set off on staggering legs across the floor. Halfway to the chair he was aiming for, he fell and lay in a gurgling heap on the carpet. Rebecca hastened to pick him up, and Francis sighed.

'I can see there'll never be any peace in this house again,' he observed as he took his son and pretended to spank him. 'And there's to be another? My darling wife, what have we done?'

'Loved each other,' she said, smiling. 'And that's what we will go on doing – for the rest of our lives.'